Khelkid

Xavier McClean

Contents

Character Portraits

Rose

Venus

Cicero

Florence

Niccolo

Cirano

The Baron

The Baroness

The Story

The following events depicted within Khelkid are just some of the nature of the 1920s, one century ago. This period of the past was tumultuous, and this is a content advisory. This book features depictions of gore, body horror, suicide, abuse, death, racism, homophobia, antisemitism, and animal death. Any stated opinions, language, or commentary offered by characters is <u>not</u> an endorsement of values or approved statement by the author. This work is fictional. Reader discretion is advised.

The Blood Price

Two figures walked together in the middle of an open field with sun-bleached grass. A subtle wind carried over the landscape as they moved in confidence of their planning. The crunch of the grass sounded beneath their shoes as their attention was directed to a strange temple that stood in the center of the field with a turquoise color. The pair noticed carved stone statues dispersed throughout that were in the forms of unusual beings. The rumors mentioned that this place held a person with an unusual talent, one who could predict events with the utmost certainty. Isolated from the rest of the world, the two wore elegant clothing that contrasted with their bland surroundings.

The first was an older man of average size with pale skin that could keep a tan in the sun. He had deceptively sharp blue eyes, a staunch handlebar mustache, a pressed suit, and top hat that covered his brown hair. His hands were covered with skin-tight black gloves, and he had a lit cigarette in his mouth. They were hardly his favorite as he preferred cigars, but for travel, cigarettes suited his needs. His aura was otherworldly as he took a sniff of the terrain around them. The second figure was a shorter woman with bronzed skin and captivating brown eyes. She wore a bright red dress that trailed behind her, along with light brown hair that reached past her shoulders. On her arms, she wore white sleeves that were formfitting. She had two large braids, and the rest of her flowing hair was held in place by a headband. She was refined and eclipsed her companion in adornments with two necklaces and assorted jewels on her. The first necklace was made of pearls and the other was handmade with a large amethyst at the center. Her voice was soft but retained authoritative diction as she spoke with poise. She surveyed the landscape and made observations while her counterpart nodded in agreement.

The two arrived at their destination and studied the construction of the temple. It was built on a north-south alignment that carried more shadows through its architecture as the day grew in length. Its entrance was well-worn with a withered wooden door in its place. The door remained slightly ajar as the man opened it further to allow his companion inside before following. The pair noticed an assortment of elaborate paintings of strange beings that matched the shapes of the statues. The man searched for additional context as he scanned various open texts and noted symbols that involved the movement of celestial bodies.

He assessed that due to the astronomical significance and orientation of the temple, it served as some form of observatory. The woman held her hand out to stop the man and quietly pointed to an elderly woman surrounded by a pile of books and charts. She wore a strange covering that was akin to an orange robe. The old woman's skin was white but held streaks of faded yellow paint. The man raised an eyebrow at the scene and snapped his fingers to gather her attention as she was buried in her studies. The man reached into his pocket and withdrew a large coin melted from gold. Gold, they assumed, would be a valid tender in these lands. As the two prepared, the woman's sleeping stirred as she awoke to see the two figures come forth.

"You can call me The Baron. My wife will be addressed as The Baroness. The pleasantries will be short. This is a professional matter, and so I hope that your discretion can be applied." The Baron extended his hand with a sly grin.

"We have searched far and wide for your abilities. Many have spoken of your talents. To see the future, are you aware of what we are asking of you?" The Baroness questioned. Her voice differed from that of her husband's with a distinct Mexican accent. It came from the region of Yucatán and was direct. Each word she spoke gave the very essence of power that exuded her status.

The woman gave a confused look at her words but guided them to move within the temple. The Baron ducked under a protruding feature of the wall and prompted his wife to follow shortly behind. He turned his head suddenly as he heard a noise come from the air, but the woman's mouth ahead remained closed.

"I am a follower of Ithedra, The Lost. I sacrificed my ability to speak for my gifts. It is only through great effort that I can communicate to you with my mind. How can you be helped today? Your donation honors our temple and her legacy," the woman mentioned as she walked to the farthest end of the room.

The Baron was mystified by such a gift and could hardly wrap his mind around such power. The Baroness received such a prompt as well where she raised an eyebrow in confusion. These abilities were unique and needed to be studied in excruciating detail. The Baron hardly saw himself as a spiritual man, but for his journey, he came to realize there was far more at stake than what mere texts could answer.

"My wife and I are searching for an object of incredible renown..." The Baron mentioned as he attempted to keep their exploits private. The Baroness was less subtle and preferred not to waste time.

"Our goal is to know if our journey has been for naught. My husband and I find ourselves to you as travelers of something we have decided to call The World Between Worlds. Are you aware of the existence of this? A place that can yield different planes of existence. We wish to document all aspects of it for the future of science... and for our own projects. What I crave the most is to study an object we have found called The Frost Gem. It seems to be a powerful object that can be converted into alternative forms of energy." The Baroness tugged at her necklace.

"An unusual request. Scholars who have come to me ask for weapons of war or how to get their leader into power. I see good things in your goal, and I am happy to help in this endeavor. My main ability allows me to see things into the future. I do not know when they will happen, but happen, all the same they do," the old woman projected to the pair.

In a brief silence, the woman grabbed a smoothed stone that held reflective properties. The woman watched as The Baroness stared into the stone and gradually saw her image contort until she broke contact with it. The Baroness held a perturbed look on her face while The Baron shot a glance of concern before his attention was grabbed once more. The Baron and Baroness descended to the floor to follow the old woman as she crouched with them.

"Do you have the date and time?" the old woman asked the pair as they sat with their legs folded.

"April 8th, 1900. My pocket watch said it was half past four, about twenty minutes or so had passed since our arrival here. What does this have to do with anything?" The Baron asked. His concerns vanished briefly as he noticed the woman nodded in understanding.

She evaluated the fates of The Baron and Baroness as her own eyes shone with a yellow light and she was offered a strange and peculiar vision. She was able to broadcast this to the pair as they observed the room around them transform into the image. The Baron stood with mouth agape. The walls of the temple and floor were now completely different textures. The trio appeared as apparitions within the vicinity of the new room they were in. It was an elegant establishment, but they were in the basement with a library that was filled to the brim with texts extracted from all over the world. The Baron looked around in confusion as he realized that the place where they were looking at was their home. He noticed glimpses of things that looked identical to his own memories and was unsure of what to make of this.

The Baroness recognized herself, wearing a similar attire to her current clothing, but one thing that stood out from the rest. In her hair, was a singular rose clipped of its thorns that remained on the outside and was tied into her hair for decoration. She hadn't thought much of it until she heard herself speak. She heard mention of a woman named Rose walking through their door. Her pupils widened as she realized the significance. She would need to locate this woman to find out the rest of their destiny. The Baroness recognized her person of interest was a black woman who wore glasses as her core attribute. She assessed Rose as studious with her blue ballpoint pen and journal that seemed to be filled to the brim with writing. She gave a satisfied grin as this seemed to be the ideal blueprint for an assistant for her work. One that was capable and willing to do the work needed to understand the greater mysteries of the world.

In time, The Baroness hoped to remove Rose of her earthly tethers and bring her into the fold completely. The three remained in silence as The Baron saw himself with a lit cigar in the corner, eying the pair and offering advice to the young woman. The pair studied every detail. Rose remained silent in this premonition and the two understood that in order to succeed in their life's work, they needed to find and employ this woman, no matter the cost. While The Baron had a dying need to understand more about the elderly woman's powers, The Baroness found herself gradually obsessed over the mysterious Rose. The Baroness' attention turned to her partner as he spoke.

"I recognize that location. It is certainly our home, but I don't understand. Considering this new evidence, I suppose we delay our search for the gem directly and to find this woman and bring her to our space. I presume that we look in the places on our list and backtrack to be sure we didn't miss her." The Baron leaned against the temple's wall.

As quick and lifelike the vision was, it was soon over and the three found themselves back in reality. The old woman's eyes quickly returned to normal as she changed her expression to one of extreme worry. The vision continued further than she was comfortable revealing to the pair. As she could see everything and deliver a path, she saw that her strange clients had much to answer for in the search to find Rose. She looked away, unable to eye them both afterward. She rarely feared for her life, but in seeing all that remained within the vicinity of their life path, there was much to be feared. On the opposing end, the pair were immensely satisfied with such a rare display of ability from the old woman. They concluded their business and it was time for them to depart. The pair debriefed with one another in earshot of the old woman.

It mattered little what she heard, as she was no longer relevant for their plans. As the pair discussed in their hubris, she realized that dark tidings awaited if they were to proceed. The old woman sought to alter fate and divert the path of ruin. She decided to go on the offensive. She took a deep breath and a low-pitched crackling sound started to reverberate through the temple. Her hands opened to reveal a bright orange light that magnified from her palm and aimed straight at The Baron's direction. In an instant, a launched orb of energy spiraled towards him as he attempted to duck out of the way. The impact of the orb collapsed a wall into itself as The Baron attempted to dodge debris. The Baroness was disoriented from the impact but rushed to support her husband.

"What in blazes!? Do you know who you're up against?!" The Baron yelled harshly. He fumbled around in his suit pocket and grasped the handle of his revolver. He quickly hid behind a ruined pillar to shield himself from a subsequent energy blast. He remained in observation, wondering what sort of measures were in place to have such power.

The Baron realized that his gun was unloaded and attempted to reload before returning fire. He carried a look of panic as he hadn't thought of being so unprepared. Two shots from his left, The Baroness landed her shots perfectly after removing a concealed pistol from the interior of her dress. She remained unmoved as her arm absorbed what little recoil emerged from the gun. One in the heart and the other in the forehead of the elderly woman as she slumped towards the floor. A pool of blood emptied around her, and The Baroness observed her handiwork. Rarely did she have to engage directly with people, but preparation in their line of work meant the difference between life and death.

"Thank you dear. I was caught unprepared... That will not happen again," The Baron bluntly stated. He wiped some dust off his pants while he evaluated her condition.

"You were fast, but I was faster. Grab what we can afford to carry. This place seems important, and I would like to understand its texts through our study." The Baroness approached him.

She gave him a gentle kiss on the cheek as she looked over a few of the now bloodied books. She grasped a small book and coursed through some illustrations that seemed appealing to her. The Baroness noticed that there was a drawing of such a gem that they searched for, but it lacked any distinct color, only being drawn in black and white. The Baroness had assumed that the Frost Gem was rightfully one of a kind, as she recalled its unique properties of everlasting snow and rendered insanity on the user. The possibility of other gems in existence was an appealing one but her focus remained on the goal.

"My dear husband, I do genuinely believe the vision we saw will give us true enlightenment for what we search for. This is in our future, but we are unsure of when this will be. It could be tomorrow or take much longer, but we will find her, no matter how long or what it takes." The Baroness looked towards the fortune teller's corpse.

As mysteriously as they entered, the couple exited the temple without another word. The Baron and Baroness took a moment to study the statues that took their attention earlier and noted the forms of the statues once more. The Baron had always considered himself a collector and scholar of antiquities, but none of these could match his studies. For every theory the two could craft about the outer universe, something else stood in the path of breaking of it entirely. The Baroness shared this disgruntled expression with her husband as the scope of their research grew more daunting by the day. The Baron's knowledge of ancient Babylonian and Greek scripts could hardly match what was written here. He withdrew a pencil and sketchbook, scavenged from the temple to copy what he viewed.

"A mystery perhaps our Rose can help us solve. Come, we must go," The Baroness proclaimed.

The two continued their walk through the field as they talked about the range of possibilities within the vision they were given. The Baron was happy to see excitement once again enter their lives that remained dull by the search for the gem. He knew that his partner was getting discouraged, and this was the adrenaline needed to invigorate their efforts. The ambient hum of a purple vortex that was their previous entry point interrupted their conversation. The vortex was an unusual entity as things around it distorted. The Baron walked through and held his hand out for her to grab. The Baroness looped her hand around and closed it tightly with the vortex closing behind them. The pair would never see this land again as they vanished off to the next world in search of Rose.

Early To Rise

The ticking sound of a grandfather clock pounded through a bedroom as a young woman slept on her back. She let out a small snore as her face was caked in sweat. Her glasses sat on a collapsing nightstand supported by long read books stacked on one another. The book's covers were torn off at the hinges and held together by staples. She awoke with her sheets sticking to her body. Summers in South Carolina were brutal and harsh as the sound of crickets made their way through the shanty wood of her home. She groaned as the sun's rays emitted through the torn curtains made with a spare picnic blanket that stretched from end to end. Her arm stretched out to touch the nightstand and barely grasped a pair of thick glasses. Her fingers delicately placed them over her eyes. She willed herself to get up and got out of bed with just a nightgown on.

Her eyes looked at the small closet left open the night before. There were only four outfits, the rest were sold some time ago to make do for much needed repairs in the house that never came. The first was a meticulously cleaned silver dress for church service with a small pocket that bulged having with a miniature Bible nestled inside. The second was an old uniform for school that she still fit in but wouldn't wear outside the house. At nineteen, she finished her required schooling for some time. The third was her work outfit, one that was marred with every questionable stain under the sun. She exited through the back door of her home through her room and felt wet grass touch her ankles. She looked below and saw it was braced with morning dew. Close to her was a bucket and spigot, she pumped water and waited for it to release. She paused for the muddy water to vanish before clean water came through. It was a rookie mistake to take water from the first batch, mud and all sorts of grime, often intermingled with the path of the local wells. A bar of soap hung on a wooden beam that jutted out from the back of the house. She looked around for any potential onlookers and undressed. She placed the soap in the bucket to lather herself and quickly dunked the filled bucket over her head as she prepared to settle into the somewhat itchy uniform waiting for her. The water and soap mixture bubbled at the bottom of her feet while she rubbed the excess off her body before stepping inside.

Still damp, she fit herself into the uniform with a small tug. She was prepared ahead of time and packed every article of clothing and spares where applicable. As she walked, her feet touched beams of the floor that creaked with weight pressed down on them. The young woman looked down and saw rotting wood and exposed nails starting to show in the foundations of their home. She entered the kitchen and saw a small bowl with flies lingering around hoping to get some nourishment. In a rush, she swatted them away before seeing her eyes dart towards a note on the table.

"Rose. Yo daddy and me already went to work, grits are on the table," Rose read.

She shrugged and crumbled up the note to toss it into the dying embers of their fireplace. Rose's eyes turned to her family's icebox, the most recent and expensive purchase in the entire house. She gave the object a glare; it was a money sink for her family but couldn't deny it wasn't useful to have around. When her parents were gone, Rose often held it open to let it cool the room just a bit more. She'd stick her head inside and feel instant relief as the ice melted from the surrounding heat. Her attention turned towards the bowl of food. She took a spoon and scraped loudly on the sides of the bowl but realized that as she was alone there was a far more efficient way to have breakfast. With nobody to chide her, she lifted the bowl and licked out the last bits with a satisfying grin. She wiped her mouth with her arm and pushed the bowl to the side.

"Just three more days. July 4th, 1925 is going to be a blessed day. We can make it to Saturday. Just a few more days of this dreadful work," Rose said. She looked at the calendar straight ahead that hung on a loose nail from the wall.

She and her friends from work saved up money from the past six months to take a week vacation to New York City and she was overjoyed. Rose's twentieth birthday was on the 4th, and they had a whole itinerary planned out. Rose couldn't help herself as she went back into her room and looked into the closet once more. While Rose often had to repair clothing, this one was store bought and far from cheap. Her treasured outfit was an elegant yellow dress with orange trim at the top, waist, and elbows. From a distance, it shone with wonder, and she was absolutely determined to have it not get any damages. Rose felt a bit guilty as she was lying to her parents for the reason of why she had the day marked. Everyone knew her birthday, but felt it was better to ask for forgiveness than permission.

Rose walked over to a cracked mirror and adjusted it to capture her entire image. She stood at about 5'6, an extra inch given depending on the shoes she wanted to wear that day. Her dark brown skin and eyes contrasted heavily from the muted white and black outfit she wore for work. Despite the rigors of her job, she always carried around lotion to stay moisturized and to keep just a small bit of sanity. As she gave a small grin to keep herself motivated for another morning, she noticed the stains left behind from breakfast. She forgot that she needed to brush her teeth and went back to the spigot, this time with some tooth powder in hand. She washed off a spare brush as well as she could and squeezed the tube. With everything taken care of, Rose used a rock to keep the back door closed before setting off for the day.

Rose walked on a simple dirt path that extended out to a few more isolated houses besides her own. Only the rich far from Rose's community could afford worthy vehicles, so walking was for most people. Everything else was used for farming. The undeveloped road was a forty-minute walk of open farms and small cabins that dotted the landscape. Rose walked past sharecroppers that started their days when the moon was still up. They offered the occasional wave as they toiled daily and Rose in return left small offerings of food on her trek home from work. The smell of manure and dust was something she was completely nose blind to as the walk to work echoed the journey to her old school that was on a nearby farm.

Though Rose felt she deserved better in life, she felt a sense of comfort and graciousness, as she knew with certainty that all her neighbors were black and had a sense of community among them. Hard times came for all, but she could trust every single one with her life. One of these neighbors was her best friend, Venus. Venus lived in a more developed area that Rose passed by daily. She usually sat on a bench that faced the road. In days past, there was a stagecoach service to ferry people from one end of the vast land to another. The lines in the road were deep and Rose could still track the old routes beneath her feet. Rose picked up the pace as she ran to Venus with a wave.

"Is that who I think it is? Hey cuz, come stay a while! How's ya mom's keeping?" Rose said happily.

Venus was the one who introduced Rose to the world of housekeeping, and both worked under a woman known as "The Mistress". Her actual title was lost on the others, but she was a rich heiress who cycled through husbands, each trying to lay a claim on her vast empire. Aside from her uniform, Venus wore a gray bonnet over her head during working hours. Venus was older than Rose by several years, as she was twenty-seven. The age gap between the pair mattered little except in the subtleties of their voices. Rose spoke to Venus with a childlike admiration while Venus was more muted, happy to engage in anything that Rose brought to mind.

"Oh, I try not to worry her much. She's got a good heart. You know what's coming up, don't we? I got your letter in the post, we finna have a great time. Though as always, I'm ready for another day. I heard the new girl was coming right before end of season. Bets on how quick she gets the rules?" Venus asked as Rose tapped her chin.

"Depends on the girl, we need a hardworking one though to push through or she'll be a problem. You know how I deal with those uppity ones from up north. The ones that think they're too good for us slow movin' colored folks. The ones that want scraps from the big house if they dance right," Rose mocked in a stuffy voice as she and Venus laughed.

"Makes sense to me, but with everything lining up the way it is lately, we'll get a problem sooner than later," Venus proposed to Rose, who nodded in agreement.

"Did you ever write to Roselia? You know, it's been a while. Maybe she and you could..." Venus went on before stopping herself short.

"She sold me down the river as far as I'm concerned," Rose said, wanting to quickly change topics. Rose liked to keep the morning discussions lighthearted and didn't want to spoil their walk to work.

"You know work be rough. The Mistress wants all hands on deck this week to get everything prepared. We do that though and we are outta here!" Rose said with a victorious clap.

Although it would take another half hour to reach their destination, Rose already recognized the familiar markings of the working estate, as it was massive. To any outsider, it was a beautiful mosaic of the highest art. The manor featured gates that have a golden trim on the top, a covered pool, an extensive garden of foreign flowers and stables for the most prized horses. It greeted its visitors with a slap of pure contrast compared to the humble farms that tried to make their way with bad soil. The Mistress' current husband placed a high stake on the conditions of thoroughbred horses and gambled often. The roads were paved and were smooth to the touch. Rose and Venus let out a paired sigh of relief as their feet were more comfortable on the smoothed asphalt. Rose felt a sense of disgust every time she walked in the midst of the Gilded Age manor, both for personal distaste in the aesthetic and the palpable reality that she worked for a former slave-holding family. Her grandparents were both slaves but didn't bother to say much of their experiences after the fact. While the times of the day promised rebirth and prosperity across the United States, Rose felt bitter as she stepped over the homeless who wedged themselves underneath trees and were sprawled out on the road. Rose felt her community was slowly being poisoned by the ills of capitalism and felt powerless to stop it.

As Rose remained in her thoughts, she looked to find Venus missing. Rose noticed that Venus walked slightly ahead of her as her pace increased. Venus had a worried look on her face as she knelt some distance away to see an old-looking dog on its last legs. The animal had patches of fur missing and sordid yellow eyes. It was emaciated and let out a small yelp. Venus was a compassionate woman who held infinite time for those in need, and this care especially extended to animals she viewed as innocent. She was an outspoken activist for the rights of animals, having traveled far and wide to take injured livestock and restore them back to health.

"Rose, look at that little doggy. Is there anything we can do to help him? Maybe we can run back and grab some water?" Venus asked. Venus kept her composure, but she was a sensitive soul and it showed in her voice.

Rose wasn't the biggest fan of domestic animals, dogs and cats upset her allergies. She let out a large sneeze as she approached the animal and kept her distance. Rose was more cynical when it came to livestock. She and her sister used to raise chickens, only to have to kill them at the behest of their parents. It was difficult to remain attached to situations like these as the most merciful thing to do was let it die in peace. Rose frowned as she knew that wasn't the answer Venus was going to accept.

"Not much we can do now, it's a nice spot. Someone will pick him up and bury him proper Venus," Rose consoled her friend. Rose sighed out of earshot as she knew Venus would want to see it again after work, if it was still alive at that point.

Venus shook her head as the two continued their walk. The two took great care not to get their uniforms any dirtier than usual, as it would be a great pain to deal with once the day began. Despite all its quirks, Venus enjoyed the housekeeping life a far greater deal than Rose did. Working for The Mistress in this slice of the world was a great deal compared to the seamstress jobs or factory jobs out there, but Rose took this as an opportunity to raise money for college and wanted to be a teacher. She'd heard plenty of tales of women getting sponsored by The Tuskegee Institute and other historically black institutions and opted to get her foot in the door, by any means necessary.

"We're late aren't we..." Rose said as she saw a group of women lined up at the front of the gate talking among themselves. She quickly sped up her walk while she gave a simple wave that was returned in kind. Although Rose felt her job was temporary, she found it difficult for her not to make friends and her presence was appreciated by the others.

"More like right on time," Venus answered with a smug expression. She looked behind her to make sure that they weren't being watched.

Rose looked among the group and practically fell over herself greeting everyone else while Venus hung back and listened for the sound of The Mistress' car. Rose held a superb amount of trust in the people she worked with. The manor was held and maintained now by thirteen women that for one reason or another fell on hard times, ten of them being black with two white women that had to take a bus to their side of town. Rumors of a new arrival swelled discussion among the workers and the identity of the mysterious group that would work while they were away. Rose usually screened out the morning talk as she was still tired, but much like the others, she noticed a whole smuggling ring out of her friend's purses.

"We managed to bring the box this time," one woman said with a giddy laugh. She placed her purse down and withdrew a snuff box.

"Celia, how do you do it? It's that musician giving you the good stuff, isn't it?" Venus prompted her to pass it over. She lifted her head to Rose and asked if she wanted to partake before passing it along to the rest. Celia was slightly younger than Venus and came from the West Coast, so she spoke with a different drawl than the rest of the staff.

"Sure, I can't stand this job sober anyway," Rose complained. She lowered her nose into the box and took a large whiff. She stuck out her tongue in disgust and let out a sneeze, much to the laugh of the others. Rose held out the box and watched as one large hand snatched it before everyone else.

"Now that's what I'm talking about! Listen, Rose is the only one here who told us that we were getting skimmed off the top. I worked two straight weeks, and they cut fifty cents! I'm a little thick in the head, but she ran the hours in that little notebook of hers. Trusted her with my life ever since!" Nora said with a hearty laugh and patted Rose's back. Nora was a heavy-set woman in her forties with red hair used to farm labor, so transitioning to housekeeping was easy. The other woman besides her was also Irish, but didn't grasp English very well, so she just communicated with nods.

"Well, she certainly got you all figured out, doesn't she Rose?" Venus teased her. Rose wasn't one to spout off her achievements much but had an immense sense of pride in what she was able to accomplish for the betterment of others when the time came.

While Rose held a small discussion with a few other women about a book she recently finished, her eyes darted to Venus, who lifted her hand up to signal that the day would soon start. The sputtering of The Mistress' car was audible from miles away when the day was silent. A cloud of smog filled the air as the vehicle stopped short for a moment before it picked up speed again. It was a gorgeous burgundy color which was driven by the butler of the estate who also served as her private driver. It held an open top as she held her nose up at the staff beneath her. The butler kept a more grounded look and nodded at the group before him. He was an elderly white man who seemed to hate his job just as much as the others. The butler honked the horn as the women moved back further away from the gate to allow them entry. The honk of the horn sounded like a dying goose and generated a few laughs that were quickly stifled.

The women watched their boss arrive in style. The Mistress wore an extravagant red silk dress with a large ruby around her neck. She had a slight overbite, and she had adorned the rest of her face with the highest quality cosmetics money could buy. In her late thirties, she still had plenty of youth left, but she already saw the need to augment her appearance to appear younger when necessary. She wore extensive jewelry that would have made her a target for robbery, had she not had the police under her beck and call as well. The Mistress sat next to her husband who was a blur of the usual Wall Street stock with a pressed suit in the heat of the day. He was a woefully uninteresting man, but served his purpose for the time being.

"How much you think one of those open tourers cost?" one of the women asked Rose in a low breath.

As the car came to a complete stop now, Rose stayed silent. She couldn't help but raise an eyebrow as she noticed one of the passengers was dressed like them but given a personal ride by The Mistress while the others were forced to walk or find other means of transportation. Rose evaluated the possibilities of their connection. She didn't look rich, but her outfit was clean. She looked to be in her mid-twenties and had blond hair with brown eyes.

"This is Taylor. Taylor is our new arrival and will be part of our new family. She is a quick learner and will be helping us prepare for the festivities. James will also be here with you today; my husband and I are going out and we will return later. You will be paid early by James at the end of the workday. The bank holiday will make it difficult for withdrawals as I have been told," The Mistress mentioned as her voice carried over to the others who waited for instructions.

As The Mistress spoke, Rose's eyes met with hers and Rose lowered her head immediately. The last thing she wanted to do was be the target of one of her rampages. She absorbed every detail of the woman's face; it was thin and almost mousey in appearance.

"Taylor, do you have any questions? As you're my niece by current marriage... Your little stunt on the property's grounds will go away after you earn your keep. Your generation has no respect. Alcohol is forbidden. We follow the laws around here," The Mistress chided Taylor.

"When you said cleaning, I didn't think I'd be working with niggers and their dirty fingerprints. That's double the work," Taylor stated. James lowered his head to open the door for her and the pair joined the others.

James' hands sat on the hood of the car as he shot an observant look at the group before him. The hum of the car continued to bellow smoke. He couldn't help but watch the visceral reaction between the rest of the women and Taylor as he mostly attended to formal duties around the house, but was privy to the various social dynamics of the group. As the new arrival, Taylor needed to quickly adapt to the rules of the road. James moved to escort the women into the estate and gave Rose a glance before waving off The Mistress. Her husband of the week left his spot in the back to take over and drove out without a word to the others. A heavy mist of dark smog filled the air as they were left to their own devices. Taylor expected to be backed up by Nora and the other woman in her sentiment, but was left high and dry while James silently opened the gate. The group could hear the man's rambling to himself as he rooted around for his keys.

"So, why are you here? You're white. This isn't what you people do. Don't you have some factory wire to get caught in?" Celia chimed in as she lit a cigarette. She took a puff and passed it to the others. While the sentiment was clear on making an example out of Taylor, James was yet to be fully trusted as he was constantly around The Mistress. They would have to wait for an opportunity to give the warm welcome Taylor deserved.

"Oh yeah? Well, what about those redheads huh?" Taylor spat while Venus looked her over.

Venus could tell she wasn't going to last long with the ire of the others making enemies already. Venus' attention turned to Rose and how she stewed in silence while her gaze was fixed on Taylor. Taylor was a marked woman already. Rose had a distaste for bullies and let no slur go unpunished if she could help it.

"Irish." Venus said as she ate a candy bar from another woman's purse.

Taylor said nothing as she heard Venus's words and scoffed. Venus's blood boiled as much as the others, but there was a lot she would be willing to deal with on the surface to keep her standard of living. It was the pact that many resigned themselves to but there were solutions to deal with such treatment.

James stood quietly as he watched the women leave to their various stations for the day. They didn't need a reminder as the place ran sufficiently well under their guidance. James prepared all meals for the day and had his pick of what to make when The Mistress was absent. James let out a groan and geared himself towards the residential home where the children slept. Taylor's eyes watched James leave as she knew she had already dug a hole for herself. Rose was hardly one to be disrespected, and while she could play nice for The Mistress, she had other plans for Taylor. Rose knew how to take advantage of a situation and she cultivated favors quickly to become an exceptional leader for the women. A few looked to see what Rose would do with someone like Taylor on board. As everyone sorted themselves to prepare for their stations, Rose remembered Nora's fondness for her and had a job for her. Venus and the others couldn't touch Taylor, but Nora and her mate Lily served as an effective intermediary. Rose only had to give a subtle glance at what was expected.

I've got a little somethin' for her. Rose thought as prepared to go to her station for the day. She grabbed a feather duster from a nearby storage container. Rose equipped it to her uniform as she looked to the library. Nora hung around while Taylor looked confused on where to go, and she took an opportunity. Nora grabbed Taylor and pinned her against the gate.

"Now you listen and you listen good, you little shite. We have a good fucking job, a really good job. You wipe the arse of these two kids of her all day and get paid a bucket load. I don't like everyone here, but if you muck this job up making problems, you're gonna be pavement." Nora raised her fist at Taylor.

"P-Please my arm. I need my arm to work." Taylor said quietly as Nora gave her a hearty punch in the face. Taylor's head resounded against the gate as it shook with the impact. With as much strength as Nora possessed compared to Taylor, it felt like she was hit with a sack of bricks with a red imprint on her. Nora was far from progressive, but she knew where her bread was buttered when it came to the others.

"You got hit by a door on the way inside, first day mistakes. Go grab a broom and act busy while we do our real work. Don't let the others catch you crying either or I'll come back." Nora commented as she gave Taylor a glare. Taylor held back tears as instructed and saw the faint outline of Rose, who looked onward with satisfaction before starting her work.

Rose found her home in the library where she enjoyed the silence of it all as she dusted the shelves and more. The library was two floors filled to the brim with books where it was clear The Mistress never read, no notes or anything but a layer of dust. Rose read a few pages at a time and spent her breaks there. She had just finished reading *The Communist Manifesto* and the phrase "You have nothing to lose but your chains" remained in her mind. The library was filled with long tables that were draped with an assortment of red and black trim that shone through stained glass windows. Rose felt that if she read her Bible here, she could truly feel the Lord's presence.

In her early experience of working here, Rose debated taking a book where none was the wiser, but she noticed that James kept an inventory of everything in the manor. It was a meticulously detailed one that hung as a poster. She closed her eyes and hummed to herself as she could vaguely hear the noise from a radio. While Rose enjoyed the tunes, she opened her eyes in a panic. It had to have been Taylor who did this, The Mistress absolutely hated the idea of the radio playing during working hours as it was filled with all sorts of distractions. Distractions were punished with docked pay and that was something she couldn't afford to lose. Rose put down her feather duster and ran through the library where she ran into Celia who had a mop in hand in a conjoined hallway.

"We need to turn that off!" Rose panicked as she noticed the radio was playing inside the manor. Celia looked at Rose with a bit of confusion as she remembered Rose had to take a sick day last week. Celia gave a small smile that disarmed Rose's panic briefly as she seemed confused. With a job as intricate as housekeeping for one of the richest families in town, losing an entire day of gossip was akin to living in a cave.

"Well, after what happened with Mister George..." One of the women interjected with a laugh as Celia had a shifty look on her face.

"Come on, you can't just lead with that. What happened?" Rose asked with a whisper. She looked over her shoulder just to confirm that the children were out of earshot. The last thing Rose wanted was for them to have their family gossip leaking through the walls and making problems for everyone else.

"Well, The Mistress doesn't know yet, but Mister George went ahead and had a little fling which grew to something much more. He still wants the money though, so little old me who witnessed such event, James who covered it up, and him came to an arrangement. An extra twenty cents for the girls on every payment and we can listen to the radio," Celia mentioned.

"Well I'll be damned! Twenty whole cents? I can buy butter for my toast?" Rose said happily as she immediately thought of her now frozen bread in the icebox at home.

"Oh yes. You'll probably want that extra scratch for all the letters you've been sending," Celia teased with a wag of her finger.

"Why, what ever would you mean?" Rose said innocently as she knew exactly what her friend was saying. Rose ran her hand through her hair as she was a terrible liar to her friends. Rose considered herself a private person but relented as she felt the gnawing desire of her co-workers to know more about her new situation. After all, Rose was understanding of everyone else and offered advice, it was only a matter of time before she had to play her cards as well. Telling stories was a good way to pass the time in between waiting for meals as they cleaned and prepared things. Everyone had their hobbies, but this was the summer of love according to the powers that be, and so love was in the discussion.

"So Rose, it's come to my attention that there's someone that we don't know about and after all, we're a family remember? Secrets don't hide easy. So come on, tell us about your shiek. I saw you a couple of weeks ago in the big town, shopping for a new dress. It was expensive too, either someone died, or you have a date," Celia commented while another woman took over sweeping duties.

"Fine. Look, I've carried a torch for much of my life, but this guy is different. Malcolm's a working man. A real man, not some wannabee jazz star who can't write his way out a paper bag. He works in a factory, a refinery specifically for crude oil-or-was it steel pressing, but he has a place in Harlem! They have to pay quite well. Three years my senior also you know. We never met, but things are going well. We talk through letters," Rose explained as she carried a bucket.

"Run this by me one more time, you've never met? You've sent letters back and forth for almost a year? Sounds like a Jane Austen book in real time. People be doing anything these days," one of the women said as she held out her hand for a bar of soap to scrub the floor. Celia passed over a bar of soap as she sized Rose up to see if she was telling the truth.

"Nope, this will be the first time we meet face to face, but the deaconess at our church is actually his aunt. What a small world. I did send him a picture of me though."

"So was our trip that we painstakingly worked so hard to do, just a means for you to finally meet Malcolm?" Celia asked while she stepped out of her friend's way. Rose looked behind her to see that she had already wasted a few minutes talking. She nodded her head over for Celia to follow so that she could dust while the two continued their discussion.

"When you say it that way, but no—We already planned on going to the city. I want to go see the dinosaurs at the museum! They seem to be presenting an open house and I want to learn more about them. Of course, hopefully we can see some famous people." Rose slid an extra duster to Celia.

"True, I do want Miss Josephine's autograph. Only you would want to see those things. I think they're scary," Celia commented as she coughed into her sleeve.

"Oh come on, they're cool[1] . They're also very dead. Besides, they have so much art you can see at the museum. Venus wants to go. You should start drawing again. I got an extra journal, so you should pick it up," Rose said, her voice getting quiet as she saw Taylor walk in with her head down holding a spray bottle and a rag. She had an impressive black eye that Rose appreciated.

"Don't talk to her." Rose said as she and Celia continued about their business.

Taylor expected the silent treatment as such but being a politician's spoiled daughter, she anticipated not having to actually do work. As far as Rose would have it, she'd make that woman's time a nightmare. Rose heard two pairs of feet making their way through the hallway. All the trained ones by now knew to stay quiet and not engage with The Mistress' children,

---

1. Phrases such as "hip" and "cool" were part of AAVE during the early 20th century and are found to be first used among young black people in the 1920s with their current meanings.

they were a time sink into an already long day but were dreadfully difficult to work with. Rose decided to dump their presence onto Taylor as Rose slowly made eye contact with a young boy already covered to the brim in spaghetti sauce. His sister was not far behind as she stared into the library with a desire to tear the place apart.

"Oh Atticus, guess what, we have a new friend today. Don't you want to spend time with her? Go on, show her your baseball collection," Rose said to Taylor.

When the mood struck, the young boy would use his baseball bat to strike things, which often included priceless art housed by The Mistress. As the boy turned his attention elsewhere for the moment, the sound of broken glass reached their ears as his sister hit glass cups against the wall enjoying the sound they made.

"Broom's in the closet. Go on, clean it up. Try not to cut yourself," Rose said with a fake smile as Taylor stood mouth agape before attempting to scramble the two.

With that taken care of, Rose lagged on the job; she learned quickly that working fast offered no benefits on top of what she had to do, and everyone else squeezed the most out of tasks for the day. Days where The Mistress left the manor were few far and between, but everyone took advantage. Without a clock, it was hard to tell the passage of time, but James made the rounds with sandwiches made with smoked ham and lettuce from the garden. Rose stuffed down the meal quickly and opted to use her time off with a much deserved nap. She stood by and leaned against a bookcase to sleep only to be woken by Venus a short time later.

"Here's your ticket for Friday for the station. I was going to give it to you on the way back, but I can't be left with that responsibility you know." Venus handed a folded piece of paper to her.

"Thank you, Venus. I'll give you the cash after we get paid." Rose studied the ticket. It was evident that Venus didn't buy a return trip at the same time which would have saved much more money, but she chose not to bring it up, they already had enough to worry about with logistics.

The women that were going on the trip packed their tickets securely in their bags before returning to work. By the end of the day, Rose and the others worked from 8-5 and lined up to receive their payment. As Taylor was the newest, she only received a paltry sum for the day's work and grumbled in irritation. She was a sight to behold, having her uniform in tatters already, just about everyone else had access to a tailor or knew how to sew themselves. The Mistress preferred to do payment by check as she found petty cash to be disgusting, but as all the women lacked bank accounts, James converted the checks to cash on their behalf. He gave a decent stack of money that no doubt already burnt a hole in their pockets. Rose was looking to hide the amount from her parents who could sniff money entering their home, even down to a few pennies.

Rose took her payment in stride and bit her tongue as she handed over her portion to Venus while Celia and a few others did the same. Rose winced at the price, the average train ticket that cost about $32.70 and that didn't include breakfast or anything else. A worthy sacrifice for New York, she'd come this far, and nothing would stop her.

Venus happily pocketed the money as the group made their goodbyes for the day and headed off to their respective homes. Venus and Rose had the longest travel time and so they also traveled together back home.

"Two more days left you know, and when you think about it, just one workday," Venus stated to Rose, who nodded happily that the day was over. The sun was still harsh on the pair as they walked along the dirt road once more, leaving the comforts of paved roads and the like behind them n ow.

As Rose predicted, Venus couldn't let go of her thoughts regarding the poor dog from this morning. It remained in its spot, unmoved as it flicked its ears to the two women. Rose kept her distance and saw that something was unusual about it. The dog's eyes were glazed over and were a yellow-orange color. She knew it wasn't natural. The dog was shaking uncontrollably as it urinated and collapsed on the ground. Venus felt nothing but sympathy and offered to try to find some relief for the poor animal. As Venus got closer, she stopped as the dog slowly got up and turned to face them. The animal opened its mouth to bark but its jaws extended out much further than before. A rupture in its back opened and revealed a large muscle with a protruding spike that flopped around as blood pooled from the opening.

"Venus?! What the hell is that? Get away now!" Rose yelled. Rose was stunned, she couldn't have imagined the dog she remembered on her pass from this morning was now a horrific monster. Venus was frozen with fear, and while she always stayed strong for Rose, she'd have to return the favor.

The dog lunged towards Venus and its unhinged jaws and loose jagged teeth ripped a portion of her left hand's skin clean off. Venus screamed and her survival instincts took over as she kicked dust in the dog's direction. The animal seemed to be overwhelmed as it moved away from Venus and headed for Rose. Rose tracked its movements with her eyes and saw that it was nearly tripping over itself to do so. Rose retreated and felt her back touch a rusted pickup truck with some farming equipment stored in the back. Rose quickly grabbed a long pitchfork that she dangled in her hands. Rose tightened her grip and swept the air to scare off the demented hound.

The dog moved towards Rose and while its jaws failed to reach, the dog gained greater control over the large protruding spike, and it moved on its own towards her. The dog was part of a symbiotic entity that hijacked its body and grew more powerful by the second. Rose barely caught the piece with her pitchfork. She felt her face caked with sweat more than usual as she barely held on from the animal's attacks. She landed a solid hit with the pitchfork, but it wasn't enough. This commotion was heard by a local farmer, who was out to feed his livestock. The man recognized Rose and Venus and approached with a loaded shotgun. Sweet relief came to both as the creature was filled with lead. It took two shots from the double barrel, but the mutant dog was torn apart. Rose went to quickly look over Venus' injury while she thanked the man for his assistance.

"I seent it come from some purple hole about a mile up north. I was headin' home from work and there it t'was. Best to keep out of trouble and not head that way. Better get her to the vet today, the good doc's going to close early for the holiday," the man said as he tipped of his hat to the pair.

Rose's priority was getting Venus some medical attention. She took slow and deliberate steps to not exacerbate Venus' injury, but she minded the time. Rose carried Venus over her shoulder as best as she could. Rose did everything in her power to not panic at the sight of her bleeding. Rose's mind raced as she wondered what could have conjured such a horrid beast.

"Venus... Stay with me now. I need your head up," Rose encouraged as Venus groggily nodded.

"That doggy..." Venus mentioned before her voice trailed off. Rose strained to lift Venus but felt a surge of adrenaline course through her as she persisted for her friend's safety. Rose could finally see the residence in the distance, just moments away before the doctor packed away for the night.

Rose yelled in a panic which prompted the door to open. The man rushed over to help Venus and Rose fumbled around in her wallet for money. In a surprising twist of fate, Venus was able to get her operation and some much-needed bandages for no cost. The veterinarian had extras he was willing to throw away and found they would be better suited before they expired. After Rose took her to the veterinarian for medicine and stitches, and guided Venus back to her home, it was time to rest.[2]

Full of sweat, Rose entered her house to the sound of laughter that emitted from the kitchen. Rose's heart remained pumping from the ordeal with the dog as she looked around to the comfort of home. Distressed, Rose placed her hand on the side of the wall and caught her breath. Rose saw her parents were halfway through a sizeable bottle of top-shelf whiskey. The two took big swigs as they were keeled over to destress from the workday. Rose was neutral when it came to alcohol. She didn't mind the taste and found the local church lambast of it irritating and ironic given the clientele, but she knew there was a point to be made. Rose wondered where it came from, most people produced their own from local stills and it wasn't nearly as potent.

She skirted by them and wanted to clean off. Before doing so, she needed to deposit some of her remaining bonus money from the end of the work-day. While her parents were busy, Rose looked under her bed and withdrew a small lockbox that stored her earnings. It was an ornate pearl lockbox that was one of the nicest things she owned. She lifted the box's flap and looked inside to notice it was barren. Rose violently shook the box as her glasses dangled off her face. Rose bit her tongue slightly as she recalled she had exactly eighteen dollars. The accumulated change was clearly stolen by her parents, and she had it for the last time.

Rose took a deep breath and looked at her parents in the other room. She saw the tiredness on their faces, her parents were in their early fifties with jet black hair but had the energy of senior citizens. Rose's mother

---

2. Black citizens in the early 20th century South were barred from nearly all public hospitals, making injuries especially dangerous. The safest place to go for basic surgeries was the veterinarian as this was seen as a suitable care facility by whites and had most medical supplies.

was a seamstress and wore a patchworked outfit that was replaced every few months, while her father sharecropped in the next town over. Their family labored and struggled to survive. Rose met the stare of her parents as she stood up and glared at them. Rose called for their attention as she attempted to muster up confidence.

"You spent eighteen whole dollars on liquor! We need to repair our floor! The walls are falling apart! I've had to wear my school threads for the past three years," Rose said in dismay. Her parents were hopelessly addicted to alcohol, every broken promise went to the dreaded drink.

Rose's mother started to laugh uncontrollably as she slammed her hand down on the table. She pointed at Rose's cheeks and shook her head. Rose was already angered at the dismissal of her comments. Rose grabbed the bottle and pressed it against her lips. She took a large swig as she felt the liquor settle in her stomach. As far as she was concerned, if it was bought with her money, she'd see how it would taste.

"You think this is funny?! You both stole my money; do you have any idea how I worked to get that?" Rose huffed at them both.

"You think you can speak to your mother that way? She works hard so that you can spend all your time reading those books from cover to cover." Rose's father rose and cracked his neck at her tone. Rose shook slightly but remained on guard.

"Stole your money. Stole... your... money... Oh, is that so? You live in our house, eat our food—You know, those grits we left out for you—and sleep in your own bed. I'd say that's damn fine compared to most people." Rose's father curled his hand to a fist. He grumbled as he lowered it to his side.

"And to think—you're twenty soon and unmarried, parading with sin among you! That best friend of yours, how uncouth at her age, you're gonna be a spinster like Venus. I've yet to see a man look at her and yet she spends all her time with that woman from the ferry. What a waste, she needs to find God," Rose's mother spat.

"You should be grateful. Where are you gonna go, hmm? We all can't just write a letter saying how we let them down and run away to California. It's been two years now, but I go to the pictures, and I don't see her on the list of actors. Your sister made her choice when she whored herself out to that white screenwriter. Hollywood! Ha! She couldn't memorize psalms, let alone screen lines," Rose's father mentioned. He reached around the table to look for a cigarette.

"Since when could I have anything that was ever my own? My name isn't even mine, you named me after her!" Rose yelled in annoyance.

"After all we do for you, we decide to have a little fun and here you are bringing a rain cloud on our sunshine. You're still going on that little holiday trip of yours? I knew you were trying to be coy, but it's on the calendar. I hear things at the market." Rose's mother asked with a raised eyebrow. Rose felt a tinge of embarrassment come over her.

"Yeah. I have the ticket bought already. I'll be away for a week, so the house is all yours." Rose placed the liquor down.

"Well, we're adults here. Say, let's plan. We can get you the money back by then, I won a good hand at dominoes. My bonus pay for the holiday should put that to rest. You know we only take when we're good for it," Rose's father mentioned as he stuck his hand into his pocket. He groggily tossed a few quarters at Rose's feet and watched her pick them up.

Rose scooped the quarters quickly and only found seventy-five cents; this was hardly the pay she wanted to get but it was better than nothing. Rose's will to fight was short as she still needed to process everything that happened today. Her home was supposed to be her peace, but it only just made matters much worse. Rose felt a strange sense of duty to not abandon the family like her sister, but each day made that choice so much more appealing. If she was the only one unable to make the tough choices, what would happen when a better opportunity struck? Would she be willing to take it?

A Long Way From Home

The next few days were a blur for Rose as her mind blocked out much of her surroundings in anticipation of her big trip to New York City. In the dead of night, she took her father's small briefcase and stuffed it to the brim with her clothes and a patchwork handbag. She decided to take a small belt of cash from the emergency fund as comeuppance for her parents' actions before. She knew it wasn't the smartest decision, but the money would be in much better hands. With twenty dollars altogether, Rose felt she was more than prepared to spend on souvenirs and other expenses. Rose paced around her room as she was unable to sleep, constantly checking outside the window for any inclination of the sun. She sat on top of her bed sheets, accompanied by the sound of crickets and other creatures that made themselves known at night.

The urge to go out was one that appealed to Rose. She knew her community well and knew she'd hardly be in danger, but carrying around money was risky regardless. She lit a candle and decided to read a book to pass the time. Although an avid churchgoer at heart, Rose couldn't keep her nose out of the latest science of the day. She felt it was her duty to understand the puzzles left behind with creation, but not many agreed with her viewpoint, so she often read alone. She snatched a scientific journal from The Mistress' library that she knew would hardly be missed this time. Rose turned to an article about climate change and the effects of the coal industry.

"Coal puts... carbon dioxide into the sky and this heats up like bacon on a stove. The snow of the Arctic has been less in previous years. Hm. Already hot here, hope it doesn't get warmer." Rose squinted to read the text. She adjusted her glasses and held the book up a bit closer.

She continued to peruse through the article with a resounding nod as she grasped some of the drawings. Rose was a budding artist herself, but she mostly chose to journal her thoughts down when possible. She held a few sketches close to her under her bed that withered in the humidity of the day. Rose could hardly be seen with a pencil, she preferred ballpoint pens above anything else. For her writing hands, they were smooth and elegant as she placed down unrecognizable cursive.

For the next few hours, Rose fell asleep until the sound of the neighbor's chicken prompted her to rise. Without much thought, she went through her morning routine and whisked herself away for the long walk to the train station. She wore her brand new dress and was excited to show it to the group. Rose had an hour ahead of her to get to the train station and wondered how quick it'd be by car. Getting a new automobile was a big neighborhood goal for a few years. She remembered when she was younger, the sharecroppers in her neighborhood all pitched in to buy an old Model T that they converted into a tractor. The foreman would take the children to school, and it was a race to see who could get the best spot in the back.

Rose noticed that Venus was missing from her home as she usually waited for her, but realized that she must have gone ahead to grab the others. Rose decided she'd meet them at the train station later as she continued her walk. She stopped briefly and opened the briefcase with her belongings and withdrew the handbag that held her most valued items, including her precious hard-earned ticket. The ground below Rose quickly morphed from spouts of mud and grass to paved road and brick. The train depot was the hub of any town and the terrain had to be nice. Any rich developers in the area from the Northeast or the oil barons of the West would have to come through here.

Just as Rose predicted, the train depot was crowded with people trying to latch on as freeloaders before the first wave of trains headed north. The huffing smell of burning coal and cow manure reached Rose's senses as she sneezed, happy to get out of the stench in just a few moments. In the distance, she heard auctioneers with microphones trying to scalp tickets for those desperate to see the lights.

"New Orleans! Did I hear New Orleans? No-How about Atlanta?!" a voice boomed with gusto. A wave of adult men in suits were clamoring to fight while their wives, daughters, and other relatives sat back in embarrassment at the sight. Rose's eyes peeled for her friends who seemed to weave in and out of view. Out of the corner of her eye, she could see Celia's signature red dress. Rose did her best to pierce through the mob as she shoved by while gripping onto her things with an iron vice. Although Rose never imagined her friends arriving on time, she was fashionably late by about twenty minutes.

"About time you showed!" Venus said, giving Rose a tight hug. Rose hardly recognized her with the detail of makeup on her face. Rose had a kit of her own but she didn't bother applying it when temperatures were still face-melting as Venus' sweat already ran down her face. She gave an instinctive look at Venus's hand; it was still wrapped up in bandages, but that wasn't going to stop her from having a great time.

"I made it just in time it'd seem! Were we waiting long!?" Rose questioned with a loud shout. Celia nodded no as she offered a cigarette to Rose.

"I'm alright for now, way too early," Rose joked as she got a laugh from Venus. Her ears kept up the search for announcements of when their train would arrive. Unlike the more updated train depots that had rotating boards that would tell when trains arrived, this one was left behind and so those that came listened through the speakers.

"Too early to start vacation, she says! May I say, what a lovely dress," Celia said. She smoked and blew out a ring much to the impressed faces of the others.

"We're actually waiting on two more. It's going to be a long trip, no stops they say, so if you've a pecking, I suggest you go for it now," Venus told Rose as she heard Rose's stomach grumble. Rose looked down in slight embarrassment. In her excitement, she forgot to make herself breakfast before coming.

"I'll get some pea-, Wait, you're the one that can't eat them, right?" Rose asked Celia as she nodded. Rose, or the others, could hardly understand why Celia acted the way she did when peanuts were around, but it scared them enough to not want to tempt fate when possible.

"Popcorn it is." Rose said to herself. She looked in the direction of a near-by concession stand. She stood in line behind a few others as she looked over to see the others conversing. An older woman stood in front of her as she was wondering what to decide. The child she carried looked at Rose. Rose smiled as a small baby boy with dark brown skin and eyes wearing striped pajamas waved to her. She knelt and kindly stuck her tongue out, intriguing the young one who also turned his tongue.

"Oh, you must be the one my little Walter is happy about," the woman said with a nice nod.

Walter, huh? That's... a name. Rose thought as she returned it with a supportive nod of her own.

"Rose! Come on! Train's boarding!" Venus yelled as Rose quickly stumbled through her order, practically jumping for the man to move quicker to fill the bag. The crowds were starting to get restless as they checked their tickets hoping in vain that theirs would arrive at the station.

"Do you want butt-" The clerk asked before Rose cut him off.

"No, I don't want butter. Just give me the popcorn and take the change." Rose withdrew a dollar. She wasn't expecting to give that much but she felt breaking it would be easier for stops along the way.

"Fifty cents for the popcorn mam," the clerk mentioned.

"Are you out of your mind?" Rose said. The huff of the train's whistle caused her to mumble as she paid the man. Rose could feel her teeth grit on themselves while she waited for the man to slowly calculate the change.

Rose practically held the man's hand as she scooped out the change and left with a small grin on her face as she withdrew her ticket. She stuffed a clump of popcorn into her mouth as she quickly swallowed. Out of breath, she saw her friends already sitting on the train with a spot reserved for her right by the window. On the rare occasions she got to leave town, Rose enjoyed seeing the best of what the wilderness had to offer. These days though, more and more of the woods she used to draw were now spaces for land development. Rose handed the crumpled ticket to the caddy.

"You can sit in any section of the train while we're up to the green line. About three hours out, you'll see a sign. Real big-can't miss it, past that you must go to the Negro section. You will be forced off the train if you do not comply, understood? Enjoy your trip," the train caddy mentioned it as he looked over Rose's ticket. Rose gave a simple nod as he lowered his arm to let her on board. His accent was different from most people. Rose could tell he was from Boston, so he stuck out like a sore thumb.

Now with a breath of fresh air, Rose smiled to her friends. The other two they were waiting on arrived in due time as well, but sat a bit further up from where they were. Rose saw Venus give them a nice wave as she settled into her space. The trio shared a small table between their seats.

"Rose. Did you bring a deck of cards?" Celia asked as she rubbed her fingers together.

"Celia, we can't play bridge or poker, there's no room. Besides, I came with twenty dollars, I'd like to keep it that way. Now if we had dominoes..." Rose said as she stretched out her legs to make a point.

The train was far more luxurious than the rest of the group expected, it had its own bathroom and concierge service, Venus really did her home-work in finding luxury for the trip. The windows were modern, as they could simply open or close with a latch. Their surroundings were filled with smog as coal began to burn and they gradually began their movement upwards. The group could hardly contain their excitement. The other two women found themselves sitting in front of the group of three as they held their hands out from above their seats.

"Now I know what you all are thinking, surely, we wouldn't go to a lovely establishment like the big city without a little giggle juice would we?" Venus said to herself as she lifted her purse.

"Fresh from The Mistress' wine cellar, a Napoleonic delight! Brewed at the ambrosia and melted on the chest of Greek gods-" Venus added on as she mocked The Mistress' terrible attempts at a posh and educated accent.

"You mean that short man made all that wine? I'll have to reconsider some things..." Celia joked as she kept looking out for any suspicious guards on the train.

Venus withdrew mason jars for the entourage and filled them to the brim. Celia held Venus as she tried to pour with the movement of the vehicle. The smell of alcohol permeated through the train, it became apparent to Rose quickly that practically everyone was on the take, and possibly the conductor himself. There was some comfort in everyone breaking the law, but she knew she'd be the first one to be scoped out as these things go.

"So what's the schedule?" Rose asked as she continued to sip her alcohol.

"Train's now left our station, but... we've got a good sixteen hours to go. Not like we can take a blimp there; I'm not made of money." Venus said as she poured another round for everyone.

Rose and the others talked happily about their plans once they arrived in the big city; there was a lot she was hoping to accomplish, and she tried her best to deflect any questions off Malcolm. Rose hadn't told him yet that she was arriving. She wanted it to be a surprise when the letter sent to his address was much closer than usual. She wrote in her journal, taking a moment to adjust her writing pattern as the train moved side to side a bit as they kept going. Not too long after, the alcohol had its effects on everyone, and they were sound asleep. Rose drifted in and out of consciousness about every twenty minutes, and she noticed that the train had come to a complete stop. She wasn't sure what the case was. The green line wouldn't be for another hour, so she and the others didn't need to move until then. What could have caused this? The train's engine purred proudly, so it wasn't a fuel issue either.

Rose rubbed her eyes and looked out the window, seeing that the train was now stopped for some time. She looked at her friends who stayed asleep and debated waking them up. She spoke lowly and hoped to get Venus' attention.

"Venus... Venus... wake up..." Rose whispered as she noticed the woman was out cold like a stone. This is something she'd have to handle on her own.

"What the... are we... no..." Rose said to herself as she noticed the shifty movement of people in the distance. She slapped herself, trying to sober up for the moment as she realized something serious was happening. Rose held her ear out hoping to hear any sort of reaction from the other passengers on the train, but nothing except a muffled conversation came to her ear. She quietly lifted the window and let some air in, and an audible conversation hit her ears. Rose opened her eyes wide as the words struck her heavily.

"You have ten seconds to open this goddamn train and give us Ophelia!" a harsh yell sounded from some distance away. Rose could make out the vague outline of a man further down the train. Although Rose could only make out one person, a passenger on the other side found that mobsters appeared. These were armed men with some goal in mind. Celia was awake next and looked at Rose with raised eyebrows, trying to piece together what was happening.

"Some mobster's girl is on this train," Rose mouthed to Celia, who tugged at her hair in frustration.

"Can't we just give her to them and leave? I support my women but I got places to be," Celia mouthed.

"You know how this goes. We'll be here a while, let's just not cause a ruckus," Rose continued to eavesdrop on the conversation.

Celia and Rose exchanged a glance at each other as the shouting match between the conductor and the mobsters went quiet. The sound of bent metal reverberated throughout the train as they were now panicking to wake up the other women. The other passengers on the train were following suit as a few windows broke with glass falling to the floor. By any means necessary, the mobsters were now dedicated to shooting their way into the train. The sound of various firearms painted the train as a hail of bullets pierced their way through layers of sheet metal. People hopelessly gathered to the floor in a vain hope to avoid the violence.

Stuck against fate, Rose and the others quietly prayed that the violence would not reach their door, but it was too late for that. A loud creaking sound reached their ears as bit by bit, a man with an enormous axe caved their way into the passengers' cabins. His face could barely be seen from the other window as he made his way onto the train. The conductor and only truly capable driver of the train was long dead as the mobsters egregiously worked their way through anyone that bothered to stand in their path. Rose and the other passengers tried their best to dislodge the doors, but they could only be activated through the conductor's side from a latch. It was going to be a long way out of here. Some men on the train used books on hand and the power of their fists to try and dislodge the advancing gangsters that now made their way to the front of the train. A few chivalrous heroes meant nothing for .45 caliber as Rose could see bits and pieces of viscera now laid out on the floor while the smell of gunpowder filled the upper chambers. She covered her ears, having not heard such rapid firing sound before as Venus and the others attempted to crawl under the seats. Her ears were ringing.

Venus and the others hoped to find an escape, but one crafty gangster shot the latch up to the backdoor and entered through, pointing his gun and letting off his magazine without a care in the world. Rose grabbed a passenger attempting to flee and held her close, pinning them both on the wall.

"If you moved an inch, you would have been a goner..." Rose said as the other woman agreed.

As luck would have it, Venus was spotted by the gangster who took a moment to address his new curiosity. He stepped on her hand with his boot and reveled as she winced in pain. Rose looked to the other end to see that he was distracted and quickly ushered the other person away.

"Well now, I can't be seen with you, but I'll give you my card. Have any of you... lovely ladies seen a woman named Ophelia. I know you're hiding little girl, or at least trying, so just answer me or my gun will find you. She's a blond type, ugly as shit, but is the boss' pride and joy," the gruff mobster inquired. Rose couldn't stand the sight of him, greasy blond hair with a mixed smell of gunpowder, booze, sweat and an ill-fitting suit.

Rose noticed the silence in the air, but as she was filled with nerves, she decided to answer the man's question to speed things along. It took everything within her to not completely stutter in fear at the devastation seen before her.

"No... We never heard of her. Please, don't kill us. This won't help you find her," Rose answered honestly, as she gripped her hand on a seat cushion.

"Ah, one of you has a mouth that can answer questions! Fantastic. Now riddle me this, where's this train heading?" the man asked, while Rose kept quiet. As Rose heard him pull the slide back on his pistol, she quickly responded to him.

"New York! We're heading to New York." Rose quickly answered, her voice quivering under the pressure.

"You've gotta' be kidding me, New York!?" the man mumbled as he heard Rose's answer.

The other gangsters at the length of the train robbed those around them as tired men and downtrodden women opened their pockets, pleading for their lives. Venus and the others knew there were plenty more passengers than men on the train, but no way was she going out like that. Further away from them, a gangster explained that if anyone acted rash, they'd have no choice but to start shooting some more.

The man Rose answered paused for a moment as he tapped his foot, while Venus slowly moved her hand away. It was clear he was thinking about something. Her hunch was confirmed as he yelled down the line. His eyes read one of the spare tickets and confirmed that Rose indeed was telling the truth.

"Wrong one! She was last seen heading for Chicago, this is New York!" the mobster shouted with an irritated shove of a nearby chair.

The other men grumbled at their mistake but still took great pleasure in terrorizing the populace. The gangster in front of the group ordered them to surrender their valuables, Rose gave up her briefcase while the others removed their bracelets and assorted adornments of value in hopes of leaving with their lives. It was hard to tell who the leader was of the bunch, but the most talkative seemed to have it all together.

"While we deal with this... situation, we're going to sit here nicely and count the loot. Any objections? If I see anything, well you know the rest," the greasy blond mobster mentioned.

Rose looked at the other women who were trying to hold back their tears and looks of anguish, she shared their pain. Their one getaway was already in smoke, but they were now too far from home to call it off. New York was going to happen one way or another. Rose knew that the rest of her party would comply, but the complicated factor was the other passengers. It didn't take long for Rose to figure that one of them would crack, as one teenage boy broke the mold by spitting on a mobster's jacket. With a resounding force, he simply grasped the boy and knocked him out with the butt of his gun. His father got up and attempted to wrestle the man and was simply shot dead by another. The noise reverberated through the train, and it rang in everyone's ears. Surrounded by death, Rose closed her eyes and tried to pray and block out the carnage. She prayed for a way out, one that could keep them safe. She hoped that with their fill of the money, they'd leave them be.

"I'm in a good mood, so-I'll give you ten minutes to run. That's right, no horseshit. Get off the train and run. We do this nice and organized..." The talkative man said as he checked his gun. With no options left, the passengers of the train piled on each other to escape and overpower the gangsters. The gambit paid off briefly as Rose and the others rushed towards the doors, with the hail of bullets just barely brushing them. They were occupied dealing with some of the other passengers stacked on top of them. The few mobsters that remained with guns trained on the outside decided to ignore the waiting order and fired at people trying to get out of windows. Their corpses fell to the ground and revealed the money that was now riddled with blood. It was a massacre of the highest order with only the pause to reload. In the chaos, Venus narrowly avoided a shot to the ankle and fell to the ground as she was dragged away by Celia while Rose lost sight of the others and ran away as fast as she could.

Past the wreckage of the stopped train, a small forest made up the rest of the remaining landscape. Rose looked behind her with tears in her eyes as she saw no sign of Venus or Celia in the carnage. She couldn't bring herself to think they were gunned down, but her immediate survival took precedent. Rose was chased by one man with a shotgun that aimed in her direction as she ran deeper into the forest. Her glasses were fogged with sweat as they barely hung onto her face. She breathed heavily and felt her chest cave in as she ignored the pain and kept on pressing. Her ornate dress was the only thing she had of value and that too, was marred with dried blood. She heard the first shot pilfer through the brush and she kept the pace going.

As Rose heard the man's search grow more frantic with bloodlust, she ran some more and noticed an unusual distortion of her surroundings. The trunks of the trees were contorted and the very grass she walked on separated to make room for her. It came with heavy surprise that this distortion grew and the color was a deep and calming blue. Rose was stunned but remained vigilant of her surroundings. As she ran, Rose noticed that this distortion followed her as she moved. A white hand with an angelic voice at the end of it beckoned for her attention.

"Rose, you no longer need to run. Grab my hand! I have been waiting all this time," the voice called out to her.

Rose could hardly hide her surprise as this voice knew her name. Delirious, Rose grabbed the hand and felt the touch. It was the touch of a woman's bare hand and Rose's eyes moved their way up to see a small grin on the woman's face. Rose looked at the woman's bronzed skin and captivating brown eyes. The two stared into each other's eyes for but a moment. She wore a bright red dress that trailed behind her along with light brown hair that reached past her shoulders. On her arms, she wore white sleeves that were form-fitting. She held two large braids and flowing hair held in place by a headband. Rose propelled herself forward into the vortex, only for it to shortly close behind her with none the wiser. The Baroness had arrived, but only one thing looked out of the ordinary. She carried a rose in her hair.

The Lone Drifter

Rose was filled with a flurry of emotions as her mind attempted to process everything that happened. In the same moment that she grabbed The Baroness' hand, Rose did not emerge to greet her, but she arrived somewhere else. She was spit out by the vortex and landed awkwardly on the ground. Rose got up and dusted herself off. She looked back to see that her means of transportation was lost. The surrounding area was completely different than the forest she saw before. Rose rubbed her eyes in confusion as she noticed the presence of cacti and other shrubbery that seemed unfamiliar to her. It didn't take long for her to realize that with the desert sands around her, she was far from her mark of the climates of home. She found herself in the vicinity of a train depot with a large sign known as Union Station. She felt a harsh but dry heat fall over her as she wiped the sweat off her forehead. Rose looked to see a smaller sign swaying as a gust of wind blew through the open concourse. She walked a bit closer and read the sign. Compared to her own train depot, the station was modern but was devoid of travelers for the moment as it was between travel times.

"Welcome to... Phoenix, Arizona," Rose read as her voice trailed off. She bit her tongue as her thoughts were true. She ended up entirely on a different coast and she needed to figure out a plan. Rose had decision paralysis. She needed to find a way to get home as soon as she could, but she also wanted to thank her mysterious benefactor. Rose knew that unless she could find herself some good fortune, she'd be stranded here without a solution. Her first instinct was to leave the depot and take a route to the city. She rushed to find an inkling of shade and was comforted by a massive red brick wall where she could travel along the shadow for a brief time.

Much to Rose's surprise, the city of Phoenix was more developed than she anticipated. Her feet met paved roads and her ears heard industry as workmen hauled concrete over to reinforce some pillars in the distance. Shopkeepers beckoned recently arrived passengers, the ones with money anyway, to shop until they dropped. Rose looked around to see that the city was vast but was sufficiently segregated, so she would need to be careful and find the safe areas. Rose walked along the sidewalk for a time before switching to the other end, not wanting to make a scene with a family headed the opposite direction.

At the edge of the street's end, Rose heard the frustrated complaints of a woman. On a further look, she seemed to have some trouble with her car as she kicked the back wheel in frustration. It was bound to leak fluid any minute. She crouched down low and crawled under the car, while her bare legs burnt in the heat of the Arizona sun. Rose saw the woman with orange hair and green eyes stare at her slightly unnerved. Her dress, which was also green, was now stained with gray and black as the exhaust deposited itself on her.

"You seem a bit frustrated. What's wrong with the..." Rose said as she studied the car's build. She noticed the car was practically ancient by their standards of the day. Her eyes met the large metal rod in front of the car while the woman beneath her continued to fiddle around with the mechanisms at the bottom.

"What on Earth is that thing. You still use a crank starter? Can you tell me what's been happening?" Rose asked in confusion. She hadn't bothered to introduce herself. She considered it better to just provide some help and in return she could ask for directions on where to go next and get a lay of the land.

"Well, I used to do the thing where I put my keys in and then it just worked. Now I don't know what to do. I came here to this awful place because I have a mission! I'm going to do it no matter what!" the woman said, trying to reassure herself with a positive attitude.

"And does that involve fixing your car? You're not doing a very good job," Rose asked as she looked around her. The heat was getting to her, and it wasn't fair to let that out on this stranger.

"Sorry, I didn't mean to be cross with you mam. It's been a long day, it's hot-Let's start over," Rose commented.

"Here I am telling you all my problems, I'm so rude! My name is Florence. What's yours hun?" Florence asked.

Rose took a moment to take in Florence's words, her accent was strange to the ears. She wasn't from her neck of the woods. She was from the city certainly with how quickly her words came out. Florence spoke with an accent that was hard to ascertain, but with each word that flew from her mouth came an assortment of facial expressions that brought life to every word of her. Her head bopped at the end of some sentences while she smiled. Rose, by comparison, spoke with much more muted expression. Her training as a housekeeper taught her to blend into the background and much like the rest of her life, to speak only when spoken too.

"I'm Rose. No special nickname or anything, just Rose. Now what you should do is try to do—" Rose explained as she grabbed the car keys and placed them into the ignition.

"Turn the keys so they face up. Get out from under there-" Rose commented as Florence shook her hair and wiped the sweat off her forehead. She had a pleasant smell that was unusual to her.

"Alright, Lord above this a mess. Take the handbrake here and push it all the way back. When's the last time you oiled this thing?" Rose asked as Florence watched attentively. Rose felt Florence's soft touch as she assisted Florence in pulling back the handbrake.

Florence bounced to the other side of the car looking for things to do while Rose held up her finger to stop her curiosity. Rose stepped to the front of the car and reached over to the hand crank with her left hand, while her right pulled on a small latch that was the choke. Rose took a deep breath as she lifted the heavy crank up and pressed inside with a hard press. She then tugged the crank twice and waited for a moment. Rose blew some air out of her mouth as she soon heard the loud whirr of the engine, and the lights flash on. Florence vanished from her view again as she adjusted the handbrake thinking the noise damaged the car. Florence went by to address Rose without realizing her error. Rose's knowledge of cars was secondhand that she picked up from her voracious reading, she had a knack for picking obscure topics to study in excruciating detail. She also held a strong desire to own her own car one day and needed to learn how to fix it.

"Oh, thank you so much! Rose, was it? Listen, how about we go for a drive. I can take you—Ahhh!" she screamed as the car slowly moved away while she attempted to chase it.

Rose stood and watched the scene unfold as she started to drift off, only to find herself being followed by the slow vehicle. Florence pounded the car horn much to the annoyance of onlookers with their faces deep in the newspapers. Rose turned around as Florence dusted off her spare seat. Florence had the car door remain open as she waved over to Rose.

I trust you know how to drive it at least. Rose thought as she gave Florence a small grin and sequestered herself in the seat. As Rose closed the door, Florence started to speed up, while Rose's hand clenched on the door until she could sit up straight.

"Welcome aboard, I am the captain of my ship that—travels on land—and in fact I drove all across Boston to get here!" Florence said happily.

"Boston? Not the first Yankee I've come across this week," Rose commented, as Florence's expression remained woefully unchanged. Rose was stunned how she managed to get this car through the dirt as far as she could. There were no highways outside of major cities, Florence had to use country roads or blind luck to find her way.

"That's right! Took me two months to get here! But cheer up, you're with Florence now. Say, where did you want to go anyway? I saw the signs on the buildings, they're not too friendly to coloreds here, but I saw some cute little town not too far away that will help you."

"Two months on the road? You can't be serious?" Rose asked Florence. Rose guided her to drive on the right side of the road.

"Well, between you and me— " Florence said as she leaned into the steering wheel, giving Rose a mischievous look.

"Hey! You! Stop that! Get out of the way you urchins!" Florence taunted a few kids playing jacks on the side of the street. Cars of the day weren't heralded for their turning ability, and Florence's clunker was hardly skilled at the task either. Rose gripped to the dashboard as she felt her stomach slosh around with Florence's sharp attempt at a turn. One of the kids raised their fist in annoyance and threw a rubber ball at the back of her car.

"As I was sayin', I came out here because in the trunk of my car comes my tool to root out evil. I've got a camera with tons of film. I'm a journalist, well, I was until my little stint at the nuthouse. You see—I used to write articles for The Times. Mostly food and fashion, how droll! I did help on a baseball article once and asked one whole question to some guy named Ruth," Florence explained.

"Ruth, as in Babe Ruth?" Rose asked with shock on her face.

"Yeah, something like that? I just see them hit the ball and I write the scores. I was more interested in... politics. Seeing how the men with the big hats make decisions that impact this country. Well, I wrote one a little close to home. My uncle's one of those men and my family decided I take a career change. After I got out, I found the mob has taken root here and I want to clean this town and expose them for the papers."

"Gangsters. Yeah, I had a run-in with them earlier. I wanted to go on vacation with my girls and then these horses' asses shot up our train and us. Whatever it takes, feel free to bring them down," Rose commented. Rose stuck her head out of the open window and looked behind her as the outskirts of the city became smaller. The heat haze distorted her vision as she saw more cacti and rolling hills with wildlife that occasionally looked at the two women driving by.

"Back in the cowboy days, there was a road here where the stagecoaches go, so it's smooth. Bumpy ride though further in." Florence pointed while using her left hand to steer.

Rose clasped her fingers on the seat while she attempted to not fly off the seat as Florence bravely sat through the bumps of the road. At their speed, the drive to this town was about a half hour long. Rose could see that it reminded her of the old dime novels in her local library, with wooden buildings, and big cattle ranches in the distance. The ground continued to be rocky beneath them as they pressed forward. A much more prosperous looking abode awaited the two women as Florence gladly stopped the vehicle, waiting for it to slide along the ground before coming to a complete stop. Rose was the first to exit and looked at Florence.

"You should work for Triple A with how much you know about these clunkers!" Florence said as she tapped the hood of her car. She covered her head and blinked harshly at the reflection from the sand and the sunlight. Rose shook out her hand to shake hers but was met with a hug instead. Rose returned it, although with a slight look of confusion on her face that vanished once she met Florence's gaze again.

"Thanks. And thanks for the ride too. It would have been a real pain to walk otherwise," Rose commented. She was more than grateful to have gotten a stranger's kind generosity, but now the thoughts of her being stuck here returned and a bit of worry came over her once more.

"Phoenix is a big city but has a lot of small roads. Hopefully we see each other again soon!" Florence stated as she got back into the car. Rose gave a supportive nod and gentle wave and walked off but turned her head back just to make sure Florence got off safely.

Alone once again, Rose immediately felt the difference from the city. Dust rose when the wind blew, practically blinding her for a moment as she fumbled around. Rose walked a good length of town to find that most of the buildings seemed completely deserted. Businesses were closed and all she could see was the occasional hanging laundry on what appeared to be people's homes. It was a humbling experience, seeing all the wood and rustic brick that stood out. Rose felt that if she waited long enough, a few tumbleweeds would blow right on by. She kept her eyes open for anything and met one soul. An older man who was reading the newspaper. He briefly met eyes with her before returning to the news at hand.

Rose walked around to finally hear some sounds of activity. The double doors of the saloon at the edge of town invited her inside and she took the plunge. She expected like the books she's read for everyone to stare at the newcomer as she entered, but nobody seemed to pay much attention. Rose mostly saw a stream of leather jackets and overalls in the vicinity and felt overdressed in what she considered casual wear. She scoped out an empty table for herself and made no real fanfare as she sat for some time before mustering up the courage to approach the bar.

The sound of music played from guitars and harmonicas was the tune of the day. Her eyes looked to see a grand piano that was covered in a thick white sheet, now stained with various liquids. She would give anything to hear something sweet from those tunes. Rose noticed their drinks in hand and her nose twitched in confirmation of her thoughts. She didn't have much respect for the police, but laws were something she didn't feel inclined to break unless she had to. After the chaos of today though, she felt that a drink was more than deserved. She placed her journal and pen down to mark her seat as she took her place in line among the drunken men challenging themselves to keep going. Rose grumbled as she only had a dollar left in her shoe as a precaution. She surrendered most of her money when she was mugged like the rest.

By now, Prohibition was the law of the land, and any self-respecting establishment was aware that the federal government was going out of their way to tamper with the domestic supply. It was one thing for Venus to bring her family's homebrewed moonshine or to steal The Mistress' good wine, but the real stuff was difficult to find. Rose hadn't realized as she eyed the selection, the group of people in front of her vanished, leaving her standing there with still not a decision made. Rose was not an experienced drinker at nineteen, a beer was a beer, but now she saw nothing but so many types of alcohol before her.

Rose was surprised to see the bartender before her was a woman like herself. She didn't consider serving alcohol to be exclusively a man's occupation, but it seemed she also owned the establishment as well, which was much rarer. The bartender had short black hair that was chopped at shoulder level, with a few scars along her cheek. Her arms were lanky, but strong, as she was used to carrying orders through the bar. She had light blue eyes. Above her was an old sign hanging off its hinges that said, "No Black or Irish need apply.". Rose eyed the sign and returned her gaze to the woman who called for her attention.

"Are you just gonna stand there with your mouth agape or you going to order something?" the woman asked Rose as she was lost in thought.

"I'll have water," Rose said simply as the bartender raised an eyebrow at her. She felt parched under the Arizona sun, and partially wanted to make sure she wasn't being tested somehow. She decided to play dumb for now.

"Honey, this is a bar. We do have the good stuff. Are you sure you don't want a drink? I can get you a glass too," the bartender asked again with some concern.

"Isn't alcohol illegal though?" Rose asked innocently. A few patrons overhearing their conversation rolled their eyes in response to her question. The doughboys from a neighboring army base that braced the bar had the same skittish reaction to doing something illegal for the first time. Rose found herself in the company of various hardened criminals that now spent their golden years in a mixture of ranching, gunsmithing, and drinking.

"So is you being in this bar by the state's decree, but as you can see, we make our own rules. I see you haven't been in Arizona long," a man joked as Rose turned her head to study his appearance. She saw a white man with a tan that held better than most. He wore a duster that was considerably weathered with some patchwork done at the bottom. His hair was gray and long, with a scraggly and unkempt look to match his beard as it approached the upper portion of his neck. His hazel eyes were trained on Rose. On his person was a holster with a gun she was unable to identify, but she could see it was a large revolver of some kind.

"So, friend, what did you say your name was? People around here call me Cicero. That's my name too," Cicero said with a chuckle.

"My name's Rose. I'm not your friend, we just met."

"Alright, well how about this. I'll buy you a whiskey, and then we can be friends." Cicero walked to the bar and placed down two quarters.

The bartender sought to remove some of the tension off Rose by vouching for Cicero's authenticity. She gave Rose a small look of pity. She certainly didn't belong, but if she had the money to pay, she'd have somewhere to stay. Visitors weren't common in their town, and she had much to say.

"His wife and I worked at the same brothel, so when I got out of that line of work, I offered a friendly discount. A discount means you still must pay Cicero! You have fine tastes and those aren't cheap!" the bartender said, raising her fist at Cicero, who simply laughed before going outside to relieve himself.

While waiting for his return, the bartender was curious at Rose's entrance. It wasn't every day someone in an expensive piece of clothing came around here. She was curious on what Rose did for work since she could hardly make enough of a return on her own expenses at the bar. Nearly everyone here wore secondhand clothing.

"So that fancy dress of yours, you make that yourself or?" the bartender asked as she adjusted her overalls. Rose took an opportunity to go over what happened as she cradled her drink in her hand.

"Oh, this! I bought it at one of those fancy European stores. I wanted to go to the big city with friends but..." Rose said, her sentence being interrupted for a moment. Rose turned around as the doors slammed loudly with Cicero appearing. Cicero returned, adjusting his belt while he meandered his way back and whistled the tune that the musicians were playing on their instruments. He whistled louder and louder as he encouraged a few others to join him.

"Cicero, can you shut your goddamn mouth for two seconds, I'm trying to hear this girl's story," the bartender complained while he frowned towards her. He dipped into his pocket and slapped down another two quarters which, she pocketed immediately, before pouring the two of them another glass.

"I hate to interrupt your sewing circle with our guest here Mavis, but if you took one look at her, she's got blood on her threads. Dry by now, but I'd ask for a doctor instead, maybe a bandage. You hurt?" Cicero commented as he sipped his whiskey.

"Yes, there's blood, but it's not my own," Rose said simply as Cicero gave her a look over. Her response caught his interest as he fixed his posture slightly. He raised an eyebrow and wondered what more Rose had to offer.

"Really now? I figured with those glasses you weren't a scrappy type, but I've been proven wrong before." Cicero lowered his hand to let Rose continue now that he had arrived.

Rose reiterated her tale while Cicero sobered up. She gave specific emphasis on the strange dog that attacked her and Venus a few days prior. Cicero's reaction brought Rose's interest to a much higher level. Rose could tell that something was amiss by his reaction, and she met that with a pause in her words. She studied the old man's expression carefully, there was familiarity with the subject.

"Run that by me again, did you say... purple hole?" Cicero said in surprise as he looked at Mavis. Cicero and the other inhabitants of the town had their fair share of issues regarding otherworldly things appearing throughout the state. Mavis shot a look at Cicero who tugged at his beard.

This was a peculiar situation; he hadn't thought the purple holes breached their neck of the woods.

"There's more. There was a blue hole also, a vortex—if you will—I went through it and some woman grabbed my hand and told me to come with her when I was running for my life. Do you have any idea what that could mean? It sounds ridiculous, I know, but if you've seen the purple ones before..." Rose reasoned. Cicero quickly downed the rest of his drink.

"Honey, the mob has been trying to squeeze into our town for quite some time, but luckily for us, everyone's packing a gun. I'm not sure how long you're gonna be staying in town, but if you have the money, get yourself a little something," Mavis recommended Rose as she tapped underneath the table. Rose's eyebrows rose as Mavis subtly teased a double-barreled shotgun with engravings on it before putting it back in its proper place.

"And if it's not the mob, it's the feds or that goddamn Baron and Baroness, succubae the both of them. Instead of blood, they come sucking for cash like vultures over a dying dog. No dignity and they've broken the union boys who used to work the copper mines here," Cicero said to Rose.

"The Baron and Baroness are Cicero's boogeyman of the week, they're rich eccentrics who buy fancy toys and don't do much, but they're harmless. They gave me the loan to build the bar and develop a lot of buildings in the city. They make jobs for us washed out outlaws." Mavis said with a shrug of her shoulders. Cicero's face became red at Mavis' comment.

"Those two are pure evil, and I don't want to hear any more about them. They're freaky. I worked for them once when I was a young man, about thirteen. I grew up in this town. I'm turning sixty-two next year and they look exactly the same. That's satanic or something. They also have been trying to squeeze our marshal so he can sell out the town, and every day that yellow-bellied pissant gets closer to doing it," Cicero grumbled as he folded his arms.

"What do you mean they look the same? If you're as old as you say..." Rose said, looking to see Mavis made her point.

"Listen to the old man if you want, but I'm not gonna challenge where my bread gets buttered," Mavis commented as she shut down the discussion before moving on to something else.

Cicero paid for the rest of his tab and Rose's as well before he got up and made his way to the entrance. Rose always needed her questions answered and decided to follow him. It took little time for Rose to catch up as Cicero felt Rose's hand on his shoulder just moments outside the bar. Rose covered her eyes as the light of the outside contrasted heavily with the interior of the bar.

"I see you made the right choice," Cicero commented as Rose nodded. Despite her appearance, Cicero could see that she was willing to handle herself in a tough situation if needed. He nestled his hand in beard in thought before letting out a burp that disgusted him. Rose made no sound as the heat dispersed again.

"Your tale about your little robbery touched my cold and hopefully still beating heart. If you're low on cash, how would you like a job?" Cicero proposed.

"What's the work? I'm a housekeeper by trade and this place could use... a lot of cleaning up," Rose said. Cicero let out a small laugh, while that was certainly true, the nature of his job was far more complicated. He cracked his knuckles and nodded to Rose.

"My work is more... show than tell. Come with me, and you'll be a lot more than a housekeeper."

Hiding In Plain Sight

Rose wasn't sure what to expect when she took Cicero's initial offer, but she needed money and would do almost anything to get it. She wondered what kind of work that Cicero implied as she looked to the ground for a moment before her attention was brought back by him. A few dust clouds rolled behind them as the sound of the bar picked up in volume. Her eyes were barely open from the rising amount of dirt on her.

"We'll get started shortly. I'm on the way to meet a client actually." Cicero coughed into his sleeve. He patted some dirt off his trousers before tipping his hat to look Rose in the eyes.

"You drink before work?" Rose asked, not in a judging manner, as she was hardly sober working for The Mistress.

Cicero nodded his head for Rose to follow. Although Rose expected to arrive at this place in a car much like how Florence drove her before, she instead saw a gray horse that strangely resembled its owner. Cicero walked over and rubbed the horse's neck as it stirred smelling Rose and her mixture of stale perfume and sweat.

"Get on the horse. From the side and not the back. He'll kick the living tar out of you if you scare him. To answer your question, only for this one. He's a regular client of mine," Cicero explained as he stepped on first and kicked his heels. Rose noticed two peculiar saddlebags strapped to the horse, and most notably, a holster as well. In Rose's area, horses were a symbol of the wealthy who bred them for racing and amusement. She didn't see them used for work, that's what she was for, The Mistress once said. She took Cicero's hand and adjusted quickly to the bumpy pace of the horse. Cicero gave no delay as he let out a quick whistle for the horse to move.

"What do you mean by regular client!?" Rose inquired, raising her voice above the sound of the horse's pattering. The desert sands lifted behind them as the two continued to ride. Rose wiped her glasses and placed them back on her face as they continued onward.

"This guy's real paranoid. He fought in the World War and he thinks people are "coming after him". This time he called my line asking me to watch the house while he sleeps. Easiest job in the world, nothing ever happens. That's what we're doing," Cicero said as Rose nodded.

Rose kept her grip on Cicero as the ride became bumpier. Cicero wasn't one for small talk, which was fine, as Rose herself could enjoy her own thoughts. Her ride with Florence was so chaotic it hardly gave her time to process everything around her, and yet, she wished to see the strange woman once again. Rose saw a well-to-do two-story dwelling constructed of brick in the distance that was their destination. Isolated from any sort of developing neighborhood, there were small mounds of cacti along the ground that greeted the two with every step. In the distance, she could see the hazy outline of the city limits for Phoenix where the distant movement of a construction crew was hard at work ever expanding. Rose turned her attention to the task at hand as Cicero stopped the horse and patted it for a moment. He got off first and then extended his hand to Rose but relented as she had already made her way to the ground.

"Rose, you see that saddlebag there? I saw you were looking at earlier. I have guns in there. You ever use one?" Cicero asked, as he patted his holster where his gun was tight and secure.

"Sometimes my sister and I would hunt possums. The meat wasn't tasty, we're just poor. Why would I... need a gun?" Rose asked with some concern on her face. Cicero put a hand on her shoulder and reached into his pocket.

"You know what, take this knife instead. I don't think we'll need it, but just in case," Cicero said which concerned Rose even more. In her hands, Rose placed a large Bowie knife with a rugged wooden handle. It was placed inside a leather covering that was snug to the touch. She couldn't help but unsheathe it as her mind raced. *Was she in the hands of a murderer? Were they going to rob someone?*

Cicero held his hand up to Rose to stay by the horse as he made a walk over. Cicero walked over slowly with his hands raised in the air while Rose watched with interest. She waited patiently and grasped the now sheathed knife to her side as she stuffed her journal and other belongings into a smaller bag she took as her own from the horse.

"Maxwell! It's Cicero. I'm here with a helper today, is that alright?" Cicero yelled as he urged Rose to come forward. Rose looked above to see a curtain move just slightly as she could feel she was being watched. The two were quiet as the faint sound of footsteps could be heard in descending volume until they suddenly stopped. Rose thought she heard at least four separate locks open as the two were met with the business end of a double-barrel shotgun. Cicero sighed as he went through this every time and held Rose still for a moment.

"How do I know you're really Cicero? A-Are you holding him hostage and having him come here to sabotage me? You sound different over the phone," Maxwell commented as he had a rigid position with his shotgun. Rose could only attempt to give a disarming smile as she listened to the two men ramble on towards one another.

"What is she doing here? She wasn't part of the deal," Maxwell said. The pitch of his voice rose.

"Listen, she's my helper. Rose is good people and she's going to help me, find what you're looking for. You were saying that something is moving in the walls of your house?" Cicero asked. He exhaled as he saw Maxwell finally lower his weapon. Shortly after, he let the two in and started the process of the locks all over. Rose studied his appearance and noted a few key details that stood out from the average person. His hair was an unkempt blond and smelled of dried tonic. He had one eye, that was blue but bloodshot, and he was not tall by any means. The other eye was covered with a tin covering that was painted to look like the rest of his face. Despite the heat, he wore a long-sleeved shirt with a drab gray color. Rose felt that a gust of wind could blow the sorry sight away if he wasn't careful.

"You will stay here and not go anywhere until the morning. Everything you will need is here. Showers, toiletries. It's all here. I need you to find it. I don't know where it is, but I hear it sometimes," Maxwell spoke while Rose and Cicero got comfortable. Rose's eyes immediately darted to a radio he had in the guest room. Cicero hung his hat on the door while he extended his hand out to Rose.

"So, this thing in the wall... You're an exterminator?" Rose asked as she attempted to piece things together. Rose could hardly keep herself together with Cicero's vagueness of it all, but she agreed to hear him out on this.

"Sure. Something like that. We'll see how tonight goes and if his story lines up with what you told me about the holes you saw, I'll tell ya. For now, just follow my orders and get paid," Cicero said as he snatched a newspaper from Maxwell's desk. As he read in relative silence, Cicero handed the spare pages he had finished or had no interest in to Rose.

Rose decided to ease her growing boredom by walking around the dwelling as she looked over her shoulder for the owner who took it on himself to close the curtains in various rooms that were not used. She admired the decor; it was an Edwardian Era inspired home with intricate tiles in the floor and tall ceilings that Rose appreciated. She wasn't used to such a spacious dwelling that used its height to keep the building cool. Rose backtracked to the room with the radio and placed her things down for the time being.

"Well, if I'm going to be here all day... May as well listen to something on the radio," Rose said to herself. She cursed herself as she didn't have any books on hand and there weren't any that she could see there. Cicero's snoring was audible from a room away as he already fell asleep where he melted into the nice chair he sat on. Rose closed the door and attempted to sound it out as her attention fell to the radio. She reached over and tuned it ever so slightly as she picked up a signal with much glee. Her hands caressed the electronic with care as she adjusted the dial with the precision of cracking a safe.

"Football? Boring. If they had baseball, now that would be something worth hearing," Rose said to herself as she decided to settle on classical music. She studied her room; it lacked a window, but she noticed an elaborate cabinet that was situated on the left-hand side closest to the door. She admired its design, which far outshined her own back home. Rose could see the wood was quite elegant in its make, it was certainly hand-carved as supposed to coming from a machine. Upon a closer look, it was probably one of the nicest things she saw in the house. It was exceptionally clean, which stood out from the rest of the room. While Maxwell's home was far from a sty, her first impulse was to grab a dustpan and feather duster.

Much to his credit, Maxwell hardly made a peep as he occasionally checked on both Rose and Cicero. Rose gathered that the man was cripplingly lonely, and he needed help from a professional than anything else. The house was remarkably well above the pay grade of someone who stayed in their house all day, but a war hero had a sizeable pension waiting for them after all. She opened the door to see the man lingering in the hallway and decided to inquire about what he asked Cicero to do.

"So... You and Cicero go back some time now. He said you call him often. What is this thing exactly you're looking for?" Rose questioned.

Maxwell turned his head and Rose was met with silence. Rose adjusted her glasses and wiped them with the edge of her sleeve. Rose sat at the end of the bed and reached over to grab a pen and her journal. She spoke once more.

"I'm here to help Cicero and I can't do that unless I know the deal. We'll be out of your hair soon," Rose reassured him.

"I hear... a scraping sound every night, like something heavy moving. It started a few weeks ago. I have nightmares sometimes, but this is different. I hear it for no reason. It comes from different levels of the house and only at night," Maxwell explained to her. He raised an eyebrow as he saw Rose's attentiveness to the situation as she recorded the words in her journal. He saw her detailed flow charts as Rose evaluated the possibilities of scenarios that came from her questioning. Cicero usually just nodded, but here he felt he was at least being taken seriously.

Rose wasn't sure what to make of Maxwell's testimony. Cicero mentioned this thing he was searching for also came through the walls. Rose's eyes scanned for any visible holes or damage that could have come out in her surroundings. She had many more questions. Her initial writings were marred with question marks on what could possibly make such a noise.

"A heavy scraping noise... You have tile floors. Have you seen any damage on them?" Rose questioned. Maxwell shrugged his shoulders and gestured to the ground that seemed quite clean. The two continued their dialogue for some time until Rose started to yawn. Maxwell took this as his chance to bother Cicero while she got some rest.

Rose's exhaustion handled the heavy lifting in having her sleep. The bed was large enough to hold a guest, but Rose noticed the absence of a large, fitted sheet. Her body rose and ebbed as she slept with her leg stuck out. She hardly remembered turning in her sleep but was jostled awake by a strange feeling on her body. In the absolute darkness of the room, Rose at long last, heard the scraping sound described by Maxwell. Rose put on her glasses just in time to see what was happening to her.

The wood of the elaborate black cabinet appeared to rise and fall as if it was a breathing creature. It moved with an unnatural flair as it forcefully moved along the ground for a moment to get closer. With a stiffened motion, the cabinet slid across the tile floor before eventually coming to a complete stop. The doors of it slammed open and a long-fitted sheet jettisoned towards Rose from the dark void. The sheet moved like a snake, attempting to wrap itself around her feet. She could hardly believe what she was witnessing as she screamed at the sight. Rose kept the sheathed knife under her pillow and quickly went to work attempting to hack it.

Outside of the room, Cicero remained asleep on the couch until in just a moment's notice, he heard Rose's scream. He cursed under his breath and looked at his revolver which was completely empty. He reached into his pocket and reloaded as quickly as he could. Ever the professional, Cicero loaded two bullets at a time, and left one to spare to prevent an accidental discharge. He called for assistance as he was finishing reloading.

"Maxwell! I think we found what you're looking for! Where in tarnation are you?!" Cicero yelled as his voice boomed through the hall. Cicero's first reaction was to get to Rose. He ran quickly, turning the corner to the guest room he'd passed so often. His finger was pressed on the hammer of his revolver as he attempted to open the door but was unable to get through. He quickly backed away and shot the doorknob off and attempted to use his shoulder to dislodge the door.

The cabinet moved with quicker momentum towards Rose as it closed its doors to brace for a charge. Rose took the knife and stabbed the air, separating the sentient sheet that withered away and returned to normal. She stood up proudly, only to realize she had simply cut the tongue of the now visibly enraged piece of storage. In the small amount of space Rose had, the cabinet advanced with breaking speed, knocking Rose directly into the wall where she bumped her head and was briefly stunned. The cabinet's secondary sheet tongue opened and hoisted Rose through the double doors and closed with a defiant slam. It began to dissipate as it lifted itself off the ground and materialized through the next wall where Cicero could see pieces of it quickly rebuilding itself through his very eyes.

"Rose! Where the hell are you!?" Cicero yelled out. He aimed and shot off twice, the bullets pierced the wood. Cicero ducked as some of the shrapnel of the wood ran in his direction. Cicero pulled the hammer of his revolver once more but was stopped by Maxwell who shot the cabinet twice with his shotgun. It was visibly damaged, but with the core remaining, it quickly rebuilt the pieces.

Rose could hear the commotion of Cicero and Maxwell as she felt the wound on her head. She came to find herself inside a separate space with white walls that were immaculate except for the floor which was stained with blood. She let out another scream as she looked around her to see the blood. Rose took a moment to calm herself down, realizing that if she could hear the others, she had to be somewhere close.

"Cicero! Can you hear me? I'm stuck in some room. The cabinet, it-it came to life, and I tried to fight it off! Wh—Now the walls are changing color to a seeping yellow?!" Rose said, hoping that her pleas could be heard. Cicero and Maxwell were bewildered at such a sight, but it came to a surprise to both that they could hear the distorted words of Rose through another plane.

"Rose! I don't want you to panic but you're being digested. Sounds like you're in a stomach of something. You have that knife?" Cicero yelled as he tried tracking down the cabinet that retreated once it noticed the resistance it received. Upon hearing her description, he realized that the two of them ran into something he felt was familiar.

"Yes! You want me to start stabbing?!" Rose asked as she looked to see that the room's walls slowly began to close in. Rose quickly realized that the blood splatters were from the walls that would crush whatever unfortunate soul wound up here. She anxiously tapped her foot hoping this solution would work in her favor.

"Yes! But only when I tell you! The cabinet is traveling through the house and if you time it wrong, you'll get stuck in a wall and that's no good. Maxwell's here with his gun," Cicero explained as he loaded his revolver. In his haste, Cicero ended up jamming his gun and needed to get the stuck bullet removed.

"Damn it, hold on!" Cicero yelled. He rushed through the door to Maxwell's kitchen. His eyes looked to a fire axe that was well suited for the job. Cicero's hands grasped the axe as he took a deep breath and swung wildly, taking out a leg of the cabinet.

Inside the space where Rose stayed, she felt the impact of Cicero's hacking as the room started to slant on an incline. Rose slowly slid down as she braced to touch the wall, only for her to fall flat as the room was corrected. While Rose could only see the confines of the white space around her, she could tell that there was some sort of permeability in between her internment and the physical realm outside. She weighed the impact of her strikes to see how well they would perform on the outside. She also heard the deafening sound of gunfire and hoped she could concentrate as Maxwell and Cicero tried to destroy the cabinet.

"Rose! I need you to do what I said now! It may get a little bumpy in there, but we need to catch it before it moves again!" Cicero said to Rose.

Rose heard Cicero's voice and looked at the knife in her hand. Rose found herself closest to the left wall. She felt the ground beneath her and while it and the walls appeared hard to the touch. She followed his instructions and stabbed with a surprisingly brutal jab. To her surprise, the hardened yellow walls made a hearty crunch sound as Rose embedded the blade into what seemed to be tissue. Rose wasn't sure if she should be disgusted or fascinated at the entity's biology that seemed ever changing. The first wall turned red while the remaining walls attempted to close in faster. Rose withdrew the knife as quickly as she could and proceeded to run and do the same to the others. The final wall was an incredibly tight squeeze as Rose could feel her arm slowly getting crushed as she attempted to manipulate the knife in her hands. Rose held it steady as the last wall changed to a blood red and began to recede. On the outside, Maxwell continued to open fire with his shotgun, reloading as he attempted to blow holes into the wood while Cicero noticed something peculiar.

The floating cabinet shook uncontrollably, and in an instant, the double doors opened to eject Rose out, albeit covered in a viscous orange solution. She landed with some due force and hit the tile floor as Cicero looked below to grab Rose. Aside from her wrist hurting, Rose got up and tried to piece together what happened. She quickly ducked as she tried to maneuver out of the way of Maxwell's shotgun. She covered her ears as he opened fire, moving the cabinet back with the impact. Much larger chunks of wood flew out as shrapnel dispersed through the house. The last shell shattered a window and Rose hid behind a piece of furniture to block herself from the glass. Out of ammunition, Maxwell scrambled to try to find a way to deal with the cabinet while Cicero spoke to them both.

"It needs pieces of itself to reform... I've got an idea. Maxwell, pick up the pieces there and run as fast as you can outside. It'll have no choice but to reform there. Rose, I need you to get to my bag and grab my dynamite. You know, the red stuff that goes boom!" Cicero yelled as Rose nodded. Rose was completely bewildered at what happened to her but set her focus on the task at hand. Behind her, Maxwell scooped up as many spare pieces of wood as he could and chucked them outside his house while Rose held her hand out to the horse.

Cicero's steed reared up at the smell of her body. Rose smelled abhorrent to animals that knew she was doused with an unnatural essence. Rose rummaged through the bag, looking through all sorts of things until she felt a round tube that had to be it. She grabbed a few sticks and ran over to Cicero who helped Maxwell toss pieces of the cursed wood out while the cabinet was beginning to rebuild itself. Now outside of the early morning, Cicero covered his eyes as the sun quickly rose and the temperature started to rise.

"Perfect. Thanks. Now what I'm gonna try to do there—" Cicero said as Rose interrupted him. He raised an eyebrow, as she quickly looked to say something.

"It has a tongue that opens out like a snake, but it's a bed sheet when those double doors open. You're gonna throw that thing in there and blow it to kingdom come right?!" Rose said, as Cicero had a sly grin.

"You learn fast. That's right! We'll bait this thing and hopefully that's the end of it. Whatever it eats, gets sent to where you were. You got spit out, so something that explodes..." Cicero remarked as he noticed Rose grabbed a few sticks of dynamite. While Cicero felt he only needed one for the job, having a few extras in case he made a mistake was a wise move.

Cicero lit a cigarette in his mouth and took a deep puff before taking his eye to the stick of dynamite in Rose's hand. Rose's gaze turned to the nearly completed vessel before the three of them as Maxwell stood by the door holding his axe. Cicero nodded to Rose as she slowly ventured over, weary of trying to avoid getting sent back to the strange place she found herself in. Rose witnessed the replication process with surprise as she noticed the legs were the first to form as it slowly boosted itself up. The distortion effect around the cabinet vanished to indicate the job was complete. Rose was determined to not be made a fool of this time as she waited patiently for the doors to open.

Rose noticed that the cabinet was still as she stared directly at it. Now outside, it seemed that with more onlookers it needed to be careful. Although it lacked eyes of any kind, Rose could tell that it had some way to sense what was nearby. She turned around and faced Cicero with her back turned. A small breeze began to pick up and remove some of the solution that was on her clothes. The scent was picked up and the cabinet slid along the desert floor, grating its wood as it did so. Rose stood closely for a moment as she waited just seconds before the familiar creak of the doors opened, and the tongue shot out attempting to lash its way around her ankle. Cicero held the burning cigarette to the dynamite and cackled with unsettling glee as he ran forward and chucked it in Rose's direction, while she rolled to the side to get away from the impact. The cabinet tongue sensed something in its grasp and scooped the dynamite as intended. Rose looked behind to see there was no explosion, so she was safe for now. Rose walked back to Cicero and wondered if one stick would truly be enough.

Cicero watched as Rose took a moment to rest. She sat on the ground and wiped her forehead seeing that for whatever reason, the cabinet remained unmoved. She adjusted her glasses and noticed something unusual was happening. Unknown to the eyes of Rose and Cicero, the stick of dynamite landed in the strange room and exploded on impact. The entity before them was bloody and beaten. There was a slight delay that was unexpected, but in due time, a gigantic explosion of fire and wood spread throughout the outside. The void of the double doors was no more as the now exposed dark entrance shriveled in the sun's light. Cicero kicked up his hat and offered his hand to Rose. He pulled her up as Rose stood in disbelief at all that she witnessed. Cicero kicked the dust off his pants and walked to Maxwell, waiting for the payment he was promised.

"You asked me earlier what my job was. You guessed correctly and you could say that I'm an exterminator of sorts. Instead of rodents and roaches, I deal with that. The unknown and mysterious," Cicero said to Rose as he continued to count the money. Rose barely registered what Cicero said to her as she attempted to process all that happened.

"Here's your cut. Nobody died so, good work. I was gonna give you twenty percent and call it a day, but I'm feeling generous. Take half." Cicero said. He opened her hand and slapped three two-dollar bills down. Rose was in shock as she now had six dollars to her name, a generous amount for her. The Lord could always provide.

"We could use your shower before we head out?" Cicero asked Maxwell as he nodded in appreciation.

"Oh, and uh, sorry about the house, you know I'm in the killing business, but I do know a good contractor," Cicero added.

The two entered and Rose went through the motions of cleaning herself as she headed to the bathroom to undress and clean. Cicero decided to go second as he and Maxwell discussed details of their encounter. As the two discussed, Rose put her head against the wall and let out a few tears of relief in the shower before packing it in and returning to her doused clothing.

Rose waited quietly for Cicero to exit and the two made their goodbyes to Maxwell.

Rose took her place on the horse and said little while Cicero rode off to town. As far as Cicero was concerned, an honest day's pay was made, and he had no regrets of how things turned out. He was a veteran after all, but for Rose, this would stay with her for quite some time. The first thing she needed to do was find a phone and the first ticket out of there. As Rose and Cicero came to the outskirts of town, Cicero stopped a bit short and dismounted his horse.

"I gave you a little extra for the bag fee. There's always some damn fee that the bankers have. I suppose that's it then. Mavis was telling me you needed to get back to your friends and the rest of the city-slickers." Cicero said as he extended his hand to Rose. Rose looked at the eccentric cowboy and returned the handshake. Although her actions were much more substantive, her tone of voice remained guarded.

"Thanks. I really appreciate it," Rose said with some hollowness in her voice. She gave a simple wave as the cowboy tipped his hat and rode off. Judging by where she was, the train station wasn't too far off for a midday train with no stops if she started walking quickly. Rose counted her money and nodded with some satisfaction, knowing that she had enough to get by and a little extra to boot.

A few days later, Cicero walked in through the saloon to spend his hard-earned cash only to see a familiar face. Despite Rose's insistence some time ago on wanting to get out of town, here she was, sitting by herself at the bartender's table. Her head was flat on the table. She didn't seem to be drunk already, but simply in deep thought of something troubling her. Cicero was intrigued and rather than give his usual snarky comments, decided to hear Rose out.

"What are you still doing here?" Cicero asked. Rose lifted her face and adjusted her glasses, pushing them back slightly with her finger. He noticed Rose was digging into her purse, but simply slid a few quarters to pay for their drinks. Cicero lit a cigarette and blew the smoke behind him as a courtesy.

"Not enough?" Cicero asked as he was cut off by Rose.

"I have more than enough by now. I wanted to go back, but somehow, I felt like I wasn't gonna get what I wanted from it. Go home and do what? The job that I can't stand, and live with my thieving parents who drain all our money on booze?" Rose protested as she waved her hands around in annoyance. Cicero shrugged his shoulders.

"I mean I already spent fifty cents on our whiskey, best to take it down. If you want some advice from an old man Rose, have you asked yourself what you really want to do? I feel like you just do what other people have told you to do. You're better than cleaning some rich person's taint."

"Yeah, I fucking know I am, that's why it makes me so annoyed," Rose grumbled as she stomached the drink.

"Is everyone your age so crass?" Cicero joked, as Rose couldn't help but roll her eyes. Cicero laughed as he downed his and waved over for another round.

"I want to go do the next job with you, Cicero. I'm not sure what I felt, but it challenged me in a way that I've never had before. The solution for anything as a housekeeper was molasses to keep the kids quiet and soap to rub everything out. It's thoughtless and thankless work. After all, I still want to go to college one day and I need to save. What I mean to say is, eventually I'll figure things out. I hope I can write my friends and let them know what happened after we got separated. I hope they're not mad." Rose scratched her nails on the wooden table.

Cicero scratched his beard as he saw Rose's brown eyes staring at him. Cicero worked alone for quite some time, but he was part of a gang once and knew that strength in numbers was always the best solution. Rose acted far better than he anticipated and could think quickly on her feet. She was green, but that was okay. He bit his tongue for a moment as he evaluated the situation and decided that he'd take Rose under his wing.

"Well in that case, I suggest we find somewhere for you to stay, don't know how you lasted this long. The only inn worth staying at in the city is full—" Cicero gestured in the vague direction past their town.

"And they're not exactly... accommodating. My wife Claudia should know somewhere for you to go," Cicero said with a pursed lip as he looked at Rose. Cicero snapped his fingers for the second bartender to fill both their drinks. As the two drank, Cicero gestured to his pocket.

"I have a list of calls I'm just starting to get around to doing. You and I are gonna run through those, but since you're on board, I'll have to show you something. Do you trust me? It will explain a lot of questions," Cicero asked. Rose nodded, happy to see she had a new lease on life.

"We'll head out first thing tomorrow."

Locked And Loaded

Rose found her accommodation less than ideal, but for the night, it would do. Cicero and Claudia didn't have guests often, so they were ill-equipped for Rose to stay somewhere for long. She woke up in a barn and rubbed her eyes. Rose's eyes met the horse she'd come to know from the day before. She shooed the curious animal away as she attempted to get bits of straw out of her hair. She thought about how much Venus and the rest of her friends would have eaten her alive for such unkempt hair, luckily, she was around folks who could care less.

Cicero's ranch was a small but proud abode; he owned two cows and a few chickens, along with two horses. He swapped between his signature gray and a beige colored horse from the barn he built with his own hands. Rose could hear rumbling around that surely was Cicero, but she was surprised this wasn't the case. Rose hummed to herself as she saw the lanky figure of Claudia through the barn window. Claudia walked towards the window and tapped it with her fist, prompting Rose to step back for a moment. She remembered the initially gaunt appearance of the woman before her, with black curled hair and a gray dress.

"Cicero is waiting for you," she said before slinking off. Rose fitted her shoes on and stepped out, still wearing her dirty dress. She felt disgusted, but hopefully could wash her clothing in good time with the best brush money could buy. Cicero waited with a toothpick in his mouth as he folded his arms. Rose stumbled out with an exhausted body as she turned to see him.

"I see you met my wife. She's more of an indoor cat than an outside one. As one would have it, after her... work... she became an undertaker for the town. So if you smell formaldehyde, that's her," Cicero said with a laugh that Rose replied kindly with a slight chuckle.

"So, what are we going to do today? I didn't have sentient furniture on my bingo board, but here we are," Rose asked.

"Bingo?" Cicero asked her with a confused look on his face. Although Rose hadn't bothered wanting to explain, she felt compelled to do so anyway. She noticed the beige horse and climbed towards the side just as she did for the gray.

"It's a game, Yankees like to play it. Malcolm told me he saw it at a carnival once. Fun little thing, you match numbers or words in a row and get a prize," Rose commented as Cicero shrugged his shoulders.

"Fascinating. That's what passes for entertainment these days. Anyway, straight to business I see. I have a list of cases to take, we're going to get you an iron worth your speed, and then we'll be heading to the mountains. There's something you need to see," Cicero explained. Cicero gave a wink to Claudia, who carried a bucket of paint as she prepared to apply a fresh new coat to a nearby wall of the house.

"I-I'm getting a gun!?" Rose asked with some surprise in her voice. Although she hadn't thought about it much, it made sense she would need something a bit better than a knife to protect herself against whatever threats may come their way. Rose looked towards Cicero's bag of fun with devious intent as she saw Cicero hold his hand out.

"Like hell, you're touching my firearms. You'll get one for now, and if the situation arises, you may get another. I'll go into the store; you tell me what you want," Cicero stated to Rose. He could see that Rose was quite stumped about what she wanted.

"In the bag there, check the catalog. It's a bit outdated but if it's not unreasonable, I'll buy it for you. Anything else though, engravings or what have you, comes out of your cut. Got it?" Cicero mentioned as he raised an eyebrow.

Rose nodded as she grasped the book and coursed through the material with interest. She studied every detail of it at a pace that impressed the cowboy as he tipped his hat. With the close of the book, the two were off to settle on what Rose decided would be her companion in time of need. The two arrived at the small town once again. Cicero waved to the many passersby who walked on foot while Rose hardly received such greetings, but she was aware of her status. The feeling was mutual as Rose stuck her gaze to Cicero. The two set the horse down while Rose and Cicero dismounted. Rose leaned against a telephone pole, observing people go by their day while Cicero knocked on the door of the gun store. While usually not open until later, Cicero was a well-paying customer and was allowed first pick of any new shipments.

Cicero met eyes with the gunsmith who raised his eyebrow at him. He got up and opened the door, letting the man inside. He could sense that Cicero was in a rush and quickly got to his cash register. The gun store, like most things in town, was a humble abode. The smith's workshop was in the back of the store and a few of the most prized pieces were kept in protective metal boxes. Glass containers housed the rest of the arms and ammunition on offer. The rest of the store had firearms with prices scratched off in chalk multiple times. Times were hard and the shopkeeper would do anything to make a sale. It also functioned as an impromptu general store, where canned goods and other implements could be bought at the same time.

"Louis, I need a beginner's pistol. Something that's good for warding off varmints if you catch my drift," Cicero stated. Louis was a rotund man with a tight-fitting tan suit and curled mustache. Louis twirled his mustache for a moment, Cicero's actual occupation was well known among the town as they housed a secret of their own. In his hands, he grasped the catalog page that Rose fixated on. Louis gave it a once over and almost rubbed his stomach in laughter.

"Cicero, this-issues' old as all hell. You live right down the street; do you not get our subscription? I can offer you a yearly— " Louis said, stopping himself as he could see Cicero growing annoyed with his offerings. Cicero turned his head to see the bored Rose outside kicking sand while she waited.

"We don't have that model anymore, but, we do have this." Louis held up a finger before going to the back for a moment. Cicero's eyes scanned the rest of the room as he noticed an assortment of new decorations, mostly with Mexican attire, but the man was paler than him. He gave no further judgements as his eyes met a pistol encased in a small briefcase.

"1908 Hammerless, this should do you just fine. I'll even throw in two magazines for free and some ammo. You know, for old times. One magazine for regular bullets, and the other for silver. Just as you've requested before," Louis offered as he winked.

"Mighty generous friend, how much is this running me?" Cicero said as he brought out his wallet. Louis gave another hearty laugh that dulled Cicero's enthusiasm.

"Hahah! Twenty dollars," Louis commented as he opened his hand. Cicero coughed in his hand for a moment as he was taken aback by the price. As his brother was in the military, he often would take advantage of his discounts. Ammunition was fairly inexpensive, but the guns themselves cost quite a bit of money.

"You're still using the LeMat? My Lord, you should melt it for scrap and get a new model. I thought you hated your sister anyway," Louis remarked, seeing the rust on Cicero's gun.

"Stopping power's too good. Just give me the oil and I'll work it. Oh, and that satchel too. She doesn't have pockets." Cicero took out his previous pay and a card to use his store bonus.

Cicero was cleaned out as far as he was concerned, but Rose kept half of the payment from the last job. It didn't matter much though; Rose was going to be his partner and she needed a good weapon to do it. Cicero arrived with a wrapped pistol in a holster for Rose. She raised her glasses for a moment to get a better look at her weapon and couldn't help but give a small bit of glee.

"Alright, here's some rules. Keep your gun holstered at all times. Keep it empty unless you know we're going for a scrape. Do not ever point it at anything you won't put to the ground. Guns are loud, if you're going to fire indoors, just be ready for it. I've also come to realize you women weren't given pockets, so you'll carry a satchel with you. Regular ammunition and magazines will be in this pouch. Silver tipped bullets will be in this pouch." Cicero instructed.

"Oh, right. Thank you. Silver? Isn't that...?" Rose questioned with a confused look on her face. She'd only heard of silver bullets from old wives' tales, she hadn't considered them to be used for anything, let alone something one could buy so easily.

"You'll know more when we get to the mountain. Get on the horse," Cicero said as Rose climbed on without delay. Cicero looked behind him with slight concern as the two continued riding. The visage of the frontier town began to disappear, and Rose questioned Cicero's tight lip. Their horse paced steadily through the scrubland as Cicero tightly maneuvered the horse through cacti and other prickly plants.

"Why all the cloak and dagger?" Rose asked as her question was left unanswered. Cicero simply pointed in the distance to a few cliffs that jutted out on the side of a mountain. The destination of Rose and Cicero was an obscure section of Camelback Mountain. A decade prior, the land was included as part of a nature preserve and left relatively undisturbed. In the olden days, Cicero knew outlaws that would hide up in these hills waiting for lawmen and their hounds to grow bored. One such enclave was a wooden cabin he and his crew stayed in many years ago.

Cicero upped the speed on his horse, rarely using the reins with such fervor as Rose practically held on for dear life. The horse vaulted over a jutted rock that stuck out some distance away as the two continued onward. Rose was unsure of what to make of her situation. She clutched her new satchel with as much protection as she could. She noticed that layers of the mountain were somewhat greener than others. When the rains were plentiful, foliage would bloom and be quite a sight for those that ventured there. Cicero stopped some distance away from the base of the mountain as they came closer. If his memory was correct, he managed to reach the back of the mountain where the sun would set.

"This is Camelback Mountain, once known as Cew S-wegiom by the locals. Here, we'll find what I've been looking for. There's a cabin up there, old now, but the desert heat keeps wood lasting a long time." Cicero dismounted. He winced as he started to climb up. The path was chosen intentionally in his younger days so that they couldn't be pursued on horseback, but it was a great pain to his joints in old age.

Rose wasn't exactly thrilled to climb in a dress and shoes, but she did her best as she hoisted herself on the jutted slabs. She took a knee and extended her hand for Cicero to grab. Much to her surprise, Cicero was lighter than she expected. The two continued onward, taking great care to not lose sight of their objective and slip below. Cicero pointed out the cabin in view, still standing after all this time. Rose was impressed at the sight. The pair walked over, and Cicero nudged the door which was shut in place. He took a deep breath and kicked as hard as he could, prying the door open. The wooden door fell off its hinges as Rose scanned the room. She noticed a few key features, most notably a now rusted cot and some expired cans of food. Her eyes darted to an arrangement of wooden bars on the left side of the room. A small otherworldly glow of purple leaked from it. Rose's eyes widened as she realized what the purple vortex truly meant. She'd only witnessed the blue one and wondered what difference this could hold.

Cicero shook his head for a moment and removed the now decaying beams of wood to reveal the purple vortex in all its glory. Rose stood in awe at the sight as she heard the snapping fingers of Cicero. He stood aside for a moment, as he focused in and saw the remains of a ravaged city. To Rose, it was unreal, she could see a window into another world plain as day. She saw ruined concrete and around the confines of the hole was a purple essence that swirled in the air.

"This, Rose, is why I do what I do. In 1899, I was with some of my friends hiding from lawmen as we all do. We went up and saw this thing appear. This is a vortex to another world. We've looked through it and were curious. One day when we were sleeping, something decided to come out and attack us. It was a relenting husk that looked human but had the appetite of a cougar. It was not of our world, but this one. I don't know what happened to it, but after that day, I noticed that there were more of these vortexes that appeared. There's two I've seen. Blue ones which just take you somewhere random, but you're still here," Cicero said, stomping the ground with his foot for emphasis.

"—but the purple ones take you to a whole new place. Monsters come from these purple ones and we need to send them back." Cicero gestured to his revolvers.

"Have you figured out what to do with these? I saw it boarded up, but that doesn't close the hole," Rose asked as she scratched her head.

"I have no idea how to close the hole. I would have figured it out by now, but the way I see it, if we send a message, maybe it'll close on its own. I have a list of places we need to go," Cicero explained to Rose. Rose agreed and helped Cicero board up the portal once more. She vowed to find a way to close them, if only to satiate her own curiosity. Every theory she'd read in magazines about science could never have prepared her for something quite like this.

"We'll come up with something. I need to go to town and get something new to wear. I'm really running out of clothes," Rose said to Cicero who shrugged his shoulders.

"Right. I actually have some things by the house. We can get that dress switched out for a pair of overalls. I can also show you my favorite part of the business. The bounty board," Cicero said to her.

Terrifying Triffids

The next few days were dedicated to Rose practicing how to shoot her gun while Cicero and Claudia offered their perspectives to help her train. The pair sat on rocking chairs on their porch while they heard the occasional crack through the air. On a successful hit, Cicero would give a thumbs up to cite his approval, while a miss was met with a gruff tone. While Cicero was itching to get started, he couldn't afford the risk of Rose being completely green with her weapon. He didn't have the money for injuries and Rose equally wanted some more familiarity. For the bigger threats, Rose needed to be in tune with her weapon. Cicero arranged a series of glass bottles for her to shoot while he lit a cigarette.

"Well, she could probably try to hit them..." Claudia joked as Cicero raised an eyebrow. Cicero knew it was a bold claim for Claudia to make considering his wife's skill level with some firearms.

"Why I do recall you nearly hitting the wall of the barn when I gave you my shotgun, honey. You may know how to handle a rifle but give it time. She'll learn," Cicero said with a doting tone.

Cicero and Claudia weren't sure how to feel regarding Rose just yet but felt some responsibility for her. It'd been several years since they were parents themselves, but they noticed Rose's rather thin frame and didn't hesitate to load her plate with potatoes and meat. The pair also had different priorities when it came to her. Cicero evaluated her potential, she was book smart, but needed to pick up the ways of the land quickly. Monster hunting required a gruff attitude, and he was afraid she wouldn't be taken seriously as his partner for negotiations. Claudia was concerned about Rose's quality of life. She knew her arrangements were awkward, as sleeping in the barn was hardly an ideal move.

"Cicero, be a dear and fix the loft upstairs. I don't care how much it costs. I think we should move her in there. Seems unfitting to be with the livestock and such," Claudia mentioned as she got up. At no charge, Claudia washed Rose's dress in a large bucket with soap and water to get some of the offending stench off. The solution bubbled as the dress sat with the dried blood slowly eating away. In the interim, Rose wore a pair of tight-fitting overalls with a few stains from the livestock.

"Yeah, I'll get on it. Just one more thing to fix around here," Cicero mumbled to himself. He straightened his back as Claudia looked towards him.

Rose continued her practice with the gun and steadily improved. As she wore glasses, Rose could focus better on one target and give a slow but accurate shot. Rose knew she needed to be faster, there was no way a monster was just going to let her shoot at it unless she was lucky. She thought about the different ways to manipulate her sidearm, but followed the standard practice to hold it straight out with one hand to keep it stable.[1] Rose also noticed that her ears started to dull a bit with the sound. It still shocked her as she felt each crack, but it was expected. She saw Cicero's head perk up as he heard more glass breaking than cracks through the air and he gave the tip of the hat in return. Rose exhausted her ammunition for the time being but had a few spares stored back in her bag.

"That's all for now. Let's head inside! Make sure your gun's un—Oh, you've already unloaded it. Good," Cicero mentioned to Rose as she nodded.

---

1. The shooting style of the early 20th century vastly differed with pistols as the style of one-armed shooting was considered effective by W. E. Fairbairn.

Rose made her way inside and saw that Cicero removed a lot of the debris that made up the interior of their home. She observed the rustic decor of everything and saw the outline of Cicero and Claudia's room. On the walls, she saw faded photographs and newspaper clippings of what appeared to be Cicero's exploits in days long since passed. Rose felt an itch crawl up her back at the state of the home, everything was still in disarray with no proper order. She found it uncouth to go and sift through other people's belongings, but her former employment embedded the need to wash and disinfect everything down to the last nub. She turned her attention to Cicero, who walked inside and threw his jacket on a nearby rack as he stretched his arms out.

"Our son lived up in the loft, so you can go take there once it's clean. Now, like I was sayin' before. Come with me to the kitchen," Cicero explained.

Rose looked at a corkboard with an assortment of notes, blurry pictures, and handwritten drawings on the wall. Rose accurately assessed that this was the so-called bounty board that Cicero mentioned before. She noticed one picture that was ripped off with only a fragment remaining, this being the cursed cabinet that they destroyed a few days ago.

"Now, up here is the bounty board. I'm a bounty hunter— legally— that is, but I'm no marshal. There's a secret number that people give to the operator if they want our services. For transparency, I'll answer the phone. People are expecting my more... matured tone over the line. Anyway, I'll gather as many details as I can and then we put it on here. I'll usually take a push pin and place the stuff we need right there," Cicero explained as he watched Rose's eyes track each piece.

"Understood. What's this? A blank piece of paper with some lines on it?" Rose asked.

"Well, that's the sign-up sheet. I reckon since I'm getting older, I expand my efforts my bit and if I find promising folks like yourself, they can write their name and the case they want to take," Cicero mentioned. Rose rubbed her hands together in anticipation but was stopped by the gentle hand of Cicero on her shoulder.

"Not yet. You're still green before you can do stuff on your own. I usually recommend teams of two, so you'll be with me. If we do get other people, some cases will need all of us, so keep that in mind."

"There's a gardener out by the city that's been having some issues. We have a rancher and his son who called in saying some kind of wild animal is causing mayhem on the farm and many more, so take your pick and see what suits you," Cicero urged Rose as he waited to see what suited her interest.

Rose gave little delay in her choice as her finger was placed on the gardener's woes. She didn't have any real preference in mind on where to start, but she knew farmland and crops well enough. The gardener's proximity to the city is also something she had in mind as she wanted to start locating her mysterious benefactor. The past few days when Rose slept, all she could recall was her voice and what she looked like. Rose pieced together that this woman wanted her here for some reason, and she needed to give her proper thanks.

While the two prepared to mount up, Rose was called by Cicero. Cicero wanted to improve Rose's equestrian skills as this was their primary method of transportation going forward. By now, the horses had gotten used to her scent and were hardly surprised when she moved close to them. Rose herself remained hesitant, but slowly built a bond with the animals. Cicero finished equipping his gear and studied Rose, who looked bright-eyed and ready to learn more.

"I think you should learn how to ride Rose. You'll take Mary and I'll take George. Mary's the blond one," Cicero declared. Rose slowly climbed off George and moved to Mary. Rose slowly walked by and rubbed the horse's neck as it stirred for a bit before returning to normal. Cicero threw Rose the spare saddle which she almost dropped as she was surprised at the weight. Rose secured it tightly on the horse and got up.

Rose and Cicero set out on the trail once more, where Cicero led with a more leisurely pace, but intent was on reaching their goal before the heat of the day. Cicero's head was on a swivel as he waved to Rose to guide Mary to follow. The horse instinctively knew to follow the other and would guide Rose back to the track when she veered off course. Rose could hear the clinking of metal in her satchel as everything started to move. Cicero noticed a particularly flat stretch of land and looked back at Rose with a sly grin. He snapped his fingers for his horse to run at a much faster speed while Rose and her horse followed. Rose gripped onto the reins as tightly as she could as the horse weaved past tight bushes and openings in the ground. She looked amazed as she and the horse were in the air for a few seconds. For the first time in a while, Rose felt genuine relief from the heat as the wind generated by the horse blew past her. Cicero cackled loudly as he noticed Rose starting to enjoy herself. Rose, on the other hand, wanted to know more about her new partner.

"You said you and Claudia have a son!? What's the rest of your family like!?" Rose yelled over the running horses.

"Family?! Well, you met Claudia already. What's there to tell? I have my younger brother Colin and then there's my sister Petunia. I grew up here, born in the New Mexico territory. My father got sold the bullshit of coming West. My older sister was a slaver, and my older brother was a pimp, so you can tell I come from good stock. The only one I talk to these days is the runt beneath me, he does something important at the Army base here. Like I give a damn. We had my son Patrick too, but he died a few years back. I got him into the business but then he had his family, and I couldn't rest knowing I'd make his wife a widow, so I cut him loose. Had a life of his own, nice wife and some city job, but got the flu. Get this, didn't wear a mask like the doctors said to and he died. It wasn't bullets or monsters that did it, just some... bug," Cicero yelled back.

"That's terrible! We get polio outbreaks back where I'm from all the time. I've been blessed so far," Rose responded.

Rose took a minute to track her progress so far with the horse as she noticed a paved road some distance away from where they were riding. A lone car breezed past them at top speed with some tired driver at the helm. It was clear they'd been driving since the night before. Rose shrugged her shoulders and looked back onto the trail; technology kept marching forward no matter what.

"Claudia and I were talkin' and I remember you mentioned your parents took your money? What's that about? Is that why you stuffed a wad of cash in your shoe?" Cicero questioned. Rose pursed her lips as she realized the bind she put herself in. After a couple drinks, Rose was more willing to bring that stuff to light, but it was engrained into her for a lady to not talk about their problems. She found it a bit surprising that Cicero bothered to remember that fact at all. Rose gave a surface level answer that she hoped would move the topic forward.

"We grew up poor. That's about it," Rose said as Cicero darted ahead.

Rose soon saw the growing urban sprawl of Phoenix before her. The number of cars on the road tripled in volume compared to their horses as homesteads vanished in place of apartment buildings and hotels. Cicero held his hand up for Rose to stop as he withdrew a map from his bag.

"Now if I remember correctly, I think we can go through the main line... over yonder and take a sharp left. Seems this person's a florist, well now... We can get paid, and I can bring Claudia some chrysanthemums, they're in season this year," Cicero remarked.

Rose and Cicero looked for a nearby post to tie their horses and put them in place. Despite the growing number of parking lots and empty areas reserved for cars, the city still knew its western roots and held fence posts handy. On the occasions these weren't found, people would tie their horses to telephone poles instead as they maintained a presence along the sidewalk.

"You know, I could never own a car. How're you supposed to tell them apart? They're all one color!" Cicero joked as Rose chuckled.

Rose and Cicero made their way to the florist's and Cicero started the proceedings while Rose hung back and looked at what was on display. She noticed an assortment of well-pruned flowers and was appreciative of the craftsmanship assigned to the pots that held them. The store was adorned with Italianesque writing and pictures as each flower held a detailed log of its origins, times of year, and what they represented. Rose hardly understood flower language, but she knew that there was a tone set depending on the type of flower given to someone along with intentions.

"Oh, you must be Cicero, I sent a letter in the mail," the florist said as he pushed up his glasses. He was rail-thin and wore a green button-down shirt that was perpetually covered in dirt. Presented behind him was a wall of awards and publications, the man was an academic from start to finish.

"You know, you can just place a call. Letters are slower to get to where I'm at. Now my partner and I are gonna go see the problem. What's got you troubled?" Cicero mentioned as he placed his hands on the man's shoulder.

"L-Let us go to the garden, and you will see what I mean," the florist said as he guided Cicero and Rose to follow.

The garden looked immaculate as each piece was carefully watered with a complicated system of pipes from captured rainwater. Rose was perplexed how well the garden was in the middle of a desert, but human ingenuity remained unmatched. Her eyes looked for anything out of the ordinary and she kept her ears primed to hear the man's tale. The florist was hardly the first place she figured to have problems like the ones she and Cicero dealt with, but she kept an open mind.

"It was a few days ago, I received word from a customer that they gathered some sort of mysterious seed. I am a botanist in the scientific tradition and therefore, I felt it was my duty to study such a piece. My customer mentioned to me they found it on a hike and after seeing some strange mysterious light, they felt compelled to bring it home," the florist explained.

"This... strange mysterious light... was the color purple?" Rose interjected.

"Why, yes it was. Have you experienced something like this?" The florist asked. Cicero nodded to confirm her statement.

The florist guided the pair to a small misshapen hole in the ground to where he originally planted the seed. Rose and Cicero exchanged a glance before looking at the mound once more. Out of the corner of his eye, Cicero noticed what looked like a broken dog kennel some distance away.

"Do you have any pets?" Cicero inquired. Rose was unsure why he was asking that question, but as she also saw the kennel, her thoughts aligned the same.

"Not at all. When I first raised the seed, it grew at an exponential rate. Within a day, I already had a full-fledged plant. It was small, but it rejected the fertilizer I gave it. It wanted... meat. Now, before you lose me, there are plants that eat insects. I have documented these in my studies, however, the meat that this plant searched for and attracted at first was birds. Pigeons are bad for business, so it was an agreeable partnership. The next day, the plant got bigger, and it started to move around. I placed it in a kennel to keep it in place. I saw your eyes dart towards it. Oh yes, it grew larger than that as well. Poked a hole clean through it," the florist continued to explain.

"As the plant fully matured, it formed to be a saguaro cactus, this makes sense given our geography, but something was terribly—" The florist mentioned. His voice was cut off by a scream that pierced through the open space of the garden.

The three left the flower shop and looked down at the block of the street. They saw a ten-foot cactus with its appendages moving as independent pieces of its body. The center of it held a mouth with sharp protruding spikes that functioned as its teeth. The abomination moved by lifting itself off the ground and using its root system to tear apart asphalt underneath it. In areas where the cactus could not root, it could consolidate its system to a giant foot and waddle to position. People in nearby cars were perplexed at the sight and attempted to honk the horn at the cactus. Some were frozen with fear as they noticed the unnatural appearance of the plant. One brave samaritan rushed to find the police station but the quickest among them was apprehended. A giant spike protruded through the ground to trip the man as it wrapped around his ankle and dragged him along the ground to lift into its mouth. The cactus lacked crushing jaws and therefore could not eat the man directly, but instead expanded its body around him and started to melt him in its digestive juices. The sight was enough to nearly make Rose sick, but a supportive look from Cicero brought her ready to battle.

Rose and Cicero ran down the street to meet with the entity. Rose's concern was in regard to the civilians getting caught in the crossfire of the pair as Cicero already started firing down range with his revolver. With a few cars headed towards its direction, the cactus moved one of its arms and launched a flurry of sharp needles. These needles held little penetrative strength, but they were enough to cause ruptures in the exposed thin car tires and send people flying onto the street as the cars overturned. The chaos of the scene emboldened the plant to uproot itself and waddle in another direction as it slammed into the wall of a building. The impact of such a heavy and large collision knocked over a few bricks and partially collapsed a nearby store. The owner attempted to escape before the mayhem continued but was swept away by a growth that emerged from the cactus as it wrapped around and launched them into a car. The pair were in a tight bind, if Rose or Cicero got too close to the cactus, they were at risk of falling into its jaws just like the first man. Running away would cause it to sprout up a spike and that could also prove dangerous.

Cicero's solution was to pepper it with enough ammunition and then get something to blow it up as he favored doing, but this required a tad more finesse from Rose's perspective. Cicero loaded in a few silver bullets as he noticed the plant had an exceptionally fast healing factor. The last few bystanders were well out of the plant's range now as Cicero guided the stragglers out while keeping the plant occupied. Cicero noticed that the plant responded to direct attacks on it and wondered how he could make it damaged long enough. He'd seen that it already was busy consuming one person.

"Is that... someone's leg dangling out of its mouth?!" Rose asked herself as she tried to calm down. Rose envisioned the cactus as a giant glass bottle and placed a few shots onto the plant. Pieces of it fell to the street as the bullets made their mark but did little to stop the cactus' rampage. The bullets that Rose first used had already been healed up and the creature remained unaffected by any other sort of damage on it.

As Rose ran to meet up with Cicero, her eyes met the pavement that started to slowly crack as a giant spike launched out of the ground, just moments from colliding with her. She felt her heart rise as she just narrowly avoided a gruesome impalement from such an entity. Rose looked to see the florist hiding behind a nearby brick wall, and occasionally poked his head out to see the progress. Rose couldn't ask for his help, they were hired to do a job and she needed to find a solution. Rose recalled she and Cicero's brief conversation with the florist and remembered his comments regarding the origins of the plant. While it remained an incredible opponent, the plant seemed to still operate under conventional conditions.

Cacti have root systems like any other ol' plant! I remember reading that plant roots can spread real far and wide. I wonder... Is my movement telling the plant where I am? It's got no ears, no eyes, as far as I can tell... It must be vibrations. Rose thought.

Rose raised an eyebrow as she decided to let out another shot but stayed still. The cactus offered no response until it felt a direct hit on itself. Its body moved all at once as it turned to face her direction. Rose observed how parts of the entity were moving independently of one another.

I was right! The cactus can detect vibrations and attack us that way. We need to figure out a way to deal with this in one fell swoop.

Rose recalled that her movements were too slow to dodge the spikes and her steps would gather the cactus' rampage, but she thought about Mary. For a few seconds, Mary and Rose were able to jump over crevices and rocks without touching the ground. Rose was willing to test the effective range of the roots as she slowly backed away before retreating into a full sprint as she yelled at Cicero.

"Cicero! I have an idea! I need you to get any people left out the way! Do you have matches on you!?" Rose yelled.

"Left pocket in George's saddlebag! I've got a case of twelve. What are you cooking up?" Cicero yelled as he crouched behind an overturned car and popped two more shots from his revolver.

A slurry of gasoline fell from the exposed tanks of the cars and coated the street with it where some dangled on the cactus' appendages. As the plant lacked any sort of smell, it was not aware of this predicament. Rose figured that she could use the speed of her horse to dodge the plant's attacks and throw a lit match onto the gasoline-covered cactus and watch it burn. Cicero reached the same conclusion as Rose did, where the plant reacted based on vibrations. Cicero took it slow as he carefully loaded his revolver. He dropped a bullet and quickly recovered it before it touched the pavement. He wasn't sure how sensitive the cactus's sense of touch was. Cicero noticed the smell of gasoline and his eyes darted to find Rose on saddleback. He raised an eyebrow but came to a look of realization as he rubbed his hands together. Cicero gave her some covering fire and then rolled along the ground to avoid a swing from the plant's arms, right before another spike rose out between his legs.

"Felt my stones rise up to my throat there," Cicero mumbled. Cicero isolated from the ongoing carnage in an alleyway and climbed a nearby ladder. As he was suspended in the air, he held little worry as he continued to shoot the plant.

Rose ducked her head to avoid the bullets given by Cicero as she urged the horse to ride onward. It was a tough sell; Mary was a horse that went her own way, but Rose laid her head on the horse to ensure the animal's safety. With one hand on the reigns, Rose held a match in her mouth as she scratched it off the box and held the lit piece. She quickly placed the matches back inside and did her best to shield the flame. The combined weight of Rose and the horse was enough to center all its attacks on the pair, but the horse's sense of hearing and instincts won the day. The horse hopped over a protruding spike from the ground and gave Rose just enough airtime to chuck the lit match onto the ground.

Rose took a deep breath as she waited for the flames to start, and she feared it wasn't enough. A few moments later, a billow of smoke came out of the erupting gasoline and headed towards the dangling plant. The cactus rampaged as it uprooted itself once more and attempted to shake off the fire, but it had already consumed one of its arms as it withered into a piece of black. Rose was aware that cacti were more resilient to fire than other plants, but a gas fire was nothing to contend with. Her eyes filled with smoke as the plant soon stopped moving and collapsed. Cicero recalled that a man was inside the now burning plant and he covered his mouth with a bandana to approach. He withdrew his Bowie knife and cut open the defeated cactus and was able to save the man inside. The digestive process was interrupted while the cactus was on the prowl and aside from a few drinks to remove the events of the day, the man was fine.

Rose observed all the damage of the streets and felt terrible. She didn't want to think about those that couldn't make it or were injured and hoped for the best. Cicero advanced towards her quickly with a proud grin on his face.

"Yeah, we've made a mess. Let's get our pay and get the hell out of here. Cleaning up is for the police to handle. Good work," Cicero said. He gave Rose a pat on the back while she remained on top of Mary. The meek florist happily opened his wallet to give Cicero twenty dollars. Cicero snatched it with speed as he looked behind him.

"Well, my business is saved. It is appreciated. I am also a member of the City Council; I can explain the situation, and everything should be fine," the man mentioned as he noticed Cicero's skittish reaction.

"Right. We should get a move on. Claudia's probably got chili brewing," Cicero waved for Rose to ride off while he meandered over to the telephone pole.

Cicero found good-byes difficult as he'd softened a bit compared to previous years. He had plenty of fight left, but much like the young Rose, accepting the loss of those as collateral damage was troublesome for sober thoughts. Cicero moved ahead of Rose to chart the way home and felt a small sense of pride in his choice of mentee. Smart, quick on her feet, and nothing left to lose was a fantastic combination for some great work to be done.

Woeful Wolves

Rose and Cicero were out filling Claudia's grocery list as the pair visited an assortment of stores. Rose took her travels to a nearby crafts store and looked for needle and thread to repair her and Cicero's clothing after combat. The smaller hunts were easy for the pair to avoid damage, but the payout was low. The pair were constantly needing to restock ammunition and other supplies as their days grew longer and longer from the homestead. She balanced her budget and looked to additionally get some stationery so she could continue to send letters to Malcolm. She prayed that he could locate her friends who she hoped journeyed to New York and to update their correspondence.

Rose was ridden with guilt as she hadn't had the means to check on Venus, Celia, or the others. Rose was excited to tell them all about her adventures and how she had much greater confidence in her abilities. On occasion, young women much like herself, would walk up and ask about the things she'd seen and how to get involved themselves. Rose and Cicero's antics were starting to reach the discussion of those that read the anecdote sections of the newspaper. The florist gave a resounding review of their quick thinking and other people delivered their testimony on the smaller cases handled with professionalism. She felt that she was doing a genuine service for the communities that lived around Arizona.

Rose and Cicero split responsibilities as the two were tasked with their lists. Rose gathered working supplies, while Cicero looked to buy produce from a corner store and ammunition from the neighboring gun store. He'd gotten the latter already and searched for salted meat and a bushel of apples for last as Claudia wanted to make a nice apple pie. Cicero rummaged around in his pocket while he looked at the scrambled list of instructions left for the pair.

"Granny Smith apples? The hell are those? Green color—Aren't apples supposed to be red?" Cicero asked.

As Cicero rummaged around looking for the treasured apples, another visitor came to the grocery store. He was woefully overdressed compared to the clientele and walked through the double doors of the establishment without a sound accompanying him. A few shoppers could hardly avert their gaze at the man's tall stature. Some wondered why someone of his status would come to this corner store as opposed to a larger supermarket with a much greater selection. The man appreciated the rustic values of the establishment and was looking for something specific. Cicero felt his breathing slow as he looked towards the entrance of the store. Bright as day, he recognized the appearance of a man that caused him to lose control over himself. The Baron appeared in the store and shopped among the commoners. Cicero looked into the man's deceptively sharp blue eyes. The glance was returned as he adjusted his staunch handlebar mustache. His pressed suit was void of dirt and his top hat was wrinkle-free.

In the middle of the store, Cicero let out a scream that unnerved a few other shoppers. He remained with his fingers pointed as he shook in utter terror. The Baron looked around and noticed eyes were on him from Cicero's outburst. He recognized most of the people in the store who were either directly under his employment or at least partially related to his ventures. The Baron built Phoenix and many other cities, but felt it was important to maintain social control. He gave a simple wave of his hand at such an accusation of wrongdoing. The Baron knew that the commoners were simplistic and any sign from authority would be enough to placate their demands.

"Just a harmless old man who lost his way. I will take him back to where he needs to go. Raise no alarm," The Baron said as his voice soothed the concerns of other shoppers.

"Why, you appear as if you've seen a ghost." The Baron looked over Cicero. The Baron was one to hardly make a scene in public, but he decided to toy with Cicero.

Cicero's shaking was so apparent, he dropped the bushel of apples in his possession. Cicero was paralyzed by fear. The bundle rolled in separate directions and was now covered with dust from the floor. The Baron noticed one roll by his heel. He knelt and dusted off the apple. In his pocket, he withdrew a dollar coin and walked towards the cashier situated at a desk in the center of the store. The Baron cared little for theatrics as he was here for business, but he decided to further assert his authority.

"Cashier. I will be paying for the bills of everyone in here, place it on my store credit and a check will be delivered to you by tomorrow," The Baron mentioned. Those that overheard his words were frantically trying to stuff their baskets with as much as possible.

The Baron took advantage of the chaos within the store so he could speak without discretion. The Baron silently walked up to the frozen Cicero and placed his hand on his shoulder. As he did so, Cicero noticed that portions of the store behind The Baron started to visually contort and cave in as if he was making a vortex with his very eyes. The two men were the same height, but Cicero felt ever smaller as he heard the man's voice. The Baron held strict control as it slowly returned to normal. His attention was centered on Cicero as he stared at him with a rage that simmered like a boiling pot.

"I know what you've been up to, Cicero. I hear how you disparage my image, and I find you... entertaining. The dithering old man who is behind the times is one of my favorite things. It doesn't matter how many of my men you and your gang have killed, or how many ventures you've taken. I am unstoppable. Little boy, you'd know better than to dip your nose into affairs that don't concern you," The Baron reveled in Cicero's lack of a response.

Unknown to The Baron and Cicero, Rose had finished her shopping early and peered into the establishment. Rose carried a puzzled look on her face as she noticed the subtle contortion on a store's shelf that vanished shortly after. She noticed Cicero was in discussion with another man and decided to not interrupt. The conversation appeared tense from her perspective. She speculated that the man before her was the owner of the store and was giving him a hard time. Rose carried a frown on her face as she could see the sweat on Cicero's face. It wasn't the usual sweat from the heat of the day, but his subdued shaking and tuckered lip meant something was surely wrong.

The Baron left Cicero with a grimace as he took the remaining apple from Cicero's basket and ate it. He took his time to chew to the core while Cicero remained immobile with fear. The Baron knew his mind had to be racing with how many of the cowboy's allies were in his pocket. There was nobody he could trust, and to erode Cicero into a paranoid pariah, is exactly what he wanted. He turned around to make his exit to the store, where Rose and The Baron briefly met each other's eyes. The Baron stopped for a second in thought before taking off.

Rose let Cicero gather himself before waving to him to meet her outside. Cicero got a new bushel of apples and salted meat and the two rode back off to the homestead. Rose didn't bother bringing up the nature of Cicero's encounter. It was obvious to her he was clearly embarrassed and decided to focus her attention on the next hunt they had scheduled. The two conversed briefly on horseback about their expectations for the next week and discussed strategies that worked and the ones that didn't. As they returned, Claudia greeted them with a warm stew that wafted into their noses.

The two ate happily while Claudia looked over the list of things brought back. While most of her hunts with Cicero were out in the city, he felt confident in expanding their operations throughout the rest of the state. Rose looked at the bounty board and saw an assignment where the two would be tasked in eliminating some sort of dog based on the blurry photographs. Rose wondered if these dogs were the same ones that attacked her and Venus back home.

"We're headed to Duncan, first thing tomorrow. It's a four-and a half-hour trip by horse so we can get there at sunrise. Get some rest, we've earned it," Cicero mentioned as he retired to sleep early.

Rose climbed up the stairs and fit what remained of her stuff into the loft. She felt the alleviating feel of the bed, and despite the stifling temperatures, fell asleep quickly. She settled into a nice routine of flipping herself on the spare sheets as the sweat started to pile on top. Without a clock to wake her, Rose kept her ears primed for any sounds from Cicero or Claudia who were early birds. After she felt enough time passed, Rose stumbled out of the loft and went about her morning routine. She was met with the quiet scraping of Cicero eating a plate of beans. He offered some but Rose was still full from an early midnight snack.

Not much later, the pair were off once again. The ride to Duncan was uneventful, and the town itself was a small blip on the map compared to the big city. Rose noted the population was only around four hundred people, it was a very small development and she wondered who would be able to afford Cicero's asking rate this time. The town held only wooden buildings with brick linings on the newest ones. She noticed a single bank with a lone teller that looked bored. Cicero's garb was recognized by some of the townsfolk as the pair rode into the further square. Rose looked at Cicero and wondered if everything truly was alright. She knew he seemed perturbed after meeting with that strange man and wondered what could have facilitated that conversation. She knew practically everyone enjoyed his presence as the gregarious figure he was.

"What took you so long?" a woman mentioned as she got Cicero's attention. Cicero raised an eyebrow and noticed her attire. She was a working professional that appeared to be a suffragette carrying pamphlets. Cicero tipped his hat and Rose lowered her head as an accompanying greeting.

"Apologies mam, the town's a bit small on our map. How can we be of service to you?" Cicero asked.

"There's a problem with our livestock, they're being attacked by wolves," the woman explained.

"Wolves? With all due respect mam, we haven't had wolves here for what, a generation at least. Hunting's brought them all down to heel. Are you sure these aren't coyotes?" Cicero asked.

"I know a wolf when I see one. I placed the call to you two weeks prior as there was one that killed our prized cow Bethany. There was some flashing purple light that came by in the sky, and then I heard howling. A sinister howling and a scratching sound."

While Cicero and the woman talked with one another, Rose looked around the town and saw she was receiving several glares from people. It wasn't anything she wasn't used to, but the amount of people that were looking at her was a bit shocking. She kept her concerns to herself for now and looked to help with the situation as best as she could.

"Their fur glistens in the light. It's not natural," one man chimed in as he was eavesdropping on their conversation.

"Not a hair in sight. Usually, they leave a little something behind," Rose said to Cicero.

Cicero nodded his head for Rose to follow as they took their horses around the town. They searched for anything out of the ordinary. The wolves were far different than anything expected. These wolves were in a pack of three that overlooked the town on a ridge. Their backs glistened, not due to the color of their fur, but because they were made of diamonds. These wolves were a marriage of organic and inorganic where their gem properties allowed them to merge with the earth and travel freely into the ground and rematerialize as solid beings. These animals were originally

Mexican wolves that found themselves in the vicinity of a purple vortex and emerged changed.

Rose noticed a particular glint hit from her glasses as the rays of the sun reflected to her eye. She instinctively covered her eyes while Cicero looked behind him. His horse reared up as its ear moved to hear the tremors below the surface. The first wolf seamlessly emerged from the sand as it reconstructed in front of them. These wolves were emboldened by their new status and held little fear for man. Smaller and more agile than gray wolves, they made quick work around the pair as their horses kept a respectable distance. Their target was a goat that was kept in a nearby barn. Rose and Cicero's first instincts were to start shooting as quickly as possible. The bullets ricocheted off the back of the animals and started placing bullet holes in wood and cracking windows.

"Great, another bulletproof—" Rose mentioned as Cicero responded.

"Only the back, the underbelly still looks natural. We'll figure out how to do this. Wait-my lasso. I have an idea," Cicero said with a sly grin.

Rose passed Cicero a lasso that was tied on her horse and the two went to work. Cicero intended to use the lasso to wrap the leg of the wolf and drag it with the force of his horse. He raised his hand and spun it around as he got a larger loop from his lasso.

"This ain't a pig, but hopefully it'll hold—What the hell!" Cicero screamed as he noticed the animal start to phase through the sand. Cicero snapped his fingers in frustration and attempted to ricochet his bullets off a metal fixture to attack the wolf. He fanned his revolver with reckless abandon as he nearly landed his mark.

Rose looked to see that two more wolves were part of the pack. They arose from the sand as well. Panicked onlookers attempted to hide wherever they could. Rose noticed that some of the properties had tile floors made of hardened earth and she wondered if the wolves could travel through tougher surfaces than sand. Rose hoped to bait one of the wolves inside a home for use to test her theory. She didn't want to violate these people's homes, but it was a cost of the job. Rose looked for a seemingly empty house as Cicero continued to ward the wolves off from the barn with the goat. Rose dismounted her horse and looked towards an empty home. It was locked, but a quick gunshot through the window allowed her to climb inside and open the door.

Cicero watched with a puzzled look on his face at Rose's actions, but knew she had something in mind. Cicero's revolver trick managed to injure one of the wolves. He withdrew his shotgun from the back of his horse and pumped two shells into the animal. Just one was enough to pierce its underbelly and it started to bleed out. Cicero reloaded and put his attention to another wolf.

"I can't get a hold on them with my lasso, they're looser than a greased cow! What are you looking in there for!?" Cicero yelled to Rose.

"The floors! They're coming up through the sand right? Let's give them something a bit harder," Rose mentioned.

Cicero decided to take the initiative and open the barn door. He nestled the tiny goat as it squirmed around but as it saw the hungry wolves, decided against making a fuss. He and the goat rode to Rose's position. The remaining two wolves let out a howl of warning to the pair for interfering with their hunt. Rose gave no mind and quickly ushered the goat into the home as a trap. The two wolves were far more careful about resurfacing as one of their own fell. While in the sand, Rose or Cicero couldn't land a hit on either one.

The two wolves could hear the conversation going on between Rose and Cicero. After some time, it stopped, and the wolves also heard no movement. The wolves resurfaced only to find Rose and Cicero with big planks of wood that collided with their heads. Rose stunned the first wolf and watched as Cicero placed two more bullets from his revolver. The animal's guts spread across the tile floor and the crackle of gems hit as the animal's back collided with the wall. The last wolf attempted to give fealty to the group as it saw it was clearly outmatched. Rose looked slightly upset but knew she had a job to do. She shot it in the stomach just as it attempted to shift back into sand. One last bullet did the job, and the wolves were no more.

As Rose and Cicero gathered themselves, some of the town started to go back to their business. Rose still felt an eerie sense from the town as the two went back to their horses. Cicero holstered his revolver and kept a steady hand on his shotgun. The woman that hired them was sequestered in the local library and stuck her head out to see that the job was done. She held a small bag with a wad of cash to deliver. Cicero raised an eyebrow as a growing crowd started to converge around them.

"The threat's gone, nothin' else is here. If you need anything—" Cicero said as he got cut off by a man.

"I didn't give you consent to enter my barn!" a rancher shouted at the pair.

Rose shot a look at Cicero as he tried to calm the man down to explain the situation. The wolves were after the goat, so he felt that taking the initiative by entering the barn was the best move. The townspeople seemed to be working themselves up in a frenzy. Cicero was used to dealing with those that had issues with his methods. He gestured to his pockets, one held some hush money, and the other was the holster of his revolvers. He was fine using either method to make sure peace was maintained.

"You want the wolves dead or not? I reckon you be grateful for what you have. Isn't your representative coming?" Cicero remarked. Cicero started to sweat a little as he saw the growing crowd of about forty people each with their own complaints.

"Bullet holes in my home! That's going to cost money to repair, not to mention that spook you have with you, can't aim for shit!" another man shouted as Rose frowned at his comment.

Rose looked at the time and noticed that the chaos of the day had already led it to an early sunset. Her arms started to sweat as her eyes looked for the woman that was supposed to pay them. The woman with the wad of cash raised her hand to wave to the others, but she was stopped by something. A group of about ten people that observed the scene came by brandishing pitchforks and shovels.

"Don't you go another inch!" a woman shouted from the crowd to the suffragette. The suffragette found herself engulfed by people much like that of Rose and Cicero.

Cicero still tried to maintain a democratic approach, while Rose attempted to bottle her growing fear. Much like home, she could see that people were starting to get antsy and she had a large target painted on her back. While the pair accomplished their goal, it wasn't a hunt without controversy. The effects of this showed as Cicero soon lost his patience with the others and Rose was put off entirely. Cicero was a known name, but Rose had started to gain some notoriety herself in the monster hunting world after her exploits with the cactus and other smaller finds. The crowd surged with anger as they raised their fists and pitchforks in the air. Cicero expected a payout as usual, but holdouts magnified in volume. The town of Duncan considered itself a proper sundown town, where they'd be cordial at best, in the day, but after-hours black people and other minorities were expected to leave. Cicero was unaware of this social transgression that he violated, and the people were rabid over it. Cicero hadn't realized that the town refused to pay him due to Rose's presence after hours.

The sneers of the crowd grew closer as Rose and Cicero felt boxed in towards their horses. The crowd kicked up sand and tossed small rocks. Cicero withdrew his revolver and cocked the hammer back. He spewed a few insults back to the bolder of the crowd. There were many times when an ungrateful populace refused to give him his due and he had no qualms about acquiring it in other ways. A holdover from his outlaw days, Cicero's persona was much different to Rose. Rose hadn't heard such a tone come from Cicero before. She wondered how much of his tales of the outlaw life were grandstanding. She realized that all those pictures of Cicero on the wall at home were wanted posters. Wanted posters that he collected and held up as a shrine to a life no longer lived.

"We did our part, now pay up. This isn't a charity," Cicero mentioned with gritted teeth.

"All you did was destroy our property value!" a man huffed with curled fists.

"Get a rope for that jigaboo and string her high!" another man shouted as he got some support from his followers.

Rose's fear was magnified as she saw the growing hatred hurled towards her. It took everything in herself to not break down into tears as they wanted. Rose was far from naive when it came to knowing her place in the world, but it filled her with an incredible sadness all the same. Rose witnessed multiple lynchings growing up and each sent her further into an emotional spiral that grew harder to get out of. Her trust in others eroded and it brought a primal sense of anguish as she looked at the contorted faces of those around her, desperate for blood. Rose looked past the scene to see growing violence on account of the suffragette that was surrounded by others. The crowd moved in on her and struck her with their fists as she attempted to defend herself. Rose could see the poor woman tossed aside as men and women alike, slapped and kicked her. She was coughing blood as the demands of the mob grew more outrageous. It was only a matter of time before the violence would head its way to Rose and Cicero. Cicero stepped forward and drew a line in the sand with his boot.

"We're getting paid. Cross that line and I'm putting you down," Cicero mentioned.

One man with a shovel marched forward in clear defiance. Cicero was unsure about the man's intelligence as he clearly meant what he said. Cicero pulled out his revolver and without hesitation, the shot of his gun rang through the air. The man's kneecap split open as he shot the man and he fell over much to the enraged crowd. As far as Cicero was concerned, he was the man with the gun and the one who'd make the decisions. His expression remained cold and unmoved as he pulled the hammer back once more. Cicero reached back for his shotgun as he felt a larger firearm would be needed to address his point.

"Go home, nigger lover!" a woman shouted from the crowd as she threw a glass bottle at Cicero. He remained unmoved as he raised his shotgun in the air.

"Next shot's going in your head and the guy right behind you, don't play with me missus!" Cicero yelled.

The standoff between Rose, Cicero, and the crowd grew to a point where even the direct threat of his shotgun wasn't enough to stem the tide. Cicero let out a pump into the crowd, but no more, as he soon feared the pair would be pursued by marshals. The smell of blood and gunpowder invigorated the crowd in a sense that he hadn't anticipated. As the suffragette laid bloody and beaten, the full extent of the crowd gave their attention to the pair. Cicero knew he didn't have the firepower or the willpower to gun down a crowd that large. Rose already mounted up on Mary and was rearing to go as the horse attempted to distance itself from the others. Cicero mounted up and the two rode off.

Not yet satisfied with their demands, a few of the angry mob started a car to pursue the pair. Rose focused on riding ahead and not looking back as she heard Cicero's revolver. Cicero was so attuned with his weapon that he didn't need to focus behind him as he let out a few rounds of cover for the pair. One bullet pierced the windshield of the car and was enough to cause the driver to crash into a nearby rock.

Without any more sounds other than the roads of the desert, Rose's tears accompanied them with each step. Rose gripped onto Mary with her head low as the horse's movements were steady. No matter how much she tried to make a difference or to improve people's outlook on her, it always boiled down to a raw and unforgiving hatred. Rose blamed herself for trying to be reasonable. She felt she needed to divorce herself from the people she saved in order to succeed at her craft. She wouldn't make that mistake again.

✦

The Merchant of Venice: I

At Union Station, a man by the name of Niccolo was on the prowl for a telephone of any sort. He was a man looking for information, with an expression of determination constantly on his face. His hair was slicked back and had an accompanying styled mustache to boot. His face was clean shaven, and his sullen brown eyes gave off a flair of mystery and intimidation. The finishing piece was a styled and pressed red suit that he often carried with a cigar. Niccolo hardly smoked but chose to keep a cigar around as a tool to disarm someone for questioning. Most people were allured by the make or the smell, and it provided the opening for conversation. He searched for a dial phone so he could call home. Niccolo's wish was granted as he moved past a few businessmen who looked down on him with their fedoras. Niccolo gave them a glare as they walked past.

"I hate this country. Bunch of stuck-up rednecks. This suit costs more than your inside-out socks." Niccolo spat lowly under his breath. He dipped into his wallet and inserted a few quarters as the fee for such a convenience.

"Hello! Operator speaking. Can I have your first and last name please?" a feminine voice spoke from the phone.

I wanted to stay in Chicago, but now they have me here in this dump. All this effort to kill one man?

"Niccolo Bianchi. Can you please transfer me to the number, WY-4670. There will be a man by the name of Enricho Bianchi, no relation, who answers the phone. He will read a letter from my organization," Niccolo stated as he saw a child looking at him. He cupped the phone in his hand as he waited on the line. Niccolo's thick accent already gained the ire of adults who had a negative opinion of Italians.

"This is Niccolo Bianchi." He stomped his foot down, irritated at the sound of a loading train in the distance. Although the operator promised complete neutrality during the call, Niccolo was paranoid that they were listening in. Niccolo was silent on the other line for a moment before another voice came to the phone.

"Enricho here. I have two letters addressed to you. The first is from your wife and the second is from on high." Enricho said as Niccolo could hear the crumbling of an envelope.

"I will read you the first. Oh boy. Niccolo, this is Alessia. From this point on, I am no longer married to you due to your status as an enemy of the state. Under Mussolini's new edict, agents have visited our home, and I will not jeopardize my or my child's standing. Both of our origins have been dubious, and it is time I make things right. Do not attempt to contact us."

Child? Is this... mine? Niccolo thought to himself. Niccolo had an assortment of thoughts at this letter, but the most important one was that of the new life he apparently sired. Niccolo was unsure of what to think. He'd been in the United States for a couple of months to help establish operations and he hadn't imagined the whirlwind of events that resulted from this. Niccolo often chose his occupation over his marriage, but he worked just as hard as anyone to secure a good life for them. He shook his head in dismay, he would have hated to be robbed of a chance at fatherhood. His internal struggles would have to wait, as he was promptly brought back to the matter at hand by Enricho over the phone.

"The Boss wants you to "greet" a man known as The Baron. He is a direct competitor to our operation. This is a personal order from up top. You have a package to deliver and there are no special instructions. Simply make sure the package is delivered. This is a big job, probably one of the biggest we've ever received. The order was conducted through a third party that requested our expertise. You'll be helping the boss' nephew Andrea establish control of the paper route while you're here also and run it in his stead. Meet him for further details," Enricho coughed as Niccolo nodded and understood the message. He blew air out of his nose in annoyance.

Although Niccolo and Enricho both spoke Italian, they conducted most correspondence in coded English to not raise suspicion from any eavesdroppers. English was the world language with the British Empire and United States at its peak. Crime or otherwise, it was essential for anyone to get anywhere.

Hmm. If I am to meet with this man called The Baron, he must have quite the bounty on his head. Shame, his head, that is-after I put a big hole in it. Niccolo tapped against some wood.

"There's a new player on the scene from Chicago. He's been quiet but is making new moves now. He goes by "The Owl", as he mostly strikes at night and sees everything in that city. Keep your wits about you Niccolo while you look to deliver the package. If he needs a delivery, make it so," Enricho mentioned.

"Yes, sir," Niccolo stated quietly.

"Try to keep this clean. The sooner you deliver the package to The Baron, the better it'll be for all of us." Enricho said, hanging up the phone immediately upon finishing. Niccolo was met with silence as he looked to find his way around the city.

For years, Niccolo felt disrespected when it came to personal matters regarding his employment with his organization. As a hitman involved with Mafia business, Niccolo often considered himself cleaning up the trash that was left behind, but a high value target like The Baron was more of his pay grade. He had every right to feel slighted prior to this call. Niccolo was seasoned, having done several killings on prominent targets over the years as a freelancer. Niccolo could speak a total of five different languages from his travels, his native Italian, English, Hungarian, Sicilian, and French, when the mood called for it. Niccolo worked as the liaison for an outfit which operated back in Italy while he and a few other trusted soldiers now served in America as a different revenue stream.

Niccolo's entry to the country was surprisingly smooth. Born in the United States on a technicality, his family left New York City to return home to Italy, but as he was born on an American ship, this complicated the circumstances of his membership within the organization. In the eyes of the government and the king, he was pure, but from those that paid him, he was an Italian-American and was kept at a respectable distance. Niccolo aspired to be much more, but fate kept him from assuming his full potential, or so he thought. This distance was a slight weakness to Niccolo, but often gave new opportunities all its own.

Niccolo's travels saw the urban sprawl of Phoenix near him. He remembered hearing before he arrived that his associate worked at a casino in the city. Day jobs for those in the business were common, it was a good way to establish an alibi for when things got hectic. Niccolo was to meet with the nephew of his handler that organized the targets he was ordered to eliminate. He rarely traveled unarmed, but smuggling a gun past the train authorities rivaled The Vatican.

In America, however, Niccolo found that guns grew on trees and the fruit was ripe for picking. He walked along the busy sidewalk and observed the traffic near him. There were large public trams that ran by on time and ferried people, but people enjoyed their personal liberties more. He was surprised how quickly the roads were clogged in such a young city. Most people in his homeland simply walked, with public transportation via gondola being the biggest way to travel. Those with power and the elite afforded to drive unimpeded. Niccolo came across the sight of a gray horse parked behind a telephone pole. It was an odd sight to see. Niccolo turned the corner of the sidewalk and looked behind to see an older man carrying groceries in the distance. He shrugged and continued his walk. Niccolo realized he hadn't bothered to bring a map of the city with him and looked somewhat lost as he also couldn't read any of the signs.

"I must remember... He worked somewhere in a casino." Niccolo spoke to himself as he saw someone give him a second glance. [1] He could tell the man was intoxicated in some fashion as his pants were filled with urine. Niccolo was aware that alcohol was illegal in the country, and yet it flowed to anyone. He wondered how easy it would be to get his hands into the industry.

"This is America! Stop speaking Spanish!" the homeless man spat at him. Niccolo groaned, he knew better than to get involved. Back home, it was easy for him and any others to stomp out any disrespect, but Niccolo wanted to keep a low profile for now and continued. He realized that gambling houses were open at night, so it would be easy to find one as he noticed various people outside of their respective stores.

At the end of the block, there was a loop in the sidewalk that led to another section of stores. Niccolo looked over his shoulder to see if he was being followed. Niccolo approached the nearby street corner and saw that he found what he was looking for. A pair of gambling dice made from metal tubing and lights reflected in the distance. It seemed to be the right location for what he remembered. Niccolo made his way over and peered inside through the glass. The light from the outside illuminated the main room. Niccolo saw that the casino had two floors, the first was filled with card tables and slot machines. The carpet was brown and held in heat from the outer window. A foolish decision. He felt his shoulder be touched by another man.

"We're not open for a couple of more hours," the man pointed out to Niccolo as he gestured to the gambling house's hours above him. Niccolo turned around and his eyes met the other man before him. Not only was

---

1. Casinos were banned by official state legislature throughout Prohibition but were constructed like most things with greased palms. To avoid legal troubles, some of these places only went by the phrase "gambling house".

he addressed in Italian, but it was also perfect and smooth. It was unmistakable. Niccolo knew him as the Underboss and lowered his head with respect. Due to the nature of his work, Niccolo was often away from the inner workings of their organization. News in the old days traveled slowly, but in the age of the telephone and telegraph, it was much easier to stay current. It appeared that after all this time, there was some restructuring to be done.

"I have answered the call of your uncle. Underboss Andrea sir, how may I be of service to you?" Niccolo asked as he waited for a sign. The lingering part of Niccolo's statement hung over him with a tinge of irritation. Niccolo harbored an intense jealousy of Andrea, he was a young man in his twenties that managed to maintain such a powerful position due to his uncle's influence. At thirty-three, Niccolo felt far more accomplished. His earnings certainly proved it, but the politics of the day kept him from being recognized.

"I want you to sit with me. See that bench there? Let us discuss," the young man explained. He turned his head to a bench a short distance away. As he walked, Niccolo examined Andrea's clothing. An important part of their work was to stay hidden in plain sight, and the stereotype of gangster clothing was already well apparent. Andrea wore a heavy black trench coat and a fedora which practically made Niccolo roll his eyes in disbelief. Niccolo could see the young man melting before his eyes but refrained from saying anything further on the matter. As the two sat, Niccolo started to speak in English, but was stopped by the raise of Andrea's hand.

"We will discuss our affairs in Italian. I don't care what the others think. As you know, back home is dealing with issues because of Mussolini. He's put pressure on our rivals in Sicily and other gangs to the south. There will only be so much time left until he comes to us in Venice. You may speak freely," Andrea paused.

"The government has already sent agents to my home. My wife divorced me over it. Divorced! The nerve! We are Italian!" Niccolo retorted.

"I was tasked here to make it so that we will have a footing unaffected by the chaos, and we will fund the efforts back home against the fascists. Perhaps if we are successful, we may indeed move operations in the States to stay. Now, for the thing that matters. You have been overlooked from promotion due to the dubious nature of your birth. This is not practical for my needs. I serve as our Underboss, and my uncle has given me permission to bestow you the rank of caporegime. You will be working for me while you fulfill your obligation. I am aware that you need to kill a man known as The Baron, is that right? For my uncle to request your services personally, that is no small feat," Andrea explained as he lowered his hand.

Niccolo froze as he wasn't sure how to take the news. His entire life with the organization he wanted recognition for his efforts. Niccolo's expectations were quite low, and he was pleasantly surprised. He'd been with a whirlwind of news, the most important still in the forefront of his mind with his apparent divorce and potential child that he felt needed to be cared for. He couldn't help but feel slightly overwhelmed.

"Thank you. Y-Yes, sir. My target is The Baron. From what I hear, he is a rich tycoon of some sort. He should be easy to find in this backwater town they call a city. I always make my payment and always capture my target. There is much work to do," Niccolo mentioned.

"Right. Well, Niccolo, the men are American-born and raised but hearty Italians. They are Picciotto and need guidance, I have about fifty of them at your disposal. They have taken the day job of copper miners some distance from the main city. Operations have been built out of the old mine, but we'll be holding liquor in there. A vehicle and weapons will be waiting for you there. Do as you wish, just make sure the money flows," Andrea informed him.

"Thank you, sir, this is very generous. What exactly will you be doing, while I accomplish these goals?" Niccolo asked as he adjusted his tie and wiped the sweat off his brow.

"My job here is pretty simple. I took a job here as the greeter of this casino, while we collect information. I want to take this city for our organization. I want to find out more about The Owl and who he is. The Americans as you know have banned alcohol sales of any kind for the foreseeable future. Vices are easy to control. My hours are on the board there, so we can discuss things outside that time." Andrea's head turned to see a gray car appear. Niccolo noted the frame and raised an eyebrow at how nice it appeared. Andrea scoffed at the sight which stopped him for a moment.

"Ah, that's my boss of this place arriving. Why don't you give him a proper welcome that I can't? He hasn't been very respectful to me as of late. He stepped on my shoes and didn't apologize." Andrea mentioned. A short man with a cigar in his mouth exited the car. The parking job was horrid, half of it was on the curb. His face was red with anger at something unrelated, but the two men were the target of his rage.

"Hey! You think you're getting extra pay for coming early? Your job is to stand outside and kiss ass of any customer here, you know that?!" the man yelled at Andrea, who only gave a passing glance to Niccolo. Niccolo advanced closer to the man.

Niccolo instinctively cracked his knuckles, and with one hand, grabbed the man's shirt. Niccolo had a lot of rage to let loose, and he needed to make a good impression in front of the Underboss. The man struggled to get out of his grip, but he felt as if he was trapped in a vice. Niccolo was a trained professional, he's squeezed many more for far less. Niccolo's face soured as his right hand clenched into a fist. He advanced with a rapid punch to the jaw that disoriented the screaming man.

"W-What the hell!? Who do you think you—" He yelled, interrupted by Niccolo, who slammed him down on the pavement below as Andrea watched with a simple nod of his head. He looked behind him and noticed a young girl with a stick of chalk was watching the commotion. The two locked eyes for a moment, and the girl continued to draw as if she'd seen nothing. Children in this city were already desensitized to such acts of violence, no parent to avert their eyes, only their common sense.

Despite Niccolo's brutality, he was an expert on restraint and stopped when the message settled in. Niccolo hardly broke a sweat as he rang out his hand while he noticed Andrea's reaction. It was evident he was still quite green and sheltered from the building blocks of criminal enterprise. He had a tactical mind, sure, but that paled in comparison to life in the field. Niccolo cracked his neck and back as a small noise accompanied it.

"Is-Is he dead?" Andrea asked in English, with a slight crack in his voice.

"No. Not unless you wanted him to be, sir. I've been in the business a long time, but I hope this will make things better. The old copper mine, I will find it and begin the work. I will return when the job is done or when you need my services again." Niccolo lowered his head, and waited to be dismissed.

Andrea whisked him off with a wave and stood at the door while his boss picked himself up. Niccolo could see the damaged man enter the casino in an attempt to patch himself up. He had a rare grin of satisfaction. Niccolo left to go down the street and start his quest to bring The Baron to mob justice.

It Howls In The Night:
I

Florence found herself inside a speakeasy, she hardly drank alcohol, but was on the search for information. For the past few days, she took refuge inside a hotel located within the center of Phoenix. Money was hardly a concern for her these days, and she used the hotel as her base of operations. Her days mostly consisted of watching people through the window or at a nearby table, but she decided to refine her approach a bit more. The establishment was homely in nature as it carried a rustic theme of the wilderness. Florence saw multiple taxidermized animals on the wooden walls with brick flooring. She saw a menu for drinks written by hand on a piece of paper nestled under a book. It was just after 5 PM, with the after-work rush headed inside. Florence saw an array of miners and seamstresses pour into the place after paying the cover charge of a nickel. She sat alone, wearing a green dress with exposed shoulders and arms. She wore a layer of lipstick and idly sat by while she heard the low ambient sound of a saxophone.

Florence's goal was to find someone willing to give her a pass to the underground. She knew that gangsters enjoyed grandstanding and would talk about their exploits at length, but she hardly wanted to be looked at as some moll. She wanted a safe and non-threatening option. On the street, she knew these people were called associates, but that was the limit of her knowledge pool. She figured that starting at a speakeasy would be the first place to start. Her eyes focused on one man that seemed a bit disheveled from the rest. He didn't seem to have any companions with him, and Florence rubbed her chin in thought.

Florence slowly motioned her way over past the eyes of a couple of others to settle close by her target. She overheard a short conversation as she palmed a small glass of wine to keep up appearances. Florence originally felt her search was going to be another fruitless night, but her ears were piqued at the idle conversation of the first man and the bartender that seemed to know each other.

"Joe—I owe a lot of money to some people," the man said. He grasped a drink poured by the bartender. Florence could smell the alcohol content from where she was as it slightly burnt her nose hairs. She figured it was just a degree from straight rubbing alcohol with how repugnant the smell was.

"Well Bill. You could always see "The Owl", I heard he's got a banker on retainer. Can give you a loan, interest free! How's the new job anyhow?" the bartender asked as he rolled up his sleeves. He gave a passing wink to Florence that was not returned as he shrugged his shoulders.

"I just started a week ago, but my boss is very generous. He comes from, uh—What's that place with the gondolas? Venice, that's right. Real strange guy," Bill mentioned.

"You said your name was Bill, right?" Florence smiled. She raised her eyebrows to catch the man's attention. The bartender did a double take at Florence as he was floored at the possibility of Bill being interesting to her. He poured a complimentary drink for Florence that she took a small sip of before passing the rest to Bill.

"Let me pay your tab. I know it's considered improper for us ladies to pass the buck, but something tells me you really need this." Florence withdrew a ten-dollar bill. She had a small grin that could erode even the densest boulders.

Bill was part of Niccolo's new entourage that was taking root in the city. He was an average looking man that seemed a bit distant minded, but overall, a good-natured person. He wore a newsboy cap, and his overalls were caked with a layer of orange dirt that never seemed to go away. Bill was stunned by Florence's kindness and beauty. The man had always been an insecure wreck and he fell apart already. He spoke to try and fill the space between him, the bartender, and her.

"Yeah, I just got a new job. I, uh, work at the copper mine to support my ma. She's older these days," Bill mentioned as he wiped the back of his neck with his hand.

"That's generous, but I don't think that dame is going to get your gambling bets settled away either," the bartender remarked as he examined the ten dollars. He gave a satisfactory nod as he stuffed it into his pocket.

"A real family man, that is so sweet. You seem to be on the straight and narrow, so tell me this—" Florence was passed yet another shot of alcohol that she passed to any other takers.

"Oh, none for me thanks. Though, I would love to know more about this job of yours!" Florence added on as she shot a glare at the bartender.

While the bartender and Florence made their differences known through non-verbal eye contact, Bill was none the wiser, as he was just happy to have someone interested in his life. He lived a rather unfulfilling life as an attempted citrus farmer but came to find that his returns were paltry compared to the crime life. Bill looked at his glass as he felt some anxiety.

"Your boss, he's from Italy?" Florence asked with a raise of her eyebrows.

Bill started to get nervous, and Florence noticed this. She changed her approach and placed her hand on his arm as a sign of reassurance. Florence could sense his inexperience and looked into his eyes with a warm smile.

"I've got family too. Sometimes, we gotta do what we need to do to make sure they're safe right?" Florence mentioned with rosy cheeks.

Florence could hardly contain her excitement as her investigative skills were coming to bear fruit. Florence pieced together that Bill's work at the mine probably coincided with the illegal alcohol dealings that supplied this speakeasy and the rest of town with their material. The copper mines transported large amounts of ore into trucks to be refined further. Florence reasoned it was highly likely they utilized creative ways to hold the alcohol, one method she read about was filling gas canisters with the solution and marking the colors differently to differentiate them from fuel. She was aware of the lengths people would go to get various liquors and she was determined to make her way to the mine with her camera. After hours, it was likely to be deserted and she could scope the surface for any sort of clue. She figured that the remote location would be enough to hide some activity going on and she could build her investigation further.

Florence idled for two additional hours while she let the conversation naturally die down between them. She ignored the call of men wanting her apartment's number and sipped some of her wine before slinking off without a trace. Her destination was to her car, which was parked right outside, and she was determined to immediately head out to scope the mine. She saw that it was sunset, and her chance was opportune. In the back of her car, she held a camera and was prepared for night photography. An avid camera enthusiast, Florence was wealthy enough to own one for the field. She was able to also study some of Jessie Beal's techniques to capture the most visible light from night shoots that would give her greater depth of her working area.[1]

---

1. Jessie Tarbox Beals was the first female night photographer and started her career in the early 1900s. She worked as a freelance news photographer and often took candid photos of normal life and did professional photos for presidents. By 1925, she was offering lectures on how to do photography.

Florence drove past the ambient quiet as she'd gotten a lay of the land in previous drives. She headed towards the outer copper mines as the city disappeared behind her. Florence couldn't help but give a giddy laugh as she had already cooked up the perfect article title for the papers. Florence drove along the empty road as she whistled to herself to keep awake. With the sun just about gone, Florence slowed her pace as she neared a steep incline that gave off the appearance of what she was looking for. In the past, much of copper mining was done underground and the old infrastructure remained, but new projects were done on the surface. Florence stopped her car and looked around to find just a few idle trucks filled with ore and wooden planks. She blew some air out of her nose with nothing exciting but planned her point of attack. She opened her car's trunk and withdrew her camera. She unboxed the device and loaded in some film. Florence walked around and found herself on top of a small mound and used this as a chance to take a photo.

Florence first took a low-lighting level photograph and followed it with a dash of flash powder. The latter use of the flash powder illuminated the mine's construction in all its glory and was caught by Florence. She was hoping to capture some movements of anything once they were developed. She could vaguely make out some unusual structure further back.

I'll have to develop these at home, but so far-nothing out of the ordinary. Florence thought.

Unknown to Florence, there were still people present in the mine's vicinity after hours. Niccolo's encampment sought to use the old mining tunnels as an operation for the men working there. It was easier to have the men retire during the workweek there than go home to their families each day with limited transportation. Niccolo entrusted the most disciplined of the men to take the first watch and two were sentries to monitor any other gang activity that tried to disrupt their operations. They offered no response to police officers or lost travelers that otherwise ended up in the area. Florence's photography was visible from a vast distance and caught the gaze of two armed guards that were on patrol.

Florence was so distracted fiddling with her camera, she hadn't noticed the two men that approached her. Her head darted up as she peered down to see a shotgun in the hands of a dusty mobster in overalls. He eyed Florence with suspicion while his partner opened up discussion.

"Hands high up—What's a woman doing here?" one of the guardsmen asked her.

"Hey, that camera you got there. The hell you doing with that?" the other man added as he wrapped his fingers around his gun.

"We gotta tell the boss about this. You're coming with us, lady," the first guardsmen ordered.

Florence's distaste for the mob was evident in her eyes but there wasn't much to do. Running was only going to be a problem and causing a scene would be even worse. She decided to play to their sense of chivalry, if any remained. Florence couldn't make up a lie on the spot that was feasible for them to believe, and she lowered her head at the sight of the gun. She complied with their demands and followed the two. As the three approached the compound, Florence found that her initial prediction was correct.

Nestled in the middle of the open surface mine, a low ambient light soon filled the center piece as the surroundings distorted into each other. Streaks of purple illuminated what remained and a vortex to another dimension was formed. Out of the purple vortex, a small gelatinous being of the same color emerged from it. The top was filled with a row of teeth as it slid across the ground and left a trail of slime behind it. Its vision was on all sides as it was filled with black dots that functioned as eyes and its eyes were trained on the nearest sign of life. It pursued without delay for its next meal.

It Howls In The Night: II

Florence sat with her back against the wall as she looked at the confines of her jail cell. It was obvious to her she was placed in some sort of interrogation area as she saw a chair nearby and some rope. The dirty stone floor contrasted heavily from her green dress. Cold to the touch, she was surprised to have some relief from the sweltering heat that otherwise plagued the rest of the region. As she was underground, she lost the ability to tell time. Her watch was subsequently stolen off her before being imprisoned. The copper facility was actually an engineering marvel, the modern rigging on top was connected an older copper mine from the early 1870s some distance away. Supported by steel beams, the best dynamite money could buy, and a few engineers that owed a lot of money, artificial tunnels were constructed to link the two together. After climbing a ladder down below, an opening led to a large man-made cave a few feet below to a steady platform. Supplies for the outfit were funneled through the main entrance of the old copper mine while the entry of people was confined to the singular ladder.

Florence saw old storage tanks now outfitted with new functionality to help store moonshine to sell at a premium. The two men from earlier remained with their shotguns. Between the two of them, whatever came their way was going to be torn to pieces. Florence whistled loudly to herself as she sat bored in the corner.

"Quiet! We said it earlier," one of the armed goons snarled at Florence. He brandished his gun as his finger lay close to the trigger. Florence knew as well as anyone else that firing guns with their rate of fire in such a small room would deafen them all, including having to deal with the rounds bouncing around. It was an idle threat. Florence eyed her captors as she noted her disgust with the leader of the bunch she learned was named Niccolo through idle conversation. As it would turn out, there were problems brewing.

Niccolo worked hard to make a well-oiled machine out of the outfit he was given management over. While they were still inexperienced with the more intricate natures of crime, Niccolo encouraged self-sufficiency and let the men sort out problems on their own. He hated to be micromanaged himself and put this into his leadership style. Niccolo only wished to be disturbed when problems really showed their head as he was busy having to plan the extensive nature of his primary work. He was woken up by another guard who was informed of their new prisoner. He raised an eyebrow in disbelief but wanted to go forward anyway. Niccolo looked up at the dirty ceiling above him as he was sprawled out on a cot simply wearing an undershirt caked with sweat. The cool air of the tunnels could only do so much. He thought about his assignment for coming here as he thought something was amiss. He was hardly one to be paranoid, but a few things seemed to not make much sense to him.

Twenty-five thousand dollars for the death of this man. No preference on the kill, no drop tag, no proof of the body either... Why does this seem odd to me? The job should be simple. This is what The Boss wants, but generally he wants things done a certain way. If he simply wants The Baron dead, they must be a serious contender. A rival syndicate I would know about, but this is just one person. Is he related to The Owl? I suppose I should go into town later and find more information about this Baron man. Niccolo thought. His pondering ended as he was interrupted by the sound of his men talking among one another.

"There's a problem down in the storage bay! The 'shines leaking and there's blood," a voice boomed down the hallway. The acoustics of the tunnels made it easy for orders to be yelled down the hall with little issue. Niccolo and the twenty men at his disposal tonight had little in the way of supplies. He needed to do a run into town and procure more before anything really dangerous happened. Niccolo sighed as he got up hearing the tail end of the man's call. Still dressed casually, Niccolo instinctively grabbed a pistol from his bag and loaded a magazine in. The new prisoner would have to wait for now. He moved in the direction of the sound until he felt a touch on his shoulders from one of his lower enforcers.

"Boss, stand back. We'll handle it," one of the men alerted Niccolo as he rallied the others to investigate.

Niccolo decided to venture ahead and follow the man's lead. He chose to lead by example and do the tasks that he asked of his men. The tunnels were vast in volume but were only wide enough for about two people at time when moving from room to room. With Niccolo's goons spread throughout the tunnels focused on different tasks, only a few at first responded to the call. Niccolo could hear the sound of footsteps increasing in volume as his enforcer neared the storage bay. Walled off with a makeshift door, he opened it and stepped inside. His eyes first came to the moonshine, the few barrels they housed were full of holes as the liquid leaked out. He noticed that these holes weren't square or round, as if someone was skimming from the top. On closer examination, it seemed like the scratches on the barrel were long stripped lines. He raised an eyebrow as they strangely looked like claw markings.

His feet were sticky as his boots were submerged in a strange purple salve that was also present. Further spatters of blood leaked onto the floor and a small drop came from above to touch the man's bald head. The enforcer locked eyes with a strange human-like creature that held elongated hair throughout its body and extended fingernails that functioned as grips to the wall. With each reach of its elongated arms, a small clump of dirt fell to the bottom. The enforcer noticed that the being in front wore some form of clothing, where a few scraps of denim remained on its body. On the creature's back was the gelatinous being that operated its host. It merged with the creature's back and embedded itself into the center of their body. A sinister low breathing sound could be heard emanating from the merged creatures as its yellow eyes pierced the man's soul.

"What in the goddamn?" The man yelled, his outburst bringing attention to the other men who quickly grabbed their weapons and converged on the situation. Two at a time made their way down quickly as they breezed past Niccolo to meet the storage bay.

Without warning, the creature detached from the wall and jumped forward to knock the man down. The gelatinous being piloted its host with a deadly precision. The unholy union stood on two legs and lifted the man with ease in one hand that was forced open. It was met with a hail of gunfire from Niccolo's men that reverberated throughout the tunnel. The host's arm swung through the air with an unnatural precision as it gripped the man's jaw and ripped it clean off. A pool of blood came as the man's body twitched before dying. His pain was immeasurable, but he could not scream. In the crossfire, their own men downed their comrade in an instant, hoping to nail blows on their adversary. Favoring the walls over the floor, it crawled on the side of the wall in a slow and menacing way. For those with a sharper eye, the face seemed almost humanoid, which unnerved them. The host's head was now completely upside down, defying the laws of its body, and blood leaked out of its eyes and mouth. It let out a horrid scream that started from a low mumble.

"Bob? Oh—Shit, it's Bob! That thing is Bob!" one man yelled over the sound of another exchange of bullets.

The acoustics of the tunnel led Florence and the others to dart their heads as they heard the cracks of bullets as they flew through the air. She stuck her tongue out in thought as she wondered what could have caused such a commotion. She was aware that gangsters were simple brutes most of the time, but there was a growing sense of panic in the space built for them. A few of the light fixtures in their room started to flicker, making a strobe effect that bothered her eyes.

"Oh, I hear the fun has started. Guns, gore, glamour! Are you going to let me out or what?" Florence said to her captors as looks of worry came on their faces. When a threat came to any outpost, it was usually taken care of quickly. As the sound of multiple magazines from their guns were spent, a deeper worry showed on the men's faces. The only people who could reasonably put up that much firepower was a battalion from the US Army, but they were clueless about their activities and were focused on enforcing the border.

"First these damn cowboys and now this broad trying to muck things up, this isn't the kind of heat we were expecting. Go find the boss to handle her, we need to go," one of the men stated as he cocked his gun back. He waited for his partner to make the first move. Florence sat happily, as from her perspective, she was in a win-win situation, all she needed now was to get her camera.

The tunnels were both a strategic advantage and a organizational nightmare, as with enough planning, a threat could be funneled into choke points where the men could bring hell to the enemy. The problem was if they managed to get overwhelmed, it would be a slaughterhouse and the die was cast long ago. Niccolo fumbled around in the growing chaos as he was swiftly reminded to check on their new hostage. He gave a reassuring look of confidence to his men before going to the interrogation area. He soon had look of confusion as he noticed a woman was in a jail cell. Given the severity of the situation, he didn't say much and chose only to lift his gun to shoot the lock. Florence covered her ears as the sound was louder than she expected but looked at the sweaty man before her.

"You need to go," Niccolo said simply but Florence refused as she needed her camera.

"Not without my camera. I told the others this, you know," she said.

While Florence now had the choice to do what she wished, her drive kept her embroiled in the ongoing chaos. She was afraid from all the noise, but she could hardly give up her goal. In just a few seconds, she evaluated that her treatment by the boss was better than these random thugs. Niccolo followed suit as he retreated out the door to find a few of his men were practically climbing on top of one another with their guns positioned on one end of the tunnel. The men took a knee and aimed their shotguns and pistols straight ahead. The flash from their muzzles lit the tunnel as a cacophony of bullets filled it in a deafening tornado. With its previous kill igniting a bloodlust within, the creature from earlier now moved towards the mass of people.

Niccolo rushed to a cache located not too far away and quickly dragged it out amidst the chaos. There were a few sticks of dynamite left from the mine's early days, some hand grenades, and a submachine gun of his own. Niccolo carried his submachine gun while Florence attempted to shield herself far behind the others. She noticed the steel beams and packed earth that made up the tunnel's integrity and assessed that with the right amount of pressure, they could make a portion of it collapse and hopefully trap that strange beast for good.

Niccolo caught on to Florence's observation as he prompted the others to slowly retreat back as they continued to open fire. For a moment, Niccolo shouted for his crew to hit the floor as he briefly held a grenade. He removed the pin and angled it at the right position for it to explode. The shockwave from the grenade managed to land its mark as the creature lost balance. With a direct hit, an explosion of gore dismembered the creature's arm as for a moment it lay still, but the appendage appeared to have a life of its own as its tendrils opened up and attached itself back to the body at hand. Trapping it would be the next suggestion, as he lodged another grenade, this time in between the steel beams. A heavy creaking sound was heard as the wall began to cave in. This much amount of dirt required a heavy amount of pressure to stay stable.

"You—Woman, grab the dynamite and bring it here! There is a box next to you!" Niccolo yelled to Florence while she turned her head at him.

"What, Oh! You mean me—" Florence said, slightly flustered at the request. Florence found the box that Niccolo referred to and looked for the aged red substance. There wasn't much left, but Florence rolled it along the ground for Niccolo to pick up.

Niccolo used a lighter to light the final stick of dynamite as his crew stumbled out of the way. With just seconds to spare, Niccolo kept his hand to the wall as he heard a shaking collapse sound as a slurry of metal and dirt started to fill the room entirely. His men cheered at the apparent defeat of such an opponent, but it was a stalemate at best. While the abomination couldn't pierce through the thick earth, its eerie howling noises remained on the other side of the wall for all to hear. Florence tugged at her collar at the sound and felt unnerved. The collapse of the wall was enough to separate the two entities, but Niccolo soon realized he was missing a few extra men. He made a frustrated kick on the ground as he was now, not only cut off from those who were as good as dead, but the alcohol storage he needed to sell was also now on the side of the monster.

Niccolo turned around and the few employees he had on disposal already went to work reinforcing the wall with whatever was on hand. He watched as massed piles of wood and scrap metal were made into a large grouping of material. Niccolo nodded as his attention soon turned to Florence, who had a grateful smile.

"Well, that was a real scrape! I should be going now!" Florence said as she tried to weasel herself out of there.

"Mmm. Not so fast. You came here for a reason and now, here you are. So, what is it? You are aware this is a dangerous place for people like you?" Niccolo mentioned.

"The truth, I can tell if you are lying."

"I'm a photographer, a journalist. I wanted to take some pictures and see what I could find, but... well, I want... revenge," Florence said. She covered her mouth slightly as she never thought to word it that way, but it was true.

Her answer intrigued Niccolo, he didn't figure someone with her demeanor could have any enemies or animosity towards anyone. Niccolo assumed immediately that Florence lived an incredibly privileged life, she owned a well-made dress and a high-quality camera. He rolled his hand to let her speak more.

"Revenge, for what? Did someone cut you off in traffic? I am a *Mafioso,* my dear. Not some letter request service," Niccolo had no qualms about revealing his identity to someone like Florence. He wanted her to be aware of what she was getting into.

"I once wrote a story about someone really powerful. They had connections... to the underground. My family is very rich and has a lot of assets. Gold, silver, you name it. When I broke the news about a corruption scandal back in 1916, I was taken in my sleep and put in a sanatorium for five years. So much was taken from me-all to silence me." Florence explained.

"Sana-what? I do not know this word." Niccolo asked with a scratch of his head.

"A hospital for the mentally insane. I was never that, only someone who wanted to say something about it. I have a nice face and am overall very pleasant to be around, but in truth, the core of me is very dark. I like to choose positivity because I think there is good in everyone, even mobsters like you," Florence stated with a cheery tone.

"How touching. What I must ask, in all sincerity, is what does this have to do with me, and my outfit? I'm running a business and right now, I've lost thirty thousand dollars worth of liquor in that tunnel there."

"I think we could work together. You have the resources and the means to get rid of the bad guys, in the way that I'd like it to be done, and I can help you. I'm a rich gal."

"I have contacts at the Times still, I could write articles about crimes that you and your gang do but instead pin them on your rivals. The police will read the papers and raid their places, while you remain completely invisible. Don't'cha think that's neat? A little devious, even? I know that someone like you has a lot of enemies, it'd be better to do things unopposed," Florence said with a smile.

Niccolo evaluated the proposal. He knew that The Owl was a big contender in running the Phoenix criminal underground, and he still needed to find out anything about The Baron. Niccolo inherited a decent number of problems, such as conflicting supply routes with Mexican gangs and the Irish who refused to do business with Italians. One extra weapon in his arsenal was a wise move to make. Florence was also completely financially independent, which meant that he didn't need to expend any resources either. Niccolo raised an eyebrow and decided to extend his hand out to her.

"A deal it is then. You will come by and do whatever it is you do with your pen, and you'll make "the bad guys" disappear? We shall see. I will let the men know you will be around more often," Niccolo commented.

"Now I must ask, two things. One, how did you find this place to begin with? Two, do you have any suggestions for the unearthly horror besides the wall?" Niccolo pondered as he took a few steps backward as a precaution.

"Well, I met this strange little man named Bill that works under you for his mother. A sweet guy, but perhaps a little loose with his words." Florence joked.

"Bill? Ah, the new employee. I was not aware he was so vocal about these things. Mmm."

"Please don't punish him, really, it was an honest mistake. I take at least some of the blame."

"As for your second question... I have a number to call, but we'll need some money." Florence looked towards the collapsed tunnel wall.

The Shadow Bouncer

Rose sat in the homestead while she read a novel she picked up from the local library. The cover was faded, but she could tell from the first page, she was on an adventure. Her nose was delighted as it picked up a smell that Claudia prepared in the kitchen. She labored tirelessly over a big bowl of rice and beans as she let the mix stir in warm water. To Rose's surprise, Cicero and Claudia had an extensive spice cabinet. She stuck her tongue out in support as she saw minced garlic and paprika join the mixture. A slab of smoked steak was Cicero's specialty. He prepared his meals way in advance with heavy amounts of salt and often used an open flame to reheat the food. Rose could feel the pangs of hunger come over her as the three would soon eat. Rose felt bad about not helping cook, but it was their insistence that she sat back and relaxed.

"Your nose hasn't left that book once child, what are you reading?" Claudia asked Rose while she continued to stir. Rose put her head up and turned her gaze to her. Rose's eyes scanned the cover once more but could make out the author's name of Bram Stoker.

"I'm reading Dracula. For... research purposes. What if we run into a vampire this time?" Rose teased. Cicero gave out an audible groan as he sat in a rocking chair. It was unknown to Rose, but Cicero could hardly stomach much horror writing as they were woefully inaccurate from what he saw.

"They slash his neck and stab him in the heart, a real thrilling adventure. I've seen vampires before, that's not how that goes usually. He's a hack," Cicero said with a righteous fervor that amused Rose highly.

"Cicero, how could you! Revealing the contents early is not welcome here," Claudia said as she instinctively ran over to Rose and playfully covered her ears.

"It's a book about a vampire, either he dies, or he wins. The book's almost thirty, she should have read it in school. I'd be shocked if it didn't have a film by now," Cicero grumbled.

His rant was blocked by a ringing sound that caused the group to look at one another. Cicero's point of view switched to the telephone that rang at the opposite end of the room. Cicero debated leaving the line unanswered, but the phone rang in louder agitation each time. While Cicero went towards the phone, he waved his hand for Claudia and Rose to eat. He would catch up shortly as his hands gripped the phone and held it up. He wondered who would bother to call him directly on a Sunday of all days. Cicero picked up the line and was about to speak, only for him to be addressed even faster.

"Is this the Grayson residence?" the voice of a worried man spoke over the phone. Claudia shot an eye at Cicero, who looked away, trying to avert his wife's gaze. He was already reprimanded once before for letting work get in the way of the things that mattered.

"We are in conversation. Who are you, and how do you have this number?" Cicero questioned while his fingers tapped on the wall for a response. He could hear the sound of some commotion in the background that the caller on the other end failed to suppress.

"What matters is I have a job for you. I heard that you are good at dealing with things of an... otherworldly nature. I run a hotel in the city on behalf of The Baron and Baroness, and there's been a hiccup before our debut next week. Do you see where I'm going with this?" The man said as Cicero let out a gruff reply.

"Our services aren't cheap you know."

Cicero felt a shake of his hand again as he heard The Baron's name. He took a deep breath and debated his acceptance for the job. Cicero looked over his shoulder at Rose eating happily while his attention came back to the phone. He felt his pocket which was a bit light. He'd finally just earned back the money spent on equipping Rose, but as he looked around the house, there were dire repairs to be made. Claudia's work was taxing as well with the materials needed for embalming becoming ever more expensive.

A little pink, but I'll live. I must be gracious. Rose thought as she ravenously stuffed down the food given to her on a plate. The mixture of beans and rice complimented the steak prepared by Cicero. Rose did her best to keep quiet as she eavesdropped on the conversation.

"Since I still have you on the line, I take it you are interested. We can afford your asking rate. In fact, this is so important, I'll offer triple if you can come tonight. I hired two additional... detectives to help sort the mess. If you can beat them, you'll be entitled to their pay as well. I just need the job done," the man pleaded as Cicero's mind already spent the pay.

"What time tonight? It's about..." Cicero said as he fiddled around in his jacket pocket for a watch. He nodded as he saw as it was just around 2 PM.

"Be at the Autumn Gardens Hotel at 9 tonight. I will let you know everything you need to there. Also, we don't have working electricity yet, so bring a flashlight." The man hung up. Cicero carried a scowl on his face having to work on his day off, but triple pay was simply too good to pass up.

"Rose, you'll need to gear up for tonight. We got a job to do later," Cicero commented.

Rose looked towards her notebook in her bag close by. She swallowed her food as her plate was nearly cleared. She had an excited look on her face as she felt invigorated to see what other strange things would come before her. She flicked open a small page and noted the doodles she'd made of the various encounters they've had. One thing still remained in her mind, which was the blue portal and the calming woman that came to her aid. She still needed to find her and give her gratitude. Cicero had no idea where to begin with that, and his concerns were focused on defeating the things that came, not finding them. Rose's eyes drifted to the bounty board as she wondered what was next on the chopping block.

"Not on the bounty board, they're paying triple. We'll be going into the city and there's a new client who wants our services. They're a hotel owner who needs us to do a little cleaning. Get some rest because we'll be up late," Cicero said as Claudia started to clean up. Rose lowered her head and gave a small thanks to the pair for cooking.

Cicero sat down and ate his meal while Rose climbed up a ladder to her makeshift loft to sleep without much fuss. She looked up at a small clock on the dresser and gave herself a few hours to sleep. She wound up the clock and set an alarm. All of her prior hunts started in the day, so a nighttime one would be a new adventure.

Rose woke up just short of her alarm, it was 7 PM which gave her more than enough time to get ready. On her nightstand was a small handheld mirror. She could only laugh as she realized she slept with a long line of drool having dried on her face. She climbed down the ladder and looked towards the kitchen counter. Her eyes sighted a large pitcher of water that she gulped down without getting a cup. Rose hadn't noticed Cicero walk in through the door as she was licking the glass to get the last drops of water while she turned around.

"You can fill it up at the spring out back and then boil it next time we come back. Anyway, here, I got you a pair of jeans from the general store. Put em on." Cicero tossed a folded pair of jeans that Rose caught. Rose raised an eyebrow as she'd never worn a pair. Overalls were common enough back on the farms of home, but jeans as they were, was a different story. Rose continued to hold the clothing as she stuck her finger inside, marveling at the pockets.

"This will take some getting used to, but it beats combat in a dress or stuffy overalls. Thank you Cicero. I didn't notice. You're carrying two guns?" Rose asked as she pointed to Cicero's holsters. Cicero patted himself down and nodded at his leather.

"Yeah, the big iron is for monsters, and the blue-steel is for anything else in my way. Remington Model 1875, this—will kill what you want dead. I can't tell you how many Pinkertons I put down with one of these." Cicero smirked. Cicero practiced his quick draw on Rose, letting her admire the gun's sheen before flipping it back into place. He waited and finished cleaning up the kitchen while Rose got herself prepared. Downstairs, Cicero talked to Rose to go over the checklist while she changed at the loft.

"Gun clean?" Cicero asked as he moved everything. He grinned as he could hear Rose tinkering away at stripping her pistol. Rose noticed there was a bit of grime and decided to use her already dirty dress as a napkin to wipe a bit away.

"Yep, super clean. Clean as a mopped floor. Very clean," Rose said as Cicero went on to the next thing.

"Magazine loaded? Sil—" Cicero started to lecture as he got cut off by Rose.

"Yes, in my bag. Silver on the right, regular on the left. Two magazines for each. Are we ready to go?" Rose asked while Cicero raised his eyebrows impressed.

Rose adjusted to her new feel, the jeans were tighter than she expected around her frame, but they felt comfortable. She hoisted her bag on her shoulder and realized that her hair was still flowing from when she slept. Using an elastic band, Rose did her best to tie back her hair so that it came behind her shoulders as Cicero waited outside. Rose stuffed her journal into another pocket of her bag. It'd been a few days since she wrote any entries in her book but was hoping to document something soon. Although Cicero found little use in the endeavor, Rose felt it was imperative to document every single hunt they encountered. As long as the portals remained open, they were at the mercy of whatever came out of them.

Cicero stood outside with his arms folded as Rose stepped up next to him. He nodded his head and waved to Claudia while Rose did the same. In the waning hours of the day, Cicero looked at his pocket watch and saw it was about 7:30. The commute to town would take just enough time. Cicero whispered to his silver horse for a moment as he placed a lantern on its neck. He used his boot to light a match and lit the wick inside, watching it brighten up with glee. Rose rode behind as usual and the two cast off without delay.

"It's a Sunday so there shouldn't be much traffic. The gasoline offends my steed, so I usually park him out of town. At least those city-slickers are nice enough to leave a hitching post out every once in a while." Cicero complained as Rose felt the wind of the horse carry on her face.

The waning sunlight was just about gone now as dusk turned to night proper. The oppressive heat of the day was instead a nice and soothing warmth. Rose hadn't seen the city at night before from a distance. In the scrubs and desert around, the growing skyline of Phoenix stood as an icon that would be eternal. Unlike all the mining towns around that were married to the work schedule, the city could afford to be open twenty-four hours, just like her treasured New York.

Rose and Cicero weaved through the dirt roads that began to taper off and lead to the familiar brick and concrete of the city. Cicero barely acknowledged the sign of a speed limit, as far as he was concerned, those only applied to motor vehicles. Assorted on the streets were attempts at parking cars that Rose was afraid one wrong move would have them flying onto the street.

"What was the hotel we were supposed to go to?" Rose asked as she saw parked cars appear in her vision while Cicero tugged on the reins of his horse.

"The Autumn Gardens Hotel. I spoke with the manager; he'll be waiting for us," Cicero explained.

Cicero felt the tap of Rose on his shoulder as he stopped the horse entirely, seeing that their destination was reached. He calmed down his horse and tied a rope to a telephone pole. Rose dismounted and prepared herself while Cicero got off his horse and meddled around in his saddlebag. He opened it up, withdrew an engraved trench gun, and loaded a few shells inside. He looked around for a moment, hoping to be discreet as he didn't want to have to explain his job to any late-night lawmen running around.

"Alright Rose. Equipment check. Here, there's a flashlight for you. I bought an extra pack of batteries, so you'll carry two. Instructions are on 'em." Cicero noted while Rose nodded. She happily placed the batteries in her bag.

"What's that over there?" Rose asked, as she pointed to see a strange car with an open trunk that seemed to house a bunch of unusual looking objects with bundles of wires attached.

"Christ almighty, it's them. I'll tell you when we get inside." Cicero explained. The two entered the lobby. Rose could tell by the pained sigh coming from Cicero's voice, there was certainly a story behind this. Cicero whistled for the manager's attention while Rose absorbed the grand scale of the lobby. It was ornate and modern, with an exquisite art deco theme. As Rose highly appreciated art, she was more than happy to see some of the newest painters from Harlem represented. The hotel manager looked up from his desk and walked over with delight to see his call was answered.

"You're early, that's a good feeling to have," the hotel manager was relieved upon seeing Cicero. His tone was more reserved seeing Rose but wasn't in much of a position to ask questions.

"Well—The problem we have is that there is something that—Okay, it's hard to explain. One of my repairmen came by yesterday to work on one of the floors and I haven't seen him since. The last thing I heard was some strange grainy sound that came through the walls. I sent The Michigan

Boys up there to investigate now. You can go ahead and join them, do the job, just get it done," the manager stated. He was starting to scare himself more as he spoke.

"Is there anything we should know before we start?" Cicero asked as he placed his hand on Rose's shoulder. He locked eyes with the hotel manager, who timidly grabbed a plan of the hotel building.

"We have ten floors here. The first two now have power, but the rest are dark. We had a circuit break and I'm not going anywhere to reset it, it's in the basement. If you have everything you need, I'd suggest you get on your way," the manager said, letting Rose and Cicero get to work.

Rose took a moment to open her bag and load her pistol. She knew nothing of what was to come but figured that being prepared was the best action. She placed her pistol back in the bag with the safety on and was ready for anything that would jump out at her. Cicero had his shotgun attached to a sling that he carried over his body while he waited for Rose. Cicero absorbed the details of the proceeding hallway before him that led up to the rooms.

"So, Rose. We'll take on the first two floors together, and then we'll pick a floor to look for. The hotel looks like a rectangle in the drawing. Long hallways, no doors are closed for the rooms either at the moment. We'll search each one and figure it out from there." Cicero explained as Rose nodded in agreement. The two walked together as they carefully oriented themselves on respective sides of the walls. Rose was on the left, and Cicero took the right side as they moved quietly. Cicero withdrew his shotgun and pointed it inside the first room, attempting to sense if anything was inside. The two stepped in unison, with Rose first checking the bathroom, while Cicero looked in the main bedroom. No signs of anything out of the ordinary here.

With the light providing plenty of cover for them, Cicero decided to talk to Rose a bit while he attempted to figure out just what they were looking for. Rose's first guess upon the hotel manager hearing a strange sound in the walls was like that of the cursed cabinet she remembered, but she saw no indications of the thing.

"Oh right, I almost forgot. Let me tell you about The Michigan Boys, they're monster hunters like us. At least, they try to be. There's not exactly a league or anything, but there are those in the business who keep tabs on what we're doing and vice versa. Usually they're just harmless, but sometimes they're just—" Cicero said. He was stopped by the sound of one of the men who burst out of the next room. A sudden noise attracted Cicero like a shark to blood in the water. Cicero's quick hands darted towards the trigger as he turned around and let out a sigh only to see a fellow hunter.

"Woah, hey now. Damn near blew my head off! Oh-It's you Cicero," a gruff older man named Dean stated. He extended his hand out while he whistled for his assistant. Rose wondered what the commotion was as she stuck her head out seeing that her section was empty. She walked by Cicero, who didn't react to her, as she stood behind him and kept her silence.

"Yessir, we're the best in the business. I'm a cryptozoologist now, studied biology, you know. I hunted a Sasquatch, right after I fought in the Philippines. Anyway, I'm showing Nate the ropes," Dean stated. Cicero could hardly keep his composure.

Rose shared the same sentiment from what she overheard, as she carried little joy for blowhards. Rose saw two men talking at Cicero while he was trying to get a move on. Rose's eyes first shifted to Dean, and then to the younger man beside him that carried a wrench. Dean was a rugged ex-soldier wearing a red flannel jacket with a stout belly and a beard with red hair. The younger Nate was right off the assembly line with a suit, slicked back black hair, and khakis. He seemed to be a mechanic of some sort based on what Rose could tell. While Rose held respect for a fellow blue-collar worker, this quickly changed with his attitude. His assistant was just as cocky as he was, a former football player from Yale. Nate scoffed at both of them, while Dean laughed in support. To Rose, they were arrogant through and through and deserved to be humbled. Her attention turned to them both as she saw the pointed finger of Dean.

"This is your partner, Cicero? This is the one who tamed the Leshy up in Flagstaff?[1] Sure, and I own Hearst. A colored girl too? But, I could be wrong. Say, why not a wager huh? If we find and take down this monster first, we'll take your pay. If you win, you'll get double the money," Dean proposed, putting his hand on Nate's shoulder.

"Dean, you were always such a child. We need to work, move out the way or I'm blasting your dick off." Cicero let out a cough. He chewed his tongue as Nate retorted.

"There's benches in the lobby if you need to sit down, old sport," Nate said with a smug grin while Cicero glared at the younger man.

"You know what—Cicero, you said it yourself. We need the money. The night is young. Why not?" Rose proposed with a faux cheery voice as Cicero slowly nodded, seeing her perspective. Cicero already had an established reputation in the monster hunting community, but Rose was untested. As far as Cicero was concerned, she was doing quite well, but when other people doubted you, word spread, and he understood above all else the need to defend oneself.

Cicero nodded, accepting the terms of the wager and the game was afoot. Despite money being on the table, cooperation when it suited them fit both teams nicely. Nobody could collect the pay at the end if there were no survivors. Rose and Cicero continued as they did for the time being, searching rooms together only to come up short. Cicero raised an eyebrow as he looked over at the two other men fiddling around with a wooden box that contained a radio with antennas attached. Rose saw his confusion and lured him over for a quick explanation.

---

1. Leshies are deities of the forests in pagan Slavic mythology. These plant creatures guard areas of important earthly power.

"They're trying to see if the monster gives off any kind of static that can be traced on there into sound. I remember the manager saying that the circuit board broke. It's a smart method, but is it the right one?" Rose questioned as she whispered into Cicero's ear. Cicero nodded, he wasn't entirely sure about the science behind it, but like most things he felt this was a bunk strategy.

"You go on ahead and check the next set of rooms. I'll back you up in a bit." Cicero watched Rose run off to the staircase. Cicero continued looking around until he heard the closing of the door showing that Rose was now absent.

Past the lighting that permeated through the bottom of the floor, Rose found herself in the darkness of the staircase. She strapped her flashlight to her body earlier and could feel its location, but she wanted to conserve battery. She slowly moved up the stairs, using her arm to look for the railing and grabbed on tight in the darkness. Rose continued to climb the stairs until she saw a flickering light emanate from the second floor. She remembered that this floor still had power and decided to go through. Rose placed her bag down and withdrew her journal and wrote down the things she observed earlier. She figured that while the rest of the building lacked power, she could retreat to the second floor as needed to refer to her notes if she couldn't see.

The architecture of the hotel was one hardly appreciated by those within it. Rose felt the walls were inviting with floral arrangements and small-scale chandeliers that were dispersed throughout the second floor of the hotel. The walls were pristine, with not a single fingerprint on them. This was a hotel clearly for those with money. She noticed a small area dedicated to open reading and some lounge chairs, a nice place to relax after the job was done. Rose noted the silence of the current floor and decided to make her way up to the third floor. Rose tapped the back of her flashlight and opened the tube; she then blew on the battery and shook it. For a few moments, the flashlight flickered on and off until it shined bright. Rose took a deep breath and headed up the stairs to the next floor.

Rose opened her bag and withdrew her pistol, while holding the flashlight in the other. The inviting atmosphere of the lit floors vanished entirely as darkness hung along the air. Rose closed her eyes and opened them as it took a moment for her vision to adjust. Despite being built the same way, the hallway felt infinitely longer than any other. Her flashlight was hardly as powerful as she'd imagined, only having a couple of extra feet in front of her for vision. She looked around for the first room of interest. The sound was so quiet she could hear her heartbeat. She took a deep breath as she felt her hands sweat.

Rose proposed to herself the first thing she would do is walk the length of the hallway. She quietly stepped forward until she felt calmer, eventually reaching to the end, confirmed by a painting. Rose looked at it and absorbed every detail, a rolling field with cows and a farmer that was typical Americana. As she willed herself to make it to the other end of the room, Rose stopped for a moment as she saw what appeared to be a strange lump in the carpet. She continued her walk but was interrupted by a unique sound that seemed to phase in and out of where she was. Rose closed her eyes and attempted to focus only for her to see a strange clump of darkness that was different from the rest. She briefly disabled her flashlight to see if her thoughts were truly correct. She opened them, and for the first time in complete darkness, she saw a single yellow eye open at the end.

Rose covered her mouth and quickly turned back on the flashlight. She looked behind her and squinted at the painting. The painting had changed; the cows were slaughtered, and the farmer was beheaded. Rose rushed to the staircase, hoping to find her way back downstairs to report to Cicero. She used her shoulder to dislodge the now stuck door. After a few heavy hits, it opened, but Rose was met with an abyss at the bottom of where she came up before. The downward stairs were gone without a trace. All she could do now was go up and see what would happen next. She held her wits about her as she hurried up the stairs to the open door, already ajar and inviting. On the fourth floor, the door closed with a heavy slam.

Cicero had his doubts as well with the hotel being far more ominous than he seemed to realize. Although he was in his early sixties, Cicero felt as if he could hear a high-pitched chime that nobody else could. Cicero loaded his revolvers as he headed back towards the lobby. He remembered there was a second set of stairs towards the front that would get him to the top of the building.

"Are you done already!?" the hotel manager asked while Cicero waved his hand. Cicero gave him a glare, as he hardly took questions on the clock.

"Do you hear that sound or what?" Cicero asked, his tone of voice growing more annoyed by the second. The panicked manager started to sweat as he was unsure of what Cicero was referring to.

"You two idiots figure out that radio yet?" Cicero taunted Dean and Nate down the hall while they adjusted the radio antenna for static. A low buzz could be heard through the room that intensified as the two looked at one another with a satisfied nod.

"Nate—Get your sorry ass up and get a move on bagging our monster. I'll meet you in a bit once I nail the signal a bit more," Dean ordered his subordinate. Nate slicked his hair back and headed for the same stairs that Rose did. He whistled as he opened the door and walked through. In the silence of the hallway, Rose could hear footsteps coming up the stairs.

"I'm up here!" Rose yelled as she let out a sigh of relief to hear someone was coming.

Rose held her breath so that her voice wouldn't betray her senses. The gait was younger and more rushed, so she was aware it wasn't Cicero, but perhaps Dean or Nate instead. She hoped the former, because a trained soldier would hopefully be more helpful against something like this. Rose saw the door open and saw a slim arm reach out with a gun in hand, before stepping inside. Rose saw that it was Nate, and while she'd rather have anyone else, backup was always a benefit. Rose looked Nate over and noticed a few things he was missing from his arsenal, most notably, a bag carrying a first aid kit. This was one of the simplest things a hunter could bring on the job. Cicero instructed Rose to keep some basics in her satchel.

"Nate! It's Rose. I saw... that thing on the floor below us. It has a big yellow eye, and it has some strange abilities I've never seen before. When it travels, these already dark rooms become harder to see. It's so thick my flashlight barely catches. It can change certain aspects of its surroundings; I saw it change a painting, and it can go into the floors." Rose waved to get the young man's attention. She pushed up her glasses to focus down the rest of the hallway as she squinted to make out his appearance. Rose's voice carried to the middle of the hallway where he was visible. Nate raised an eyebrow at Rose's words, with his hand still on the gun.

"What do you mean go into the floors? Describe it in more detail, or this is pointless," Nate asked with irritation in his voice. Rose gestured to the carpet to illustrate her point. Nate kicked the carpet he stood on and searched for an entry hole. Other than a layer of dust that had already accumulated from the carpet, nothing out of the ordinary was seen. He glared at Rose seeing that tidbit as a waste of time.

"You'll see what I mean. Here's what we're gonna do. I'll search these rooms here and you can do the other end. We'll meet in the middle. If you see it, call for help." Rose moved past Nate and grabbed her flashlight out of her bag. Rose took a deep breath and watched as the piercing glow of the light moved the room. Against her better judgment, she peeked out her head for a moment to make sure Nate was fine before focusing back on the task. She could only hope Cicero's luck was better. Rose knew full well what she saw; the being had some sort of sentience and was clearly playing tricks on her.

In the lobby, Cicero moved to the set of stairs he hoped to find. Instead of heading up to Rose, however, he figured it would be better to locate the power breaker and reset the power for the hotel. Cicero realized that this would be much easier to locate their monster of the week instead of fumbling around in the dark.

"Hey! Wait. You better make room for two," the voice of Dean called forth as Cicero turned around.

Cicero tipped his hat as he saw the man withdraw a large revolver. Cicero wasn't aware of the brand, but he knew it certainly packed a punch. Cicero debated whether or not Dean actually wanted to play fair, but backup was welcome. The two ventured down the stairs, with Cicero's flashlight leading the way. He smacked the end to reignite the light once more as he noticed it started to flicker already. The basement of the hotel was deceptively long but compact at the same time. It was a long tunnel with cracked walls that went to a neighboring building. The sound of their footsteps echoed through the tunnel as wafts of dust filled their noses. Cicero held back a sneeze with years of trained restraint and took a short breath.

Cicero held out his hand to stop Dean for a moment as he noticed a strange lump in the distance. He felt his age betrayed his sight, but on further examination, he realized that this was a body. Cicero recalled the hotel manager's words about having someone on call to repair something in the hotel, but how did they end up here? Dean was breathing heavily over Cicero's shoulder as he pushed past him to continue walking. Cicero felt himself jostled further by the impatient Dean.

"Come on Cicero, quit lollygagging and get on with it!" Dean demanded as he scoffed at Cicero's delay.

The body Cicero sighted earlier already had signs of decay, he'd been dead for a couple of days. Cicero grimaced at the sight but there was nothing more that could be done. This beast would have to pay for taking an innocent and it would in due time. Dean and Cicero continued down the tunnel without much thought. At the end of the hallway, a sudden clambering of footsteps made Cicero freeze in place. He was certain that only he and Dean were present. In the distance, past the range of Cicero's flashlight, a humanoid figure inched towards them. The agony of their face was contorted and unrecognizable as their body was construed in multiple ways, as if it was being manipulated by something.

The footsteps increased in volume and prompted Cicero to turn around. Rather than remove his shotgun, Cicero withdrew his LeMat revolver, loaded with silver bullets, and trained it on the figure. As it slowly made its way, Cicero opened fire with his bullets reaching the void beyond them. The loud firing noise and smoke filled the tunnel but landed its mark. Dean fired his revolver off as well, as the two winced with the acoustics of the tunnel not generous to their ears.

The lead shot off by the two reached the now revived maintenance worker as pieces of flesh fell to the ground. The heavier of the bullets reached the corpse's legs, breaking them and causing it to crawl along the floor. In its place where blood lay, a swirling black liquid took its place. Without issue, the corpse floated above the ground, towards the two with increased speed. Cicero switched to his other revolver, still unable to see what lay beyond them while Dean struggled to reload. The sound of a few dropped bullets was obscured by Cicero's blind firing. Cicero prompted Dean to follow him as his pace increased.

Cicero cursed to himself as he hadn't bothered to look at the schematics of the basement, there was more to this tunnel than he realized. It was a much larger labyrinth than he anticipated. Cicero lost sight of Dean as the two split ways in a panic to avoid the floating corpse. Cicero noted that the appendages that were blown off by his revolver were now replaced with some sort of strange black energy that radiated from the body. He found the breaker and quickly reset the power. At the end of his rope, Cicero moved to a nearby ladder and hoped this would be an escape from the currently unkillable entity.

On the surface, Rose found herself with a unique problem. She was restricted onto the carpet as she felt her legs grew heavier while she continued to move closer to Nate. Rose looked below her and noticed that the carpet she was on turned into heavy cement. Her legs were caked with cement as she attempted to move, but the substance hardened at a supernatural rate. Rose attempted to bash at the cement with the butt of her pistol. Beyond her range of motion, Nate only saw a normal carpet and a dark hallway. Rose was bashing her leg for no reason, and this action caused great discomfort to him.

"What the hell are you doing? Why are you bashing your own leg?" Nate asked as he saw Rose grow more panicked. Rose came to the conclusion that the changes made in the surrounding areas had to be localized to the person that was experiencing them in some way, but she was beyond confused on why this only happened to one and not the other.

The entity sucked additional light out of the room as it grew to a larger fast-moving ball that torpedoed itself through walls. As it was a being of shadows, it left no physical damage on the walls other than the sound of broken debris from the speed it produced. The whirlwind that ensued knocked over a loose painting that fell to the floor. A nearby flower vase fell behind Nate and startled him. A low hiss of words that blended together started to fill the room, with different messages for both of them.

"Get out of my fucking head!" Nate yelled. He curled his hand into a fist and punched the wall. He took a knee and vibrated violently like a fever shake.

Rose saw that the lights installed on the ceiling flickered on occasion, and streaks of light that illuminated the hallway contorted their shadowy assailant. The creature prioritized large streaks of light in an attempt to dislodge them, as it started to wrap around a dim light bulb. As it wrapped itself around the light, parts of it started to evaporate before darkness was restored once more and it went back to its original size. As this floor was one which previously had no power, she had some relief as she hoped the rest of the hotel's electricity would be complete. Rose attempted to get Nate's attention as he was slowly unraveling mentally. Rose saw the growing sweat on his face as he started to hyperventilate. She looked past the gruff attitude of the young man before her and raised the pitch of her voice to be more soothing. For better or for worse, Rose knew that her life was also in this person's hands, and she needed him to focus.

"It's okay, we're going to be fine. Now something important, I know it looks strange, but I need you to lift me up to the side—" Rose's eyes tracked the sporadic movement of the shadowy figure. Behind Rose, the shadow contorted in size as it spawned a large black hand and disembodied jaws with jagged teeth that made a crunching sound as it grew closer to the pair's location. Rose lost her breath as she felt the shadowy hand constrict her stomach. She was lifted into the air while she signaled for Nate's attention.

"Nate! Help me out here! The thing's coming right for me!" Rose pleaded as he remained unmoved.

From Nate's perspective, Rose was still on the carpet for no particular reason. The two's visions of the scene differed entirely as Rose was presented with a different vision of Nate that stood like a frozen deer. Rose was unable to tell if it was due to him being green or a more callous decision to buy time for himself. Rose felt herself pinned against the wall by the sentient entrails of shadow, and instinctively used her knife to get out the way, but it merely phased through. Undeterred, Rose fiddled around in her holster, just barely grasping her gun before it fell to the floor. Rose shot the floor and was let go by the shadow. Her ears rang with a sharp pain as she could hear nothing for a second. In the brief moment before she hit the ground, she saw that while the bullet phased through the shadow with ease, the flash from the muzzle caused the creature discomfort. She quickly equipped her flashlight and went on the offensive as the creature started its ascent to another floor.

Out of the creature's influence, Rose and Nate could once again see the same plane. Rose said nothing more as she walked to the staircase, and he followed shortly behind. He let out a few warning shots from his revolver as he saw a speck of darkness flee. Rose hardly thought the creature was on the run, but instead leading them into a much more dangerous trap.

Now on the eighth floor, the pair emerged to a normal hallway. Rose was puzzled as she looked around to find nothing out of the ordinary. She fiddled around in the dark and squinted to write a few pieces of information with a ballpoint pen based on what she'd seen during the brief moment of peace. Rose held her ear to the wall and rubbed it for any disturbance. Nate hardly found it worth cooperating with Rose as out of the glint of his eye, he saw a tease from the shadowy creature. Despite his tendency to freeze up, he hatched a plan to get rid of the beast and thought of the money he wanted. Just like her, Nate was there for a paycheck.

"You're slowing me down, so I'm pressing ahead. Don't wait up." Nate cut ahead of Rose. Rose bit her tongue in frustration as splitting up was the last thing she wanted to do.

Rose recalled that the shadowy figure seemed to have a drastic aversion to light of any form. While she could still see, the creature was able to darken the areas it occupied. She looked along the walls for a sign of a window or anything that could be useful. The rooms had windows that were reinforced with a deadbolt and heavy curtains, but it was too dangerous for her to go through the motions of that alone. While the other floors lacked windows, she was aware that the highest floor held access to the roof, and this was her hopeful vantage point. Rose had no idea how long she'd been at the hunt with Cicero, keeping time was practically impossible. Rose hoped to use the sun's rays as a way to dissolve the creature for good.

"What the—!" Nate yelled, before the black ball entered through his eye sockets.

The pain was immeasurable as he rolled on the ground in an attempt to dislodge the thing. Nate was now blind, and the shadowy entity spiraled around his head like a miniature planet. His eyes were consumed by a rift of darkness and any words of his were met with a resounding echo. Nate was humbled by the stains of a suppressed past revealed to him, the darkest of memories supplanted all thought. As he gave into despair, the void grew larger and started to suck Rose in. She dug her heels into the ground as much as she could, but felt herself slowly drifting towards the insidious mass.

His arms reached out in an attempt to grab Rose. Where his physical hands could not reach, the shadowy figure grafted onto Nate's body and used it as an extension to grab Rose. Nate was powerless as the shadow formed a large hand and lifted Rose up to launch her into the wall.

Rose felt the impact of her body hit the wall as she got herself up and felt pain surge throughout her body. She groaned in irritation as she felt her afflicted bone freeze up her right arm. The possessed Nate let out a horrific moan that sent a shiver throughout Rose's body. Nate attempted to dislodge the beast but was helpless to its whims as its voice grew louder.

"Kill... Kill. Kill!" the disembodied voice threatened as Nate's mouth remained closed.

The hand that attacked her clasped itself around her throat and started to squeeze. Rose's eyes started to fade as she felt her breathing get heavy. As Rose felt the life within her squeeze out, her hand shook as she barely grasped the trigger. She shot a bullet into the void that used to be Nate's face and felt a gradual release. Rose hadn't bothered to think any further about it, she was focused on survival only. Out of nowhere, Rose discovered that she had been moved to the end of the hallway by the shadowy hand. Rose ran quickly as she used the carpet to her advantage to speed up. To propel itself further, the shadow ejected itself from Nate's body and made an assortment of physical surfaces appear on the wall. It bounced from side to side as it gained further momentum as it chased Rose.

Rose shot her gun behind her as she rushed to the end of the hallway to reach the stairs. Rose was covered in sweat as she dropped her satchel for less resistance and barely made it. She whisked past the ninth floor and at long last reached the penthouse suite. The tenth floor only had one room and one other door that opened out towards the roof. As Rose continued, she dashed and felt a grip around her foot as she was slowly dragged back. Rose let out a panicked scream as she dug her nails into the ground and attempted to jostle out. With a sly kick, she dislodged her shoe and hobbled over to the locked door. She used her last bullet in the magazine to shoot off the lock. Rose swung the door open and was met with the open expanse of the early sunrise.

Rose never felt better seeing the few precious seconds of twilight as the tendrils of the shadowy being emerged from the open door and attempted to grab her. Rose advanced to the middle of the roof and as she heard the wind of the early morning rise, the streaks of the Arizona sun came to save her. The bold shadow creature was humbled by the quickly increasing amounts of light as it writhed in pain from reaching to Rose. Rose took a deep breath as she saw the lights of the penthouse suite glow with a resounding hum. The shadow being was assaulted by natural light and that of the high-quality bulbs on the top floor. With nothing left to grasp, the being vanished into thin air and the room was silent.

Rose found with the power on in the entirety of the building, it meant that Cicero must have succeeded in resetting the basement's breaker. Her first thoughts were of his well-being, but as she went to reclaim her stuff, she went to check on Nate's condition. Rose entered the eighth floor where she left in a mad dash and covered her mouth in horror; the lone bullet she shot at the shadowy beast, popped his head in the chaos. Rose noticed a sole bullet went clean through his forehead to the other side. She let out a guttural scream that reverberated through the staircase. Rose was soon joined by Cicero, who made his way back up the stairs to find Rose. He was out of breath as he didn't trust the elevator to carry him up.

"Been looking all over for you—" Cicero said as his eyes shifted towards Rose. Cicero looked over the body with a raised eyebrow. He studied it closely, tapping it with his boot to be sure. Nate's corpse was still warm, Cicero wasn't sure how to break the news to Dean. A bit of blood leaked through the exit wound of her bullet. Cicero scratched his head as he tried to piece together the scenario as Rose stumbled over her words.

"Cicero, I'm a murderer! He's dead because of me! I panicked; I could have done something about it," Rose stated, looking over the faceless hunter that lay still.

Every time I make a mistake, someone dies. It wasn't me this time, but someone did, and I have to live with that. Rose thought. She hoped to hear some reassurance from Cicero, but the old cowboy had a much more callous outlook to on-the-job casualties.

"Clean shot. Not how I would have done it but hey, problem solved." Cicero looked over the body. Rose was beyond appalled with Cicero's gruff response to a casualty on the job.

"It gets easier, besides—Alright, maybe I shouldn't have said that but I'm right. They know what they signed up for. I'll handle things, just get your stuff and meet me in the lobby. Partners die often, it's part of the business," Cicero said as he tried to pat Rose's shoulder in support.

Rose was beside with grief as her attempts to survive brought the death of someone under her watch. Rose didn't think she could ever have the heart or the will to take a life, she'd always find a solution that kept the peace if she could help it. Rose idled in the lobby while Cicero smoothed over things with Dean. The two men were hardly emotional on the matter, but Cicero greased the man's pockets with some money to pay for the funeral and any other fees. As Cicero concluded his business, he tapped Rose's shoulder and the two walked over to the receptionist at the hotel. Rose's eyes were still red with tears as she blamed herself for the outcome of today.

"It's taken care of. You'll want to get someone to clean the walls as a precaution. Tunnels too," Cicero mentioned as he raised an eyebrow to the man.

"I must admit, I did not expect this to be handled in such a fiscally responsible manner. Your pay will be distributed forthwith in a—" The man mentioned while Cicero held up his finger.

"Cash. Cold hard money. You got that?" Cicero grunted.

"Our employers will send you the money as requested. Not to worry, your address is already in our ledger." The man mentioned, which gave Cicero a shudder. The fact that The Baron had any knowledge of his primary residence was terrifying. He looked behind him as he saw Rose trying to get her word in and stepped aside.

"I... have one question for you," Rose asked as she broke her silence.

"Did you happen to find a purple vortex before the sightings of this entity? We have found a number of things just like that come from those."

"Not at all, it seemed to have just shown up one day and is now... no more, thanks to you both. Once again, I will forward your success to the relevant parties, and you will be paid," the man explained as he gestured for the pair to leave.

Rose and Cicero were both concerned on the man's answer on how the entity was independent of a vortex. The pair decided to table their discussions for the time being and take advantage of the early morning to get breakfast before retiring for the day back at the homestead. The pair left and headed for a bistro that's been the talk of the town owned by a man named Cirano.

The Owl: I

Rose and Cicero walked out to find their senses bombarded by the rapidly increasing temperatures of downtown Phoenix. Cicero rubbed his stomach as he had little to eat since the previous day, and this sentiment was shared by Rose. Rose noted that Cirano's was a good place to eat with a wide selection and was accommodating to those that could pay. The early crowd before the morning commute to work was present as businessmen looked into the daily paper and talked about all sorts of things that were of little interest. Rose was curious at the format of the establishment, her eyes darted to a sign that said, "Seat yourselves." Rose had been to few restaurants and each one always required an escort. As Rose sat down, two people relocated to a further table with a glare while Cicero returned with two glasses of water that were also self-serve. Rose felt relief as she took a sip of the calming water. It was some of the freshest she'd had ever, and it lacked the aftertaste of Cicero's spigot. The pair felt strangely calm as a cloud gave brief relief to the sun that came over their heads. Rose looked around and admired the decorations. They were remarkably modern with a rustic atmosphere built by brick. Rose and Cicero looked at one another while they waited to be served. The wait staff were occupied fulfilling the copious amount of coffee orders and the preparation of pastries. While advertised as a bistro to cater to a certain crowd, Cirano's functioned more as an all-purpose restaurant where it had a rotating breakfast and lunch menu.

As the two waited, Rose felt they were being ignored for obvious reasons, but her mind changed as she saw a man approach the pair. Cicero turned around in his seat to see what Rose looked at and saw a middle-aged man with a gray shirt and newsboy cap. He wore a black apron on top and looked like he hadn't slept in weeks. Cicero bit his tongue as he studied the man. He wondered how much money he truly made off the restaurant business, everything was amazing and yet affordable to someone of their pay grade. Cicero was hardly cheap, but he prepared practically everything at home with Claudia.

"Oh, you must be the—" Rose said as she was cut off.

"The owner? Yeah, placed is named after me too. I see you lack a menu, what do you want to order? Breakfast items and lunch are the same, just different drinks, so you can order what you want," Cirano mentioned.

"Well, what do you have?" Cicero said as he raised an eyebrow.

Cirano listed off an assortment of things at a speed that bewildered the pair. Rose admired the meticulous nature put into his business. She was curious about the size of the kitchen, among other things, but all she wanted was some chicken and waffles. Rose ordered while Cicero pondered his decision with a tug of his beard.

"Give me a steak with a piece of hard toast. I'll take a medium. I'm not a bloodhound, but I'm not looking for leather either," Cicero said as Cirano nodded. Cicero was mildly impressed that he remembered the orders without needing to write them down like the juvenile wait staff. He also appreciated a boss that would work with his employees rather than lord over them like an overseer. Cicero removed his jacket and placed it on the chair.

Rose and Cicero had nothing left but idle time to discuss things around them. The pair started talking some more as they waited for their food. In the interim for their orders being prepared, a young woman delivered a covered plate of cookies with frosting on them that looked delightful to Rose's eyes. They were a dark brown color that she hadn't seen before.

She licked her lips as she quickly scooped one into her mouth and felt the slightly sticky nature. Cicero studied their table and the rest of the restaurant while Rose ate. While they chose outdoor seating, there was also generous accommodation inside as well.

"So, this place is run by a man? And there's all these... frilly napkins? They have flowers on 'em, what use are flowers on napkins? They're just gonna get dirty. Lit candles in the middle of the day?! I'm not telling any hard truths, but I didn't take him to be a dandy. What do you think?" Cicero questioned.

"Cicero, I didn't take you for a gossip! You can't just ask that!" Rose looked behind her to hope nobody was listening.

"It's not a problem, we're here eating, it's just an observation. Why—Look at this Rose! These cookies have better frosting on them than my wife's cooking and she's baked for years! Oh, are these made of chocolate?!" Cicero said with a cheery voice as he bit into one.

"Right, I forgot one piece of information. Before we headed to the hotel, I got a call while you were asleep. Some man was on the line and was willing to pay us for a job out by the copper mines further out west. Best part? We don't have to kill it, they just want us to investigate what happened. Apparently, those miners trapped some beast from a purple hole using a cave-in. Pretty clever if you ask me," Cicero mentioned.

The pair received their food and ate happily as they debriefed on the previous night's events. A few eavesdropping waitresses talked among themselves in confusion, but one remembered the incident with the cactus and wondered if these were the same people involved with such a thing. Rose and Cicero looked at one another to see who would foot the bill, and Rose withdrew ten dollars. Cicero had a smug expression as Rose truly appreciated their partnership. Once all else was taken care of, the pair left a generous tip for Cirano's service and hospitality. The owner himself did not partake, he scooped up the collection and placed into it the tip jar to be split among the employees. The breakfast shift ended later, and a new cycle of lunch staff came by ready to work.

Cirano looked over his establishment with pride as he assisted in kneading dough. Cirano was a prideful man who had an axe to grind with many but captured the hearts of those with his pastries and other food items. It was frequented by the well-off and less fortunate, though at different times of the day. A shrewd businessman, he took any patron willing to come forward. He kept a tight and clean ship with well-paid and trained employees. Despite being the owner of a profitable operation, his real aims lay elsewhere. Cirano walked around, giving affirmative nods to his subordinates. To help sell the atmosphere, Cirano looked to his newest purchase. A phonograph that played classical or contemporary music was attached to a glass stand that its sound accompanied them through the restaurant. He and his crew were preparing for the hectic lunch rush but today was an unusual day.

After surveying their newest points of economic conquest, The Baron and Baroness chose to patron this location this afternoon. The two walked in tandem, with her grasping his arm as they scanned the perimeter. The sun was high, and The Baroness wore a beautiful lavender sundress that was the eye of all that passed by. Her husband wore a tan suit that took the desert heat far better than the usual black. The two had long cultivated their image slowly but surely as well established and admired titans of industry. Many of their rivals were bought out or put under the ground which allowed them to participate with the common masses undisturbed.

"We haven't been on this side of town in some time. An associate told me that Cirano's seems to be the best in town. Shall we?" The Baron asked, as The Baroness moved the two of them in the bistro's direction.

While there was a sizable number of customers before them, none compared in importance to the two that arrived. The Baron and Baroness stood in silence as their eyes tracked a waitress who was attending to their other customers. While quite young, she was aware of the rumors regarding their reputation. Their opinion of the bistro could sink it to the ground if she were to falter here. Her palms started to sweat, and she wiped them quickly on her apron before lowering her head in acknowledgment.

"Give us your best table and grab us Cirano, there are things to be discussed," The Baron tipped his hat as the nervous waitress quickly led them to their table. The two waited as the waitress cleaned off the table with robotic precision. The Baron went for the first chair to pull for his wife and then he sat down. In the same breath, another waitress came by with complimentary bread fresh from the oven. Two menus were placed on either end as cold glasses of water were offered. The Baron reached for his wallet, but the delay in her response signaled that the drinks were free.

The two sampled the bread, taking great care to use the associated fork and knives provided. The two ate silently as they waited for their associate to come by. Out of the pair's view, Cirano felt his shoulder be tapped by the young waitress who informed him of their new arrivals. Cirano took a deep breath from his task and prompted the waitress to pour drinks while he took care of his guests. The Baron and Baroness raised an eyebrow at Cirano's attire. Despite being the owner, he wore an apron and was knee-deep in flour like that of the commons.

"Word travels quickly. A man who takes care of business, foreign and domestic, is one to keep good company, wouldn't you say? I'm looking to buy you and your services. You are, the, Cirano are you not? If I'm mistaken, my business will go elsewhere," The Baron teased. Cirano was incredibly nervous as he understood The Baron's relevance on the culinary scene and his role in industry. In his spare time, The Baron wrote storied reviews of places he'd dined at that gathered the attention of those around the world. For Cirano, this was akin to his favorite team making it to the NFL Championship. He needed to choose his responses carefully.

"R-Right. Welcome to Cirano's, what are you looking to buy?" Cirano muttered. He attempted to maintain his cover as best as he could. He knew that his other endeavors treaded on the toes of business conducted by The

Baron. The Baron was brutal with his enemies and Cirano hardly wanted a war on his hands with The Baron's inner circle specifically. The Baron kept going as he overwhelmed Cirano with his aura.

"You are the third biggest earner for the Chicago branch, if my research is correct. This has given you a lot of attention, but yet, you remain below where your standing should be." The Baron eyed Cirano.

In his many years of negotiating, The Baron knew Cirano's story before he could speak. He sensed ambition in his heart that could under the right circumstances, be built up to support his needs. The Baron and Baroness earned political enemies over the years they've built their empire, and that included unpredictable agents such as mobsters wanting to encroach on their city. While many were easy to buy non-aggression for a time, the pair lacked the muscle needed to enforce their apparatus. The police in these parts were too fickle and incompetent to perform the more delicate tasks.

The Baroness saw Cirano start to freeze up, so she decided to appeal to his ego. She held a look of approval at the organization and aesthetic values of the restaurant's design.

"I wanted to give my thanks for such fine hospitality. The decor is exquisite and inviting," The Baroness said. She lifted an empty glass to be filled with red wine. Without a second thought, Cirano snapped his fingers for the most expensive one he could. While he didn't have a particular special, he hoped the taste would hold over well. Cirano stood with his arms folded as he looked towards the couple.

"It is appreciated. You know, my father always told me baking was for women. I decided to think for myself—" Cirano said, getting interrupted by The Baroness' soothing tone.

"Yes. You took a risk made of your own destiny, and now you have a successful business. This is one of the best bread loaves I've ever sampled, and I have been to France proper at least ten times. Well done. Our discussion though, is we have come to give you an offer," The Baroness complimented, her eyes gesturing to her husband, who grasped the bottom of his chin in thought. Cirano was confused, he wasn't in any position to sell his restaurant and lacked the time to be a private chef.

Cirano had a look of surprise on his face that he used a nearby menu to suppress. Cirano was ignorant of either party's true status in the crime world, he only confidently knew of their affairs in the dining world above all else. The rumors were just rumors, and wanting to make an accusation of their crime networks would be a show of bad faith. Cirano knew that the information said by The Baron was true, and he wondered how quickly he became compromised.

"I think you have mistaken me. I'm but a legitimate businessman—" Cirano coughed in attempt to alert a nearby waitress to intervene. The Baron caught wind of the ruse and raised his hand.

"Hey uh, bud, should we be talking about this kind of business in daylight hours? I'm a man of means but my restaurant needs to keep up good reviews," Cirano mentioned with a tone of desperation at the behest of his customers.

"I know exactly who you are. We can discuss business freely here. You are The Owl, and you've caused quite a ruckus for my supply route," The Baron opened as he lifted an eyebrow at Cirano's reaction. He further emphasized his point with a smug grin as he gestured his arm out to guide his eyes.

"Look to your left, and then to your right. Everyone working in your kitchen is on my payroll, one way or another. Your waitresses grind long hours to buy my precious gems, so that one day, they can see themselves in my image. Only you can change the world, that's what they say," The Baroness said. She leaned back in the chair and folded her arms behind her. The Baroness referenced one of her magazine's latest issues that featured a reflective film that let the reader impose their image on the model, surrounded by a life of luxury. It was a message that was supposed to encourage self-confidence but also draw people to buy more of her gem line

.

How did they know? Who could have squealed? Cirano had a look of surprise on his face that he couldn't suppress. Cirano gripped his hand into a fist that nearly bled with the amount of nerves he had about his situation.

"Don't consider yourself with the opinions of the sheep. You are a man of means, but do you have power? I'll let you in on a secret. See that man there? Works for me," The Baron pointed out a man in the distance waiting for a tram. His head turned to face Cirano as he continued to speak.

"Your bus boys. Work for me. Every guest here at your lunch shift is on my take. This includes your personal driver that you share a special connection with. Nothing said here will compromise your... standing," The Baron mentioned. Cirano decided to pull a bluff in an attempt to save face. He dropped the innocent baker persona and took on the true visage of The Owl. He cracked his fingers together as he yawned from the tired workday.

"I know who you are. My services don't come cheap. You never want to cheap out on a nice car, short your waiter, or your bill collector. All of those things can give you a bad day. I'll say this. There's plenty of crews who can do what you want, but you get what you paid for. Why not work with us? You've got the cash, and I got the time. Let's break some bread," Cirano mentioned as The Baron was pleased. He saw The Baron raise his head with the truth now revealed.

The Baroness waited patiently as she sipped her wine for the prompt. Her thoughts on the matter still centered on finally reuniting with Rose, but she first needed to protect her investments. The Baroness established a series of trusts that were self-sustaining so she could fund her ventures into gathering resources to acquire The Frost Gem. While her husband also supported this endeavor, The Baron was centered on dominating the railroad industry, and proposed a grand railway independent of the US government and the yoke of inefficient companies that took much of his time.

"It's a simple security measure. My wife and I own an immeasurable amount of assets in the state of Arizona. Someone with your intellect and firepower should keep a healthy... deterrent from my competition. Dear, if you would," The Baron mentioned.

"Our terms are simple. In my pocketbook, I hold an envelope with one hundred and fifty-thousand dollars encased inside. On agreement for working with us, the entire sum of money is yours. Tax-free. With our partnership and patronage, anything you or your associates may need can be purchased without scrutiny. Machine guns? Legal fees? Health insurance? All these can be taken care of. Divest from the Chicago branch and work for us," The Baroness offered. The Baroness's glare was soul-reading as she watched Cirano debate the cost and benefits in his head. Accepting the offer would basically be open warfare against the higher-ups back in Chicago, but with this nest egg, he could get the best of the best.

How... How did he know!? Fine, let's think this through. Let's see what happens. They have my attention. Cirano mulled over as he met the stares of both as not even the wind offered reprieve from the awkward silence. His hand slowly reached over to the envelope and stopped short for a moment.

I've never seen this much come my way before. This is... Cirano thought. The proposal was inviting, but cold cash could be found anywhere if he tried hard enough. He needed to know just how serious this was, and his answer soon came from The Baroness.

"Your silence tells us plenty. Cirano, it's one thing to be good, but in order to be great, you must take risks. Your father probably told you as well that working as a laborer in your station was best for you. This is spite and jealousy for his own shortcomings. The restaurant is but a steppingstone to your greatness," The Baroness said, her counterpart nodded in agreement. The Baron could only continue to be impressed at his wife's ability to turn a situation to their favor in the manner she did. The moment of truth arrived for them both as Cirano grasped the money and quickly stuffed it into his pocket. The pair gave each other a satisfied expression as The Baron turned once more to address their new employee.

"For now, operate as you are. We do not wish to declare war on the other factions yet. There is a small matter to be addressed at your leisure. There's a small hamlet not far from here that occupies land I wish to develop for my railway. An eyesore from miles away from the splendor of the city, filled with retirees and degenerates. A dossier will be provided. Make it known that if they refuse to sell, there will be consequences for it," The Baron ordered.

As the three continued to talk, the Baron and Baroness ordered their meals which came out swiftly. Cirano bowed out leaving the two to discuss things on their own. Cirano greeted the rest of his guests, bouncing from table to table. Shortly after, The Baron looked over his meal, a club sandwich with a side of bacon and devoured it wholeheartedly. He looked at his wife's meal which was an ornate pasta dish and grumbled slightly at his clearly inferior pick. She scooped up a small piece with a spoon and placed it on her husband's plate before speaking once more.

"I received word from the manager at the Autumn Gates Hotel while you were out. The entity of concern was removed by two hunters. These were not the incompetent fools originally hired but two new entrants." The Baroness wiped her mouth with a napkin. Sitting outside, the sound of automobiles picked up in the distance before tapering off again. The Baroness fanned herself as she waited for her husband's response.

"Enlighten me dear. We have our hands in many pots. Who are these two hunters?" The Baron inquired as he sipped a glass of water. He swished around the ice cubes hoping to cool the drink quicker than anticipated.

"One is a veteran, known as Cicero. The old man who tries to tarnish our reputation. A pesky one, but at least he seems to be only confined in this place. He was seen with a Negro girl who fits the description of who we have been searching for. My precious Rose. I've been hoping to find her soon, but with everything we had to do, I've been neglectful on the search.

Our daughter needs a home," The Baroness stated, with her hands still as she grasped the table. The proposition of finding the next step of her plan was immensely intoxicating and she was filled with excitement.

"Ah, yes. I am very familiar with Cicero. I gave him a good scare the other day in the department store. He and his father worked in my copper mine back in the '70s. It was a good starting project after a lull of travel, but not my best work," The Baron scoffed. His wife's words entered his mind once more and he was prompted to raise an important question.

"You think she is the one?" The Baron said lowly, moving his head close to the table.

"I do. We have traveled to many worlds, some like ours, some far stranger. I have sought out every rendition of this girl and yet I feel that the original is upon us here. How odd it is, we are both our originals. It would only make sense for another to come from here as well."

"I suggest husband, we test this theory by giving her an invitation to the manor. The job is done, and payment will be given, but I have a test I wish to enact."

One last call was made for Cirano as closing time neared. Ever down on his luck, Bill approached the restaurant and took a deep breath. His work with Niccolo wasn't enough to pay off the debts he owed. Bill took the bartender's advice and decided to opt out for the loan, but he knew it was going to cost him more than what he'd have to pay back. Bill was loyal to Niccolo, but he needed to think of his survival first.

Cirano was in deep conversation with his personal driver, George, who idled by at a table. Cirano playfully winked to him as he saved a slice of cake for him. He gave a warm smile to Cirano, as in the late hours, only a skeleton crew remained that knew his truth. George held a small cup of coffee and noted Bill's appearance. He nodded his head and assessed from his attire that this was for business matters. Cirano raised his eyebrows as he received the signal. He dismissed the rest of his staff while one young lady remained stacking dishes.

"You can go home Nancy. I'll close up here," Cirano said to the tired student. She left without a word. The desperate Bill tugged at his suit collar as he humbly lowered his head.

"'Scuse me, are you Cirano?" Bill asked.

"Yeah. That's me. The hell do you want? If you're looking for food, the last cheesecake is out." Cirano mentioned, as he was sure that wasn't Bill's actual intention. Cirano instinctively placed his hand on George's left shoulder.

"I wanted to see The Owl for myself," Bill opened with a nod of respect. Cirano returned with a nod of his own for him to enter inside. Cirano lit a cigarette for himself, and one for Bill, while George remained on the outside. The door closed as the pair looked at each other. Bill was filled with sweat already from the nerves of it all.

"What do you do Bill? As in, your real job. I know you're a soldier of someone's crew," Cirano asked judgingly. Cirano knew Bill already from his appearance as his own mobsters frequented the same speakeasy. It was important for him to keep tabs on the members of other crews, should he find them to have some value for his own efforts, or to get rid of them.

"Well, I-I work for Niccolo sir. I'm really good with a shotgun and staying out of trouble. Though there's a problem," Bill said. Bill was covered in sweat already at the prospect of talking to Cirano. It was nerve-wracking for him to do so as talking to a boss so casually was usually a sign for the worse.

"So—My understanding is that you work for a rival family and yet, you come asking me for aid? What can you offer me that will benefit?" Cirano demanded.

"I wouldn't come here if I didn't have anything to offer you-It's just been hard. I need money. I can offer my services. I know you have hired guns, so I won't give that. I can give you some info. I know your boys have had trouble south of the border, but I have an in," Bill proposed.

"Niccolo? I don't follow. Oh, you must mean Andrea. Ha! A foreign two-bit crew with not much to show for it. Though, their exploits in Mexico are appealing. I'll give you the money. I don't like rats in my restaurant Bill, but you look like a mouse to me. Small and unassuming. I'll give the payment out in increments. How much do you owe anyway?" Cirano asked. He assumed the loan was going to be a paltry sum that could be easily resolved but was shocked by Bill's hesitation.

"I owe ten thousand dollars to some Irishmen," Bill commented lowly as his eyes hit the floor. Bill started to hyperventilate but calmed himself down as Cirano stared him down in utter confusion.

"Genuinely, how the fuck do you owe that much money? Did you spend it on whores or something?! Do you do heroin?" Cirano asked in shock.

"I'm a gambling man sir," Bill tried to hold back his tears out of embarrassment.

Cirano looked deep into Bill's eyes and could see the anguish on his face. For some reason, it reminded him of when he first met George and before his job could provide him with some security. Unlike George though, Bill was a slave to his vices, and this gave him little sympathy.

"You know, my father's a gambling man too. I just hope you have better luck than he does," Cirano threatened as the two shook hands and the deal was made.

To Rob A Bank

Niccolo waited outside the copper mine with his pocket watch as he scanned the desert for a lone car to come by. He and Florence arranged for her to come by around noon to ensure she wasn't followed. Lunch time was the perfect cover for her as those that would, even remotely, suspect her of anything were busy feeding themselves and cared little of her antics. Florence had been a subject over the past few days as she got herself acquainted with the intricacies of mob life. Under Niccolo's watchful eye, Florence observed the tools of the trade. She saw the distillation of alcohol and was marveled at the lengths it took to get it into the country and the hands of reliable sellers. She took an inquisitive look at the men's weaponry and was subject to hours of Niccolo's enforcers trying to impress her with stories. Niccolo wondered if Florence really the stomach had to do what she was going to do. His ex-wife was affiliated with the crime life and had a hardness that he couldn't see in Florence.

As far as he witnessed, his men ranged from offensive perverts to doting paternalistic ones that tried to keep their crassness to themselves when she was around. The first time Florence showed up, she brought little more than a notebook and lipstick. This earned a few jeers from the rest of the men and provided an ill-needed headache for Niccolo. Niccolo knew that she'd have a lot to write about today. Florence was privy to the planning of a bank heist that Niccolo and Andrea mapped out for some time. The schedules were memorized for each teller and the transfer of money from a secured truck. The bank was going to be filled to the brim with cash as it aligned with the pay period. For Niccolo's men, this was going to be their payday and a little extra.

Niccolo heard the obnoxious honking horn of Florence's car as he walked over to acknowledge her. Florence gave her horn one last ring as she waved to Niccolo and the rest of the men that bothered to come by. While Florence drove by a mound to hide her vehicle, a few of the gangsters talked among themselves, confused at Niccolo's insistence on keeping her around. As it was still working hours, the mine's primary function was still open. The sound of heavy machinery whirred down for the lunch rush as a tractor strapped with large plates moved large quantities of sand.

"The boss is from Italy proper, you know how they are with dames. Personally, I think it's a distraction, but she's a looker. Might give her my address— " One man said as he looked over his shoulder to see his boss glaring at him. He gulped in his throat, while prompting the others to remain focused on guarding the outfit.

Niccolo raised his head in surprise as Florence dressed much more muted than usual. Her usual green dress was replaced with a sordid gray that looked as rugged as everyone else's clothes. She wore a small hat that housed her orange hair and wagged a finger to catch his attention. Niccolo walked by and was puzzled as Florence quickly moved behind her car. He heard some rummaging through her trunk.

"I am a performer, and I will play the part I need," Florence grinned.

"I brought this, just in case!" Florence said. She reached into her trunk and withdrew a baseball bat with nails embedded in it.

"W-Where on Earth did you get this?" Niccolo questioned. He wasn't sure whether to be impressed by Florence's creativity or terrified. She seemed to really embrace the role of an observer to the highest degree.

"And expose my secrets to you? Why, I never!" Florence laughed as she met Niccolo's eyes.

Niccolo turned to call his men to prepare their vehicles needed for the venture. While he watched his more seasoned gangsters equip the newer hires, he spoke to Florence about another matter that concerned them both.

"I confirmed the call with those people you recommended me. They will be coming later tonight, so after the heist, we can meet with them and figure out our second problem. They asked for a lot of money, money that I don't like giving them, so hopefully the venture today will provide what they ask for," Niccolo mentioned.

Now that Florence had woven her way into working with Niccolo, she was excited for her first day into the realm of organized crime. She had her camera ready, and while she wasn't able to take any pictures of Niccolo himself, she was happy to turn in any photos of those he sought to deal with. The pair moved to Niccolo's personal vehicle that came stocked with bulletproof plating on the sides and reinforced glass windows. Niccolo had a number of people out for him personally in the underground, and it never hurt to be careful. Although Niccolo prided himself as an excellent driver, he rarely had to do such a task when he was at the mine, much to his disappointment. One of Niccolo's hobbies was watching drag racing, and he always wanted to be in the back of an incredibly fast car. Niccolo waited by the vehicle as he blew some air into the small opening of his suit to cool himself. Niccolo snapped his fingers as the men scrambled to see who would be responsible for herding the boss. The humble Bill dusted off his working jeans and gave a nod of acknowledgement to Florence and Niccolo.

Bill received a gentle wave from Florence as he carried a burlap sack towards the pair. He and the other men prepared a set of masks to cover their faces of varying sizes that he passed onward. There was a group of about fifteen men for the bank job, and each one made a smaller incision with a switchblade to fit their eyes. Bill rested his shotgun on the ground away from the others while he helped Florence fit her mask and Niccolo's.

"Very helpful. Though we don't need to wear them until we actually reach the bank," Niccolo mentioned as he gave Bill a pat on the shoulder.

Niccolo understood he made Bill nervous, but he valued his eagerness. While most of his mobsters liked to make a spectacle out of a hit and run or causing ruckus, Bill did what he was told and came back home with the loot.

"Oh—Sorry boss, I figured since we were going for the truck, it'd be best to be prepared," Bill commented.

As the men armed up and went into their positions in separate cars, Florence was escorted into their car by Niccolo. Bill and another man took point at the front of the vehicle while the pair hung back. Niccolo's trunk was prepped with spare ammo for his submachine gun and a few other implements. He held explosives to breach the interior safe and a pair of hearty gloves to disguise his fingerprints. For the more refined searches, he also had his men apply a solvent on their hands that made identifying fingerprints more difficult. Niccolo was aware of the growing countermeasures put in place by the police they couldn't afford to bribe and sought to ensure there were no mistakes. Florence's arrival with the party came as a mixed reaction, but it was common practice for women to be used in operations as the police delayed elevating hostilities, which made her a perfect element for the robbery.

The cars drove off in a single-file line as an armed convoy. Niccolo and Florence were in the middle of four cars. Two cars were to divert the money truck into a section of town where they could dispatch the vehicle, while his own and the back car handled the bank robbery itself. Niccolo knew it would be some time before the pair would arrive in town to cause a scene. He remembered there was a county fair that was going to be a great distraction for his plans.

In the silence of the car, Niccolo attempted to understand some of Florence's view on things. He had a basic knowledge of what she was like, but her philosophy confused him. He wondered how someone so cheery could brace themselves for the hard tasks it takes with the crime world. Though Florence was only an observer, Niccolo naturally treated this like any other normal session of business. Florence would be in disguise, so he had no issues with her being in town. Bill kept his hands on the wheel while the other guard looked at his pistol in boredom.

"I have to ask. You agreed to work with me, yes. Does it bother you? The things that I do? People will die if they don't give us the money Florence," Niccolo asked.

"I noticed your men try to tiptoe around me what they do. That's not really needed. I'm not gonna tell you what to do Nicki, your business, your house and such. To say, oh the humanity when you kill detritus in the streets, really is disingenuous. You're a lion at the zoo, and I can't get sad when you eat other animals. We're both useful to the other, so it doesn't matter how I feel." Florence adjusted her position in the seat.

Regardless of how she felt, Florence's experiences at the sanitarium destroyed much of her innocence on how the world worked. She'd seen death by neglect, which was worse than anything else she'd imagine. At least here, they died for a reason. If they were smart, they would comply with these armed thugs and leave with their lives. Florence was an avid reader of events in the paper, aside from her own work, and she kept a mental log on all sorts of specific details. Her esoteric knowledge intrigued Niccolo as she showed signs of familiarity to specific terms he used when addressing the men.

"Besides, the bankers are the real criminals," Florence stated with a smug grin that got a small chuckle from the front seats.

"You know, for being the boss, I figured your thing was to plan and hang back." She watched the endless stream of cacti out the window.

"It's about respect mostly. Anything I ask the men should be possible by my hand. Killing people is as natural as breathing to me. I have a few rugged men like the ones in our company, but many are just starting out," Niccolo explained as he felt for his pistol.

"Your wives know you do this sort of thing? There's a flower shop by the bank, you could go there after and—" Florence started to say as she was cut off by a harsh sound.

The first car in the convoy stopped quickly as the rest shortly followed after. The group was stopped by a few other trucks that carried supplies. The main road into town was temporarily blocked off for access to the fair and a police checkpoint was established to make sure the lines remained in an orderly fashion. Niccolo cursed under his breath as he saw the attendant looked like he cared about his job. While Florence expected Niccolo or his men to simply gun down the attendant, there was more finesse involved than that. Niccolo only intended for problems to get killed, but those that were workable could be reasoned with. Niccolo instructed everyone to remain attentive to the checkpoint and comply with all demands. The first car in the convoy advanced without issue, while Bill kept his hands clenched on the wheel.

"Sir. State your reason for entry." The attendant precisely examined the vehicle. He saw the group present and ordered a deputy with opening the truck.

"I-I'm here on company time on account of my boss," Bill mentioned with a worried grin.

Niccolo remained calm as despite carrying ammunition and an illegal firearm, the boxes that they were contained in caused no alarm. He held his breath as the police were searching for liquor and they had nothing of the sort. The man gave a curious shake but opted to let it be. The clink of glasses was far more important to the men who earned bonuses for every bootlegger that was caught coming into town. The man raised an eyebrow at Niccolo's attire but came to a realization as he looked at Bill's clothing. The police officer gathered that they were related to the mine on the outskirts of town and must have come to see the fair. Bill was a local and looked trustworthy enough. With a disarming smile, he won over the attendant's goodwill.

"Oh-You know they offer a discount for miners? Your boss back there must be clocking your every move, eh? Give them a good time, you boys do good work," the police officer mentioned to Bill.

The other cars sped through checking without a problem and Niccolo instructed the others to prepare. As the group drove into town, Florence recognized the hotel where she currently resided. She held the edge of her seat as their pace increased with little regard for traffic. Bill bobbed and weaved the car around and followed the lead as sections of the town were packed with people. Niccolo instructed Bill to find an alleyway to park the cars without issue. Bill complied with the utmost efficiency as he settled them into a smaller section of town. The bank itself was one block away, and they parked with a few minutes to spare before the transfer would start.

Niccolo hoped to use the first team to distract the truck and rob them blind, while he focused on the crown jewel that remained inside. He reiterated the plan and waved his hand for Florence, Bill, and four other men to come with him. Bill gave Florence a bag to hold the money while he loaded everyone else with their armaments.

"Team A is focused on the truck, we will go and go through the doors. There is one in the back. I will use an explosive for the safe if the person can't crack the code," Niccolo ordered as they went into formation. The group ventured quickly into a sprint as they tried to get there. A few onlookers pointed at the scene, where a man brandished his gun for them to look the other way.

The excitement of the rush was hard to contain for Florence as she felt her heart pounding. The group made it to the exterior of the bank and pooled inside. Bill was called up by Niccolo to use his shotgun to blast off the lock. It made a loud metallic boom that rang through the outside. The group was on borrowed time as Niccolo felt at least one police officer would try to be brave and stop them. Bill advanced in first and aimed his shotgun at the ceiling. A small crowd of about twelve people were inside and feared for their lives with screams. The rest of Niccolo's men saw it fit to start bashing the desk and overturning anything of value from the worker's desks.

"The second time this week I've been robbed!" one woman shouted.

"Shut the hell up, bitch! Put your valuables in this sack," one of the men ordered as he pushed Florence forward. Florence's bright green eyes stuck out of the mask as she watched well-to-do women take out their most precious valuables and stuff them in her burlap sack. While Florence felt bad, she recognized these were some of the more opulent people that could afford to lose stuff.

"I'm tired of you mobster thugs thinking you can just do this to people!" a man shouted as he threw a stapler at Niccolo. Niccolo felt the impact of the stapler hit him in the face and opened fire on the man without prejudice. He let out a stream of three bullets to fell the man instantly as he fell forward. The recoil of the gun moved Niccolo's arms up as he corrected his angle. A few casings dropped as he did so and filled the room all at once with its sound. Niccolo used his submachine gun to herd the group of now petrified people into a corner of the wall. He was beyond his amount of patience as his mind was on the objective.

"This is how things are going to go. You-are going to tell me where your safe is and open it. Any other heroes end up like him there," Niccolo threatened with his submachine gun. He shot one bullet that cracked through the room and hurt the other's ears.

"S-Sir, I don't know how to tell you this, but we have no money." The bank teller advanced with his hands up.

"What the fuck are you talking about?" Bill asked as he nodded his head with the shotgun. He stood back-to-back with another man, who watched the front entrance for the police to make their inevitable visit.

"We got robbed earlier this week by The Owl, sir. You'd have to wait until the money truck comes again," the bank teller mentioned with honesty.

Niccolo was stunned at how such a move was made without their knowledge. He and Andrea had kept this within the confines of their gang and those responsible, but he was also aware that The Owl had his own ventures in the city. An opportunity like this bank was just as likely a target for him as for them. Niccolo gritted his teeth in frustration, he gunned someone down for virtually no benefit. He decided to stall for time until he could come up with another plan. In a few moments, he slowly retreated backwards while Florence quietly followed. Niccolo urged the group to run back to the car and provide reinforcements for the truck that was to come.

In the absence that came with the group leaving the bank, the police were alerted by the yell of a woman who shouted for assistance. The few guards not posted at the ongoing fair were mobilized. Niccolo and the others went into the car and drove off. The other two cars that convened with the truck met right on schedule. Two of the gunners drove next to the truck and shot at it. The guns were poised outside the window as lead started to fly. Most made their mark on the large metal, but some pieces ricocheted as the movement between the two vehicles varied. Passersby that witnessed the event attempted to hit the sidewalk to avoid the ensuing chaos. Bits of debris started to accumulate as loose bullets pierced windows. Niccolo tried tracing the route that he remembered the other cars took as Bill continued to drive.

"There's people in the way—" Bill commented as he realized there was a crowd from the fair that grouped near some shops.

"Drive through them you lummox, they can move if they want to live!" the other man shouted to Bill. Bill had a small frown but relented as he started to advance at a quicker speed.

One person was struck by the hood of Bill's driving, but the group managed to converge with the other cars. The first two were parked side to side and walled off a section. Two gunners were poised outside the window, one sharpshooter with a sniper rifle to kill the driver and another carrying a rifle to be a counter for police marksmen. Niccolo and the others arrived just in time to prepare into position. The green truck carried a large outlet of cash and was a slower moving vehicle than they anticipated. The usual trucks were fast and light, this was a fortress on wheels. Niccolo figured the explosive meant for the safe could be repurposed for the truck instead. The truck barreled through with surprising durability as a flurry of bullets ricochet off and collided with glass.

Bits and pieces of cracks sounded through the air as the truck came by. Bill followed the truck and sped up as Niccolo set his submachine gun to fully auto and started to fire at the vehicle. Florence covered her ears at the awful sound and swerved back and forth. She had plenty to talk about in her next article, if she lived through this. Niccolo ripped a grenade and tossed it at the bottom of the truck behind them. The explosion was enough to knock the truck off course, but it remained steady. The sniper in the car pierced the glass of the truck and shot the driver in the head. His body flailed on the wheel and the massive truck overturned to collide with a nearby building. The wreck was palpable, but Niccolo was convinced some of the money remained.

Niccolo called the rest of his men over as they used hammers and other tools to break through the reinforced hull. A generous amount was saved, but as Florence was called to scoop the loot, more police officers started coming to the scene. The few of Niccolo's men left by the car opened fire and downed a few cops on horseback. By now, the amount of chaos that reverberated in their misadventure was known throughout the city as the fair was soon under heavier security. Concerns about multiple gunmen, both from The Owl and Niccolo's crew, called for a response from the National Guard.

Niccolo knew he couldn't contend with forces from the United States Army and made the wise decision to pack as much money as they could before getting too greedy. Florence could hardly carry the sack as it dragged on the ground behind her, but she felt some adrenaline rush as she scooped the hefty sum into the car. Niccolo's priority as the boss was to get himself out as quickly as possible, while the others dealt with the growing presence. In the safety of the car now headed back to a safehouse to lay low, Niccolo laughed as he counted the loot. He felt the stacks in his hand and studied the faces of the various presidents on them. Although the bank itself was a bust, they were still able to earn more than enough to pay off their next phase of the plan.

Later that night, the rest of Niccolo's forces managed to either skirt by or were placed under arrest. Niccolo had organized jailbreaks in the past in his previous jobs and would eventually return for his men when the time came. With everything finally settled, Florence was busy as she wrote her day out from start to finish. Niccolo idled as he heard the sound of horses rather than that of an automobile. He was surprised by the appearance, but he saw two people arrive. Niccolo snapped his fingers to get Florence's attention as they greeted the two visitors.

"Name's Cicero. I think we spoke over the phone. Here's Rose. You said you had what kind of problem now?" Cicero asked as he looked over Niccolo with distrust. Rose's response was different as she saw Florence's face light up.

"Rose! My sweetie! Remember me, little ol' Florence!? You missed me!" Florence ran and gave Rose a tight hug. Cicero and Niccolo both looked at each other as the pair caught up. The men's greetings were riddled with disinterest of the other as they were more inclined to their current partners.

"Yes cowboy, we do have something of interest. I'll take you to the wall," Niccolo mentioned. Niccolo looked over his shoulder to make sure neither were followed.

"Did you hear about what happened in town Florence? Cicero and I were at the fair to buy this oil for his wife and then everything went haywire!" Rose recalled.

"Oh, well, you might hear something about that," Florence teased, much to Niccolo's annoyance.

The four went to the wall, as Cicero and Rose readied their weapons. Niccolo detailed the encounter while Florence went in her bag and gave the pair reference photos. Cicero raised an eyebrow as he noticed a particular ooze that emitted from the wall. It secreted a black and purple tar that started to bubble.

"Uh, how long has this been on the other side of this wall?" Cicero asked.

"About a week or so?" Florence mentioned with low confidence.

Rose bent down and felt the integrity of the nearby rocks in the packed dirt. She felt they were eroding in their hardness as the rocks were softer closest to the ooze than non-affected rocks. She figured the slime acted as some sort of melting agent that could possibly destroy the cave-in dirt after some time and they'd have a much larger problem on their hands. Rose was unsure of how to tackle the situation but advised that relocating the men to a secondary location would be better. Rose and Cicero could also smell the distinct smell of moonshine peer through the ooze as well. The two gathered quickly that the copper mine had other things going on, but they were paid to hunt monsters, not stop crimes.

"Depending on what... this all is, you should move your "mining operations" somewhere else for a while," Rose mentioned to Niccolo.

"Unless you want us to blow that wall to kingdom come, you ain't getting through to the beast. Tell ya what, it's getting late. Rose and I need to go and you call us for what needs to be done. It came from a purple hole, so we share your concerns." Cicero mentioned.

"Fine, do what you need to do. My concern is with The Owl, and I can't have disturbances in my business like these beasts. I am a Mafioso, yes, but he's a real problem," Niccolo admitted.

Rose tapped Cicero's arm in recognition of The Owl. Both Rose and Cicero recalled how some of The Owl's men came by and brandished machine guns to the small town that they frequented. Rose saw the fear in their eyes and her own as well, as townspeople were lined up to the wall. Mavis' bar was spared only for the rush of looting the booze and harassing the patrons inside. The old and feeble outlaws that lived in the town were seen as a roadblock to the last true bastion of progress. As they were being squeezed by the Mafia for The Baron's aims, it churned their stomachs in disgust. The good people of Cicero's town that provided her with aid were ones that stuck with Rose through her time there. As Rose continued to work with Cicero, she maintained a good heart, but the practicality of the twentieth century wore at her like any other. She and Cicero couldn't supply a fight on their own, they needed bodies and weapons.

"We are aware of The Owl as well. That sidewinder is trying to hurt my people, and I won't stand for it," Cicero said as he clenched his fist. Niccolo nodded in agreement as he liked Cicero's display of strength.

"An agreement can be made between us. You will help us get rid of the monsters and I'll see what I can do about keeping The Owl out of your little town," Niccolo mentioned while Florence studied their reactions. Niccolo was in a good mood with his profits to cover the costs to Andrea, in addition to providing a little extra for himself.

Rose and Cicero shook hands with Niccolo while Florence gave Rose a hug. She respectfully nodded her head downwards to Cicero as the three were escorted out by Niccolo's men. Florence settled into her car to get back to her hotel for the night, while Rose and Cicero had a lengthy ride home.

"What do you think about them for backup on the next job? Or perhaps the piano at Mavis' place?" Rose asked Cicero as he shrugged his shoulders.

"That's a four-man job at least, from what I understand. I appreciate you taking the lead on that one. You're really growing into your own out here," Cicero admitted happily.

On the way back home, Rose felt she had something to say. Although she was mostly happy with today's events, Rose thought about Cicero's encounter once again at the grocery store and the face he held back at the hotel. His scared expression of the mere mention of The Baron was enough to put him on edge. Rose was aware by now that The Baron carried a reputation from multiple parties, but she wondered what gave her mentor such grief. Cicero stopped his horse as he turned around to see what the problem was.

"Need a break? Well Rose, color me impressed. Mary's taking a liking to you. She used to buck me off every now and again," Cicero said with a chuckle.

"You know, we'll be on our tenth job together soon. Not too shabby wouldn't you say? So, thank you kindly Cicero. It's been a challenge, but I used to work with horses at the old place. Though, something's been fixed on my mind, and we need to talk about it. That man with the top hat and the pressed suit looked at you with such scorn in his eyes. It's as if he knew of you. I remember at the bar you mentioned something about him, but I don't recall everything. Things just started to come together for me. You both have a history and it's real nasty," Rose assessed as she locked eyes with Cicero.

"What of it? Those were just stories. Not much to tell. I see folks passing all the time, really it's nothin'," Cicero said. His attempts to lie weren't landing.

"When we were in town last week or so at the store, I saw you drop your bag, and your palms started to sweat. You clutched your chest and gasped for air. Now I'm no fool, not much makes you yellow. The killer furniture and the ghost snakes didn't do it, so I knew this was serious." Rose wagged her finger.

"You don't need to be—" Cicero proclaimed as he was interrupted by Rose.

"Be what? I'm your partner, right? I'm supposed to learn from you. We're a team. Let me help you," Rose pleaded. She crossed her arms and shook her head at Cicero's insistence of trying to shield her from the truth.

"Alright, I'll give it up. You've been a good steady hand, and the truth is something I owe you. That man with the top hat and pressed suit you saw at the general store? That man's simply called The Baron. Now this is where people go and point and laugh at me, you can join them if you so choose. I'm in my early sixties. I worked for The Baron when I was young, I started at ten and ended at thirteen. He ran a copper mine much like the one from earlier, and I earned a good dollar a day. Honest work, until it wasn't. Eventually, The Baron's venture turned to be a wash. My father also worked at the mine, and while he was a cold man, he's still my pa. The Baron ensured us the operation was safe, this is what we agreed to signing up for. It was-some thing for the railway that got built back in the 70s," Cicero coughed.

"I'm very confused. This man's certainly older, but he looks no older than my daddy. Go on, say your piece and I'll hold my thoughts to the end," Rose commented as she let Cicero finish. Rose was unsure of what to think about all this as she determined to figure out the truth and what she was getting into.

"Someone got paid somewhere, there was an explosion, a planned cave-in, that destroyed the equipment and trapped everyone else. I was thin as a rail and crawled out of the wreckage, but everyone else suffocated or starved. The people in that town where I grew up, they all lost someone to him. The Baron pocketed the insurance money and the families got nothin', thanks to a tiny thing in the fine print," Cicero spat.

"Now one day, he just shows up out of nowhere in my town, with my people, almost fifty years later and doesn't look a day older! How can you explain that? Everyone in this town thinks I'm crazy for it. I'm the only one who remembers, and I can't get any respect about it. He just appears like a ghost and leaves whenever his work is done. His wife does the same thing, there's something foul here. This will never end until I put them in the ground. This old outlaw never played nice with the cops, so we're gonna get dirty."

"At first, I wouldn't believe a single word that came out of your mouth, but from what I've seen, this is just another Tuesday. For some reason, his wife seems mighty fond of me. She sent an envelope that came in the mail. She outlined that the three of us share something in common and in order to hear more, I'd have to listen and see what she has to say. I was going to accept her offer and go to their manor. We can find out more there and I'll tell you everything we need to take him down. You got me a job to earn my keep and hold some dignity. Let's set things right for your town." Rose adjusted the reins of her horse.

"This is a dangerous undertaking. The Baron as I remember him is a man of means, and my gang shot, chopped, and exploded our way through all those that worked for him as we tried to find him. You know danger, but most people can't even get a whiff of the man before you never hear from them again," Cicero huffed, giving Rose one last warning of what she was undertaking.

"I'm not most people, Cicero. Never have been, but I understand the concern. For now, let's play it by ear and do what we can. I'm not backing out of this one." Rose placed her hand on his shoulder. Rose and Cicero nodded to one another in acknowledgment of the other.

A Realized Prophecy

Rose took her previous conversation with Cicero to heart as she and Claudia looked into the mirror. Rose was expected to go to the manor of The Baron and Baroness, and she could begin the long task of finding information. She could hardly hide her nerves; she was beyond stressed about the prospect. She knew her way around rich white folks with ease, but there was something unsettling in the air surrounding this meeting. Rose looked to make sure every aspect of herself was on the up and up. Her nails were trimmed, she used a dab of perfume to freshen up, and looked at the state of her best dress. Claudia did her best to remove the stains out of her initial orange dress with multiple washes and every detergent she could think of.

"Well, you ain't meeting Queen Victoria, it'll do," Claudia said with a hearty pat on Rose's shoulder. Cicero lit a cigarette and huffed in annoyance. He held the letter in his hands with contempt as the black and gold envelope shone in the light of their home.

"Any reason why she shouldn't take Mary? I don't want that Niccolo fella giving her the wrong idea. You know Italians are illegal immigrants, right?" Cicero complained to Claudia.

"Cicero, dear. I know you love that horse as does Rose, but she's going to a very important place. It's hot as blazes out today and she needs to not be a complete ball of sweat."

Rose kept quiet as the two discussed what they'd expect from her. The trio came up with a plan where Cicero and Claudia would venture out to spend the day in town and to find them if anything went awry or was strange. It was the best they could come up with and agreed. Cicero took a more protective stance when it came to Rose meeting with others for obvious reasons, but he felt genuine concern for her life if The Baron was involved. He knew that The Baron knew how important she was to him and his way of life.

Niccolo was outside as he stuck his head out of the car window. He gave a slight frown as he looked at the state of Cicero's home. While Niccolo hardly had the best accommodations at the mine, he was able to afford rather lavish hotels with the amount of money made from his schemes. Niccolo left the car running as he stepped out and walked up to the porch. Inside the house, Cicero saw him approach their home. Cicero walked over and looked at him before ushering Rose out to the front.

"Relax cowboy, Rose is in safe hands." Niccolo smiled as he pulled her towards him. Niccolo wanted nothing more than to leave to drop her off to return to his duties.

"Thanks for taking me up there, Niccolo. I know you're busy these days," Rose said as Niccolo opened the car door for her.

"It's funny you happen to have gotten the eye of The Baron. I've been looking for him for some time," Niccolo alluded to his work. Rose slowly shook her head at his statement.

"Seems he has a lot of enemies, The Baron that is. You and Cicero both hate him? Why not work together. If you're looking for money, he probably won't take it, he just hates the man that much," Rose commented.

"You make a lot of assumptions, but I work alone for now."

Niccolo kept his hand on the wheel as he darted to try to avoid traffic. Cicero outlined the address to Niccolo previously over the phone and was enamored by their location. Niccolo could tell he was in the right place by the architecture alone that outclassed anything he'd seen in the city. He was eerily reminded of the villas in Rome with the amount of dedication placed into their construction. The Baron and Baroness lived in a developed, flattened suburb with a small community of other rich socialites to keep up appearances. The extent of their owned property included a lounge that was carved into the base of a nearby mountain and was hardly an inconspicuous location. Niccolo could hardly contain his shock at such an immaculate venue. He anticipated it to be stocked to the brim with armed guards, but the road up was far less packed. Niccolo and Rose made little conversation as they both shared a glance at the scale of the establishment.

Niccolo parked the car to a sudden stop as he recognized the twin statues mentioned in Cicero's description of the property. Rose got herself out and looked around at the unsettling atmosphere of the neighborhood. Rose didn't see an ounce of color other than herself and knew quickly this was in one of the many segregated parts of Phoenix. It felt foreign, as she'd already known a good deal of the city, but the planned structures of her surroundings radiated a bygone era of wealth and prosperity. Rose recognized that she walked from the smoothed paved road to seeing grass, grass in the middle of the desert that required exuberant amounts of water to maintain.

"The cowboy wants details regarding The Baron, I am sure. Though if you happen to give some information to me first, I can make it worth your while. Someone else will collect you once you're done, I have things to do," Niccolo mentioned before he took off.

The Baron and Baroness' home held an area of over ten thousand square feet with cement tile blocks and alternating square glass windows. Rose walked to the low door and saw a doorbell. She pressed it and heard a remarkable chime. After what felt like an eternity, the door slowly opened, and The Baron emerged. He didn't wear a pressed suit but wore leisurewear that was made of high-quality silk.

"It appears you've gotten our invitation. Rose, my dear, come in and shelter yourself from the elements. It is a hot day today," The Baron urged her.

Rose couldn't help but open her mouth in awe at the interior decoration of the manor. The floors were made of ceramic tile with a brown orange that remained ever cool. The furniture was impeccably white as The Baron led her along into a route of the home. The house's expanse was enough to host an entire crowd of around forty people with absolute comfort. She noticed a pit dug into the center of the home that held a bunch of couches and a small fireplace meant for conversation. The west wing of the manor held a reflecting pool that Rose could see through the glass. The backyard was an extensive garden that featured an assortment of flowers of this world, and of others, that the pair procured in their travels.

"Rose. I take it you understand that we're here to discuss manners of business, but I wanted to get your opinion on something. I value your intellectual pursuits from what I have seen of your ability," The Baron mentioned while Rose's eyes darted to a wall of ornate paintings. Rose froze as she felt the interaction of The Baron talking directly to her. She recalled Cicero's hatred of the man, but compared to those she saved, she wasn't met with contempt or disgust.

"These paintings... They are so... beautiful. Did you make these? I recognize some, but others are unknown to my eyes. Haven't gone to many museums, but I see the oil paints hold up well," Rose commented.

"Oh, you appreciate the arts?" The Baron asked as he took a second to grab two glasses of wine from a nearby table. Rose grabbed the glass by the stalk with her hands in a fist. Rose looked around to find any sort of wait staff or anything, but she noticed the entire manor was empty. Rose noticed that although she had one in hand, The Baron had yet to drink. She pursed her eyes and placed the piece on a diamond encrusted coaster. The Baron lifted an eyebrow and sampled his drink.

"The wine is not as good this year. A shame when you have machines doing the pressing," He noticed Rose gave no response. Both of their eyes wandered to a luxurious oil painting with exceptional strokes. The scene depicted two Greek gods in courtship in the vastness of space with a few known planets.

"This painting by Morgaine Durand, I used to court my wife. It may come as a surprise to you, but I personally knew the man himself. That stroke in the left-hand corner comes from the shock of a loved one's demise, not a drunken stupor. Many experts claim it's the latter, but I know better." The Baron lit a cigar and watched as the smoke hung through the room. Rose raised an eyebrow and started to go look elsewhere.

"I understand you may have heard things about me, but I have also heard things about you. Rose, you have been important to me and my wife for some time now. We are of your world, but from a much darker time. How much do you wish to see what is fiction and what is fact?" The Baron stated. He saw that Rose remained still and was hesitant to listen.

"I was young once, born in the frontier of New Amsterdam, in the year 1680. It was a harsh winter. It was in 1708 that my life ultimately changed, I tracked down the last coven of witches that survived the trials of Salem. While many women and men were unjustly murdered for speaking against power, there was just cause for their demise. Few of the souls killed were indeed correct in their feats. Magic or as the call of the day says, energy, exists all around us and can be manipulated for various aims," The Baron opened.

Rose could hardly believe such drivel most of the time, but the matter of conviction coming from the man's voice was otherworldly. Rose remembered all she'd seen so far with Cicero and felt she now had an explanation for what they'd dealt with before. Her expression grew sour as she remembered the swirling vortex of purple in the mountain cabin and others. The existence of magic, in whatever form this was, needed to be categorized and understood. This was not only for her peace of mind, but for the rest of the world. Rose tensed up and formed a fist to channel her anxiety. She spoke and made conversation.

"So, this is all your fault then! These... anomalies... that I've had to deal with come from you. Why? Why are you doing this?" Rose pleaded as The Baron looked at her with indifference.

"Why, what do you mean? I know that you have a different impression of me, so allow me to introduce myself to you in good faith. I am aware you are a woman of both faith and science, much like my wife. People these days find this pairing to be contradictory, but perhaps it is this union that makes things stronger. Come and follow me. She will be waiting downstairs." The Baron said as he stood aside, waiting for Rose to start her walk. He studied Rose's posture and other traits as they continued. He looked for confidence and certainty of her words.

The Baron continued his lecture while Rose felt herself shrink in the vast labyrinthine style of the mansion. The walls were held with high ceilings and adorned with far more paintings and photographs showcasing their extensive travels. Rose felt this section of the house was more of a museum than a proper living space as she noticed the number of objects placed in protective glass, the originals, that would be worth countless amounts.

"That isn't to say, there are no differences between the two. Magic is contorting energy for the things that energy wasn't meant to do. Energy is to be consumed; magic, however, creates something new," The Baron said. He approached behind her with surprising speed. Rose felt her back jump up. In front of her, Rose saw a gilded door with what appeared to be encrusting gold trim throughout.

With a nod from The Baron as he tipped his top hat to Rose, she laid her hand on the fashioned doorknob and opened it for the two to enter. The staircase revealed an extensive library and repository of various things collected in their travels. In any other time, Rose would have cried tears of joy. The staircase was covered with a purple carpet that contrasted the two's outfits. Hunched over in the distance was an elegant woman with flowers in her hair and an expensive necklace of pearls. Rose's heart raced as she recognized the woman that saved her. All at once, she was filled with emotion as she silently walked up to The Baroness. She was practically shaking from awe and gratitude.

"You-You saved me. Thank you... so much!" Rose said, surprised at the volume of her voice. She was relieved to see that her savior was right in front of her. The experience was surreal. She recalled it all, the chaos of the mobsters and the derailed train. Her pure exhaustion as the world around her turned blue and out came her hand to rescue her.

"Rose answered the call. She is a skeptical one, but all lambs can be shown the way, can they not?" The Baron said to The Baroness as he walked over and gave her a passionate kiss.

If Cicero's words remained true, Rose was utterly confused at how such a woman could find herself in the yoke of The Baron. She felt conflict immediately, but she needed to have an open mind. Rose remembered the letter's statement, that they shared a gift in common and she needed to know what exactly this meant. Rose's eyes looked towards the vast amount of information at her disposal. To her, it was Alexandria's library reborn. Her attention was called back as she saw the eye-stunningly white teeth of The Baroness in a smile.

"It is good you accepted our invitation, you know. I would have found you in person, but there were things I needed to attend to." The Baroness spoke to Rose, who could only offer a nod. Although Rose was hot arriving at the home, she felt relieved as a small gust of wind blew on her skin. She looked around for a fan of any sort but was surprised at how cold the air felt.

"You seem to be marveled. Air conditioning is truly the peak of engineering," The Baroness smiled.

She walked over to Rose with one hand in a fist as she clutched something. Rose was prompted to leave her hand out as The Baroness revealed an odd gemstone. Rose saw she had one on her neck that was clearly an amethyst, but the other stone she was unsure of. The room was well-lit with several light fixtures providing enough for the three to see one another. Rose noticed that there was a scattered workstation at the base of the massive library shelves and some loose tools.

"I have just finished making this. Do you remember the color of the void of which you traveled here?" The Baroness asked.

"It was a dark blue color. What does this mean exactly?" Rose questioned as she looked behind her to see The Baron standing close by. He leaned on the nearby wall as he watched the two of them discuss.

"I am a physicist by trade, self-taught. These vortexes have two colors we have designated in our research. Blue vortexes are a form of travel in the same plane of existence, but purple vortexes are the bridge between the known worlds. This is why I was able to bring you to Phoenix, but there was a problem. When I grabbed you, my intention was for you to come here in this very room. Instead, you were in town, but further than anticipated. We have come to believe; this was an act of your subconscious attempting to save you from the unknown. I am one to adjust for any polarity, but what you emitted was strange. Rose, you are safe now with us. These occurrences you have encountered come not of this world, but of others. My husband and I have the power to manipulate these but only the ones we have created. There is a chance for these to appear naturally," The Baroness paused for a sign of acknowledgment from Rose before continuing.

"All I've seen are these purple ones that are coupled with these strange beasts. When I was home, I was attacked by one, I thought it was just a local problem, but it seems to be everywhere now. What are your thoughts on why that is? Has this always been happening or is this new?" Rose asked in curiosity.

"Well Rose, that's where you come in. You seem to possess a peculiar quirk, the ability to manipulate these as you avoided my grasp. If you would, I would like you to stand over there and close your eyes," The Baroness doted. She still had much to explain to Rose and sought to make the most of her visit.

As Rose moved into place, The Baroness soon realized that she finally was in the position she witnessed a long time ago in the temple of the fortune teller. The vision she saw of herself, her husband, and Rose finally came to fruition. She needed to know now where her destiny would lead and with Rose at her side, she felt immensely powerful. The Baroness looked to her necklace and stuck her index finger and thumb together giving an intense focus. The amethyst around her necklace started to glow and Rose resisted the urge to open her eyes until instructed. A pre-determined space conjured by The Baroness took form as a mold of light and a spiral of visible purple color formed in the room. At the center of it all, a foggy afterimage appeared, until all it once it became clear.

"Every bit of magic requires a conduit. My husband and I have this ability by will as well, but it is less tear on the body when done this way. I have been unwell recently, but this will pass. Observe Rose. I have brought forth a new reality at random. One of many. Come with me and I will show you what has been laid out for us. To understand your gift," The Baroness urged Rose to follow. Rose stood with her mouth agape at such a sight. The Baron opted to stay behind as he went to conjure a portal of his own. This one was blue and remained in the same room. Rose only caught a glimpse of it and wondered where he was going.

Her attention was brought back to her current objective as she stepped through the portal to find The Baroness in the middle of an open field. She looked around and noticed a horde of round pink-haired entities with a single blue eye. They were harmless and bounced around without a care in the world. Much like cows on the road, Rose noticed that these creatures gave her attention as they walked by. They made small muttering noises as they approached her. Rose was distracted by how cute these creatures were and she felt shock that these were one of the first things that didn't try to actively kill her. Rose's head turned as she heard The Baroness' whistle. She ran past the grass while one of the pink creatures lingered behind in curiosity at their new visitor. The Baroness used this dimension as a jumpstart for her to go on further ventures. It was a stable realm with only these passive creatures as the inhabitants.

The Baroness chose this place first for the two to talk in relative quiet. She knew there was a lot of information for Rose to absorb and opted to guide her in the most efficient way possible. The Baroness knew much about Rose, but only what she could tell on the surface. She had known other Roses before in her twenty-five-year long search, but this one was different. Rose walked over to see The Baroness with her legs folded as she offered a space for Rose to sit in front of her.

"I have one question for you. You knew my name before I met you. That, I remember. I want to know what happened with that. Did I look some-one you knew?" Rose questioned with genuine confusion. The mystical qualities and wonder of The Baroness started to erode slightly as Rose's mental wall started to close her off. She had no reason to distrust her, but she remembered her intentions for this visit and to dissect every word given to her with the utmost care.

"You have a familiar face, but we never met, until now. Rose. What if I told you that there were a million of you existing at the same time? When the world was formed, many others like ours remain, and yet we were told we were unique individuals. This was a lie on the cosmic order. There are in fact, living and breathing copies of you. When you come to a dimension where the lie is exposed, you are faced with a choice. Which one will remain? You or the other? I always choose myself." The Baroness stepped closer to Rose.

"What... do you mean by that?" Rose rubbed the back of her neck.

"In every realm, dimension, Rose, there is one of you. The one to break the barrier and expose the lie, is the original. I am the original *Aquetzalli*. The order of the universe dislikes us. There are forces out there that do not take kindly to what we are trying to achieve. I have killed others of my name. I have taken their energy as my own for balance must be had. Their years that were and ever will be are now mine. I have not truly died of hunger, thirst, or assault. When I have, I arrive all the same back with the life of a lesser *Aquetzalli* killed in my place," The Baroness stated. The Baroness hoped by revealing her original name, she could build further trust in the uneasy woman before her.

"W-What?" Rose muttered. She could hardly make sense of it all, she was already floored by the idea of other dimensions existing in such a raw state. She hadn't imagined that there were others of her around. Did they all suffer in the same way she did? While Rose counted herself as particularly eloquent with her thoughts, she was on the verge of having an existential crisis. She placed her hand on her forehead in thought at The Baroness' words. She closed her eyes to give herself a mental reset and tried to rationalize all that was given to her.

"I appreciate the respect, but I'm unsure of what you want. You both mentioned the gift, and I understand somewhat of what this all seems to mean. There clearly is something else at play, but I just want a straight answer," Rose mentioned as she was trying to stall for time.

"I decided to speak with you as there is potential to be had here. We know what you and Cicero have been doing to some extent, but I wish to know simply what your goals are. What do you, Rose, want. I know many people have never asked about what you want out of your life. Your origin is a curious one. A young cleaner who worked under the thumb of others, now participates in the destruction of ethereal beasts and beings that we have encountered. This makes one curious," The Baroness mentioned as she looked at her nails.

"Rose. Can you answer something for me? How are you doing? I mean, that in the truest sense of the word. How are you doing? The land where you stay is not your home, this is known to me."

"Fine. I'm fine. I miss my friends mostly, but this work I do is fulfilling and it gives me some dignity. I'm used to cleaning tables, washing dirty laundry, and people ruffling my feathers, so it's a nice change of pace," Rose said honestly.

"And the work with Cicero? Has that been satisfactory?"

"The work's fine. I like the thrill of it, trying to figure out how to get rid of the next danger that comes our way. No matter what, I always do my due diligence to save the people in the towns that we work with. I-I think I'm doing a good job. Cicero tells me that and I'm inclined to believe that. Though, not everyone seems to feel that way," Rose said with a crack in her voice.

"Can you tell me about that? You seem to be doing a service for people, why would they not be appreciative?" The Baroness looked into Rose's eyes. Rose found the line of questioning strange, but endearing. The Baroness had just met her and showed genuine concern.

"Well—There was this one time. A horrid place called Duncan. Not too far from here-rather, back on our world. A place filled with awful people. Cicero and I finished the job as we expected, and instead of being remotely grateful, the crowd hungered for me. They wanted to hang me! They wanted to kill me! Me!" Rose's voice heightened in pitch. Rose's heart raced as she recalled the harrowing experience. It was undoubtedly traumatic, and she found it hard to keep herself grounded as that tension resurfaced. The Baroness looked at Rose's reddened eyes and spoke softly.

"My sweet Rose, you must know by now The American Dream isn't dead but working as intended. It was never meant for people like us, the ostracized and ridiculed. Is this what you want your life to be? Your work is thankless, you are run out of town by an ungrateful rabble. Rose, there are people—out there, dangerous people who want nothing more than to dispose of you and stomp out your gift from the world. Only I can give you the means to navigate it and the strength of your abilities. I implore you, go where you are wanted. My husband and I will always allow you to access our manor. Come, take a hug," The Baroness beckoned Rose. The Baroness kept her arms open as Rose walked over to her and embraced her.

My sweet Rose. Nobody will hurt you anymore. I will mold you into an instrument of my command once I'm done with you. The Baroness thought with a grin.

Rose felt comfortable as she slowly removed herself from the vice-like grip of The Baroness. Now she had a moment to truly observe her and could see that The Baroness came from a point of understanding. Rose's interactions with those that were non-white were minimal at best in Phoenix, and she constantly distanced herself from people to maintain self-preservation. The Baroness was a port in the storm of someone who seemed to understand exactly where she was coming from. Rose considered The Baroness' words as her mind scrambled to find how this could benefit her current work with Cicero. Rose recalled The Baroness mentioning her innate ability to manipulate these vortexes and thought about the purple ones that remained. While Rose and Cicero focused on removal, she could do some serious preventative work by closing them with mastery of her power. The pair rose together to return to the manor.

The Baron waited for them both with a change of clothes as he wore his usual black suit and tie. As the two entered through the portal, The Baroness used her hand to clamp it shut and the rift vanished behind them. While Rose thought it was time for her to depart, this was only the first half of their venture.

"While you were away, I arranged for reservations at our favorite café across the ocean. Have you been to Paris, Rose? It's cleaned up considerably since The Great War," The Baron said as he offered his hand to her.

Rose almost let out a laugh at such a question. It was obvious to all parties that The Baron was pulling her leg, but under the illuminated night sky, the smell of Paris hit her nose just as any other. She could hardly believe how her day was going, the industrial air of French industry floated around her as she saw crowds of tourists clamoring for the next destination. Rose was steadily impressed that this ability could give her unparalleled travel to anywhere she desired if she could master it. Rose's mind, which centered on saving money, already calculated what she'd be able to gain from never having to take a train again. She could simply go wherever she wanted and take who she wanted. All those trips to the Florida Keys that Venus fantasied about could be possible, and she thought of all the places she'd want to take Malcolm as she recalled in her letters.

The trio were guided inside with little issue. It was an upscale establishment with all sorts of strange sculptures that Rose found interesting. An array of decorative bronzes were the centerpieces of the room. The heat of the kitchen's flame filled the rest of the room as low ambience played from a harp. Rose's ears were exposed to an outpour of French as they were sat down. Rose sat across from both The Baron and Baroness, who looked at her with wide eyes. She took in the atmosphere. The Baroness ordered, in French, a round of red wine for them and some bread while they got situated. Rose felt the soft touch of The Baroness' touch grace her cheeks.

"Rose, I noticed you seem to have a gaunt frame in your face. Please don't be modest and eat until you are full. I need you at your strongest," The Baroness gently recommended as they waited.

"We want to offer you a job. I want you to be trained so that you can use your gift to help us. My wife and I seek an important artifact known as The Frost Gem and we hope to employ your help in acquiring such an item. It's an unusual proposal, as it's far from what I am used to, but I think you'll come to understand its importance." The Baron lifted his hand for the waiter to return at a later time.

"It holds a special property. I have built my wealth off jewels and the manufacturing of these products for some time, but The Frost Gem is no mere diamond. This artifact comes from another universe, and it holds an unbelievable amount of energy. Do you know what this means Rose? Our dependence on oil and gasoline to power our world will no longer be required. This is transformational to our very understanding of science. We can build a better world with your gift, and you would be responsible for the things that come later. The two of us are experienced travelers of

The World Between Worlds, that is to say-what we've labeled these dimensions that are between each other. With our influence in local political and economic matters, things have bogged down for us significantly. I want you to log and document everything you've seen from these vortexes and deliver it to us in a report. You will be compensated for these efforts of course," The Baroness mentioned.

"I see. As it turns out, I've already kept a personal log of what Cicero and I have encountered for any future visits, I believe that it's certainly possible to give you what you're looking for. Though, I must ask, how will my "gift" be used in this way?" Rose asked with skepticism.

"There's also something else to consider. I've seen the papers and know the writing on the wall. There's a gang war brewing between "The Owl" and some other factions of gangsters in the city. How am I supposed to know I'll be safe doing this for you?" Rose added on.

"Your gift will be used to help you in the battles that matter most. As I mentioned before, there are forces that exist that would want to impede the idea of unlimited free energy that are far scarier than some run of the mill pickpocket. What I ask of you may require flexible morals. Do you think if it were to your survival, you could take a life?" The Baroness asked seriously. Her tone shocked Rose as she sat up straight.

"I don't consider myself bloodthirsty or violent, I like to talk things out. Though, I've come to realize that there's some people who just won't take no for an answer, or like what I have to say. If it came between that and myself, I'd always choose myself." Rose echoed the previous conversation she had with The Baroness.

"Good," The Baroness stated in satisfaction.

The waiter returned after The Baron's dismissal and placed the wine down for the three to drink. Rose lifted her glass as the other two clinked them together. As far as Rose was concerned, she didn't need to compromise her morals to support herself and get what she needed for success. She thought about the reason why she'd gotten a job to begin with, her desire to be a science teacher and all that came with it. An honest day's work for a dishonest dollar hardly made a difference. Only an idiot would spurn down the opportunity of a lifetime, and she felt some semblance of debt towards The Baroness for saving her life.

"I take this as your agreement to get started. Your training will be conducted at night. You are to go during the weekend to the manor. My wife has a freer schedule than mine, so she will take the bulk of your sessions, but you will have time with me. I think we're going to get along well," The Baron dictated to Rose.

"Rose —When offered a glass of wine, grasp it beneath your fingers. I noticed you held it by encircling your hands around it. Your training's started already," The Baroness mentioned with a cheery tone.

"One last thing. We were going to have a gala for our anniversary this year. I will forward the details when the time is nigh. I would like you to come as the newest member of our partnership. Feel free to bring anyone you wish. Use the conduit given to you to harness your internal stability for your first assignment. If you can generate a portal of your own, we will have much to discuss," The Baron let the message hang. Rose understood the tone of his statement.

Rose sat in her chair in deep thought as she realized she'd fallen right into a precarious partnership. She dreaded the conversation to have with Cicero regarding everything, but she realized that there'd be a golden opportunity for them to still plan. Her primary concern was keeping the town safe from The Owl's gangsters that threatened their way of life. She knew that the truth behind the complexities of The Baron's and Cicero's rivalry would have to wait for now. Rose couldn't help but wonder how far the extent of her abilities could go, and with all she'd seen, it would be impossible to leave this behind. Rose looked into her wineglass and accepted the consequences as they came.

Bad Dreams

Rose had gotten through the hurdle of talking to Cicero regarding her new employment with The Baron and Baroness. Rose anticipated a drawn-out conversation, but Cicero came from a point of maturity that impressed her from the old cowboy. Rose knew that Cicero always kept a calm head, but his hatred for The Baron and Baroness ran thick and she couldn't blame him for it. As she offered her perspective on their conversation, Rose understood that Cicero found her new connection with them as a way to gain their trust long enough for her to get essential information to taking them down. Although Rose found herself tired, her weekend work with The Baron and Baroness didn't inhibit their schedule for bounties.

The pair held a settled routine and with a nest egg slowly filling up, Cicero opted for them to take some much needed rest. Rose walked into the kitchen and snacked on a slightly stale piece of bread. As she chewed her food, she noted the various decorations on the wall. The first were Cicero's weapons aside from his shotgun, he had a lever action rifle with a box magazine and a large two-handed sword with a leather handle. She hadn't seen him use any of these and wondered if these were relics from his more colorful past. Rose's attention was brought next to a mounted animal. She knew that Cicero wasn't much of an animal hunter; he was very knowledgeable about nature and held a grand respect for wildlife. She saw a taxidermized grizzly bear head with sharp teeth and wondered how it got there. Cicero raised an eyebrow as he noticed it caught Rose's eye and filled in the details.

"The bear ain't mine. It's Claudia's. Her father was some big game hunter and since he had all girls, she was the tomboy of the family. I may be a hardass when it comes to killing freaks, but I could never put one between the eyes," Cicero admitted to Rose. Cicero sat in a chair and raised his head up to get a better look at Rose, who pointed towards the bounty board.

"We're not huntin' today, so do what you like except that. I know you're an eager beaver most of the time." Cicero opened a newspaper.

Rose nodded as she was happy to get a break. She felt herself run ragged by the amount of effort put into their latest quests. She also thought about the walled-off problem still at Niccolo's copper mine. Rose and Cicero were avoiding that area until they could workshop a solution that would benefit the four of them, but nothing seemed appealing. Rose went out for a short walk around the property to stretch her legs. As she paced around, Rose enjoyed the ambient sound of a short gust of wind. She made her way to the barn to feed the horses, but paused as she noticed something unusual.

Shit. Rose thought as she saw a small glimpse of purple come from the barn. She heard the worried neigh of Mary as she reared up towards the entrance of the barn. Rose opened the door and watched as the horse immediately ran off a short distance away before stopping by a nearby cactus. Rose snapped her fingers and gently called the horse back over as she wondered what could have spooked it.

"Cicero!" Rose shouted as she heard a quick rumbling from the house. Cicero stumbled out as he looked to find what was the problem.

"We..."

"You have got to be joking. A purple hole? Right in my goddamn barn? I guess we're hunting today. Go grab your iron and meet me here. We'll go looking around for varmints," Cicero ordered.

Rose did as she was told and returned. By now, Rose and Cicero could just use non-verbal contact to go over the plan. Cicero nodded his head as he'd cover the back of the house, while Rose would check the barn and the front of the house. The two quietly pursued the potential target. Rose looked to the sand and tried to find any semblance of prints. She or Cicero had no idea what they were up against, as they noticed no signs of damage or real disturbances. Rose checked the barn and saw, other than the slightly disturbed George, nothing out of the ordinary. The open purple hole seemed to decrease in size as if it was being manipulated. Rose wondered if this was the aspect of her power that was mentioned by The Baroness. She tried to lift her hand and concentrate, but she only ended up exhausting herself as she did so, with no visible effect. Rose looked up to find Mary reared once again, and wondered if the horses were detecting something they weren't.

"You see anything on your side?" Cicero asked.

"None that I can see, no damages, nothing. Maybe it's not here at all, but it went somewhere else?" Rose inquired as she holstered her sidearm.

Cicero looked through every inch of the house and saw nothing was amiss. He mumbled to himself as he remained slightly paranoid about the outcome. He went to grab some tools from a nearby box and attached some spare wooden boards to reinforce the barn. For now, the horses would linger on the outside just in case anything else came from the new portal. With nowhere else to look, Cicero called off the search but vowed to remain vigilant for the rest of the day. Rose chose to retire early up in the loft where she worked on letters to send Malcolm and Venus describing her escapades.

Rose idled with her thoughts in a book until the light of day brought itself to night. She heard the final rumblings of Cicero as he got ready for bed. Claudia was feeling ill and spent the entirety of the day in bed. Rose wished she could do more for her, but she wanted to avoid getting sick at all costs. Her thoughts lay on her performance over the past few weeks and saw steady improvement. The balance between keeping the demands of Cicero and The Baroness slowly eroded at Rose's stamina, but she had plenty of resolve. Rose felt more exhausted than usual as she yawned and sprawled out on the sheets. Rose fell asleep and let her creative mind take hold.

Rose had vivid dreams when she was inspired by media or went through something particularly traumatic that kept her mind racing. On occasion, she even had awareness of her existence within this dream and found that she could influence their direction. She found herself in a long corridor that was black and aligned with gold trim. As she walked, an accompanying electric light shone with an amber tone that reflected off the pieces. The space was large and inviting as it resembled that of the art deco seen in New York. Her footsteps were accompanied by the low sound of smooth jazz, something she'd only heard a few times on the radio as she drifted to sleep. Rose found as she walked down the corridor, sections of the wall opened on their own as if they were a door. Rose continued her pace and found a bronze pedestal that stood in the center of the room. She raised an eyebrow as she studied the piece and saw a weapon lay at the center. Rose patted her side and realized that she lacked her pistol. She grabbed it from the pedestal, and two magazines materialized in her hand. Rose could she tell was dreaming, but she didn't know how to get out. She felt herself inside a labyrinth that expanded at every step. As she loaded the pistol and admired its sheen underneath the light, the jazz continued to play as a pair of double doors opened.

Rose entered the room and the doors slammed with a wide boom. She looked around her and saw a few of her former monster adversaries reborn before her. She fired her pistol with fury as the sound filled the room and the smell of gunpowder and blood accompanied it. These were mere shadows of what she once faced, and Rose hardly batted an eyelid at them. Satisfied with the spilled blood, the room's next set of doors opened without delay. Rose continued this process until she noticed that she seemed to circle around paths she'd already been through. One such room was different, with a new door standing in its place. As Rose opened it, she only saw a small open square in the ground and was compelled to go through it.

The tight-fitting square allowed Rose to enter a deeper form of her subconscious mind where things drifted in and out of existence. Repressed memories and the deeper fears lived in this layer and was one Rose was not keen to stay in. Rose fell into a room of gray where the sounds of her mind reverberated out of the walls, a prison of sound. She fell to her knees as the sounds grew louder in volume until she felt her very insides contort. Her skin peeled back, piece by piece, as she felt a rupture below. She heard a scream that wasn't her own. Rose's eyes opened and she was filled with sweat. She fumbled around in the dark and rolled off the bed as she heard the scream coming from Cicero and Claudia's room. Rose had forgotten Claudia suffered from night terrors, but she felt grateful as the woman's piercing scream set her back to reality. In the still night, Rose left her dwelling and went down the stairs to grab a class of water to cool down. As she leaned on the awning, she noticed a peculiar circumstance. The cup left on Cicero's table moved slightly to the right on its own.

Rose's eyes narrowed as she focused in on the strange movement. She held her breath as she heard a low scraping sound from the cup that grew louder as it slammed against the wall. The cup broke into fragments and fell to the floor. Rose rushed into the kitchen, her footsteps, loud as could be. Other things in the kitchen started to move, but in a haphazard way that made little sense to her. Rose knew it was far from her delusions from just waking up, there was a real problem at hand. She wasn't sure how to handle it, shooting inside her own home was hardly a worthy solution. The groggy sounds of Cicero stumbling in his pajamas would have been a humorous sight to Rose on any other occasion. As he entered the kitchen, he saw a hand towel dangling above the pair.

"What...?" Cicero asked in confusion as his eyes widened to an unnerving sound. He heard the loud pattering of feet descend as the invisible entity headed towards the floor. It skirted past the pair and made its way to the sleeping Claudia. Cicero gave chase as he went back, while Rose found an unusual solution in the corner of her eye. She looked at a half-open carton of flour. Rose rushed in with Cicero as she emptied the solution of flour onto the bed where Claudia remained. She revealed a creature that resembled a centipede. Instead of antennas, there was nothing more than a small void that it was using to suck the energy out of the trio as they slept through the night. Claudia woke up in a stir as she coughed from the flour placed on her, while Rose took the golden opportunity to grab the creature by the tail and knock it to the floor. As it lay stunned, Cicero took the opportunity to give it a hard stomp with a hiking boot and the creature was no more. Far from their usual hunts, Cicero couldn't help but laugh at such a sight.

"Honey, you get cleaned up. I'll get the flour out the sheets." Cicero gave Claudia a hug.

"I'm heading back to bed. Y'all sleep well." Rose winked and headed back up to the loft for some sound sleep.

The Merchant of Venice: II

Niccolo and Florence were walking to a nearby cafe to debrief on the current phase of their next plan. As Niccolo's outfit settled after the bank heist and dispersed the truck's money into reputable channels, he was ready to start his new advance towards claiming more territory. Niccolo found his exploits with Rose and Cicero to be more enjoyable than he anticipated, but his primary goal remained. The Baron still remained at large, and The Owl was still an unknown entity. At first, Niccolo doubted the aspects of his partnership with Florence. His outlook changed as he tuned onto the radio to hear bust after bust of lowlifes that tried to undermine his criminal enterprise.

Just as Florence predicted, her yellow journalism was enough to send the bloodhounds of the law on her behalf and obscured Niccolo's activity. The Irish mob were no longer a problem in the western sector of the city as they were crushed by police dogs and fire hoses and the balance of power shifted significantly. Right as Niccolo started to make his moves, however, he ran into a roadblock regarding The Owl's activities. The pair spent many a sleepless night as they both tried to understand him and the motivation behind his outfit. His suppliers were still unknown as his realm of influence passed by everyone and questioning led them nowhere. Florence assumed that her uncle held some sort of connection to this man as one of the biggest power players in Phoenix, while Niccolo realized that his competition consolidated under The Owl's control.

Florence walked ahead with a blissful pace to her step as she encouraged Niccolo to match her speed. She hadn't realized the bustle of the city always had something to offer. Though it was the peak of the workday, there was a growing crowd of interested patrons that decided to have their lunch to hear what was going on. Florence watched as an array of people gathered around a few men and a blonde woman took a small podium. Their voices echoed as a small microphone arrangement was made. A crowd that seemed to be unending interrupted their walk.

"We want a pure white Christian city! Vote for Blackstone Shaw III! Not only will he clean up crime in this city, but he'll send those monsters back to Hell!" a man in a white cloak shouted. The hoots and hollers of like-minded individuals who gave claps and synchronized cheers accompanied his shouting. In less than a generation after the government wiped them clean, the changing tides of politics brought a resurgence of Klan ideology and power.

"Ugh, disgusting," Florence remarked as she saw the growing assembly. With a recent change in local government, the Klu Klux Klan was able to rally in the streets openly as they actively recruited for more to come join their ranks. Locals embraced the Klan as they championed a pro-Prohibitionist approach and the expulsion of undesirables. The mob factions hardly were involved in social endeavors, but the fanaticism of the Klan gave them issues as well. Despite their championing of virtue, the Klan operated as a direct competitor to their ambitions and targeted suppliers. Niccolo's inherited alliance with the organizations in Mexico came under heavy fire. The chaos of anti-immigration made a perfect smokescreen for illegal dealings that were justified under a court of law. Niccolo hadn't interacted with them before, but he heard to some degree, the amount of violence that spewed from them in Chicago.

"Who are these people and what are they doing?" Niccolo asked.

Florence gritted her teeth as she heard the same vitriol regurgitated for another audience. Her native Boston was just as unruly when it came to the demands of the white majority. She attempted to cover her ears as Niccolo grabbed her arm and attempted to ford the growing crowd. Each passing step grew tighter as the crowd became a blob that swallowed the small city street. The pair groaned as every day there was some new distraction that kept the busiest roads in town clogged. Niccolo saw many bare faces, but as the words of the man grew louder, the faces of those present vanished into the crowd. The day was hot, but it mattered little as the crowd was fired up.

"Lynch the tar baby! Roast the coals of the pedophiles in the Catholic Church! Damn wops stealing our jobs and our poisoning our way of life! We want a stronger and united White America! I'm not the one you want to see, but hear my words, for the great and mighty Blackstone Shaw approaches us!" the man yelled. He embroiled the crowd further.

The crowd threw their hats in the air as Florence and Niccolo noticed the crowd parted for the man running for election. Blackstone Shaw was a rotund man who ran on a campaign of a clean and corruption-free town and was surprisingly steadfast to his morals. He wore a pressed tan suit that contrasted with the growing sea of white around him. His money was clean and so were his shoes, but his heart was filled with mindless rage and hatred for those he considered undesirable in his city. As Blackstone Shaw approached, he was accompanied by a group of hooded men that held picket signs with obscenities and campaign slogans for the man in question. Niccolo offered no comment on the signs but was curious about what was written on them. Florence's journalistic curiosity entranced her to stay and listen to the man's drivel while Niccolo started to look slightly uncomfortable. As he turned around, he noticed more faces were now covered with hoods.

"Ladies and gentlemen, I advocate for you to consider a strong vote this year. Ladies, with your newly earned right to vote, I assure you that your

children will have a secure future and today I offer you some promises,"
Blackstone said, as his bass-filled voice sounded through the intercom.

"I've heard all sorts of things, but my first day in office, I plan to root
out the evils that plague Phoenix and the rest of the slop! What evil lurks
within this city, you may ask!? The Baron says this is his city! I disagree.
How can we follow the guidance of someone backed by the Jews of Wall
Street, hmm? Their gold is tainted and so is The Baron for accepting them
into our city. The creatures of the night, I've heard about in the newspapers
will be rooted out by our stalwart police force and regulars from the army
base," Blackstone commented with a hearty laugh.

As Blackstone went on, Florence felt she'd seen far enough to write a
scathing review of the proceedings. She took Niccolo's hand and barged
through the crowd as she attempted to make it towards the other side.
Florence was aware that while the mayor-to-be held a clean record, his associates were far more guilty. She looked for any familiar faces and recognized
just a few shopkeepers from her travels that were part of the crowd. One
of the men gave a perturbed look underneath the hood as Florence gently
tugged Niccolo away. A break in the crowd led to a less populated section
of the sidewalk where the pair emerged enroute to their destination. A few
unhooded members of The Klan passed out pamphlets to passersby, some
curious were asking questions while the disinterested ones left without
another word. Florence was stopped by one man, who gave a large smile
at the pair.

"Oh, I'm not a Jehovah's Witness—" Florence said in jest at their appearance.

"Mam, please take this and have a wonderful day. Sir," the man said as
Niccolo remained quiet. He handed Florence a pamphlet. The pair walked
off and now headed towards the cafe. The rambunctious crowd continued
to shout slurs beyond comprehension as they were embroiled with rage.

"What does that say?" Niccolo inquired as he pointed to the paper in
Florence's hands. He tried making sense of the political drawings but came

up woefully short on his analysis. Italian politics were hard enough to understand, let alone that of a different country.

"Remove the... Oh, that's a mean word. I won't say that," Florence crumpled the piece of paper and threw it aside into a nearby trash can.

"So that's who these people are. I got a call from an associate of mine past the border, people like those men in the white there, lynched my supplier across the wall a few nights ago. I owe some crews a significant favor from putting the money to getting Andrea out of jail for card fixing. A debt I'll have to repay," Niccolo noted as he adjusted his suit.

Niccolo opened the door to the cafe as he watched Florence walk past him. His eyes surveyed the perimeter of the establishment and saw a mixture of clientele that intrigued him. He made no eye contact but noticed an Irish captain enjoying a meal with his family. Niccolo wasn't particularly fond of the Irish but held no qualms with this man as their territory didn't overlap. Niccolo instinctively pulled out Florence's chair near the window as the pair sat down. Niccolo noticed an assortment of other patrons that occupied the establishment that seemed to be all types. White collar workers, seamstresses, and miners all found a home here and something to eat. Florence was quick to make her decision as she always ordered a club sandwich with extra lettuce. Florence gave Niccolo a confused look as she noticed he held the menu upside down. As Niccolo met her gaze, she quickly changed it to a small smile.

"You sure can speak it, but your English is lousy! Why not just tell me what you want?" Florence said.

Niccolo remained quiet as he pointed to a piece of cake. He chewed his tongue at the prospect. He remained in thought as he studied Florence's appearance. He was interrupted by Florence's voice.

"Why the long face Nicki? You've seen my work speaks for itself. You know how many people got put in the paddy wagon because of me?" Florence teased. Florence's journalism was the bane of small crews that remained sloppy but could bribe the police to hide their handiwork. Niccolo noticed that the usual routes that required a territory tax were duty-free, much to his and the other men's satisfaction.

"That I cannot deny. It just bothers me that no matter how close I get, I always seem to be this close to figuring something out," Niccolo admitted.

"Every one of my jobs doesn't go exactly the way I want it. I've been in this game a long time now, twenty years at least. I started as a teenager, but somehow The Owl always has his grubby hands on my work," Niccolo explained. His fingers patted the table as he wondered where to go from here.

"You know, it doesn't always have to be a man pulling the strings. Maybe that's why they haven't been caught yet. What if The Owl's, a whole group with mobsters and helpers at their beck and call? That could be why they manage to hit so many places at once the way they do," Florence questioned.

As Niccolo and Florence debated the possibilities, three cars converged close to the cafe. Two cars were black while the middle was a dark green. A group of six men exited the car. The crowd listening to the mayor's speech finally dispersed and the roads were free once more, but chaos would soon reign supreme once again in the city. The police were routinely paid off to ignore crimes in certain sectors when applicable, and this was no different. The first of the two men in black cars left the vehicle and approached the green car. Cirano was escorted out of his vehicle. In traditional fashion, Cirano rode in the back of the car where he was received with his signature weapons, a bulldog revolver and a sawn-off shotgun in the backseat that were wrapped together with cloth.

As George drove, Cirano examined his weapons to make sure they were in working order. Unlike a few of the other leaders, who saw their vehicles as disposable, Cirano spared no expense for his. The body of the car was reinforced with bulletproof plating and thick glass windows powered by a hand crank. He wore a burgundy suit with a black hat and red feather on the outside. His left hand wore rings on each of his fingers, taken from the rival bosses he'd murdered on his way to the top. Cirano's appearance demanded respect from those that saw him as onlookers panicked and attempted to run away through the alley. A boss dressed his best for a hit done personally, and anyone with common sense knew this.

The cafe fell still as the silhouettes of the men appeared. Right by the window, Florence and Niccolo saw the face of Cirano appear before them. Cirano rarely attacked in the day, but he needed to send a message to the restaurant owners. Niccolo soon realized that the target in mind was the Irish captain, but he wondered what sort of action would warrant a response. He assumed that Cirano would simply enter the facility and apprehend the man this way, but he had other plans. Niccolo's pupils widened as he realized the stance he was in. Niccolo quickly urged Florence to hit the floor. The owner of the restaurant withdrew a shotgun and pumped it, the only action he could afford to do. He knew his fate was sealed. He hoped to use a deterrent with force to ward the gangsters away. Niccolo scanned the floor as a few trapped patrons were in a panic. Running outside was suicidal, and the back entrance was walled off by the man holding the shotgun. The standoff was palpable as they remained on the defensive and waited for the next move.

The Irishman brought out a pistol as he debated taking the family with him but looked at it dead center. His eyes were filled with rage as he saw Cirano light a cigar and give a wink. Niccolo watched as the man mouthed *"Not my fucking kids!"* through the glass. Cirano tossed his pocket watch and gave a countdown for the man to say good-bye. The man gave a panicked shout in a language Niccolo couldn't understand as he stood up and shot. The crack of the bullets caused a scene among those in the café who screamed. Cirano didn't move as the man's bullets were woefully inaccurate. He found such a plead to be completely pathetic.

"Light it up," Cirano said plainly. His entourage of four men each brandished their submachine guns. After ten seconds passed, a hail of bullets erupted through the glass and wall of the diner. Those that weren't on the ground, were torn to ribbons with the assault. The following hail of bullets was a thunderous crack as shards of glass and metal flew everywhere within the small space. Florence laid onto Niccolo as she vibrated in anxiety. Niccolo's eyes remained open as he absorbed every bit of Cirano's brutality. Nearby, the walls were riddled with holes and the smell of gunpowder surrounded them. Sounds of piercing flesh came as tears of those in pain shouted out and were subsequently silenced with the next bit. The owner was long dead, with a large hole in his head and blood that seeped onto the floor from the bullets. The rest of his body and subsequent patrons were torn to pieces as arms and legs were strewn throughout.

They all have choppers, every single last one of 'em. How am I getting out of this alive? Nicki... Florence thought as she opened her eyes in shock. She scanned the space and noticed there was another short path past their table that led to the bathroom. She evaluated an escape that banked on there being a window in the back. It was a bold move, but something else she needed to do came to mind.

In between reloads, Florence saw that the violence ceased, and her eyes darted to the table with the family. In a last-minute act of defiance, she saw the Irishman's wife shield a young baby covered in blood but remained alive with a harsh cry. She broke her stance from Niccolo and slowly crawled underneath to grab them. Just by grip of her fingernail, Florence slid the child across the ground to her corner. Niccolo's thoughts were on the dropped shotgun. He knew that if Florence and him saw The Owl, it was apparent that he saw them as well. Niccolo debated his next move as another flurry of bullets came right before the pair remained quiet for another five minutes.

Once the dust settled and the engines of the cars that housed The Owl and his men were off, Niccolo slowly helped himself up the wall. He extended his hand to Florence as the pair scooted by to see her plan. She held the baby tightly to her. A few injured survivors of the ordeal used napkins to clean their wounds as they struggled to avoid the debris and more. The sounds of the police sirens never came to them as they wondered what evil was unleashed in their young city. Those that heard the noises from the bathroom locked the door and attempted to protect themselves. Niccolo used his shoulder to breach inside the men's bathroom and saw an open window that led out to a small space that opened to a bigger alleyway. It was a tight fit, as Florence barely fit through with the child in tow. Niccolo undressed himself and tossed his clothes through the opening before exiting. He quickly redressed and looked at Florence.

"We need to get rid of this child. Drop her off anywhere, and I need to get to a phone. Your residence is not far from here, yes? We will split up for now, for your safety. I will need to get back to base. Wash off at your hotel and stay there until I get a better understanding of things," Niccolo mentioned as he smelled himself. He could use a bath as well and thought of the safehouse. Niccolo and Florence parted ways as agreed.

A few hours later, Rose and Cicero idled around their home as their eyes were constantly locked to the telephone. As they were working on longer solutions for their backlog of creatures, the pair hoped for a clean and simple hunt. Rose was drawing random sketches of her adventures in the corners of her notebook while Cicero played solitaire. Rose gave a passing glance at the phone while she shook her pen for additional ink. As Cicero put away his cards in frustration, the pair's call was answered with a loud ring. Cicero rushed towards the phone as he was eager for more income. Cicero raised an eyebrow as he heard some muddled words in another language on the other line.

"Cowboy? Ah, this is Niccolo. I have a job for you," Niccolo commented.

"Look, you helped us out with a few tips here and there, and I appreciate that, but I don't need your dirty money," Cicero stated through the line. Cicero looked behind him to see the judgmental faces of Rose and now Claudia looking back at him. He gave a gruff sigh as he felt compelled to hear Niccolo out. Cicero hardly was one to talk when it came to morals, he

was a walking fossil of the Wild West and all the ills that came with such a ti
me.

"Listen cowboy, I'm going to say this again in case the hair in your ears blocked my words. The payment for this job will be two hundred dollars," Niccolo mentioned.

"Well now—What exactly did you have in mind?" Cicero asked as his tone lightened up.

"Don't wear that dreadful ensemble of yours. You will be provided a suit and hat, as we're going to operate with discretion. I will arrive with Bill and explain things further." Niccolo commented. Cicero hung up the phone and explained the mechanics of his next job to Rose.

Once the details were finalized, Rose bit her tongue on the matter, but she felt the breather could work out for her. She needed to continue practicing her training for The Baron and Baroness as she neglected portal conjuring while hunting with Cicero. Cicero later heard a knock on the door as the familiar whirr of Niccolo's car spewing smoke came by. Bill remained in the car while Niccolo approached the premises. As Niccolo walked by, he could see Rose's small hand wave from a nearby window.

"Come on in!" Rose said happily as Cicero frowned.

Cicero felt slightly uncomfortable as he slowly lifted his arm up to let Niccolo inside. Cicero nearly did a double take as Niccolo took off his shoes and left them outside. As Niccolo met eyes with Claudia, he gave a low bow of his head. Cicero was so used to cleaning up sand and dirt from everyone else, he hadn't considered such a gesture even possible. Although he still held significant bias, Cicero's opinion could be swayed by the little things that often went unappreciated.

"What, no moll by your side today?" Cicero teased as he used his finger to draw Florence's figure. Niccolo bit his tongue at Cicero's statement and shook his head. His attention was better left for Rose, and he was intrigued by what she was working on.

"What are you drawing? Oh-These are very good. Say, mind drawing something for me? I ran into The Owl today and I want to get a depiction of the man. Here's what I have in mind. He is a tired looking man with a suit and a hat with a feather in it. White male, with some stubble-like an aftershave," Niccolo started to say as Rose quickly shifted to a new piece of paper in her notebook.

"Anything else you can tell me?" Rose held her hand out for a cigarette. Cicero rummaged in his pocket and handed her one. She chose not to smoke indoors for safety reasons but kept a few on hand as she used them to calm down on occasion before the bigger hunts.

"Older than me, at least by about ten—no—maybe fifteen years. He's certainly established as far as gangsters go, long-lived in this line of work." Niccolo explained.

"He sounds middle-aged, so I'll draw some little crows' feet there, like so. You know, he looks a lot like Cirano... the owner of that one restaurant in town," Rose felt a sudden burst of realization. Niccolo snatched the piece of paper and nearly crumpled it as he studied every detail. If he could get it printed on a poster and use it for target practice, he would in a heartbeat.

"You are tellings me that boy-lover Cirano is The-Fucking-Owl?" Niccolo looked over Rose's sketch of him. It wasn't a perfect rendition, but it was more than enough for him to realize what he was up against. Niccolo was so rattled that his mastery of English started to erode as he begrudgingly cursed in Italian.

"You know, now that I see it, this makes sense with what Mavis told me. Last time I went to fill up our satchels with ammunition, she was telling me about some folks that came to shake down patrons at the bar. These must have been people working for The Owl, I mean Cirano. So, what's our next move?" Cicero questioned.

"We need to get this sketch to Florence. She can send it through the papers, and we can get him arrested! I was thinking of how many people go to this restaurant, some are especially important, there's no way the police don't do an investigation and can put this to bed," Rose assessed. Niccolo and Cicero shared a laugh at Rose's answer. While the idea would have worked for a small fry, Cirano operated on a completely different level than the others. This was known by all parties, but the idea of extra pressure into the game was a worthy play by Rose to isolate Cirano and help save the town.

"Rose, my smart one, I must tell you something crucial. The police will not help us, you understand, both me and the cowboy are wanted by the government. Not only that, Cirano is the police. He owns them. When his men do crimes, the police hardly show up and when they do, it'll be me in a jail cell, if I'm lucky. There's only one way this goes," Niccolo commented.

Rose grumbled at their response but given the evidence she'd seen in the papers; their reaction was well-warranted. The government could be a ruthless asset when compelled to do something but otherwise remain pitiful to act. Rose vowed to do more planning while she saw Niccolo and Cicero off. She could only wonder what the other two were off to do, while she waited for Claudia to return to her duties before practicing her conjuring once more.

Niccolo and Cicero were led towards the car by Bill where Niccolo prompted him to deliver the instructions for the job. As Bill explained, Niccolo removed an assortment of masks for the group to wear over their heads. Cicero changed from his usual wares into the suit and hat that Niccolo provided. He looked at himself as he felt slightly disheveled from his usual appearance.

"The boss wants us to place a house call to some members of The Klu Klux Klan about an hour from out here. We're here for information, but if a few happen to resist, nothing of value's lost. There's a camp of them in the mountains for a retreat. You bought your gun?" Bill explained.

"Well damn, why didn't you say so? I always carry an iron on me." Cicero grabbed his revolver from his old pants. Niccolo gave a devious grin as he was curious to see if Rose's car side stories about Cicero's exploits were true.

The trio remained quiet as they headed towards their destination. Bill observed the movement of vultures in the sky as they patrolled looking for a meal. The movement of the car jostled the three around as it attempted to make do on the dirt road. Cicero wondered what sort of mess Niccolo got himself into when it came to dealing with the Klan. He was aware of their disdain towards his foreign nature. Cicero had his own battles with them as they targeted his hometown in years past for sheltering an injured man on the trail. Cicero also felt especially guilty after what happened in Duncan and decided a proactive approach would work better. Cicero looked over his revolvers as he locked eyes with Niccolo. Niccolo brandished his Thompson, much to Cicero's disapproval.

Such a loud thing, is he trying to invite the whole neighborhood? Cicero thought. The sun started to wane as the three neared their location.

"Once it hits twilight, we will take the car up the climb and visit the camp. Just pass these hills." Niccolo said briefly.

A few exchanged cigarettes between the men were enough to pass the time. Bill felt uncomfortable with the silence and talked some about the surrounding nature while Cicero filled in the details. Cicero always had an interest in being a park ranger, but being in league with his gang forbade him from joining any sort of government organization. Niccolo checked the sky as he felt the time was soon near. The purple vistas of the Arizona sunset soon faded instead to a resounding dark blue that was shown over the sky. In the distance, a small bit of light from the city resonated.

"Where'd you say they were now? I don't see a thing over—Oh." Cicero said as he noticed a giant wooden cross burning in the distance.

The group got into the car and headed towards a few haphazardly parked cars on the hill. All black, Bill made sure to park a slight distance away from the others to make sure their vehicle was unharmed. The men took no time in gathering their firearms and advanced towards the camp. Cicero heard drunken singing and the clinking of alcohol bottles as he adjusted his mask. One of the sober Klansmen sighted them in the distance and raised a fist in the air with a rifle in hand. He aimed it at the men before him. The rest of the lot attempted to get into formation.

"Who the hell are you?" one of the men asked.

Cicero let out two shots with his revolver before the others could blink. Niccolo hardly masked his surprise as the rustic old man carried a deadly trigger finger. The first of his bullets pierced straight through the skull of one of the men, while the second disarmed the man with the rifle. The sound from Cicero's revolver reverberated throughout the canyon as the first man hit the floor. The drunken men were unsure to do, as some bumbled around and attempted to make sense of their situation. In the three sources of light present at the camp, Cicero, Niccolo, and Bill stood side by side with their guns towards the group. Running wasn't an option now.

"Now, my question is this. Which one of you lynched a man named Lorenzo Vera? Was it one of you? Or-I can make this easy and just assume it was all of you," Niccolo threatened as he stepped closer with his gun out. The rest of the men, a group of ten, were aware of the deadly power that such a submachine gun possessed. They were in awe at how a man acquired such a weapon. Cirano's outfit was given a blank check to buy whatever they needed, but firepower like that was rare.

"I don't know what you're talking about!" one of the men yelled, while Niccolo shot at the grass for them to comply. The impact from the bullets kicked up dirt in their faces. The muzzle flash was bright enough to qualify as a signal flare as a few of the men covered their eyes from the stark light change.

"He-Here! I'll answer, for pete's sake, I have a family!" one of the uniformed men said as he crawled towards the group. His eyes were filled with tears as he wet himself. He looked to his right and found the rest of the men held up by Cicero. He gave a small whimper as he noticed Cicero ordering them to empty their pockets of any valuables. Cicero was more than happy to relieve them of their hard-earned dollars from their regular job.

"You think you're so fucking tough, do you? You gonna shoot me for talking a big game? You and that wop, I can tell his garlic breath from here!" another bold Klansman from the group threatened Niccolo. Niccolo lifted an eyebrow under the mask as his gaze turned to Cicero. Niccolo didn't need to convey the dynamic, he was the boss for this job and Cicero served as a capable enforcer.

"Wasn't on my list of things to do today, but what the hell." Cicero let loose another blast from his Remington. The bullet lodged itself straight into the second man's neck as a portion of his head hung on by a spare muscle tendon. Niccolo couldn't help but let out a small laugh at the sight. Cicero came off as a simple curmudgeon, but Niccolo could see he held a taste for blood still so deep down. Those bedtime stories of his exploits from Rose turned out to be far more than he expected. He wished that half his men wouldn't hesitate with the way Cicero shot.

"Bill? It's me-Charlie! Why are you with these tomfools?" one of the Klansmen said as he recognized Bill from the group. Aside from his voice as he barked orders to the hostages, Bill wore the same pair of worn-down black shoes everywhere he went, it was one of his personality quirks that made it difficult for him to stay incognito.

"Listen, sirs, I'm not trying to die today. Here—I'll give you the compound's location. The man that ordered the hit," the man said as he slowly watched Cicero's revolver track his movements. He fumbled around for a pen in his pocket and withdrew it. As Cicero kept the gun trained, he wrote down some instructions and the address on a piece of cloth.

Niccolo walked over and grabbed the piece of cloth. He gave a nod as he passed it to Bill. Bill looked over the directions and felt a cold sweat come over him. Bill realized that the instructions given by the KKK member weren't for his own organization, but that of Cirano's main warehouse. Bill was aware that Cirano hadn't placed any order for the killing of any

Mexican opposition, in fact it was the opposite, he was trying to court their support. Bill gritted his teeth as he was in a compromised position. He was aware that Niccolo was ignorant about the location of Cirano's warehouse, and calling out the man would put an unnecessary risk on him. Bill had done everything he could to avert suspicion and he needed to remain hidden.

"Uh, boss. We got what we needed. I say we ice him," Bill said. He hoped to use the opportunity to tie up a loose end.

"Good idea. You do it," Niccolo ordered as he waited for Bill to blast the man with his shotgun.

Bill took a deep breath and gunned down the Klansman in a pool of his own blood. Niccolo watched as the man's intestines poured out and shards of flesh were rendered to pieces from the blast. Bill fell quiet as Niccolo watched the remaining men squirm before the three soon left. One of the hostages spit towards Niccolo as he turned around, the gesture loud enough to be heard in the silent air. Once he was in the car, Niccolo ordered Bill to make a pass of the campsite as he used up the rest of his magazine through the window, leaving the group shot and scarred to pieces as a reminder. The survivors, if any, would be able to tell what happened that night at the ridge while the vultures could happily feed.

As Bill, Niccolo, and Cicero drove off, the car was silent once more. Cicero's eyes remained bloodshot as the carnage invigorated him in a way he hadn't felt in a long time. Niccolo didn't see himself as any arbiter of justice but felt relieved to get one loose end out the way as he needed Mexican support to strike at Cirano's operation. Niccolo reached into his pocket and handed Cicero the money as promised, with a little extra. The familiar mounds of sand and flat roads soon gave way from the small spots of precious green from the campsites.

"I'm surprised cowboy, you may yet be good for us. If my men shot half as good as you, I'd own Chicago by nightfall. Consider training the men if you're looking for some fast cash..." Niccolo teased as he placed his hand on Bill's shoulder.

"Bill, you are a good man. I would love to see you take captain rank someday. Though, I have two questions. I caught that one of them knew who you were, were you one of them in a past life? And remind me of the place we need to go," Niccolo commented.

"Just lads from grade school, nothing more, nothing less. It's down by the east end of town... last I recall. Can't say for certain." Bill's arms locked up on the wheel from the pressure. Niccolo felt satisfied by his answer for now.

"Bill, drop the cowboy off to his home. As for me, take me to base and I will handle the rest from here," Niccolo said.

The Owl: II

At 1 in the morning, Cirano awoke from his sleep to address his more important matters. A list of instructions for the restaurant's delayed opening stuck out of his typewriter. He ripped it off without a second thought and placed it on his desk. At a timely manner, Cirano heard a knock on the door in his apartment. Cirano rubbed his drowsy eyes and quickly fit into his pressed suit and fedora to put on his head while his baker's clothes remained draped over a spare couch. He opened the door and saw that George had arrived. He quickly looked to see if he was being followed and invited him inside.

"There's a situation at the warehouse, so I came to pick you up as soon as I could. Please, get dressed. I'll tell you more." George turned his head to obscure his condition.

Cirano had an exuberant amount of money but remained mentally trapped as he eked out an existence in his apartment. Cirano's apartment hardly matched the idealist lifestyle of the larger-than-life gangster. His apartment was sequestered in a calm area of the city and decorated with vintage furniture from days gone by. The walls were lined with various items kept in meticulous frames. Cirano walked past photos from years gone by. A door slightly open ajar had multiple fitted suits that hung up some distance behind him.

"George? Honey, why are you here at this hour? Work doesn't start until 5— " Cirano's eyes adjusted to the changing light. He knelt and looked at the man's face with disdain.

Is… that blood on his head? Cirano thought.

Cirano was angry with the events of the earlier day but was too busy with the restaurant to address them until now. As he met the brisk air of the cool night, he surveyed the kingdom he'd built for some time. The Baron and Baroness ruled in the day, but at night, Cirano was the one who made the orders as far as he was concerned. Cirano had a trusted circle of lieutenants he enlisted to keep his operation going throughout the entirety of Arizona. While he was based in Phoenix, Cirano had eyes and ears in Yuma, Tucson, and was working his way to Flagstaff. All of these were good ventures for the branch, but there were concerns on his end.

As Cirano and George walked in tandem to the car, a drunken man walked by with a cracked liquor bottle. Cirano gave no mind to this, but noticed George's reaction as his hands shook. He was clearly perturbed by the man in some fashion, and Cirano wondered what the case was. The streets were mostly empty, save for a few late travelers that attempted to find their way home from a flickering streetlight.

"He's been following me all night from his car, he didn't see my turn signal. I tried to book him, I tried to apologize, I even threw a few quarters for him to leave but he won't leave me be," George complained as he looked away from Cirano.

"You're the one who cut me off in traffic! Come on, bring it up!" the man yelled as he pointed at George. He curled his hands up and started to sway around as he held back vomit.

"So, you got cut off in traffic, and the thing you decide to do, is stew on this all day, waiting like a child who didn't get a toy from the corner store. Well, we've got a sale going on." Cirano cracked his knuckles. Cirano walked over and punched the man in the jaw. He stopped as he let the hit from the first attack settle in. The man swayed from the impact. He raised his fist again, this time, with a much harder swing as he knocked the man's tooth out.

"Bullies always say you're the villain when you fight back, you remind me a lot of my father—you know. My father sold our apartment in Chicago because he became a Mormon and decided for us to homestead out in Utah. It was me, my mother, and him. Starving. For days. For what, you might ask?" Cirano narrated as he curled his fist. Cirano was known to go on unrelated tangents as he let out his anger on the man before him. Despite knowing that he needed to be in a rush, this was currently a far better use of his time.

George could only watch in silence as Cirano continued to beat the man senseless. He could hear tears coming from the other side of the street. An elderly man sitting on his porch with a cigar witnessed the encounter and was shaken with fear as Cirano slowly turned his head to him. The air was palpable as Cirano used his boot to stomp his target's head in.

"And what the hell do you want?" Cirano withdrew his pistol from his suit pocket. He enjoyed the accompanying scream from the old man as he let loose a few bullets that pierced the quiet of the neighborhood. The ricochet of the bullets hit a brick wall before stopping. Cirano gave a cold grin to the man in full confidence that he would remain quiet at the scene of the crime.

Without further delay, Cirano and George headed towards the warehouse. Cirano saw that George drove with extreme speed as he ignored red lights and any yield signs. Cirano wondered what the news was that required such cryptic information. He was usually given a phone call or a dossier with information, but George had sworn to secrecy regarding the nature of this visit. He could only look at Cirano through the rearview mirror with a low nod in understanding. The warehouse was on the edge of the city and operated as a car repair shop during daylight hours. At night, they ran liquor shipments throughout the rest of the state and provided security details for packages bought by The Baron for his grand railway project. One of many fronts now under Cirano's upkeep, this was his main area of operations aside from his restaurant.

Cirano exited the car and headed straight to his office. He held a look of confusion as he saw that the light under his door was on, and the door was unlocked. Cirano was the only one who had entry into his office as he carried a single key. George quickly left the warehouse to adjust the parking spot of the car while Cirano was left alone. Cirano opened the door and saw The Baroness wearing an elegant gray dress that stood out in the drab office.

"Mam. W-What are you doing here? I didn't receive any correspondence," Cirano asked in shock as The Baroness waited by his desk.

"I came to check on things and make sure our investment has been worth the aid. Is this a problem?" The Baroness asked.

The Baroness was keenly aware of problems that started to interfere with her husband's work. Infighting between the established peace of the various factions with a claim on the city and other territories grew to be a large issue. Supply trucks ended up being absorbed by the outfits and the resources allocated didn't match the output given. The Baron was also aware of the monster problem that rooted itself on certain sections of the road. He was aware of Rose and Cicero's occupation and had anonymously enlisted their services before, but there was much more than they could handle alone. There was a growing need to negotiate a sit-down for the last crucial months of the project. The Baron rarely left his work and started to grow frustrated, a fate all, including his wife, wanted to avoid.

"Not at all. It's just—" Cirano mentioned as he held his hand up. Cirano's head turned towards his window as he heard the halting screech of a few other cars. Cirano opened his drawer and revealed a revolver as he heard the ambient noises of gunfire in the distance.

Outside of his office, Cirano's outfit was under siege by a few members of the Mexican gangs that Niccolo allied with. After Niccolo delivered the information given to him by the KKK, the Mexican gangs decided to set an example on what they assumed to be their outpost. Niccolo had no reason to assume that the information given was faulty. Cirano's outpost was especially well hidden, so those that arrived were unaware they had struck the lion's den. Cirano was dumbfounded at the information breach as he'd done just about everything aside from changing city maps to keep this place obscured.

"Mam, we need to get you to safety right now. I'm not sure what's going on, but we have a room for you," Cirano offered as he extended his hand.

"I'm fine standing here," The Baroness coldly stated. Cirano was surprised at her answer and how calm she was. The Baroness' ear was primed towards the sound of the men that shouted various explicit statements in Spanish, but also a rallying cry for the fallen that they depended on. The Baroness shot a look at Cirano as he postured himself up by a window.

Cirano let out a few rounds as he blindly fired into the establishment. He heard automatic rifles as he ducked, avoiding a fair bit of shrapnel that came by as The Baroness continued to observe. These were subsequently snuffed out as Cirano heard the satisfying hum of returning fire from his men armed with submachine guns. The tactical advantage was easy as the amount of firepower allowed one of Cirano's men to take on at least three at once. Soon after, the gunfire ceased and there was a break in the violence. Cirano heard pained Spanish screams and gave a satisfied laugh at the competency of his men. Cirano soon heard victory come from the rest of the outpost. Two survivors from the opposing gangs were going to be held as collateral while the rest would be buried out in the desert. This jovial occasion was not shared by The Baroness, who seemed perturbed by what she witnessed.

"Cirano. I have some critiques to offer regarding the state of the warehouse," The Baroness opened.

"It's all part of the game here. Of course, madam, what would you like to address?" Cirano asked as he chewed his tongue.

"I saw your surprise at such an attack. Do you not have intelligence on the other factions and their plans? This place is not supposed to exist and yet here we are. May I remind you; my husband and I hired you to help secure our assets. I am running a business. I gave you an exuberant amount of money. Your men are also not military trained, I noticed on my way here they lacked specific procedures I was looking for. I arrived armed and was not searched. None of these men know who I look like," The Baroness commented as she gestured towards the interior of her dress.

"I figured the men just assumed a dame wasn't going to be any fuss. Anyone looking to be any trouble we take care of quickly," Cirano admitted. He found it a bit ludicrous that The Baroness insisted she be searched like a common criminal, rather than have any other status, given her background.

"That was your first mistake. Anarchists use women all the time to smuggle explosives, and this is an auto repair shop. A firefight was risky, what if something blew up? Protestors have blown up my factories. Hire regulars that have experience from The Great War or at least, The Spanish-American War who are crack shots. You may see enterprise as mere business, but I see it as war. A war I intend to win. Your men also do not respect you in a way I find adequate. I noticed their idle chatter was surrounding rumors regarding your... tendencies. I will not go further into this, but I need a stronger hand to account for externalities that put my assets at risk," The Baroness mentioned. She studied Cirano's stone reaction as he gripped the corner of his desk.

"With all due respect mam, it's expected the men have autonomy, it's how we do things. They pay their tribute and go home, this isn't grade school. None of us are friends, and trust me, they know respect. I popped a guy's face clean off for mouthing off last week. What the guys talk about doesn't concern me as long as the product flows."

"It has not flowed, that is why I'm here to begin with. That may be how things are done in the thieves and degenerates of the Mafia, but you are not an associate anymore. Your side projects are not important. You are my property, Cirano. That is what you agreed to when you took our investment. Run it to our specifications. Be lucky I arrived instead today.

The railway will continue completion and I will not have my husband upset," she threatened.

"Of course..." Cirano mumbled.

"Prior to this engagement we witnessed, I placed a folder on your desk. These are the latest updates regarding the railway project and some information I picked up from various socials. All these members have wives and after some wine, they get to talking. Douse the fires where they are. My husband will be calling the other factions soon, so be weary, we want to be on top."

Cirano grumbled as he gave a nod of admission to The Baroness' direction. The last thing Cirano wanted to do was be reprimanded, he valued his direct control and hated to be reined in. He looked towards his desk and glanced at the beige folder that held a number of papers inside. Cirano found paperwork to be immensely boring as he preferred the more bombastic parts of being a mob boss, or whatever his current position was now. He always found his directives changing.

"Excellent work. Now, I'm going to retrieve my daughter. I lack a pocket watch, but I can tell I'm late. She will be sorely disappointed after I chided her being late to do the same. I don't like hypocrisy. Good night." The Baroness walked off. She enjoyed Cirano's confused face as he hadn't the slightest idea of the daughter she referred to.

As The Baroness approached the exit to the office, Cirano held out his hand for a quick explanation. Though he was under their employ, Cirano attempted to view their working relationship as cordial. The Baron and Baroness were the pinnacle of success, and while Cirano did well for himself, he knew that he could be better. Accepting their offer was just a steppingstone for his own ambition, and he wondered what sacrifices they took to reach such a position. Cirano piqued The Baroness' interest as his tone changed from his next question.

"Your daughter, what's her name? Does she know about all this?" Cirano asked. Cirano had questions regarding this aspect. He always kept his criminal activity hidden from his remaining family, especially that of his father, and wondered how things would be different if he revealed that information.

"Why are you concerned? I'm not one to tell you how to bake a cake?" The Baroness asked as she turned to face him.

Jesus Christ, she gives me the willies. Cirano thought. He looked to quickly disarm The Baroness' suspicions.

"I'm just making idle conversation mam. Didn't think with your projects you had the time for that," Cirano commented as he noticed The Baroness nod in agreement.

"She doesn't know. Though, if it ever came to be, she'd laude me for it. After all, we keep the crime contained and the streets cleaned," The Baroness recounted as she turned to the door.

"I'm doing all the work, cunt." Cirano mumbled as he noticed The Baroness remain still. She turned her head and offered an unnerving glare. Cirano felt a chill come up his spine as he realized his error and hoped she hadn't heard.

"Hmm? Did you say something?" The Baroness asked, as she knew fully well he was disgruntled.

"No..." Cirano said with a shake of his head. The Baroness gave a passing grin before she headed out the doors. She gave an affirmative close to the doors and summoned a portal to vanish without a trace.

Left with his own thoughts, Cirano immediately threw the things off his desk in a rage. He was understandably upset about the lack of security in his own outpost, but to be disrespected in such a way gnawed at him. This wouldn't be the first time that Cirano had dealt with such treatment, but his solution for it would need to be different. In his former life, Cirano could just beat or kill his way out, but The Baron and Baroness were untouchable. He gathered his things off the floor and organized the table. Cirano started to go through the documents that held little appeal, but his interest grew as he saw the very back of the packet. He removed the paper clip that held the documents together as he was curious to find what was present. Cirano already grew annoyed as he saw that information was being hidden from him. He never felt more disrespected and now he wanted to find out everything there was.

"What the hell is this?" Cirano asked as he looked at a piece of paper covered with black marker. He held it up towards the light and noticed that some of the content was redacted. The Baron and Baroness hardly accounted for anyone else to read their documents on retrieval, as only specific sections of the paper were relegated for Cirano to read.

Not one to be outdone, Cirano was resourceful. Cirano ripped the last page off and placed a fresh sheet of paper on top. He grabbed a nearby lead pencil and slowly traced over the shaping of the letters that appeared on another piece of paper. The light from his desk slowly illuminated the remaining letters.

"The Portal Project..." Cirano mumbled as he continued to transcribe the details. Cirano's hands started to shake as he read more about The Baron and Baroness' observations regarding portal travel and the utility that came with teaching Rose her abilities. He was disturbed as he finally understood the extent of their presence. That cold feeling that emanated from both of his clients was unnatural. He was dealing with something otherworldly.

Is it true? These people can just... No. There's no way. I need some proof.

Cirano quickly saw an opportunity as he rubbed his hands together. Cirano looked over a series of photographs that were attached in a subsequent envelope embedded further into the packet. He was unsure of how The Baroness would have made such an error, but decided it was best to remain quiet. Cirano wondered if this information was a test of some sort as he looked around, subconsciously imagining the pair flanking him. Cirano raised an eyebrow as he noticed these images were in full color. He hadn't seen such clarity from a photograph before. He saw an image of Rose summoning both blue and purple portals with each hand

and wondered what it meant. An accompanying dossier was present with non-redacted text. This was a grave mistake left behind in the copious amounts of documents under the watch of The Baroness regarding her experimentation. The Baroness wrote her notes in English for The Baron to read, as it was his first language, despite knowing several others.

"Subject R-26 had shown increased proficiency in blue portals. Moving from place to place will be easy. Purple portals still need much work. Other worlds exhaust subject and food is required as catalyst. Hypothesis: This is likely not needed when under duress," Cirano read further.

Though The Baron and Baroness were out of his yoke as his current employer, Rose remained a curiosity for the mobster. She was an easy face to recognize, the two interacted briefly, and she was now the favorite of The Baroness. If someone with the ability to conjure a universe from will was under his control, he could use it to wrestle control from anyone and be his own man. Cirano realized that done correctly, he could become a literal god without trying. Cirano was a creative man when the time came, and he wondered of all the possibilities that could be achieved with such raw power. Cirano gave a low laugh to himself as all he needed to do was play the lapdog for now and his time to strike would come later.

"Oh, this is something special. If this is the case, then I could simply bide my time and wait for that little girl to come by once again. I'll get things prepared but for now... I need to figure out who got the location of this place. Someone's gonna croak for this." Cirano cracked his knuckles.

New York's Finest

In New York City, Venus was the only one who stayed behind after the women's venture for Rose's birthday. It'd been months by now. While the others scrounged together money to return to their jobs back in South Carolina before they were swept up by new hires, Venus remained as she found a new calling. She was able to secure a place of her own after landing a job as a greeter at the American Museum of Natural History and took a generous loan from a family member to make ends meet. She stood at the steps of her tenement housing and her mind drifted to Rose.

I know that girl's got herself somethin' going on, but I wish I knew. I wrote letters to home but nothing's arrived here. Where could she be? Venus thought. Venus walked down the busy avenue as she took in the sights of the big city. For a long time, she hadn't imagined how much there could be in this city, but even the sprawling felt small as she weaved past crowds of people that gave no heed to her existence. She found herself in a cavern of conformity with all the pressed suits of the men and carbon copy designs of the women accompanying them. Venus felt a slight daze as she wafted through the smog, where the uplifted skyscrapers looked over her. The calm of the South was ripped apart by a blast to the ears of street peddlers, crashed cars, and arguments of those standing around.

Venus felt herself brushed by someone and felt her once strapped purse now missing. She turned around and saw just the back of their head. It was a man with a newsboy cap that ran through the crowd with a hearty elbow as Venus came shortly behind him. Venus was well aware of the risks, but what little remained of her money was in there. She rushed past, knocking over people in a fit of rage. She nearly slipped on an upturned slab in the ground. As she got a closer look, she grew even angrier as the man that robbed her was also black. Of all things, why her? She knew why, the police wouldn't give a damn and she looked like an easy target.

"Thief!" Venus yelled out, as a few patrons standing by saw the scene. Her resourceful thinking led a kind woman to guide Venus on where the man went, and she pursued. Although Venus felt the tide change, she felt far less confident as she noticed her thief had an accomplice, this time armed with a crowbar. Nobody was willing to get involved, and she knew she'd have to surrender her money.

"You've got a lot of nerve runnin' your mouth like that. I can take some teeth out and leave home with a little extra, hmm? What say you?" the man with the crowbar threatened.

Just down the road, a group of steel workers closing out for the day made their way home. Their iconic yellow helmets stood out from the sea of gray and brown that accompanied them. A few hardly considered themselves vigilantes, but they cared about the city and community they lived in. One of these men broke away from the pack as they headed home to see the lost Venus. Thieves were a known entity and often preyed on the wives of those that worked long hours. Nothing was better reprieve to the steel workers after working a long day than to deliver a well-earned beatdown. The tense situation was broken by the presence of one man who held a pickaxe from splitting coal.

"Who the hell do you think you are? You stupid or something?" the man shouted as he held the pickaxe. Venus turned around to see her temporary savior as she quickly moved away. The man gave a low whistle to signal to any other listeners nearby of what was happening. The robber that threatened Venus felt a cold rush come over them.

"Y-You know what, this isn't worth it. Take your damned money," the pickpocket said. He looked behind him to make sure he could make a quick getaway. The man vanished without a trace and the steelworker wiped his dark face with the back of his hand.

"Thanks for the tough break there. I've got just a couple of dollars to my name. I just feared that pickpocket was going to do a lot worse. I'm Venus. Yours?" Venus said with a handshake as she grasped her savior's hand.

"Yeah, I'm glad that worked. They've been causing trouble for weeks, but I know they're scared because they started robbing white folks too," the man said. He shook her hand slowly and paused as he knew the name sounded familiar.

"Malcolm— " Malcolm said before getting cut off by Venus.

"Hargrave?" Venus questioned as Malcolm was shocked she knew his surname. Malcolm looked around to make sure nobody else heard him before speaking further.

"Well... yes. If you know my name, then you must be Rosie's Venus. Not many of us with that sorta name. The sister planet that orbits her world, as she told me," Malcolm said. Venus covered her mouth in embarrassment at such a cute nickname for her. Venus knew better than to eavesdrop on Rose's letters, but she just had to be nosy.

"Actually, this isn't the first time I saw you. I saw you at the library last week, if you're anything like Rose, they are hiring you know."

"Yeah, I already told you I was broke but I have a job. It's honest work, but I was trying to use the phone in there to call for anything. I can't go back home, and I haven't been able to contact Rose at all. I have to do something." Venus said in dismay.

"Well, I do get letters from her. One came from... Arizona? I couldn't believe it, but I saw that frilly handwriting and knew it had to be her. Look, I'm off the clock. Let's grab something and kill time. We might have to walk some though before we can find a place. Relax, I'll buy," Malcolm reassured Venus with a wink.

"What's the deal with that woman who runs the library anyway? I saw a tank crew that was laxer than her," Venus joked as she heard Malcolm sigh.

"Yeah, that's Tasha. I wanted to get a book on dinosaurs, Rose was telling me all about those in the last few letters, so I could catch up. Lost my library card and she refused to hand out a new one. I press steel for a living, it gets covered in ash! Though, she's not all prickles and thorns. She runs a speak, you know," Malcolm mentioned. As the pair walked, Malcolm took the side of the street while Venus was able to walk in the interior of the piece.

"You'd think after I fixed the radiator, I'd get at least a discount. Guess I can't blame her, I'm not the main clientele after all," Malcolm lit a cigarette from his pocket. He shook it slightly as the end had a clump of tar on it from the mill. Venus' expression remained confused as Malcolm spoke. Venus hadn't paid much attention prior, but she found that Malcolm seemed to have a fairly hushed accent compared to her own. He spoke with his own idioms that eluded her and was hardly one to have a drawl or speaking style like that of home.

"You've been in the city how long and you don't know about Tasha's? Look, skinny is, it's a bar for women by women. She does serve men, only in the daytime though. I'm that guy, so I usually can get a few stiff ones at a decent price. If that's your thing, go by after hours and see her there. Just be sure you can handle your liquor. I don't see you hauling steel like me any time soon Venus," Malcolm laughed.

"Now how does one happen to find this establishment, hmm?" Venus asked as she sized Malcolm up. She stepped closer to him as she felt safe in his presence. A sigh of relief came over her some as Malcolm seemed like a genuine soul. Though, her curiosity was at its peak as she had the source of Rose's affection right in her presence. She wanted to inquire some about Rose's writings and their subsequent relationship. Rose held an idealistic perspective in just about anything she did, and Venus wondered how much this reflected reality.

"It's not a cakewalk, I can tell you that much. Though since we share a mutual interest, let me help you out and take you there. I've got a few hours before I'm supposed to head out to greener pastures. You're going to want to find a door that ain't a door. It looks like a furniture cabinet. The bouncer stays outside the establishment and is leaned against the wall. He's a greaseball so you'll know you're close. The whole block is black otherwise. Mind you, Tasha's also has a password every week. Just hang around 10 PM at the end of the road, any will do, and look in the sky. If you see the moon, look for the phase and tell that to the bouncer. If there's nothing, say New Moon and you'll be golden," Malcolm explained as Venus nodded her head.

Malcolm and Venus continued to talk as they passed a number of streets and Malcolm's depiction of Tasha's establishment started to reveal itself. Venus raised an eyebrow as she looked for the apparent furniture cabinet door that was aligned next to a wall. Malcolm snapped his fingers to get her attention and nodded his head. It was still daylight out, so the pair were able to go in without any issue. The speakeasy was a humble establishment, and it was some time until the owner herself would make an appearance. The interior looked like a log cabin complete with a fireplace that wasn't lit. Wooden floors and chairs with rugs were an accompanying piece of the decor.

Venus saw that the walls were rubbed with a solution to give it a rustic smell that was appreciated by her nose. Low lit candles and lanterns above their heads projected an inviting glow that filled the room with an otherworldly sense of peace. A phonograph at low volume played the latest in smooth jazz, as Harlem was just down the corner and new artists were trying to get their sound heard. Tasha's was a place accompanied by both the poor and the rich, as even the occasional white actor or actress bothered to make an appearance through town. Venus and Malcolm sat on stumps covered with fine rugs, the smallest nooks were in the corners to provide privacy. The menu itself was also especially classy, with names of special cocktails after national parks.

Venus ordered straight vodka, which came as a surprise to Malcolm who tensed his fingers at the sight. He was a notorious lightweight among the rest of the men and palmed two beers that were doing their work. The two enjoyed the ambiance as a few early regulars came by. Venus waited a few moments for the drink to settle before she snapped the trap of a conversation.

"So, Malcolm. What's the skinny with you and Rose? Really. How come you never came and visited us? Hell, I feel half of our trek here was to meet you. You know, the man's supposed to be the pursuer, last I checked," she remarked as she sipped her drink. Venus mischievously knew she was burying into his skin a bit. Venus paid special attention to Malcolm's reaction and wondered how much was really happening between them.

"Look, are you—I like Rose a lot. I really do. It's just... there's so much going on. The mill, we might be going on strike soon and I'll be more broke than you. Though you know how strikes here get solved. The company just hires out the army and it's real bloody. Rose, she wants a lot, and so quickly. I send one letter and I get four in the mail." Malcolm rubbed the back of his neck. He grimaced slightly as he knew how fanatically Venus took care of Rose.

"Does she not deserve it?" Venus mentioned with a flair of defensiveness. She felt her hands clasp against the glass. She noticed that Malcolm saw this and took a deeper swig of his beer.

"The truth is really all I can give. She's done a lot for me, feelings-wise and all. It's difficult to accept that space when you've never had it. I go out in the world and I'm just some random nigga to these people, but when I talk to Rosie—I feel like the President. I have a job to do here, and I can't give Rose the life she wants, not like this. There's a lot I need to do first to get myself out of this rat race. I have to breathe before we both drown," Malcolm mentioned. Malcolm felt a tinge of insecurity in his own path. He was a competent worker and did his due diligence, but Rose had a variety of esoteric interests he hadn't ever heard of. All he knew was expenses and the prospect of giving someone else the same level of energy was a daunting task as work winded him down to a husk of a man. He found it compelling that his co-workers cited their families as their source of strength through terrible workweeks, but he could hardly find such a shine.

"These sound like excuses, Malcolm. Almost a year to make a choice seems simple to me. You seem like a pretty decisive fella," Venus remarked as she looked at her nails.

"I'm trying my hardest. Venus, let me ask you something. Genuinely, just you and I in the room. I know for a fact, you'd stab me with this fork if I broke Rose's heart like that. I just can't make promises like that. She thinks we belong together. What am I supposed to do, tell her to wait around until I don't live payday to payday? That could be years. The best should be for her, regardless of if it's me or not. For her to be loved and cherished. It'd be great if it was me, but I have to be realistic. She makes me gifts by hand and sends them in the post, gets me all sorts of little knick-knacks to put in my matchbox of an apartment. Nothing I can do would even match that," Malcolm said as he rubbed his temples.

"I don't think you understand how Rose works. She's accommodating to a fault. She'd crawl through broken glass rather than change course if she feels there's still a reason to keep going. It's a stubbornness that's both somewhat scary and inspiring all at the same time. She doesn't fall into this stuff easily, and now, you seem to be the subject. I like you Malcolm, and I'll give you this advice. As someone who knows women more than you ever will, whatever you choose to do regarding Rose, I'd make that decision with the utmost severity. If you do decide to cut her loose, I wonder what the future holds. You have no scorn from me or her friends of course, we're mature people, but she will rise to a height that eclipses any skyscraper. You don't have to be her rock, but you should be there if you feel something is there." Venus snapped her fingers for another drink.

The two shared another drink in silence for some time until Malcolm checked his watch and saw that the night crew was starting to arrive. Venus decided to end the night with Malcolm on a peace offering and gave him a tight hug before he left. Her night had just begun as she continued to stay and study the clientele. A bar made by women for women was an interesting prospect as she angled herself on a stump and enjoyed her half-drunk stupor. Venus' thoughts regarding where she was in the world were something she had time to develop, and she found that an atmosphere like this one is what she favored the most. It came in stages, she found that the touch of a woman provided more fulfillment than what she'd seen for others. She felt compelled in the confines of her old life to at least entertain men, but now she could bypass that entirely, and build a tight network.

Venus had incredibly powerful charisma as she was able to weave her way into getting free drinks by singing, something she only done on occasion at work. Now without the expectation, she could do it whenever she wanted. Her attention was brought by one particularly wealthy woman who remained as low-profile as a rich person could be. Venus saw a shorter woman with bronzed skin and captivating brown eyes. She usually favored red but wore a solid sapphire dress that trailed behind her, along with light brown hair that reached past her shoulders. Her headband held a singular rose. She was captivated by the woman's entrance and needed to know if her thoughts were true.

This has to be her. I must be dreaming. The Baroness of Baroness Gems & Ends? Here!? In this bar, with me in it? Venus thought. Venus assumed her mind was playing tricks on her. She boldly went over and addressed her with an open hand. The worst thing she could do was be briefly embarrassed by her mistaken identity.

"Mam, I must say, you have an exquisite taste in gems. The way the amethyst lines up with the pearls is reminiscent of the 1915 Summerset Edition! First, not Second. The Second had to be recalled because of war shortages to help the Allies! I'd recognize that design anywhere. Wait, are you!?" Venus said as she tried to cover her mouth but failed miserably. Venus could hardly believe her shock as she couldn't afford any of the gems she'd seen in magazines but could see them in her sleep.

"Yes, I'm her. Always nice to see a fan of my work. I hope you don't mind me intruding on this space. I just happened to be in town for an expo and wanted to get a good red before I return home to my husband. I have much work to do," The Baroness acknowledged.

"I-I'm Venus! I-If you need anything, ever in the city, please. Do not hesitate!" Venus stuttered as she grabbed the woman's hand. Venus noticed that The Baroness gave her a look of judgement that she hoped panned out to be in good fortune. To be evaluated by such a powerful influence was something not taken lightly.

"You... have a good soul Venus. I pray that it remains that way for those that depend on you," The Baroness mentioned as her attention was brought back to the barkeep. With the usual red wine as requested, the woman took a corner of her own and gave a nod to Venus in acknowledgment of their encounter.

Venus' interaction was more than enough to cause a stir as the owner herself raised an eyebrow from the opposing end of the room. This attention was kept periodically as the hours of the speakeasy started to wane in activity. Only the most dedicated regulars remained now at the bar while many packed up shop and stumbled home. The cities were a dangerous place at night, let alone daytime, but a system was put in place to make sure the inebriated arrived home without issue. Tasha remained a curious witness to such an interaction. This mysterious visitor was among the richest in the area and yet, this random person caught her attention. There needed to be more and she was bound to find it one way or another.

"I'm surprised. The Baroness never talks to anyone here, but she gave you a full conversation. What's special about you?" Tasha asked as she leaned closer to Venus. The scent of whiskey on her breath was more than enough to tell Venus she could still feel adventurous.

"You must be Tasha. I can tell you about it as I was looking to talk to the owner some about the area. Let's say I'm new here. Interested?" Venus asked with a raise of her eyebrows. Tasha looked over at the nearby rack with a faux fur coat that called out to the pair. The night could be frigid and doubling up was common.

"I'll grab my coat."

Museum Madness

Rose stood awake on her bed as her eyes slowly drifted over to the necklace given to her by The Baroness. It'd been some time since she thought about it but studied its pulsating glow. The amethyst, once placed under her bed, produced an inviting light. She had been so occupied with her other tasks, she nearly forgot about the main assignment given to her, which was conjuring a portal with this device. With the chaos of the weekend finally coming to a close, she decided to invest this endeavor. She thought about what to do next. She clasped her hands over the gem.

I'm supposed to think of somewhere to go, and this will take me there? Just like that, I'll go wherever I want? Rose thought.

Rose had been trying to contact her friends for some time, and while she managed to contact Celia and a few others that were aware of the situation, Venus remained missing from her letters and phone calls. Rose knew that it couldn't have been intentional, but life makes all busy. Rose also thought that her own letters somehow failed the cross-country voyage to the Deep South. She decided that her target to conjure a portal was to find her friend.

Rose stepped outside away from the idle conversation of Cicero and Claudia to embark on her endeavor. Rose closed her eyes and clutched the conduit tightly. She felt a feeling like a developing sneeze as the surrounding area started to slightly contort. While Rose remained steady, the artifact in her possession did not react at all. Rose was doing this solely on her own will, as she was unable to make the artifact work by her touch. The amethyst's glow contained the ultimate price to make portal conjuration, gathered souls from various other worlds. A successful use of the artifact would have drained the amethyst of its hearty glow. Rose lacked the heart of a killer and could not make this bond happen, she found her own path instead.

Rose could hear the vortex generate in front of her as she slowly opened her eyes with a satisfied grin. Rose looked inside through the portal and noted the strange architecture. It seemed nothing like the buildings of home. Rose stepped through the portal and closed it behind her, the action almost second nature as she folded her fingers and the loop's hum vanished. She now found herself in a dimly lit room. Rose heard the strange sound of giggling, but the voice wasn't one she expected. Rose found herself in what appeared to be a kitchen in a low-lit tenement apartment. Rose was confused, her thoughts were on Venus, so why would she be in this place? It looked nothing like home. Did she make a mistake? Rose's thoughts were interrupted as she heard a scream from the other end of the room. A woman with nothing more than a bath towel on saw Rose's shadow from the room. With a flick of the light switch, Rose froze as the other woman pointed a finger in her direction.

"W-Who are you! H-How did you get in here?!" the woman frantically asked Rose. Rose bit her tongue in embarrassment. This was a perfectly valid question, as she pleaded for some grace. She had no idea how she could possibly explain her predicament. Her heart raced as she heard a second pair of footsteps and Rose nearly gasped as she saw Venus come up behind the other woman. The pair gave each other a surprised look. Venus' look was more of confusion as her apartment had two reinforced locks.

I clearly didn't think this through. I figured I'd be outside, of course, my hole is gone.

"V-Venus? This is... your house...?" Rose said as she looked around and back at Venus.

The situation at hand was embarrassing on its own for all parties, Rose averted her eyes to preserve the pair's modesty. She hadn't really thought she was breaking and entering, but it sure looked that way to the pair. Rose anticipated having to explain all that happened over the past couple of months past their separation, but not in this particular manner.

"R... Rose?! Let me get dressed and we-we should talk," Venus said as she left Tasha and Rose to look at one another. Rose could only give a slightly worried look as she evaluated the pair's relationship.

After what felt like an eternity from Rose's perspective, Venus shook her head and laughed nervously. She was fully dressed in a skirt while the pair walked down the stairs and sat on the outside stoop. There was nothing outside aside from the occasional car that passed by the pair. Rose took the left side while Venus took the right. The wait between the pair was palpable, Rose had gone through all this effort to find Venus and wasn't sure where to start. Venus scrounged around and saw a pack of cigarettes; she offered one to Rose, who accepted graciously, while Venus abstained. She took the lighter and watched Rose settle as both felt the cold stone beneath them.

"Well, as you can see, I got a bit of a different life now. What happened Rose? Where did you go? We were all worried sick." Venus opened.

"It's a very long story, but I can put it up. After we split off from those mobsters, some woman rescued me in a blue light and I know it sounds, ridiculous when I say it— " Rose spoke as she stopped suddenly.

"Speak with some pride honey, I'm still listenin', finish your tale." Venus commented. Venus could tell that Rose was different, if not slightly lost, as she stared into her brown eyes. She'd seen and experienced things without words.

"—but she dragged me through that hole, and I ended up actually in Phoenix, Arizona of all places. At the time I didn't know why, but she wanted me there for something. Now I know, we share this gift. I can make these holes appear, but some are blue, and others are— " Rose continued as Venus cut in.

"Purple?" Venus asked with a raise of her eyebrow.

"I saw a small glimpse of blue light from the edge of my bed when you came in. So, I knew you wasn't wasting my time. At the museum I work, I saw a light much like that, but it was purple. I don't know what it means." Venus answered Rose.

"You telling me you saw a purple light? Venus, that's what I do. I take care of all the bad things that come through those. Remember that dog that bit you? If I only knew back then what the hell I knew now. I'm a rough and tumble girl now and get paid to do it real quick like," Rose asked Venus as her eyes looked to her healed arm.

"Well, you've done well for yourself. That's a good thing. I like that. I know you wrote to Celia and the others, but you didn't get anything from me. I did find out where you were though. On account of meeting your Hercules, Malcolm don't live too far from here. He actually saved me some time ago from some hoods that didn't know better." Venus explained. Venus grinned as she could see Rose immediately light another cigarette to soothe her nerves. She knew Rose's mind had to be racing on how close she was.

"Though, I have my thoughts. I'll keep that to myself. All I'll say is that we had a nice conversation and reminded him that you are a very nice girl. I think he's a good listener, so don't worry about that." Venus winked.

"You're right, I wrote to the others. I wrote to you too, but I never got a letter from you, makes sense given where you're at now. I assumed you were busy; I didn't know you made a life for yourself here and all. I didn't wanna intrude, but who is that woman in your house? She wasn't dressed." Rose raised her shoulders. She attempted to save face. Rose was aware of the vitriol given by her parents regarding Venus in their small town, but realized very quickly it was an environment not worth keeping.

"Well. I'm not really sure how to word it, but Tasha's my lover. She's not really a label person, but she's sweet on me and treats me well. Maybe it's a bit early to call it that, but that's my life now." Venus explained. Her eyes looked towards the street rather than Rose. Rose knew better than to center the conversation around herself, given the sensitivity of the matter, but she considered herself Venus' best friend. It was a guttural reaction that came from her.

"You didn't tell me? Why?" Rose asked, her voice cracked slightly as her throat was dry. She rubbed the back of her neck as she didn't want to come off as needy or abrasive, but she felt left out in the cold.

"Rose, it's—I was going to, on the train, Celia was aware, but I still needed to figure stuff out. It's not that I don't trust you, I do more than anyone else. You came here, looking for me, specifically. I don't know how you found me at all, but you did, and I appreciate that. You know how our town is, all that dark stuff behind it. I wasn't afraid of you, you've always worn your heart on your sleeve. The girls helped me wherever they could too. I just wasn't sure if I could have my faith and my true love also. That's a hard struggle. Tasha doesn't believe in God; she thinks He left a long time ago for people like us. What do you think? As somebody not like me, but like me?" Venus commented. Rose remained quiet for a moment to process the answer to such a loaded question.

"Looking back, the timing don't matter. I'm just happy you feel today's the time to say so and with little ol' me. Oh Venus, I always knew you didn't pay attention in Sunday School. All you need is to know that God's love is everywhere. Don't matter one bit if you have honey or vinegar in your tank. The word of the prophet is all I care about, and He never said a word about that. That said, if He did, I think we'd have a good conversation." Rose opened her hand for Venus to grab it also.

"I feel safe with you Rose. Thank you. There's just one thing I need to ask you now. Remember how I said I worked at the museum not too far by? I'm a greeter there, but, sometimes I get to stick around at night, and I see things happening. I want you to get to the bottom of it, and hearing what you do, I think I can do it safely," Venus offered.

"I don't have my gun, but I guess that won't be an issue. What's going on?" Rose asked as Venus looked surprised. Venus hadn't considered Rose to be much of a sharpshooter, but growth came in all forms.

"Come with me and I'll explain everything," Venus mentioned as the two made their way to the American Museum of Natural History.

Rose and Venus walked past the bustling lights of the remaining skyscrapers that remained ever open. The pair arrived at the southern facade. Rose watched as Venus fiddled around and saw a loose brick that housed the museum's spare key. The custodial staff used it to get in and out of the growing institution as they cycled through washes and got supplies. As Venus opened the door, Rose's jaw dropped as she saw an incredible display before her. She walked in to see the design of a triumphal arch built in the Roman tradition. She looked like a lost child as Venus happily watched Rose bounce around looking at the various pieces of art and other exhibit pieces.

"Down there on the west side of the museum is Hall of The Age Of Man, a bunch of models of cavemen, things like that. You've got the planets up ahead, a bit boring if you ask me, and a bunch of other stuff. I'm not a tour guide, I just do greetings," Venus explained.

"So—What exactly did you need me to do Venus?" Rose asked as she looked at the miniatures on display.

"We've had a problem with our mummy. There's a lot of hearsay goin' on, but basically, these men in suits come by with a mummy, but it looks nothing like anything we've seen before. The archaeologist on staff says this person doesn't have any related Egyptian items at all, but we wrote the plaque to say that he did anyway. On the second floor—Oh no." Venus explained as she looked towards the staircase. Venus noticed that past Rose, noticeable piles of sand started to develop along the stairwell. Venus called over Rose to run towards her as the two looked in confusion. Rose saw the familiar streak of purple light fill the upstairs hallway.

"Venus, I need you to tell me what exactly is happening." Rose mentioned.

"At first, not much did. Things started moving around out of place, but our security guard at the time ended up missing. Gone, all there was left was a skeleton," Venus explained. Rose grumbled; she'd definitely be at a disadvantage without her pistol.

The museum was currently closed for renovations in the East Hall, so nobody was in danger yet, but the time to act was nigh. Venus recalled that after the purple portal appeared and closed itself off, she witnessed a beam of light jettison throughout the interior of the museum the second week she'd been here. It was concentrated on the tomb of the obscure mummy, but one smaller streak of light reflected into The Hall of The Age Of Man.

Rose and Venus climbed past the stairs to make their way to the Egyptology wing of the museum. The mummy was already in a rage, summoning small tornadoes of sand that buffeted the two women. The mummy's limbs unnaturally held in place as they slowly rotated back and forth in its attempts to move. Rose had no knowledge of hieroglyphs, nor did Venus, but within the glimpse of her eye, she noticed that the mummy summoned runes that materialized as it spoke. These same runes matched the documented ones written in the annals of The Baron and Baroness' library.

It's a full moon tonight! I shoulda known. This shit happens when the moon is at its peak. Rose thought.

Venus felt her heart jump out of her chest as she felt Rose grab her to a different section of the museum. The sound of thrown apart artifacts and priceless vases filled the area as the mummy went on its rampage. Rose felt a slight sigh of relief as nothing else seemed to have life in the museum other than the mummy, but the longer it continued to happen, the more trouble they'd have. She wanted to make sure the mummy didn't leave the confines of the museum. Rose signaled to Venus she had an idea. Rose called her over and asked if she had any access to the back rooms where things were held. She noticed that the museum pieces seemed to have weapons on display in the Corridor of Conquerors section, detailing an assortment of weapons.

"Those are just replicas, but we do have some real ones maybe in a room. What are you cookin' up honey?" Venus asked as she ducked to see a random vase tossed down the stairwell.

As the full moon reached its peak, a break of the glass came as a man lumbered down the hallway on the floor below Rose and Venus. He seemed confused by his surroundings but understood that this was now home. He was a short, but stocky man with a beard. He had an eye missing and held a club in one hand. The model once made of wax, resin, and other materials seemed to have life as much as anyone else around him. He looked as real as anyone else. His skin was bronze and looked as it if was baked by the sun, despite years in storage. He could even speak, though his call fell on deaf ears as none could understand him. He let out a low bellow that sounded like a moan more than anything else.

As Rose and Venus ventured downstairs to find the key to the backroom, the pair exchanged a glance as they saw broken glass on the floor. Venus ventured ahead first but let out a scream as she saw a missing and now broken exhibit from the west side of the hall. Venus turned her head to find the prehistoric man given life once again. Venus came to realize that whatever forces at play were making the mummy rise again, also seemed to have affected this exhibit as well. While the rest of the statues remained as they were, the primary model walked among the living.

"R-R-Rose! Come over here now!" Venus yelled as she heard the clack of Rose's feet against the smoothed floor. Venus shook in fear as she saw the man observing his surroundings. She looked to Rose and saw her calm which also soothed her as well.

"Oh, I know what he is. He's a Neanderthal. They're supposed to be a little thick in the head, maybe literally, but he doesn't seem so bad. Hell, he might want to help us out," Rose mentioned. She stood in surprise as the Neanderthal walked towards the pair. He pointed to their skin with a grin, it was as if he was aware of others like them once. The man spoke, which he abruptly stopped doing, as he saw the reaction of Rose and Venus absolutely befuddled.

"Well, he's not tryin' to kill us I guess. Maybe that big club can help somehow? If we can get you to the back room, there's some weapons from The War Museum we have on loan. Great War stuff, a bit odd to put modern things in a museum, but what do I know." Venus proposed.

Rose, Venus, and their new Neanderthal friend put their heads together to solve their predicament. He was enamored by the pair's clothing as he compared his own. He walked around the interior of the room and looked at the other statues with a sense of longing. It was obvious that he considered these kin somehow, but in what way? Rose hadn't thought something like that would even cross a caveman's mind.

"Should we give him a name?" Rose proposed as she watched the Neanderthal man eye a stuffed mammoth. He seemed to examine it and look in slight disbelief at how it was built. It looked off from his perspective. Rose found it amusing and wondered what someone who'd seen such an animal would think about how they built them.

"Rose!? We don't have time for that! We have to stop this thing, do whatever you need to do!" Venus said in a panic. Rose held out her hand and placed it on Venus' shoulder.

"Venus, it's just a little rude, he's gonna be helping us. I've been on several jobs solo, and I'll tell you this. For some reason, the mummy right now just wants to keep its own little space. It hasn't destroyed the roof or anything yet, so we got little to fear. For now. Anyway, I came up with a name. I like Gork," Rose said.

Rose let out a little whistle which got the Neanderthal's attention. Gork came by with the club in his hand as he attempted to give an idea of what his thoughts were. While Gork couldn't understand the others either, he attempted to use his hands and tapped the ground with his foot. Rose looked to Venus as the pair still needed to get to the back room with the shipments but had no idea where to start. Finding a spare key was easy enough for the entrance, but the valuable stuff was harder to find. The keys were usually kept on the curator's person, so there needed to be a way to get into the office. Rose followed Venus and looked behind her as Gork followed behind them silently. The trio approached a door that Venus believed to be the back room that she spoke about earlier. The handle of the door was a bronzed nub that faltered as they remained stumped. Rose attempted to jostle the door open. Rose knew that she could certainly use a portal to get through, but she remained ill-confident in her abilities. It was by sheer luck from her perspective that she was able to get here at all. There was still much practice to do.

Rose was happy to have Gork on board as he saw the two struggling to open the door. He looked at his club and waited for the pair to back away before using his strength to slowly smash the door handle past the hinges. Venus was impressed as she gently moved the door ajar for the three to enter. While Rose was focused on finding a tool, the room itself could be appreciated. The room itself was a stuffy enclosure filled with a layer of dust and grime that painted the floor. The drab tan and gray structure was a far cry from the streaks of color that were on exhibition at the entrance. The room held a collection of manuscripts and other tomes that hadn't been examined in the slightest, with a bounty of interesting artifacts exhumed from the latest archaeological digs of the day. Egyptomania was the call of the day, so most of the items inside were related to this region.

Without delay, Rose's eyes scanned for the best weapon for the job. Venus calmly grabbed Gork's arm and held him to stay. Rose found the promised Great War armory; these were working pieces that hadn't yet been trimmed down for presentation purposes. She saw an exposed gun nearby, Rose couldn't recognize the make, but an idea formed in her mind. She grabbed the bolt action rifle with a bayonet attached. Rose was only trained on pistols for the most part, but she wanted to experiment, and this was the only weapon around with ammunition located in a nearby crate. She had ten rounds and needed to make them count.

"You know how to use a gun like that?" Venus asked with some concern.

I don't, but I've seen Cicero do this a number of times. All I need to do is—Aha. That's it. Rose thought as she nodded her head in confidence to Venus' statement.

The three exited the room as Rose took great care of the weapon. She was surprised at the rifle's heft for what it was, but it would be their saving grace. Rose remembered the rising sand tornadoes generated from the mummy but found that they now favored a new strategy as they headed up the staircase. The being summoned sand golems that slowly lumbered over to the trio from the end of the hallway. Gork ran ahead with his club and engaged with one of them, swiping hard and dismembering the pillar of sand to the floor. He quickly saw the futility in such an endeavor as the rest of the sand quickly built itself up but served to be an effective distraction. As Rose approached closer, the mummy started to summon more runes that were visible in the air. Rose shot the gun first and missed entirely as she felt her ears ring from the sound. She felt the impact of the rifle dig into her shoulder as she adjusted her position. The heft of the rifle worked in her benefit where she used it to offset her reaction to the recoil.

"Rose! The mummy is guarding some sorta object?" Venus called out as she hid behind a pillar and pointed. Venus had a sharp eye as she noticed that amid the mummy's destruction, there was a short reveal of a tan-colored gem embedded inside of it.

Rose continued to shoot as Venus called out an opening. As Rose adjusted her aim, the bullets pierced through the mummy and the detached limbs also melted to sand. It was a mind-boggling experience as the pair tried to figure out what was happening. Gork saw an opportunity as Rose looked to aim for the strange gem lodged in the center. The caveman gave a mighty yell that distracted the mummy as he lifted his arm and tossed the club. The impact of the throw and the device was enough to knock it off center. The formerly levitating mummy fell to the floor and its summoned sand golems evaporated. Venus watched Rose take the initiative as she used the bayonet to stab the mummy through the back. The precious gem, that was all worth this fighting, was knocked away and the sand started to vanish. The mummy withered to nothing more than a few wrappings left behind. Venus felt a sigh of relief but also grave concern at the wreck of the museum.

"This gem? The hell is it?" Venus asked, as Rose raised an eyebrow of concern. Rose remembered that The Baroness hired her to help find a similar looking gem, but one she called The Frost Gem. She wondered if this was part of a set or something greater.

For some reason, Rose felt compelled to touch it, but she decided to refrain. Gork held the gem in his hands with a gentle pose as he neared Rose and Venus with the object. The tan glow that emitted from it was now inert. Rose assured Venus that this wasn't her mess to deal with and to get home as soon as they could. Gork remained sentient under the moon's power, but once day returned, he would once again be part of the statues. Rose and Venus gave their good-byes to their new Neanderthal friend as he went back to his holding place. Rose and Venus exchanged a tight hug at the museum's entrance and as they did so, a blue portal appeared. Rose made her way and was set to return to her dwelling in Phoenix with all she learned.

The Sitdown

N iccolo sat in the car as he was accompanied by Bill and two other men that served as his personal guard. It was a somber moment for the outfit as Andrea was in critical condition from a drive-by the previous day. A few of the other gangsters stayed behind as family admittance to oversee his visit as protection, in case anyone came forward to finish the job. The police walled off a section of a nearby street to investigate the current crime while Niccolo waited. Shards of glass and overturned bullet casings were collected by the growing number of officers. Niccolo felt uncomfortable as he skated by from the efforts of the overworked police force. He looked out the window of the vehicle and noticed one of the men exit the facility and rush towards the car. He rolled down the window and motioned for the man to deliver the news directly to his ear so that the others were spared. Niccolo had just received word regarding his new position as acting underboss in Andrea's condition.

"How did this happen to begin with? I was busy with an errand," Niccolo voiced to his subordinates.

"Can you believe it boss? Nearly forty-thousand people in this city and we've managed to piss on the shoes of everyone," Bill mentioned.

"Well—Thing is, from what I'm aware of, it started wit' those fucking paddies not knowing their place. They had something going on with The Owl and his crew and the boss got caught in the mix. No respect, he takes two shots right in the chest. Praise the Lord above he's still standing. Things will be alright, right?" Frank explained.

Frank was a shorter man compared to Bill and Niccolo, he served as the outfit's tax collector but started to find himself within Niccolo's inner circle. Frank knew how to keep his mouth shut compared to the others and didn't pry into affairs often. Niccolo counted on him to distribute proper payment to the men, and he remained airtight under pressure from lawmen. He was in his early fifties and wore thick glasses that drew attention from his oddly youthful, slicked back hair that was a dark brown.

"Thank you, Frank," Niccolo commented as Bill didn't answer his question at all. He placed his hand to his temple as he relayed directions for Bill to drive.

Niccolo's time spent with Rose and the others conflicted heavily with his time at the mine. Niccolo, much like Cirano, opted to give the men autonomy as they knew the city and related territories better than anyone else. Niccolo felt a sense of guilt as he neglected keeping an eye on the boss, where the reality was he still remained green on the field. A shot like this is what Niccolo feared the most as the fallout from the don's nephew was going to be catastrophic. Niccolo was hardly prepared for a war on his hands, but his outfit would be an embarrassment if action wasn't taken quickly. Niccolo looked at his hands. He had spent a great deal of effort shaking down those that had any dealings with Florence's uncle as he agreed to do for her. Much like The Baron, Florence's uncle found himself embedded in the rail industry as a mogul looking to get a quick buck. Niccolo found it fulfilling work as he trailed businessmen from the shadows and dragged them to the darkest subsections of the city for questioning. He also needed to keep tabs on his primary purpose of assassinating The Baron for the bounty. A lot of important people depended on his efforts and the pressure was mounting on him. Niccolo punched the dashboard in irritation.

I have to attend this meeting in Andrea's place, and I don't know the first thing about this... There must be blood for this if no answers are given. Niccolo thought. Niccolo thought about a plan of action but soon fell asleep as he felt the bumps of the road.

Sometime later, Bill's stop of the car jolted the other guards awake as they kept their guns handy. Bill pointed out a growing mass of people that were parked in front of other cars. From what he could tell, they were gathered for a while. On a closer look, Bill could see representatives from all the other factions that had a hold on the city. He saw the Irish and Sicilians, hooded Klansmen, and lastly the Mexicans and Mormons in heated discussion. Bill took a deep breath as he anticipated this would be a long day. Niccolo echoed this sentiment as he wiped off some drool that leaked to his suit. In the growing group of individuals that arrived, Niccolo exited the car flanked by Bill and the other associates with their weapons. Niccolo found a niche to step forward and remained quiet as he surveyed the arrangement of opposing men.

"This man calls us all here and has the audacity to show up late, bah! The Church would never stiff anyone in such a manner," one of the Mormons mentioned as he dusted some dirt off his suit. A few of the other faction representatives shared the same resentment as they wondered what was going to happen.

A lone car sped off in the distance that gradually grew larger as the men dispersed to give room. Niccolo was aware that Cirano had to have been involved as his crew was currently missing from the arrangements and looked around to see if there was a trap of some sort. The land surrounding them was nothing but flat desert, a sniper's glint would be easy to spot from such a vast distance. Niccolo kept his composure as the others in his outfit started to talk among themselves. Niccolo raised an eyebrow as he met Cirano's eye through the glint of the lowered window. The opportunity Niccolo was waiting for was here. He had all the evidence he needed to bring Cirano to task and hopefully enact some concessions out of him for the bloodshed. Niccolo watched as a few other men emerged from the car. The last man to exit the vehicle was The Baron himself. Niccolo covered his mouth in surprise at the reveal. His suspicions were racing as he met eyes with the man. The cacophony of the others surrounding him stopped immediately as the man in black emerged and clapped for their attention.

"Hello all. I'm Archibald Conway. Some of you may know me as The Baron. I've gathered you all here today because I am to establish a working peace for the time being. Heed my directive." The Baron adjusted his tie.

For many, including Niccolo, this was the first time they ever witnessed The Baron directly. Cirano and a few of his associates surrounded The Baron with smug grins as all the attention was placed on them. As the man running the show, The Baron's aura was imposing as he guided attention with the utmost authority. Any breath out of place was met with a soul-melting gaze that cut through the gangsters. The Baron's demeanor was a living contradiction. He exuded intimidation but was incredibly amicable as he organized the list of grievances that were held to those that remained. This was a peace mission rather than a declaration of war, and so The Baron offered respect with the tip of his hat. Niccolo knew right away why he needed to die. His cunning mastery to weave the factions to perpetual warfare and to stop it by will was enough to disrupt any plans for his organization making in-roads. Niccolo's ire was reserved mostly for the smug Cirano, who looked at the other gangs with disdain for his time being wasted. Niccolo would bide his time to wait and then make it known that he was ready.

It's really him. Perhaps this was intervention that put me on the path. I have a gun on me, and I can see his face and yet I am unable to shoot. The Baron does not know I am to kill him and yet he traps me. Niccolo kept his eyes trained on The Baron's mannerisms. Niccolo's attention was taken by the Klansmen who he had experience with earlier. He wondered if these were part of the same group that he and Cicero gunned down.

"Now hold on now Archibald! We were next. I recall last sitdown you gave those border hoppers over there, rail exclusivity up until 1927, south of Tucson? I demand we have full exclusive rights of the zone. We're bleeding over here! We've got a majority in the state legislature and we're shipping citrus that goes on your rail! You want my advice? I suggest you start listening or there's gonna be problems," one of the Klansmen mentioned. The Baron scoffed at the attempted insubordination before him.

"I take no advice from those with family ties so tight you can use them as rope. Use it to hang yourself if you address me with such a tone again. It's already within the city's charter that Negroes and other non-white races are not allowed to buy property north of Van Buren. A vote I helped arrange for your cooperation. You've caught me in a good mood, so I will allot your group a toll booth under my permit for an exchange rate of 5%, no lower or higher," The Baron dismissed with a raise of his hand.

Cirano enjoyed the unfolding drama. Cirano had his opinions regarding the factions, he got along with the Mormons best given his childhood upbringing. He knew how they worked and the products that they appreciated purchasing. They were reliable customers and made capable trading partners, but this was The Baron's decision making of who earned what. The Mexican drug trade was growing with various generals feuding over portions of territory. Niccolo had the foresight to reach out early and maintain relations with smaller lords which came in dividends for his cause. Cirano knew that The Baron was also a visionary, as he could acquire surplus arms from the United States government that embedded its hands into Mexican affairs. The Baron could hardly care about foreign politics, but he couldn't resist being a diplomat if it filled his ambitions.

"As for us—The Owl and his outfit killed one of our leading men! Fucking kids died in broad daylight! Where's your heart, we want tribute for this Archibald!" one of the Irishmen declared as he raised a fist. Niccolo nodded his head in a rare showing of solidarity. Cirano's outbursts against those he perceived as competition constantly were an uproar against those that wanted to achieve balance. Cirano weaponized the police force to protect his image and used them to such an extreme it caused resentment from the other factions.

"I will allot you a sum of ten thousand dollars for a non-aggression pact. This will let you bury the bodies and pay for the funerals. This is more than a sufficient sum considering your group's antics overseas. Consider this a mercy, I have contacts in the British Empire that would benefit from such important information regarding your families," The Baron threatened as the men meekly nodded in acceptance of this agreement.

Niccolo hardly was a patient man, but he knew better than as an upstart to interrupt the chain of command. Niccolo eyed the rest of the groups and reassured his men that their concerns would be met. Eventually, The Baron looked to see if all parties were addressed as his eyes reached the absent Niccolo. The Baron snapped his fingers as he urged Niccolo to speak loudly and clearly.

"You. Come forward. What will bring your party to peace? I understand your branch is minuscule here, but the European market is another matter. Is it money you seek?" The Baron mentioned.

"I don't want your money. I want him to be accountable. My underboss, Andrea, was shot by your subordinate. The wound is fatal." Niccolo mentioned to The Baron as he pointed a finger directly to Cirano. Cirano's eyes sized up Niccolo as he held a further smug expression.

The Baron raised an eyebrow at Niccolo's response. This was an intriguing one as he didn't expect such a blunt and simplistic answer. The Baron laughed at the folly of youth and felt somewhat impressed that Niccolo felt his own earnings would be more than enough to support him. A more serious matter entered The Baron's thoughts, however, as he looked to Cirano to explain himself. Cirano was already proving to be a liability as his temper was hard to control. He'd already claimed the life of one faction leader and while the Irish were easy to bribe, he knew Niccolo seemed to have a burning integrity. The worst kinds of people to negotiate with were those that were arrogant and those that had a goal larger than themselves.

"I-didn't do a damn thing. Though, I understand why you're mad. If blood is what you want..." Cirano teased. He withdrew his pistol and aimed it at Niccolo. Cirano stepped forward as he saw Bill move close to Niccolo with his shotgun prepared.

It was considered terrible form to openly display a firearm during a sitdown, but Cirano cared little for social convention. He was used to being the boss and operating under The Baron's heel started to wear out its welcome as the two came to disagreement on presentation. The Baron was cold and calculating when it came to business, while Cirano reacted solely off instinct. Niccolo felt his heart race as he stood his ground while the other men watched in intrigue. Cirano gave a wink and slowly moved his arm to the direction of his lieutenant's head and shot him dead on the spot. The crack of the gun rang through everyone's ears as they remained quiet at the outburst. The man fell flat to the sand as the weight of his body made a thump. A trail of blood leaked from the exit wound on the side of his head. The viscous solution melded into the desert sand to produce a disgusting rustic mix. Cirano's insistence on this was the knowledge that the man's sheer incompetency to control his own route is what led to the death to begin with. The eyes of the remaining men turned to The Baron to see how he would react with his meeting derailed by Cirano's shortsighted judgement. Cirano wiped his suit clean of the blood.

"What the?" Another man yelled as he brought out his revolver. He nodded his head as others followed suit; their guns pointed at their respective enemies.

The Baron was the only one who refrained from drawing their weapon as he scanned the crowd. He remained perfectly calm due to his knowledge that this was just showmanship. The Baron didn't need to concern himself with hapless bravado that the men required to prove themselves worthy to the other. He crushed a small pebble beneath his shoes as his frustration started to show.

"Cirano, I have no time for your games. This is business. Let the adults talk," The Baron lectured. Cirano shot The Baron a look at his reprimand but bit his tongue as he did so.

"Now, I understand we have a bit of a disagreement. Let me remind you, I have a railway that needs to be completed by the end of the year and I intend to make my due. Given the need to prepare for things at home, I've decided to replace your workers on my project with an import of Chinamen. Twice the labor for half the cost, that's just business." The Baron dictated. He felt a slew of complaints as every faction now was further annoyed with losing competition to growing Chinatown in the center of Phoenix. The Chinese gangs were more established in California than Arizona and lacked a real presence, making it open season for any upstarts to try to muscle in.

"We additionally need to do something regarding the monsters that have been attacking. We all read the papers here. Ignorance gets us nowhere. These strange entities are interrupting our flow of capital. War is not profitable right now for any of us. Focus on maintaining your domestic supply and eliminate the monsters as they come. I will contact you again when the weather is fair... if you catch my drift," The Baron declared.

The Baron received the silent nods of his guests as the meeting was declared over with the final word. Without anything more, the disgruntled parties who earned some and lost some were never truly satisfied. It was in The Baron's best interest to keep everyone just on the edge of their sanity. The influence that The Baron had kept a tight leash so that no faction could truly expand more than their piece of the pie, and each one remained subservient. The men poured out in increments as they waited for their respective rivals to leave. A flurry of glares and scowls accompanied them as they retreated to their territories.

Niccolo and his group were the last to leave as he stood with his back to the car. Bill and Frank flanked Niccolo on each side as they lowered their heads to hear the next move. Niccolo remembered a statement that Rose made some time ago. He and Cicero shared a common enemy in The Baron, and this extended to Cirano as well. Niccolo recalled that while his pride and distrust were what originally led him to work on his own, there was utility in working together. Cicero had the entire backing of a small town that he grew up in, but he needed to earn his trust fully.

Each of the denizens were rugged, hardened, and most importantly, armed criminals that Niccolo felt could be disposable. He needed to construct a united front against Cirano's forces. If he could stage the battlefield to be this small town, Niccolo could easily draft the people to assist in his war and he would be free to pick up the spoils. Niccolo knew their time was over, so it was a matter of picking which master they could have. He felt he'd be merciful and could provide something new at the behest of Cicero's concerns. Niccolo was ignorant about which groups found themselves allied with Cirano; his offensive personality made it difficult to make lasting deals, but unpredictability was dangerous.

"We've done enough today. We should regroup for now and talk with the rest of the men. They will need to hear this," Niccolo mentioned. He waved his hand for Bill to drive the car and head back to town. As they were on the road, Frank opened discussion as Bill gave them both a worried look from the driver's seat.

"What do we do, boss, if Andrea dies? That looked bad," Frank commented. He twiddled his thumbs as he knew the outcome regarding the war but wanted to see what Niccolo would do. Niccolo was not yet Underboss by the branch, but in the eyes of their current family, he was their best bet.

"At this rate, not if, but when. We can't sit idle and let them make a mockery of us. War is coming, but I'm going to need help," Niccolo declared as he looked out the window.

The car approached the city limits and soon made its way to the hospital. Niccolo already felt a grave feeling in his heart as he saw the sullen heads of the men that waited outside the hospital. Niccolo needed no verbal confirmation that Andrea died of his wounds, two .45 caliber bullets shot clean through, and it was a miracle he survived this long. He'd been chewed out before for mismanagement, but the death of Andrea was going to be something difficult to get through. He needed to bring something big and fast. Niccolo's resolve sharpened as he realized he could give his superiors back home the best gift they could ask for, Cirano's business. Countless customers came by and were a revolving door of profit. Niccolo wanted the man's head for himself, and he would do anything he needed to get it. He also considered The Baron's warning regarding the monsters that be, and he felt it was his time to truly do his part. In due time, he would go home and tell Cicero that he was ready to help with the next monster hunt.

Teaching Takes Time: I

Under Cicero's nose in the dead of night, Rose's rebellious streak led her to the hand of The Baroness once more. For her safety amid the growing gang war, Rose was rarely let out of the house at night aside from being on the job. Although she knew the dangers of her life, she felt restricted and with her growing masteries of her gift, it was only a matter of time. The pair had a favored dimension that the two would meet to harness her training of traversing other universes. Rose learned how to conjure this one on her own with assistance, but struggled to envision other landscapes just yet. It was an empty field with a singular large tree that had massive roots that spread throughout the landscape.

The leaves gave a subtle blue glow as the wind blew in the distance. It provided ample shade and remained perpetually in dusk as it was just light enough to practice. The Baroness waited as promised, wearing an elegant nightgown that accompanied the timing of their meeting. The Baroness stood at the base of one of these large roots and waited as she saw the frame of Rose gradually appear in her vision. In the times that she was unable to appear, The Baroness would leave a journal with instructions at the base of the tree and a checklist that Rose was to fill out upon completion.

"It would seem you and I both had to sneak out?" Rose casually asked The Baroness as she teased her outfit.

"I couldn't sleep. Sometimes, I have these night terrors that keep me awake. I've had them for centuries, so I don't think they vanish anytime soon," The Baroness mentioned. Her posture remained ever poised as she waited for Rose's response. She could tell Rose grew much more comfortable with their dynamic, which is what she wanted the most out of her.

"There's monsters out there that thrive on that sort of thing you know, wanting to enter your mind as you sleep. I took on a Conscious Consumer some time ago that was bothering Claudia. Who'd think some flour would do the trick?" Rose mentioned. The Baroness' still expression gave Rose a moment to collect her thoughts and explain the process.

"Conscious Consumer. I-I come up with names for the things you told me to document, do you not like it?" Rose asked in a slight panic. Rose always had to be perfect in the confines of her old life. Mistakes were something that were punished harshly, and this sentiment carried with her to most avenues. She didn't pride herself as a perfectionist but knew that the deck was stacked against her from birth. She had to impress and excel if only to be given a passing glance.

"Interesting. A personal touch to ensure the job is done well is always appreciated. Now, I noticed you seem to have news in your heart," The Baroness mentioned. Rose's reluctance on the situation was known as she unconsciously tucked her lip in, trying to dodge the issue. Her adventures with Venus opened a new perspective to her current occupation, but she also needed to discuss important affairs in the city.

"Before we begin training, could we talk about some things? It's been some time. I've had questions for a while, and your reluctance to answer them recently gives me some pause," Rose opened truthfully.

"You are my daughter... in a metaphorical sense, of course. You can tell me anything," The Baroness offered with an open hand and warm smile. Rose felt a tinge of discomfort at her statement, but suppressed this to the best of her ability. The issue of her own parents remained a sensitive subject.

"I heard there was a string of murders in town, and you were seen in the area for at least two. What's up with that? Are you in danger? Is someone after us? I need to know what we're up against to keep you safe," Rose asked. The Baroness felt a tinge of surprise come up her back. She opted to keep a distinct separation from her underground activities when it came to Rose. She feared that Rose's kind heart would supersede her desires to learn her powers and enact her plans.

"Oh Rose. It's my job to keep you safe. You must learn to develop your abilities, that is all I need you to do. An unfortunate reality of someone in my position is that they think they can reach my husband by targeting me. These are nothing more than political rivals that want to get a rise out of him. I assure you, I am safe, and there is nothing more to talk about on this matter. Given all you know, if anything, I am the danger." The Baroness squeezed Rose on the cheek. She let Rose continue her questions, she found intellectual engagement essential to the process. The Baroness liked that Rose could question her surroundings and what she saw to a degree. She wanted a protégé and eventual partner, not a lapdog that offered little perspective.

"I also thought about what you told me when we first talked about the gift. You said you killed the others of yourself... What were they like? To meet someone who's you, doesn't that seem odd? Why would they attack you?" Rose asked. The Baroness smiled, as it was obvious that Rose was trying to reassure herself of her goodness. It was an admirable trait, but The Baroness knew that Rose would have to embrace the darkness to succeed.

"I'm certain there were others that had the same idea, I was just the best one. In truth, most were awful, sniveling, and too privileged to be of any use to my ambitions. They were not... the circumstances of my upbringing... and they did not evolve in the same way I am now in the twentieth century. You may see it as greed, but I see it as a necessary evil for stability. For clarity Rose, I'm not speaking of eugenics where purging the weak is seen as an ideal, but a far more pragmatic solution for the stability of the worlds we travel in freely. There are others of you, those that I thought that held promise... You have a good heart, who's to say the other Roses do? Hmm?" The Baroness reasoned.

"I'm a bit worried about traveling into the city for my other work. I keep my ears to the papers, and I hear that Cirano's men are making progress in the gang war. A girl like me, with all those eyes and ears trained on me? They've been proper-so far, but something gives me the willies. Hard to believe that such a kind looking baker is really wicked, but it's true that the brightest flowers are the deadliest," Rose mentioned as she locked eyes with her. She studied The Baroness' reaction.

So, she knows that Cirano is The Owl. I wonder how much else she knows? Clever, she'll reveal that to me in time. The Baroness thought.

"Cirano is... an interesting man. I know little of his background, but I am aware he seems to be related to the violence that's threatening the city. The mobs favor his location. My hands are tied as far as that situation goes. Say the rumors are true, if he endangers you in any way, I can gather resources that will make—Do we understand each other?" The Baroness commented as she cut herself off. Seeds of doubt started to enter Rose's mind regarding The Baroness' ignorance of the mob activity going on, but she remained cheerful in front of the woman. The Baroness cut their discussion short as their primary focus was on their lesson for the night.

"Before we begin. I noticed you arrived late last time we met, but I said nothing of it. Try not to do that again. You are aware my time is precious," The Baroness chided Rose. Rose humbly lowered her head in acknowledgment of her error.

"I apologize. This was not meant in disrespect, I met with Venus-I told you about her, and things took a little long. There was a mummy, and some sort of gem dropped from it when I defeated it. It wasn't the thing you hired me for, so I gave it to the museum to examine," Rose mentioned.

The Baroness felt the back of her neck stand on end as she heard the word gem come from Rose's mouth. The concept of multiples that she once considered a theory was now on the table. She kept this excitement to herself, but knew that if this gem existed, The Frost Gem certainly remained. Any others that exhibited such properties needed to be hers, no matter the cost.

"Of course. Hand me your conduit so I can evaluate your performance as you were told to practice," The Baroness mentioned as Rose handed over the amethyst.

The Baroness lifted an eyebrow as she examined Rose and then back at the object. She moved it along the back of her palm as she closed her eyes and took a deep breath. She was able to assess the depth of the conduit as she filled it with souls in the basement of her manor. She took great care to forge such an artifact for its primary use of opening weakened portions of the universe for travel. From Rose's perspective, The Baroness appeared to be doing nothing more than parlor tricks, but she saw a small glow within it as she touched it. The Baroness opened her eyes at last with a puzzled look on her face.

This is peculiar. It's completely full. At her experience level? Did she fail? No. That's not it. I need to think a bit harder. From what she told me—Ah yes. She managed to procure a portal all her own. Very good. The Baroness concluded.

"You and I have some fun planned tonight. I've come to realize I've been coddling your performance when your skill seems to increase exponentially. We will test these limits," The Baroness proposed. The Baroness summoned a purple portal for the pair to exit from their initial land. The Baroness donned sunglasses as she waited for Rose to emerge behind her. The comfortable darkness of the twilight grove gave way to an unyielding blast of sunshine.

Rose saw a tall mountain range and felt the warmth of the open day before them. Her eyes needed a moment to adjust to such a stark change. Rose had never felt air so pure as she was away from the smog of the city and the fresh scent of manure she'd grown accustomed to. The tips of the mountain top were adjacent to the clouds themselves as a small amount of snow accompanied them. The grass beneath her wrapped around her feet with an invitation to sit down as she took every step forward. The hills accentuated her speech, elevating it to a volume where even a low whisper was an audible echo. Her surroundings were a marvel of nature that suspended her in thought until her attention was grabbed once more. The Baroness grasped Rose's hand and walked over to the edge of a cliff where she could see the outline of a small town at the base of the mountain. She anticipated a descent of some sort, but what The Baroness offered was far more extravagant in its nature.

The Baroness took a deep breath as she focused, opting to show Rose the portal making process. It started as simple as Rose did hers, where she still used the movement of her hands to demonstrate but made a slicing motion. Rose noticed that the portal generated by The Baroness had split into two. Two portals were common enough by now for her, an exit point and an entry point, but two more came with it. These portals were suspended in random placements in the air. Rose was confused at such an orientation, where would she emerge from? The Baroness lifted a finger for Rose's question to remain paused. The Baroness rushed at a deceptive speed and jumped off the cliff, much to Rose's shock. Rose wasn't sure what to make of this as she saw The Baroness descend before her very eyes. Rose noticed that each of the portals were arranged in a particular way that carried with the wind. The bottom of where The Baroness jumped off was a portal as well. In total, she made five with each of these connecting to one another as part of a network. An intensified blue hue filled the sky.

Rose could hardly hide her surprise as The Baroness hopped between them with ease. As she moved from one, the momentum of the previous portal combined with her velocity gave her increasing speed. The movement of The Baroness was beyond impressive as she took the opportunity to showcase her proficiency to the shocked Rose. In the moment the pair locked eyes from a distance, she gave Rose a wink as she prepared for her grandiose finish. Not far from Rose's location, she noticed another open that was the sixth. The Baroness barreled through and maintained the landing despite her rush of speed. The momentum that carried her was reflected with a gust of wind that shot out the portal for her.

"Like a cat, you'll always emerge on your feet if you place your exit point near a solid surface. Use this to your advantage. All that speed you've acquired doesn't just burn away. It must be used and channeled into something else. Connective force is incredibly powerful. Rose. I want you to jump off this cliff and enter the hole I have summoned for you." The Baroness dictated.

She did all of that in a nightgown? My goose is cooked for this exercise. Rose thought. Her eyes were still racing as she attempted to understand the mechanisms behind it all. Rose recalled that her mentor was a self-trained physicist, and it was by design that she could do all of this, but Rose lacked such thought. She wondered if The Baroness would challenge her in some way, she had to be careful.

"Eventually, you'll reach a level of expertise and synthesis with your environment where you can do this..." The Baroness teased with a grin as she dusted off her nightgown.

Rose gulped as she willed herself to walk towards the depths below. The edge of the cliff felt further with each step as her legs became hardened tree trunks. Rose lacked a fear of heights, but she feared the aftermath of her own ability disrupting the process. Rose offered a prayer as she envisioned the path to take. Her trust in The Baroness was enough of a grounding force to guide her forward, much to the latter's anticipation. Rose had never felt a fall with such speed before as gusts of air went through her eardrums. She felt a pop as the altitude changed. Her eyes opened to see the gaping void call to her as the first portal came without a hitch. Rose had to fight the instinct to wrestle away from the flow set for her. The back of Rose's mind assured her that her status would shield her for the time being from any serious harm. The rush of jumping from multiple portals was an invigorating perspective as she barely held onto her glasses. Her clothes flew in the wind but she felt little resistance as the portals carried their own propulsion. She wondered about the utility of such a move with herself being unable to generate so many at a time.

On the ground, The Baroness watched with intrigue. She allowed Rose to loop around three times and familiarize herself with the course. Her eyes remained trained on Rose and she adjusted the trajectory of the portals. She removed the last one that Rose exited and wanted to test Rose's ability to think on the fly. Rose would have to generate a new portal in the amount of time she exited to complete the loop. The Baroness folded her arms and watched closely.

Rose enjoyed her flexibility as she was able to manipulate herself to flip with the momentum. As she turned, she gave a gasp as she realized her previous opening was gone. Rose hadn't anticipated her own abilities tampering with the route she was given, she needed to course correct. Rose had limited time to do so as she attempted to get herself back on track. Her delay in fixing her position drastically launched her out of the course and into a freefall. She fell perpendicularly to the other portals that remained up. Her arms dangled as she did so, and she was unable to form the circle movement she commonly used. Rose looked around her as she started to panic, she needed the movement still as her speed continued to increase. In a moment of clarity, she ran her tongue in a circle in her mouth. Her control of her energy became more precise as lesser amounts were needed. To her surprise, she saw the familiar contorting of her surroundings and summoned a portal. The opening of the portal was only a few feet above her rapidly descending location, but each second was precious before touching the ground.

Wait, I can use this to climb up. Was that the test?

Rose attempted to remember what The Baroness mentioned about connective force and momentum. Rose kept the current one she had and placed a new portal right below her to keep a constant loop. As she was able to regulate her speed again, Rose moved down each portal slightly, gaining just a bit more speed from her descent. Rose did this for some time until she felt she was ready to use this force to reach the mountain's summit once more. Rose let herself fall with a large amount of speed as she placed the exit of her portal much higher than her current position. It was at an angle, so she could fall closer to where she needed to accurately land. Rose envisioned the grass where she first reached this new world. Rose anticipated a few scrapes from this move, all worth it to touch the ground. Rose exited through this portal and emerged back to where she started her exercise. She rolled along the ground and felt a surging pain through her ribs. She felt every crack of her body as she attempted to get up. She was covered with grass stains and loose dirt that was impacted her landing.

Very resourceful. She clearly saw that I tampered with the course, and she didn't need to be saved. Self-reliance will take her far. The Baroness thought. The Baroness turned around to hear Rose's arrival and made her concern known to the young woman. She offered a satisfied grin that Rose accepted as victory for the day.

Just as Rose felt the first time seeing the hand of her mentor all that time ago, she felt a sense of wonder come across her. Her concerns remained in the back of her mind, but she buried them deep for now. Just what more secrets did The Baroness have to teach her? Rose needed to know more, and they both knew it. Rose wanted to expand their relationship beyond the classroom or the secrecy of the mansion, but knew that was currently not viable. The pair looked at one another with a solemn acknowledgment that neither could address the other in public for the time being. The Baroness took these feelings into account as she offered her guidance and inserted herself further into Rose's affairs to isolate her from the others. Only she could provide the guidance and provide the support that Rose needed.

"Nothing's broken. You've earned some rest my dear. Tomorrow, we will do purple portals. It's time for you to be able to truly help our endeavors for The Frost Gem," The Baroness stated as she held her hand out to Rose.

Now that Rose had a growing mastery on her work with blue portals, her efforts to understand the complexities regarding their purple counterparts was something on her list to achieve. Rose's body was exhausted, she spent all day in bed without as much of an acknowledgment of what went on below her before the next night. She could still feel the slight rise and fall of her stomach churn from the maze of portals constructed for herself. Rose followed her given instructions by The Baroness the night before and went again to the twilight realm. Rose saw that rather than the elegance that came with The Baroness' reflective clothing, a dark and foreboding figure stood in wait as the twilight filled.

The Baron with a stiff black suit slowly lifted his head in acknowledgement to Rose's outline in the distance. Rose emerged some distance from The Baron and gave a slow wave as she realized who was there. Rose made her way to walk to The Baron but was stopped as she noticed something peculiar appear in front of her. The Baron only walked a few feet before seamlessly making his way to Rose. Instantaneously, The Baron appeared from a blue portal he summoned to appear right in front of her, as if he teleported before her very eyes. His hands remained in his pockets as he stood, where his entrance vanished at the same speed. Rose kept quiet as her relationship regarding The Baron was more complicated. Rose trusted Cicero a great deal and she made a promise to keep his town safe.

"Hello Rose. I take it you were expecting someone else? You will be with me today. My wife is out on essential business. I've reached a point where I can step away from my projects for now," The Baron explained. He realized that with the amount of time spent in proportion to one another, he spent little time with Rose as his grand railway was developing. The last thing he wanted to do was neglect her training and decided to address her from that point.

"Come, take my hand. There are things you must see. I'm aware you are proficient with a sidearm and that my wife has shown how to use an ability such as mine, but I have something in mind more... cerebral." The Baron beckoned Rose. He took her silence with grace; it was fair as the two lacked much time together with the bulk of her training done with his better half.

"I am going to teach you how to travel between universes. You will watch what I do, learn how to navigate them and at the end, you will be able to conjure a new reality with your very mind," The Baron explained as he placed his hand onto her shoulder.

Rose was curter with The Baron in her demeanor as she was firmly in Cicero's camp, but she minded their scale of difference. It was an odd pairing as she felt powerless to truly stop any known wrongdoing, but as one of only two mentors for her abilities, it was one that came at a price. Rose was drawn to the mastery of these skills and this is something The Baron knew well. Rose's desire for knowledge trumped anything else as she wanted to reach her potential, the one that was sought out by them to begin with. She started to internalize her importance and had a growing confidence develop.

"I've had some difficulty with the purple portals, I'll admit that. Only through practice really, I've been able to get here, but the rest doesn't make much sense to me," Rose said.

The silence met from The Baron prompted Rose to show how she'd been doing so far. Rose struggled to find the world she was looking for. She was paralyzed with decisions. It was one thing to imagine a new world, but to find it, bring herself to it, and to bend the rules of that universe for her to enter was a daunting task. The Baron watched silently in focus as he evaluated Rose's form. Rose tried to manually trace out the portal with her fingers. As she strained, The Baron noticed small purple sparks materialize in front of the pair that fizzled out to nothing more.

"Again." The Baron snapped his fingers to stop Rose's progress.

Rose could feel pressure applied on her as she felt the piercing stare of The Baron. She knew that the man wasn't one to mince his words, he truly saw her potential in learning their gift. Unknown to Rose, The Baron recalled a time when he also had difficulty with spawning a purple portal. The Baron felt that discipline in the form of yelling and dictating instructions like a drill sergeant was an antiquated method of learning. He knew her energy was overflowing and needed to be course corrected like a river. The Baron walked up to Rose and took a knee as he placed himself next to her in the same position. He offered a piece of advice.

"Imagine, something in your life that you've always wanted to change. This is what the witches of Salem once told me. For me, it was the death of my siblings. You see, portal conjuring can come from important events within one's life. My wife advised you earlier to think of someone you missed, and this is how you entered New York. Purple vortexes are the gateway to new universes that differ from our own. Some in slight ways, but others, much so. In this case, I am asking you to find an alternative to the life you have now. I know there's plenty, you have suffered a great deal," The Baron reasoned as he gathered Rose's attention. He took her palm and lightly cracked her stiff fingers as he spoke.

"For us, my wife and I, portal making in a new universe is like roulette. We can get close to what we want, but never exactly. This keeps travel interesting, but it has its disadvantages. In fact, we found The Frost Gem about one hundred and fifty years ago or so. We lost the dimension and have been looking for it ever since. You suffer from the opposite problem. You seem to be able to find any universe you conjure in your mind, but if you are unable to think of it, it remains hidden to you. For now, I will lead. You will follow," The Baron said as he took a deep breath. With a snap of his fingers and a bit of concentration, the area surrounding them started to contort and a purple light started to emit.

The Baron and Rose entered through his portal to the back alleys of a nearby suburb. Rose was unsure of what to expect as she had never traveled with The Baron before. While The Baroness craved excitement with her wish of scaling tall mountains granted at the behest of Rose, a calm suburb was a big surprise for her. As Rose got her bearings, The Baron locked eyes with Rose and made a nod towards a general store in the distance with friendly locals. Rose anticipated some sort of dangerous twist, but The Baron had assured her violence would not be needed to solve her problem. Rose had conditioned herself to see most things in this world as a threat, and for good reason, but with The Baron's assuredness, she knew she was needed and wouldn't be put into harm's way.

"I have taken us to a place much like the one we call home, but there is something amiss. I am curious if your senses can pick it up. Your test starts now," The Baron instructed.

"Not much looks different. I see blue skies, people wearing our dress, though, we look underdressed for the occasion," Rose said while The Baron watched closely. The Baron motioned for her to move forward. He allowed Rose to lead while he trailed behind in observation.

The Baron's aura exuded raw power and mystique regardless of where he traveled as he trailed behind Rose. Rose decided to enter the store and look around for anything out of the ordinary while The Baron remained quiet. Rose's eyes scanned fruits and vegetables. The prices were contemporary to what she remembered at the general store with Cicero. The idle conversation of other shoppers was in English, with no identifiable accents to think of. Rose started to wonder if The Baron truly was messing with her, but she remembered they entered through a purple vortex. Rose walked up to a nearby wall and was drawn to a painting on it while The Baron examined a piece of bread in his hand. Rose noticed the painting was a calendar, and while the text was legible, she raised an eyebrow at the days. The days of the week were completely different.

"I know what's the problem," Rose said as the curious ear of The Baron came to her attention.

"The calendar's all wrong. The days of the week—Mothyday? Tiresday? Once is a fluke, but there's intention here." Rose assessed.

"Excellent work, Rose. One of the most dangerous aspects of multiverse travel is finding places familiar to your original home. You may mistake them for what you are in, but these are not safe refuges. As you are one of countless others, to the universe, that is, there are copies of you that will range from neutral... to a problem. Whether or not, you are proactive in finding yourself and wiping away this presence, the universe cannot stand for a rule of two. One must die or be removed to fill in the void. Do you follow?" The Baron lectured. He was impressed as such a small detail would usually go unnoticed. The Baron valued that aspect of Rose, the meticulous details of her notes and other things reminded him of how he micromanaged his company.

"At my age, I have no such worries, but my footprint has been left in multiple locations over the centuries. At a certain point, depending on how often, and the extent of your travels, you will cease to age. You may even cease to die, permanently at least. One must die or fill the void. If you are killed, your essence will be filled by the Rose of another world, who was snuffed out, and you can return home." The Baron continued. He paused to hear Rose's input.

"I... don't understand. Am I truly me then?" Rose asked as she started to get worried. The Baron placed a hand on her shoulder that eerily removed her doubts. Rose hadn't anticipated having an existential crisis in the middle of a grocery store.

"Of course, you are. You are the only one who has this gift. When you are reborn, everything comes with you. The inner consciousness, the blood, the guts, all of it. You wake up, just as you are, and while one world may not have another Rose... You are the most important, and the universe recognizes this." The Baron reassured her.

The Baron could tell that Rose still had questions that needed to be answered. He explained the resurrection process to the best of his ability. He informed Rose that her resurgence into the world would be seen as natural and not probe many questions. Rose would appear as normal, possibly in different clothing, in an area where she has spent a long time. Those that are asked about her are unable to recall her arrival and each give a different story as if they were given false memories. The Baron likened this as a defensive measure of their powers to ensure their safety in a vulnerable state. Outside of their immediate vicinity, the events of the world continued as normal, but the path of regularity would soon follow. The Baron found that the effectiveness of this smokescreen faded over time. The Baron had resurrected countless times, and death was an inconvenience more than anything else. As he concluded, he looked at Rose

.

"But, why me? Genuinely. If there are thousands of Rose Carpenters out there— " Rose said before she was cut off by The Baron with his hand. All her questions would soon be answered, but not in the public eye.

As their instructions were done in this area, The Baron bought a few apples for the road and continued their discussion outside the venue. The pair walked down a paved sidewalk where the locals happily gave them waves. It unsettled Rose to see people so cheery and she wondered what lay beneath. People were never happy to see her, and she was aware The Baron had a laundry list of enemies, regardless of dimension. The Baron prompted discussion between the two as he looked behind him to see they were not followed as outsiders. The Baron found a nearby bench for the two to sit as they earned some rest.

"Not all of you are born exactly in the same fashion, but they are you. Twenty-five years ago, my wife and I visited a fortune teller who foretold us of our greeting to you. Bound by fate, remember? We were shown a vision of us three standing at my manor just like when you first saw us. I did not know how long it would take." The Baron lit a cigar. He took a mighty puff and blew out a ring of smoke. He extended his hand to Rose to partake, one of the ultimate signs of trust that The Baron could exude on a person. Rose knew better than to deny such a request at that moment and she felt a smoke that smooth was worth having. The Baron continued his anecdote.

"In 1912, we spurned an invitation to the Titanic to go on a better vacation and stumbled upon a Rose who fit the description of what we sought. We returned later in 1918, thinking she was the one, as she needed to age into the vision. We taught her things, but there was a problem. She could not conjure with the strength that you do, for you, it is as simple as breathing. She was a teenager that came from rich stock, so we understood the undertaking. Someone who was used to luxury. The family was not inviting to our questioning, so I removed them from the equation. Orphans are much more compliant with demands. Though, her eagerness and rash actions to do the unwilling and unsavory brought concern to us both. Your reluctance shows me that you have the strength and intelligence to handle multiverse matters with competence. The time will come when striking is necessary, but that is not now," The Baron mentioned as Rose passed the cigar over.

"Despite what you may think regarding my ventures in business enterprise, I am a sane man. Destroying the stability of what makes us prosperous for personal goals is a foolish endeavor. I simply wish to be the richest man. I provide jobs, infrastructure, and more. You see my dealing with the Southern Pacific Railway will bring unparalleled prosperity to Phoenix at last," The Baron reflected on his progress.

"Am I supposed to just ignore what's been going on here? You've destroyed how many lives for something like wealth? You will die, one day, and you can't take it with you. The pursuit of wealth isn't sane, there will always be something worth more to you and you must have it. Regardless of what it takes. That's how it works. That's how it always works, and someone like me has to suffer for it," Rose retorted.

"There are those who do fall between the cracks, but merit is what separates the wheat from the chaff. Rose, you are a humble woman who neglects her own talents and skillsets. You survived this far, it's high time you understood your purpose in this world. It's not of this world, but every world. To experience, to travel, to document all you survey. Your goals? You have infinite resources to do it, you must be willing to make the hard choice, and that is why my wife and I are here. To teach you. You stand here because you want to know what it's like. You've accepted that the people I crush beneath my feet are worth this knowledge. You may not see it that way, but it's the truth. Grandstanding and moralism will get you nowhere. You are here to learn," The Baron expressed. He let the words hang over Rose. Rose felt a cold feeling as she suppressed a shake that came over her. She balled her hand into a fist and buried her emotions.

"I too once had a mentor when I lived on the frontier. I understand your attachment, but it's one that must leave. He taught you basic skills, but if you want to thrive, I implore you, move in with us. Accept our knowledge." The Baron placed his hand on Rose's shoulder. The Baron looked her over as Rose kept a neutral expression.

"I want you to try something for me. Eat this apple I bought from the store and tell me how it tastes." The Baron commented.

Rose gently took the apple from The Baron and took a girthy bite. To Rose, it seemed utterly the same, but as she bit into the other, the taste was abhorrent. Rose nearly spit it out instantaneously as she half expected a worm to come out.

"Hmm. I was afraid this was going to happen. You're not seasoned yet with your external travels in places such as these. Take this other apple, it's from our Earth, so you can be replenished." The Baron passed Rose a red apple from his bag.

"While we can pass through the realms without issue, the realms themselves may object to our presence. Remember how I mentioned that there are others of you out there? Lesser and lurking in the shadows. This realm is saying you are not welcome. I propose you fix that as soon as you can." The Baron warned as he dictated instructions to her.

"In other news. As you know, our gala event is two weeks from today. It goes without saying I expect you to look your best on arrival. Of course, all your little friends you've made in the city can accompany you, if they choose. I prefer you are comfortable above all else. This is more than just the celebration of our love; this is your initiation into our family. This is why you learn the trade. The Romans adopted adults all the time, and I'd say we're better than them by now," The Baron said.

"How long have you two been married?" Rose asked, attempting to deflect the subject. She hadn't realized how far deep The Baron and Baroness were willing to go for their dreams. Rose felt uncomfortable being referred to as her daughter by The Baroness despite her admiration.

"We tell the public twenty years, but it's actually two hundred. When you find someone you love Rose, it matters little how much of the life you've lived before them. Your destinies intertwine and there is only one path forward," The Baron commented as he adjusted his top hat.

While The Baron took a break for Rose's training, they were far from finished. Away from prying eyes, the pair went to the site of an active volcano through a portal generated by The Baron. He gave Rose an - affirmative pat on the back as he wiped the sweat off his brow. Rose felt assaulted by the whiplash from settings between the calm suburb and nearly coughing her lungs out. The amount of ash that erupted nearly blinded her as she was rubbing her eyes. The Baron stood triumphantly, but found it difficult to also match his distaste for the surrounding area.

"As you can see, we stand at the precipice of a nearby volcanic eruption. Rose, I am going to close the portal behind us, and you will whisk us to safety. Unlike you, I am unable to die as you well know. Melting by lava or suffocating by volcanic ash is more of a minor annoyance. Though, I would hate to get my skin scalded for such a time. Good luck," The Baron commented.

Rose barely registered The Baron's statement as she continued to cough but nodded anyway. She tried to imagine the crisp air of the mountain that she enjoyed with The Baroness earlier. The rolling hills and high sun with swaying grass were appealing. Rose struggled to concentrate, but the ongoing threat of annihilation was a proper motivator. Rose felt a tinge of power surge within her as her fingers started to glow an illustrious purple. She took it slow as she knew panicking was only going to make things worse. Rose's coughing subsided as behind her, the ash and dust started to curl in on itself, the starting process to the appearance of such a portal. The ambient glow of purple contrasted with the dark soot that flew among them. As Rose turned around, she was met with the stark contrast of the mountain she desperately wished to go. A place with pure air, driven by both desperation and a desire to meet her set expectations. Her reward would soon come as The Baron gave a slow clap of praise. He guided Rose through the portal and nodded as Rose closed it behind her with ease.

"Wonderful work Rose. I will see you when the gala is nigh. For now, I have some duties to attend to. Be well. Make sure you dress your best." The Baron tipped his hat. He extended his hand to shake for Rose.

As Rose watched The Baron depart, she felt something placed in her hand. She felt a piece of paper and as she unraveled it, nearly fainted at the sight of a one hundred dollar bill all her own.

Beethoven's 5th

The local barkeep Mavis enjoyed the early quiet of her establishment as she cleaned up the venue from the previous drunken brawl. Bits of glass and stale beer riddled the floor with reckless abandon; it was a sordid sight for anyone who valued their hygiene. She attempted to hide her stress from the ongoing gang war as she grabbed a mop and started to clean the wooden panels below. In her haste, the bucket of soap fell to the floor all at once, and she stomped her foot down in frustration. Her doubts in The Baron and Baroness' true generosity started to take root, as she constantly needed to take out additional loans to cover the costs of supplies. Cirano's men considered any bar within the outskirts of the city as competition for the alcohol trade and Mavis was forced at gunpoint to offer up twenty percent of all her income in a brown envelope. She could hardly complain as her work was outright illegal, but she felt something needed to change, and fast. Mavis gave her ire towards the piano sequestered in the corner with scorn.

"That little girl and Cicero are gonna deal with you real soon. Maybe then you'll stop driving away my customers," Mavis complained as she looked towards the inanimate piano. The woman looked up from her monotonous circling of the mop to see Rose and Cicero standing by in the entrance. The pair came prepared with full satchels for an outright onslaught as they were used to dealing with from the usual.

"Did a tornado bust in this place? It's at least twice as awful as usual—" Cicero opened.

"Cut the shit, Cicero. Now's not the time. I need that thing taken care of, I'm bleeding money and nobody wants to come to the bar since that thing took out one of the tourists," Mavis groaned.

"I don't have the faintest idea of where to start. All I know is that it eats people from what you wrote down. Lord, have mercy what on Earth happened here!?" Rose commented. She retreated a healthy distance away from the piano. Rose's demeanor calmed as she saw the piano was in stasis once more.

"Everyone's got a gun here, but I don't think that's necessary," Mavis explained.

"Come again?" Rose asked. The first thing she did was hover her hand over her holster.

"Everyone in this town tried to come up with some way to deal with that damn thing. We blew it up, it reformed. We set it on fire, it reformed. We tried hauling down river? It came back the next day! That thing is cursed. If you play the wrong note, it opens up and bites your finger clean off. If you're lucky," Mavis huffed. Mavis heard fragments of Cicero's escapades with Rose whenever he went to town to resupply. She wondered if the two really had the gusto to deliver as they have for countless others.

Cicero let Rose and Mavis hypothesize scenarios regarding the piano as he helped himself to the beer tap and gave a hearty drink from his glass. Cicero remained calm as he felt a slight buzz from the brew. He called for Rose's attention with the snap of his fingers.

"Remember how I said this was a four-man job? I decided to listen to your advice, I called up a favor a little while ago." Cicero explained to Rose as he gestured to the double doors.

Rose had a small grin as she heard the familiar sound of a nearby car. Rose recognized Niccolo's car from anywhere as the engine let out a unique purr that set it across the rest. Florence entered first, her bright red hair and green eyes that gave much needed contrast to the drab room. She wore a teal dress that gathered the group's attention. Monster hunting in a dress was already hard enough for Rose, as she preferred pants or overalls, but this was her first time. Niccolo came behind her with a raised eyebrow as he observed the various markings of the floor and tinged his nose in disgust. His usual red suit was replaced with a more muted gray that hardly hid his clandestine activities; dried blood was present on the sleeves.

"Well cowboy, we made it despite your directions. This hunting, shall we start?" Niccolo gave the pair a nod while Florence smiled.

"I understand you've had run-ins with gangsters before and you managed to quell that entity in your mine once and for all, but the stuff we normally deal with is a bit past that. A steady hand is what's going to get us out all alive. Any suggestions? The piano there is our target," Cicero mentioned to Florence and Niccolo, as Rose continued to observe the piano for any signs of movement. Rose withdrew her notebook from her bag and started to sketch the known details about the encounter.

"Just a suggestion, but I'm pretty good at the piano. I could give a crack at it and see what it sings to me. Music is like a language, some people speak it and others don't, you know?" Florence said as she raised her hands and moved her fingers.

While Cicero and Niccolo both shared a glance of confusion, Rose was able to piece together Florence's logic. It was known by all parties that the piano was alive in some way, even when it remained inanimate, and their failure to communicate with the being led to terrible outcomes. Rose was not musically gifted and wouldn't find herself anywhere close to it. Niccolo went to draw his pistol out of distrust of the object but was stopped by the hand of Rose on his arm. Rose gave Niccolo a reassuring look as she felt confident in at least entertaining Florence's suggestion.

"Ah, what the hell. What song do you want, there should be a book with something there for you to work with." Cicero prompted Rose to help him look for sheet music.

"Oh, I can't read music. I'll scoot my little butt on the bench there and play from the heart. Works every time! Give it a chance," Florence said with a wave of her hand. She calmly approached the piano.

Rose and Cicero both let out a cough of concern at Florence's carefree attitude towards the situation. While the pair looked to find Niccolo to be a port in the storm, he agreed with her stance. Niccolo couldn't help but laugh at Florence's comment much to Rose and Cicero's growing discomfort. Mavis made a knot in her hair from the anxiety of going near the piano alone.

"Oh Florence, that is very amusing. You all will have to trust her, she can do amazing things under pressure, I have seen it myself. She also can forget what she had for breakfast. We shall see which one shows up today." Niccolo lit a cigar from his pocket.

The piano that housed itself in Mavis' bar was once an ordinary instrument built from oak and had a spruce soundboard. The object was obsolete in more ways than one, but it gave a specific type of grandeur that was appreciated by Mavis. It arrived wrapped in a large bow with an associated anonymous message attached. In the bar's early days, she and her father often used it to host competitions for the best songs accompanied by the band. One day, the piano needed repairing and was sent away to return in the same fashion. The instrument returned with an unforeseen sentience; it held an aura that enticed any interested parties with its siren song to come forward. A wrong chord triggers the piano into a state of frenzy as the keys become daggers in an attempt to scrape off their flesh until they were no more. The piano itself could move, slowly and tirelessly making its way towards the disaffected player to finish the song or die trying.

Florence walked to the side of the piano and moved the sheet off it, revealing the piece on full display. Her eyes scanned the keys and saw faded blood on the ivory before them. This was the mark of others that failed, but she remained determined as ever. She let out a deep breath and closed her eyes as she imagined what she wanted to play. Florence recalled an earlier memory, one of a time she usually liked to put behind her. Her mind drifted to the sanitarium where she stayed and heard a peculiar melody. There was no outside media, so Florence replicated what came from a broken heart, much like her own, in those days. As she started to play, the piano's chords recognized a new subject had entered its vicinity. Florence was aware what a wrong note gave, but what was the indication of a right one e?

Out of the four observers, Rose was stunned at Florence's display. While Rose considered herself adaptable to think on the fly, composing a symphony from scratch with no traditional background in music seemed to be a herculean task. She couldn't wrap her mind around such a display but gently encouraged Florence to keep going with a silent raise of her thumbs in support. Cicero and Niccolo were more muted in their implicit agreement to jump at a moment's notice the piano started to act up, but the melody was appreciated. Cicero tried to figure out what made the difference between Florence's wistful movements and that of the assortment of talented musicians who all were attacked by such an entity.

Niccolo kept his cigar in his mouth as he watched Florence sway in what seemed to be zen. It was an unusual thing for him to witness. She always seemed to be over-enthusiastically cheerful and energetic, but he was aware of what remained underneath. The notes that came from Florence were a ballad of conflicting emotions that could never manifest in such a space. Florence occasionally bopped her head back, looking upside down at the others with a big smile on her face as she continued to play. Niccolo knew of Florence's internment to a more intimate degree than the others given their partnership and it was something met with understanding. As Cicero remained stumped and Rose wondering where it would end, Niccolo realized he'd determined why the piano hadn't reacted in such a manner.

Her fingers are so graceful, her eyes, her eyes are so... reflective. She seems relaxed with poise. Though she struggles on occasion, the piano does not react. It's not looking for perfection, it seeks... originality. Niccolo thought.

Niccolo found that the piano wanted an authentic song, nothing that it'd ever seen before. Covers and countless retellings of popular media throughout the ages were ones that drove it to anger. Cicero's suggestions from the song book were all popular and were perfect from start to finish. The lid of the piano started to stir, but as Florence's fingers made an assortment of sharp and flat tones, the usual ruckus made from it was absent.

Niccolo noticed the movement of something light brown in the opening of the grand piano's strings as Florence played. It appeared to look like some sort of rodent. He stepped closer to Florence but kept his silence as he didn't want to disturb her ongoing melody. The risk for this action was immense as if he agitated the piano, Florence would likely lose this chance and a finger in the process. Niccolo was a trained hitman and he could easily hold himself still on command. Akin to using a sniper rifle, he cupped his hand and grabbed the small rodent-like creature with deadly accuracy.

"Ah-ha!" Niccolo clenched his hand into a fist. He tightly wound his fingers around the being's neck. Rose and Cicero went over to Niccolo as Florence's playing was interrupted. Niccolo took a closer look at his prisoner and saw what appeared to be a chipmunk but held soulless black eyes. It appeared to be pacified from Florence's notes as it remained in Niccolo's captivity.

"The thing in my hand was inside the piano! I am sure that is what has been making it go mad! Florence, hit anything, any key!" Niccolo pleaded with her. Florence complied with Niccolo's request and marveled at the fact that regardless of what she did, the piano remained motionless. Rose was stunned as she quickly opened her notebook and started to write details.

"Well now. That little burrowing varmint seems to have some sort of magic attached to it. I'll call this one The Puppeteer. It burrows into objects and turns them into demented things," Rose mentioned. Cicero quickly went to grab a spare bag to house the animal in as Niccolo went by him and placed it inside.

"Still got that sledgehammer round back Mavis?" Cicero asked as the bartender gave an affirmative nod.

Cicero volunteered to end the creature's existence as he went to smash the felt bag with extreme prejudice. Florence averted her gaze slightly as she disliked the movement of the beast inside while the hammer crashed down. A resounding crush of guts and bone with a tiny scream afterwards accompanied the sound. It took little effort to finish the job as Cicero wiped his forehead clean of sweat. He was impressed with both Florence and Niccolo's resourcefulness on the job and called for a drink.

Mavis was more than appreciative as she hugged Cicero tightly and left a kiss on the cheek in gratitude. She quickly went to pour some glasses for the four and mentioned that the tab would be covered for tonight. Rose was happy to have her pick of the selection where money was no object. She also appreciated that the four had the bar to themselves before the usual crowd would make their way in through the night. Rose, Cicero, and Niccolo shared glasses of whiskey, while Florence abstained. She instead had a cup of fruit juice, much to Cicero's ridicule. He could hardly contain his laughter at the sight.

"I don't drink much, for I try to be a Sober Sally when I can! That's what all the leading health experts say you know. It must be a special occasion for me to drink!" Florence said as she looked at the other three and their glasses. Rose grinned; she appreciated that Florence went by the beat of her own drum no matter what.

"Sober Sally... Oh brother," Cicero dismissed.

"It's a special occasion that we're alive in the first place." Rose rubbed her arm.

Cicero clinked his glass against the table in agreement and slammed back his drink. Cicero looked to Rose and Niccolo to follow through without delay. As they did so, Florence opted to learn more about her allies' expertise on the supernatural. Her mind was focused on the Mafia conflict, but the creatures of the otherworldly were of great interest to her.

"Cicero, I have to ask... Are the ape-men real? The ones with the big feet and furry bodies. I always wanted to know," Florence asked as she sipped her juice. Florence's curious expression turned sour as Rose and Cicero shared a laugh for some time.

"Well Florence, that's a complicated matter. If you're referring to the collective tall tales that make up American Sasquatch, they're gone. Someone killed the last one in 1840, and they won't shut the hell up about it, I grew up hearing tales about it by the fire," Cicero explained.

"Now hold on, Nicki back me up, don't you have creatures like those that are white in Europe? I saw in the papers they got the scalp of one," Florence commented.

"You mean Yeti? I have heard of those yes, but those are legend surely. Though if the cowboy thinks otherwise..." Niccolo mentioned as he slammed down his whiskey.

"Can't say I've been up to the Himalayas, but that'd be a fine hunt, wouldn't you say? Too bad everyone that goes up there freezes to death. Imagine that, nobody disproves the theory," Cicero said. Rose felt a slight shudder as she recalled The Baroness' vision of a desolate and frozen landscape to find the item she desired the most. A place that cold was an ill-inviting endeavor to the hot climate Rose was born and raised.

"Then-how does nobody know about these things if they're everywhere? This should be breaking news in the paper! Put it on the radio!" Florence yelled.

"We—Our community that is, is more than happy to talk about the stuff we find. Whether or not the public chooses to believe us is another. We get plenty of calls, so there's people who believe in what Cicero and I are doing." Rose concluded as she turned to Cicero in agreement.

"I'd be richer than The Baron if I was the only one in the business of hunting monsters, but some folks don't understand. The authorities for one. You solve a problem and oh, there's a breaking and entering charge. Public endangerment, the works. Bunch'a bullshit if you ask me," Cicero added.

"Either way today, y'all did good work and I didn't have to fire a shot. That was our last case for a while, so until I get more calls, we'll see," Cicero mentioned.

Cicero snapped his fingers for another round for all parties involved. He felt confident knowing that Niccolo and Florence could eventually be trained to be competent substitutes for either he or Rose, just as he envisioned. For now, the old cowboy would sit back with victory at hand and enjoy all they'd earn that night.

Burning Rubber

With a lull in cases over the past couple of weeks, the stir-crazy Rose looked for any excuse to leave the house. While Florence attempted to help Cicero and Claudia with small errands in exchange for using their typewriter, Niccolo quietly exited to work on his own endeavors for the time being. Rose couldn't be caught dead painting a fence or feeding the chickens for the fifth time. She creeped up behind Niccolo as he headed to his car parked outside the homestead. Niccolo had his head in the trunk rifling around through goods as Rose stood some distance away. Niccolo gave a sigh as he just wanted to spend some time alone. The stress was weary on his face and his concern looked to his car.

While Bill usually served as Niccolo's personal driver, he called out sick, and Niccolo didn't mind driving on his own. The driving part was easy, but the mechanical aspects of car repair were lost on him, other than hitting a wrench for the desired result. As a capo, Niccolo was far busier than he anticipated having to gear up with more direct blows with Cirano's men. With the death of the underboss came a resounding level of changes that swept through the organization. Niccolo was working to eye a successor to himself in the meantime as he was split between containing the monsters that threatened his bottom line and the outfit itself. Cirano's alliances were being drawn quicker than Niccolo could keep track of, but he needed something to keep his mind at ease.

Niccolo favored a joyride every now and again, but he grumbled to himself as when he attempted to start the car, there was hardly any sound.

He angrily hit the roof of the car and kicked some sand aside as he cursed in Italian, much to Rose's amusement.

"Trouble with your car? I could give a look at it. Wouldn't be the first time I helped with that sorta thing," Rose commented. Niccolo stood still and pretended that he didn't hear Rose. He already found it embarrassing enough that he would need to grovel to use Cicero's toolbox.

"You seem to know many things. Tell me then, what is wrong with my car." Niccolo said as he waved his hand to her while his back remained turned.

Rose moved right aside from Niccolo and opened the car door as she surveyed the interior. She sniffed the leather and coughed as it baked in the heat of the Arizonan sun. Her eyes looked at a pipe that seemed loose. She could tell that Niccolo got into a collision at some point due to the impact damage on the metal. Rose realized the problem while Niccolo remained confused.

"Do you have any schematics for your vehicle? Most automobiles have them, if you want to know what part you need to replace," Rose asked.

"Reading isn't really our style at the mine," Niccolo recalled.

"When's the last time you cleaned your exhaust? It looks horrid. Also, your pack nut's out of place. Just a minute. I can go get the box from Cicero's barn."

"My... Right." Niccolo said with a crumb of defeat in his voice.

Rose returned with Cicero's toolbox. Niccolo could see the faint outline of the cowboy in the distance as he jeered. Cicero was busy feeding the horses while Rose went to grab the box. She went to work and grabbed an L-shaped piece of metal to graft onto the pipe and keep the nut in place. As she relocked the loose pack nut inside, she clamped the metal piece hard in the small opening between the two. Rose gave it a quick slap with the back of her hand to test her handiwork and it held.

"Thank you." Niccolo commented as Rose started the car. Rose bowed sarcastically as she offered her knowledge for a price.

"No good deed goes unpunished, so what is it you want?" Niccolo asked as he tapped his foot. He rubbed the back of his head which was filled with sweat. Rose tipped her glasses down with a playful expression.

"I'm bored. Dreadfully bored. Venus is busy and can't come to the phone, everyone else is stuck doing tasks. Are we going to beat up somebody that owes you money? Ooh, are we gonna run some rum to Mexico?!" Rose noticed Niccolo had a surprised look on his face with how forward she was.

I wasn't aware she had such a craving for this stuff. She must find it appealing like those people who run in front of trains for the thrill. I can't risk taking her anywhere near the mine right now and I would never hear the end of it from the cowboy, so fine. To town we will go. I can take her shopping; it works for Florence. Niccolo thought.

"Haha—Well, I just was going to get groceries. The men at my operation need to eat after all. But we'll see what happens." Niccolo stated as he decided to let Rose tag along.

Niccolo stepped into the car and waited as she opened the second door and settled inside. Rose could smell Florence's strong perfume still linger in the back of the car and sneezed which made Niccolo laugh slightly. She looked around and saw behind her a few magazine drums for Niccolo's weapon, along with a few other implements. Rose had been in the car plenty as Niccolo ferried her to The Baron and Baroness before, but with her mastery of her new ability, this wasn't needed anymore. Niccolo sought to increase the car's defensive abilities by opting for reinforced plating and a faster engine, as fast as a car of his model and make could get. Niccolo arranged for the vehicle to make an extra twenty miles-per-hour and had every intention of using it.

"I see you brought your toy Niccolo. I don't leave home without mine either," Rose hinted as she placed her satchel over herself.

"You and Florence both have that look on your face. You know the one where you take my time with something random." Niccolo commented.

Niccolo hated to admit it but in lieu of the sounds of nature accompanying him, he was getting used to a co-pilot. He checked the time, briefly referring to his pocket watch.

"I know that pocket watch model, a couple of my clients who were in the War have them. Did you fight? You certainly handle weapons like you did," Rose questioned. Niccolo stuffed it back into his suit as he took the wheel.

The way out of Cicero's homestead was a rough one, unsuitable for motor vehicles as Rose grasped the side of the car door. She shook in place while the car traversed from side to side until it reached the flattened street. With the road straight, the path to the city became clearer. Niccolo exchanged quick glances with a working crew that was placing up signs for directions, a much-needed thing for weary travelers. Rose noticed they were prison laborers from their clothing that were clearly transplants as they attempted to stay cool in the sun. With not much ahead of them now, Niccolo put the car under cruise control. Rose felt a slight tinge of fear as Niccolo casually laid back with his arms nearly folded in satisfaction on the road.

"Neat huh? I'm sure you know this, but not all cars have this feature, they say you can keep the same speed uphill or downhill. They call it cruise control," Niccolo noted as Rose studied the handle of the car. He heard from Florence about Rose's affinity for cars and attempted to pique her interest with some extra details.

"To answer your question, I trained for my king as all Italian men do but I was a man of honor, so my activities caught up to me and put me in prison in '15. I did not fight in the war, but my brother did. I have multiple sisters at home." Niccolo commented as he honked the horn of his car for another to speed up. His eyes were peeled to the road as Rose looked out the window. Without any room to pass on the asphalt, he increased on the gas and sped ahead of the car in front. He continued with his story as he veered back onto the road.

"Half-brother, my father was a cheating bastard, but that distinction is not important at home. Growing up with Durante was annoying, he was top of his class at everything, and I did not do well. Whatever he wanted, he would get. We are the same age and yet Mother favored him best. When the time came and we were of age, Durante said "Niccolo, be a soldier with me! Join *Corpo Aeronautico Militare*! Join *Arditi*! I got gassed for practice and it burnt off my fucking mustache, took months to grow back. I decided to sign up for army to try appease her, and yet I was not her darling." Niccolo added on as he noticed Rose's silence. Niccolo was astounded at how well of a listener Rose was as he continued to tell his story, Florence could hardly stay focused and would ask a million questions.

"Anyway, Durate received a big party before getting his designation at Ionzo, we were all very happy for him. I think he arrived on the eve of the second battle. Yes... second battle. There were twelve, just so you know. A month in between them give or take. I'd get letters and eventually they stopped coming. I don't know what any of them said. I heard from his commanding officer that he died like a rat, his skin flayed by the gas. He was only three hours from home. As a boy, I used to cross that route in an afternoon but now it's just a crater. I asked this man how he lived to give me such information. Durate took his place on the charge. I wanted to kill him, but I could not. For some reason, I always hear his laugh when I go to bed." Niccolo commented as he spat out the window.

"There are only two people I hate on this planet, this being Mussolini who has separated me from my ex-wife and Luigi Cardona, the worst general in human history. I don't even hate The Baron, far from it. I admire his work ethic, a shame I'll have to put a bullet in his head." Niccolo raised an eyebrow.

As Rose's eyes started to tear, she sucked them in and continued to look out of the window. Rose felt she should have been grateful. Niccolo's brother died a horrible death and yet she remained estranged to the only family she had left. Niccolo patted her shoulder while keeping a hand on the wheel as the familiar sight of industrialization came to them. He let out an annoyed sigh as there was now bumper to bumper traffic due to road work being done on a few interconnected streets. Niccolo honked the horn as he picked at his hair in rage.

"You would make a terrible gangster. Too much empathy, but that is a good thing for people your age," Niccolo remarked.

"You speak English very well, I know that's a bit rude to say but... why so?" Rose asked as she was puzzled.

"The English own half the world and I would like to own that half. Nothing gets done without knowings it. It is encouraged in Europe to speak more than one language. Though, I am not native and make mistakes, I know enough. I also needed to learn before coming here to do my work," Niccolo commented.

Rose was about to reply but stopped as she saw Niccolo get cut off by another car. Normally, this raised little concern as the city was known for terrible drivers, but the car seemed to operate on its own. The front seat was completely empty. The steering wheel operated on its own and the car hardly emitted any smoke. A few drivers voiced their displeasure to the car that passed them by with a flurry of insults that gradually morphed into confusion. The car was far faster than anything else the pair ever witnessed, with an acceleration that could challenge the best race cars of the day. The car left with a loud honk that resonated in the streets.

Despite representing one of the most basic cars on the market, it still managed to garner the impressions of all those that witnessed it. The metal remained infinitely polished as sand and grime were repelled from the body of the vehicle. Niccolo eyed the vehicle and saw it emitted a strange desire to be challenged. The excitement that he looked for on the road brought the imagery of the drag racing he enjoyed so much. Niccolo saw the road narrow as he thought about what he had witnessed. He tempered these expectations as he needed to keep his mind on the objective.

"Did you..." Rose mentioned with a low whisper.

"Yes, I saw it. Not our problem," Niccolo commented as he saw Rose's frown. Rose felt obligated to stop any paranormal activity if she could help it. Rose was also curious about the origins of this superpowered automobile, it was an old Model T, but had an unnatural ability to go at high speeds.

"Niccolo, we have to go fix this and see what's the problem. People could get hurt if we sit idle and do nothing!" Rose commented. Niccolo remembered what he needed to do in order to butter Cicero up for the alliance he was plotting to make. This also included getting on Rose's good side, so he would need to play the hero for today.

"I last saw the car go left; we can see what to do about it from there," Niccolo replied as he changed course.

The wake of the rogue Model T was already causing issues by the time Rose and Niccolo arrived. The vehicle completely ignored traffic laws and caused a disturbance as the pair watched police vehicles attempt to corner the machine. Just as the police cars were getting closer, the ghost car waited and then diverted at the perfect moment, causing a collision between the two. Niccolo had a tinge of worry as he felt Rose was going to push them right into danger. Rose tapped Niccolo's shoulder to keep driving and keep sight of the car. Niccolo honked the horn to get the opposing vehicle's attention as it slowed down to taunt the pair before going off. Niccolo held the wheel with one hand as he gripped his pistol out the window and started shooting. Civilians that passed by started to run in a panic from both the ongoing car and Niccolo's violation of public disturbance.

Niccolo groaned as he could hardly make his mark having to drive and shoot at the same time. Niccolo attempted to shoot out the tire of the car so that it would slow down, but it was difficult to aim. He looked to Rose to see if she would take over and drive, but she had another idea in mind. As she stewed in thought while Niccolo hopelessly lost track of the car, Rose tapped his arm.

"I have an idea! We're never going to catch it at this rate, but what if we don't have to?" Rose questioned.

Rose concentrated on their position and the last location of the car. She anticipated the car could drive at a speed of about two and a half times their rate if the car was going full speed. She planned to use portals to teleport their car into the opposing direction of the rogue ghost car. In doing so, she would be able to use the impact from the portal to ram the vehicle to tilt it over and try to make it stop long enough for the pair to figure out what controlled the vehicle. Niccolo found himself not only having to contend with the traffic caused by the car, but the panicked drivers around him. Each close call was nail-biting for the man as he swerved through a few lanes. Niccolo did his best to signal where he'd be turning and stopped short just as the tram nearly cut them off. He gave a deep breath as he felt his heart race.

Rose kept her ears pinned for any sounds as she heard the ghost car already causing havoc on another section of the road. For some reason, it decided to have a personal vendetta against other cars that honked towards it and rammed them at full speed. Rose covered her mouth in fear as she saw a man get flung out of the window from the impact. The other car crunched on impact as the Ghost Model T remained unaffected by the collision. A wreck was awaiting them as the car noticed their persistence.

Rose looked at the smoldering heap of overturned cars and confused people attempting to run to safety from the road. She had to rethink her strategy as approaching the car to ram it was only going to end in their deaths. Rose honked the horn and the car waited for them to get closer before speeding off once again. She concentrated and timed the presence of a portal to move them closer to make a right turn at the end of the street. Rose anticipated that the car would stay on the track and not try to collide or cut corners along the street. Niccolo proposed driving through a nearby alleyway for a surprise attack, but Rose already accounted for this.

"Wonderful idea! Now, what do we do when we get close to it?" Niccolo asked as he could hardly hide his surprise as they skipped most of the street.

"Ramming it is not an option. Get me close and I'm gonna send that thing to the ocean," Rose explained.

Niccolo complied with Rose's directions as she saw his attempts to dodge what remained of traffic on the road. He narrowly avoided a red light as he peered into the distance to see the outline of the car. Rose was preparing to do as she promised and with one more boost, the pair were on the opposing side of the car. She only had one shot to do this, as she minded the amount of gas left in Niccolo's tank before the car would speed off again without warning. She closed her eyes and summoned an opposing portal that was parallel to their orientation and ahead of the opposing car. Rose left a smug grin on her face as she looked through the rearview mirror and saw the car going full speed into the portal that appeared right in front. Rose had imagined the Atlantic Ocean; she'd seen it at least twice in her youth and the ghost car sank at a quick rate while water started to seep from the portal and flow into the local sewer. Rose quickly closed both active portals and gave a sigh of relief at her expertise.

"Thanks, Niccolo. You and Florence can really pull your weight. Take three dollars from my purse for gas, that should be more than enough for a full tank," Rose proposed as Niccolo happily accepted the payment.

"Now, I think you said you wanted to get some food for your men? I know a great grocery store," Rose commented.

Niccolo stretched as he felt the rush of monster hunting. He could hardly believe this is how both Rose and Cicero made their living, but she was a natural. Niccolo parked the car at a nearby gas station and looked into his wallet to pay for the price. Rose sat back, happy to look at her surroundings for a time while Niccolo pumped the gas. He let out a muted chuckle as he recalled the entire endeavor. He never imagined himself getting attached to the others and their antics, but there was something interesting about this arrangement, and decided to stick around.

The Shepherd's Shotgun

Rose and Cicero found themselves in the town of Yuma, a far cry from their more local cases in Phoenix. With Rose much more comfortable in her portal ability, traveling further distances for jobs was hardly a concern for the pair. The town of Yuma housed a lone mission on the edge of town that requested their aid. The pair's exploits grew from just a local scene to top bidding and Cicero was happy for the business. Rose wondered what a church could possibly need for their skill set, but as a believer herself, she was more than willing to help. The blue portal remained open as Cicero gathered his bearings, it was the first time he'd walked through and noticed the stark change in scenery. Cicero was befuddled by the sprawl of the town that boomed under trade. In his youth, Cicero recalled Yuma being a blip on the map that was hardly relevant until the Southern Pacific Railroad brought jobs to the area.

"In my day this place was a dump, what the hell happened?" Cicero asked as he looked around.

Rose gave a small chuckle as she watched Cicero pat himself down to make sure everything with him was still present. Just down the road, an open market with a bunch of sellers hosting local produce called their ears. Rose walked ahead and closed the vortex behind her as she urged Cicero to keep up. The two felt the unusually sweltering heat accompanied with a blow of humidity from the Colorado River. Rose hadn't expected such a distant place to be a boom town either, but the people were vibrant and authentic to her in a way that the big city of Phoenix lacked. Authenticity was something she always appreciated as she admired the bounties of citrus that she wanted to bite her mouth into. Her thoughts of spending her money on a large orange to juice it proper were interrupted by Cicero.

"Back when I worked for The Baron, I heard stories from some of the old-timers in the mine. This used to be Quechua land, back when the Spanish were trying to convert people-didn't work out too well. The Fort came and pacified the region, but now I think they have a reservation. Our clients aren't them, but they're close enough by. They make good jewelry out of topaz," Cicero explained to Rose.

Rose raised her arm and pointed in the distance as she recalled the directions to the mission. She saw a solid black iron gate and fencing that walled itself off from the rest of the town. The mission's buildings were a mosaic of adobe and stone that was resistant to fire, an adaptation kept out of concern for angry crowds to their presence. The mission was a far humbler abode than anticipated. There were four buildings, the main chapel, sleeping quarters for the nuns and priests, and two structures that remained unknown to them. Cicero noticed that the gate was open ajar to let them inside. He led first, and once he felt it was secure, let Rose follow right behind him. Rose noticed an assortment of relics and saintly imagery on display that elicited different reactions from the pair. Cicero was agnostic at best and found the whole thing ostentatious; the presence of gold and silver ingots left a sour taste in his mouth. As a devout Baptist, Rose had her opinions regarding Catholics as well.

Grandma always told me to never trust a man with a short service. Well, we're all friends here today. Let's see what they got to offer. Rose thought.

A lone woman holding a broom lifted her head from her task to see Rose and Cicero present. Rose recognized her as Mexican and struggled to remember even basic greetings in Spanish. She felt a sigh of relief as Cicero placed a hand on her shoulder and spoke on their behalf.

"Where's Father Sarmiento? He's supposed to be paying us a big sum for his problem." Cicero asked as the woman nodded. He was taken aback as she received a response in English.

"I will summon him, please stay here." The nun bowed and the broom fell to the floor.

Rose felt an unusual feeling emerge from the mission as it felt unusually quiet. After some time, the pair were met by a slightly overweight Mexican man. He was the head priest, with only a purple cloak behind him to differentiate himself from the rest of the people present. Rose studied his appearance carefully. He was an older man, roughly in his early fifties with a gut. He had a curled gray mustache and slicked hair. The priest hardly wore any sort of jewelry; this was reserved for the decor of the establishment. He and Rose stood almost eye to eye in height, as he gave a nice grin.

"You answered my call, and from so far away! The Lord is helpful for us today. Come inside and I will let you know what you are needed for," Father Sarmiento mentioned.

The interior of the cathedral had a stained-glass window from the front that reflected rays of light in the interior with the pews. On the front were multiple crucifixes and the main venue where the sermons were delivered. In the quiet of the church, Father Sarmiento was joined by the earlier nun. The four remained quiet as Father Sarmiento nodded his head to gather Rose's and Cicero's attention. He leaned back on a supporting pillar to the cathedral as he wiped his sweat from the ongoing heat. Another nun in the distance opened the back door to attempt to gather some air flow.

"To be honest, I wasn't sure we needed this, but there's nothing else for us to do. Well, we could use a donation to our missionary fund. We have made some purchases that The Vatican has not sanctioned. Mrs. Rose, and Mr. Cicero, can I take you to our nunnery?" Father Sarmiento explained.

"Sure, why not. Tea and crumpets before we go solve your job? I'm sure you've pilfered enough pockets already to get the fee paid," Cicero taunted as he let the man escort the pair.

"It's not one of ours, that is the problem. Our usual ways of solving things is—" Father Sarmiento opened as he turned around to see a question coming from Rose.

"Did you see a flash of purple, Father? A portal to another world? These usually accompany strange occurrences here," Rose asked.

"Purple portal? No—No such thing. As far as I have been told," the priest continued. Rose and Cicero exchanged a worried glance.

"I have done extensive research before hiring you both, you helped a friend of mine once. A florist in the big city recommended your services. No, I ask your help for demons. Demons that require more than holy water to vanish." He mentioned as he paused. This is where he usually heard ridicule in his statements. The priest adjusted his pace as he made room for an accompanying nun.

"Demons? Now, I'm willing to believe a lot of things, but demons...? A bit out there for me." Cicero commented as Rose shook her head. Cicero reserved his complete judgement on the matter, it was likely they mistook some sort of creature for a demon.

"Well, I offer this question. Miss Rose. You are a believer in God, Jesus, and his sacrifice, yes? I see it in your eyes. We may differ on some things, but our love remains the same. I must tell you this, if we live in a world where great good can be done, great evil unfortunately lives with it. I want to keep this town safe, even if they disparage our presence." Father Sarmiento mentioned.

"Now, normally, men are not allowed to enter the nunnery, but these are desperate times. I am not a military man, but a few of our nuns served as guerrilla fighters for Pancho Villa's forces a few years back. They made the call for us to move from holy water to silver bullets and walls of salt." The priest explained as he stopped by the door.

The accompanying nun walked past the others and offered a quickly paced knock. She alerted the other residents in the building to their new visitors. Cicero raised an eyebrow as he heard hushed Spanish spoken, his fluency diminished as he aged but he was able to understand far more than Rose. The head priest opened the door to a group of nuns postured around a Russian Maxim 1910 gun, with wheels, ammunition, and more. It was a remarkable specimen, having served in both World War 1 and the Russian Civil War. The nuns acquainted themselves with the piece as they were in debate on how to effectively field it.

Rose saw while most of the nuns were established older women, there were a few young ones around her age. The nuns gently approached the group and the more experienced in speaking in English asked Rose all sorts of questions. They admired her dress as they hardly were given much room to accessorize.

Rose had her mouth agape as she was floored by the possibility of any religious building holding a weapon of that caliber. She scratched her head as she noted the amount of firepower. Rose and Cicero both expected to have to do the bulk of the work, but having experienced hands was a worthy endeavor. Rose felt more comfortable about what she was asked to do with some extra support. Rose looked to see Cicero share the same dumbfounded remark. He'd seen piles of ammunition just stacked in organized caches.

"Well, shit. Looks like I'd go to service more often. What exactly are you up against, US Army regulars?!" Cicero remarked as he looked at the sheen of the gun.

"We wanted to get a Browning, but we needed to buy ammunition for the convent. The locked building you passed is our armory. We have old Winchesters saved from the days they were fighting Indians, but they now fill God's will. Our brothers and sisters down south were generous dealers, but to protect our way of life, the shepherd must fight off the coyotes, pumas, and jackals." Father Sarmiento mentioned with a curled-up fist.

"Color me impressed, Father, I had all your types pinned as yellow. Though, I must ask. When you said demons, what exactly did you mean?" Cicero asked, now more invested in the man's claim.

"Our demon of question is a Chinamen; he was very devout and went to our services for years. One day, he arrived with a fever, and naturally we tried to do our best. We had a doctor on staff at the time. His problem was beyond... mortal means. So, we decided to do a routine exorcism," the priest explained.

"Oh, right, a routine exorcism. Please, go on," Cicero commented. Rose pursed her lips at Cicero's reaction. The other nuns started to go quiet as the head priest continued to explain the conditions of the mission.

"His body started to spin and contort in ways we thought not possible. When the sun is red in the sky, he awakens, and the reign of terror commences. The last time we tried this, we lost two good priests. We have him chained and placed under a cement blockage. We remove it once to administer food. He seems to eat, but nothing else comes out. Now... with the gang war between The Owl and the other factions breaking loose in the big city, the lust for blood is unable to be controlled and I fear he may strike tonight. We are separated by miles of desert, but gang violence has struck here also. This is why I called you both to serve as experienced monster hunters," Father Sarmiento added.

As the trio left the nunnery, the remaining nuns continued to work maintenance on the big gun. Once again entering the cathedral, Father Sarmiento escorted Rose and Cicero to the storage area that served as the basement. A sole light bulb flickered and produced patchwork illumination for the three to see. A solid coffin that reinforced the body and weighed it down with iron chains was present. Rose felt a rush of sheer terror as she saw the display. Cicero was less animated in his reaction, but he felt his nerves run cold.

"You think this will happen tonight?!" Rose asked as she received only a wall of silence from the priest. She turned to see only the man's brown eyes staring back at her. She took a deep breath and tried to calm her nerves.

"Are you the only priest here? Where are the others?" Cicero questioned.

"The two we had to bury, but my successor is currently on a missionary trip. He has arranged the smuggling of ammunition to our building but is currently away. It's the nuns and myself for now," the priest answered with worry.

"It's half past three according to my pocket watch. We'll get prepared and be ready," Cicero commented. He went back up the stairs with Rose close behind.

The afternoon waned quickly as the priest warned where the midday started to turn red as described. Cicero saw that the nuns made good on their end by securing sandbags and more as they were postured up against the machine gun. A lone phonograph beyond them played a Spanish opera. Music was played throughout the mission at full blast to keep morale high. It was believed that music produced by the saints could quell the demon, but Rose and Cicero felt different. Unknown to the group, down below in the basement, a large cracking sound occurred. The nightmare had just begun.

Rose and Cicero remained together as they grasped their respective handguns and accompanied Father Sarmiento who held a double-barrel shotgun. Rose admired the sheen of the weapon, it was encrusted with brass and held various religious iconography. As the three arrived at where the basement was, there was a pause to see if today would truly be the day. The priest looked at Rose and Cicero. He volunteered to go first but was stopped by Rose's hand. The man locked eyes with her and Rose spoke.

"I'll go down there first. I'm the quickest out of us here and can run back up if I see anything out of the ordinary. Cicero, I want you out by the pews." Rose took a deep breath. She felt around for a cigarette but remained empty. Cicero tipped his hat and saw Rose off.

Rose descended the stairs with her pistol held out. Rose immediately noticed a stark change in scenery. In the depths of the decrepit basement, an unsettling contrast emerged as she noticed a bright and blinding light from the opposing end of the room. The light flickered and pulsated with shifting shadows on the damp walls. Rose looked behind her and saw that her own shadow had completely vanished.

"There's... something strange! The restraints are all gone, but it seems to be in some sort of prison!" Rose called from downstairs. Cicero's old ears didn't hear her words from down there, so she assumed he was occupied with another task. Rose felt compelled to approach as she laid eyes on the being. Her primary task was overridden as she heard a low melody play within her head. Rose felt an unusually icy feeling on the back of her neck as she realized the extent of what was happening to her.

It was calling to her. The transformation was complete. The shell that housed the infected man was a prison of gold, a pulsating entity with two large eyes that soon shattered as an unholy creature emerged from its cocoon of carnage. The being used the man as a host, but what remained of his body was no more. Rose saw the demon emerge from the shell and recoiled at how it looked perched on all fours in its full form. It shifted around the room, limbs undulating like a tentacle in its wake. The demon's body was covered in strange tattoos that seemed to move and writhe with every gesture. Rose saw its white coloration, a lightly feathered body that appeared like down on a goose. Its fingers were long and hooked with jagged claws, ready to rip flesh asunder.

She... has... given... life beyond. The demon spoke into Rose's mind as he then rattled off some command in a guttural language that made Rose's skin crawl. Her eyes started to roll back into her head, and she attempted to step back but found herself completely immobilized. Rose gathered her willpower and conjured a portal to fall through the basement floor. She propelled herself just a few feet backwards from the creature's influence. The air grew frigid as it hulked towards her. The creature took a breath, but its chest and body did not move. It was almost as if it was unneeded. The harbinger of doom as depicted by the priest came to reality. Rose ran away up the stairs and shot a few bullets behind her to buy her time.

It took little time for Cicero to know what happened as he instinctively whipped out his LeMat revolver as he saw Rose run right past him. As instructed, Cicero propped himself up by the pews and hid behind one of the pillar walls. He could hear the spider-like puttering of the demon as he moved through the closed door. The very essence of the wood bent to the creature's will. Cicero clenched his hand into a fist as he emerged to see the demon find itself in the main chapel. Cicero took the offensive and let out two hits of his revolver. The first missed and ricocheted off a piece of stained glass that littered onto the creature's body. The second bullet was an effective hit on the right foot. It groaned in physical pain, but found that with blood, it could restore itself.

He will never come back. You failed. You failed. The demon projected into Cicero's mind. Cicero let out a curdled yell as he tried to get the creature's influence out of his mind. The distraction was enough for the creature to leap onto Cicero and pin him to the floor. Cicero felt his eyes slowly start to turn back, much like that of Rose's. The creature's mouth was devoid of teeth but instead operated with a sucking motion that generated enough force to leave injuries. Cicero attempted to punch the demon off him as he was too close for the discharge of his revolver. The recoil alone would be enough to knock himself out if he wasn't careful.

Cicero restored control over his body as he faced the threat head on through pure grit. For a split second, Cicero saw the creature transfigure as it revealed the stripped away flesh of the possessed man. His face emerged from the center of the demon and was riddled with blood. The blood seeped from the rear end of the creature towards the floor. Cicero could hardly mask his disgust as the demon continued to contort. He held out his gun and shot once more to silence the screams that reverberated in his mind. Out of the cacophony, a foreign voice called out to him that filled the chapel for but a moment.

"Help... me..." The voice called out in Mandarin.

Cicero saw that the possessed man was in deep sorrow as he called out for any answer to his plea. Cicero rarely froze, but he was unsure of what to do. The man attempted to regain control from the demon as the fused combination fought with itself. Cicero kept his gun out as there was no telling when the battle was lost. Cicero watched as pews fell over with the internal battle that commenced. Various statuettes and precious sculptures fell to the floor in pieces as there was an epic struggle between them.

Cicero watched in vain hope that the man could overcome, just long enough to die with some sanity left within him. Cicero prepared for the next shot. The body of the demon lay still, as if it were frozen in time. Cicero slowly moved over to get a better glance and immediately sidestepped, as the man was no more. The demon had won and lunged straight towards him. Cicero fired the shot and the crack pierced, but it was a traded wound. Cicero's arm was bloodied from the creature's encounter. It came again with a ravenous hunger to feed.

"Damn, my arm!" Cicero winced as he traded blows with the creature. Cicero felt a large batch of blood leak from his body as he kicked the demon off him. With Cicero's blood, the creature recovered what remained that was shot off from the silver bullet. As Cicero retreated, he saw that it came again for another round. Cicero prepared for the worst as his gun had a jam. Out of the corner of his eye, however, a light in the darkness came by. The stained glass reflected the dusk of the outside as the shadows continued through the chapel.

"Asmodeus! Foul demon of this temple, face my wrath! Cicero, aid for you my friend!" Father Sarmiento mentioned as he prompted Cicero to duck. With the blast of his double-barrel shotgun, the demon was knocked back and attempted to crawl up the walls to recover strength.

Rose heard the commotion in the chapel as she was earlier outside with the nuns. She saw them mobilizing and getting ready to construct a wall of salt to trap the being. Rose's primary concern was keeping the demon contained in the confines of the mission and making sure it didn't get out.

She entered the cathedral and saw Cicero bleeding while he was helped by the head priest. Rose tried to get their attention. She raised an eyebrow at Cicero's reaction.

"Rose! Look above you!" Cicero called out. Rose turned her head to see the demon sequestered on the roof. She gave a slightly regretful look to the priest as she was damaging a holy site. Rose peppered a few bullets that pierced the being's skin.

Rose realized that attacking the demon directly wasn't going to do much as she saw its skin slowly repairing itself. Rose shot one of the supporting wooden beams, and prayed that it wouldn't collapse the roof, as the demon was jostled from the speed of the falling one to the floor. As the demon hurdled towards the three, Rose stepped in front of Cicero and Father Sarmiento. She quickly conjured a blue portal for the creature to jump through and find itself on the outside of the chapel. Rose urged the pair to come quickly and join her outside before it got too far. Rose sent the demon forward out close towards the firing range of the nuns with their Maxim gun. The three were enthralled to see that Rose's gambit paid off with the demon trapped in the square given to it. Rose was surprised that the salt wall actually held up and the demon refused to move. She closed the portal quickly as the creature lunged within its space.

The cathartic roar of the machine gun sounded off as the nuns supported the belt-feed. A rhythmic organization was present as Rose, Cicero, and Father Sarmiento opened fire on the creature in support. It took a large firing line of the four. As the bullets rained down on the demon, a chorus of gunfire deflated its ethereal hide. The impact from the gun sent bits and pieces of flesh in all directions as it vanished and melted into silver dust. Smoke from the gun dissipated from the sides as the bullets continued. The demon contorted and convulsed as it attempted in vain to sway the nuns with its telepathy, but their faith and conviction kept them focused. The creature unveiled unearthly moans of agony until it was nothing more than a puddle.

As the creature was once a man, the nuns scooped what remained of the debris and looked to Father Sarmiento to give a burial. The man had no next of kin and had left much of his assets to the church.

"When I was down there... The demon spoke to me. It told me, "She has given life beyond." What does that mean? On its body, I saw engravings of strange text. It was marked with something, or I guess, by someone," Rose asked as a nun went to treat Cicero's injury with bandages.

"I do not know. The scripture remains cryptic, but you and Mister Cicero are resourceful people. It will be found out. As always, we must prepare for the next mass. Our contribution will be sent to you in the mail," Father Sarmiento commented.

"By the way, your secret is safe with us. Consider it a confession. Your... ability to make the holes," the priest added.

Rose and Cicero gave their respective goodbyes as the nuns surrounded Father Sarmiento. Rose and Cicero walked towards the back of the chapel and Rose conjured a portal for them to return to Cicero's homestead back on the outskirts of Phoenix. Cicero decided to keep his message given to him by the demon a secret. He had a feeling what the creature alluded to and wanted to not think about it anymore. The pair hoped that would be the end of their blows with demons, but the concerns of these messages kept Rose up at night. Just who was the one that gave life to the man? Is Hell a place one can truly come and go?

Go Forth And Prosper

After their slew of cases, Rose and Cicero were in town as the two decided to go watch a movie together. Some downtime was much needed for the duo as they were running ragged from their errands and needed time to think of a plan of action for the upcoming gala that The Baron and Baroness were hosting. Rose was waiting on her best dress to be cleaned at the washers, while Cicero checked on the details for a pressed suit. Cicero's ticket intended for Claudia became Rose's as she was busy with work and Cicero wanted to catch a midweek show to save a quick buck. The ever-resourceful cowboy tilted his hat as he and Rose approached the theater.

Rose covered her eyes as she was blinded by a series of flashing lights that signaled to the world. The bright lights were a stark contrast to the overcast late afternoon, where streaks of orange sunlight escaped the barrier of clouds above. The entrance to the theater was free to access as the usher took their tickets inside for the venue. Rose and Cicero stepped into the room and looked around. A slew of posters detailing the newest pictures and their prices attached were on the flanking sides of the walls. Rose was paralyzed with indecision.

"So, you've ever seen a picture before?" Cicero asked.

"Well, no. We never had a theater where I grew up. First time for everything," Rose commented. Rose turned around as she heard Florence's voice emerge from a nearby bathroom.

"Florence! Hey there!" Rose waved as she walked out.

Florence wore a dress with floral arrangements sewed in of various flowers. It was a port in the storm for the drab fashion Rose noticed people wore on their daily commute. She walked by with a bright grin as she immediately hugged Rose and made her way to Cicero. Cicero grumbled as he opened for a hug as well. Cicero felt his bones crack as Florence smeared a tinge of makeup on his jacket with her tight grip.

"Oh, my lovely Rose, hello! Nicki's here too, he went to go buy snacks. Wait, I got a big old popcorn, we can share! We're all seeing the same picture, right? Go Forth and Prosper?" Florence asked. Florence's attention turned to Cicero, who had his sights on the ticketmaster.

The usher that manned the lobby was busy with his nose embedded in a dime novel. Cicero walked over and snapped his fingers to get the man's attention. He slowly moved his head to meet Cicero's as he sat on a stool and reached over to a drawer.

"I came by the other day and bought these tickets in advance for two, but we want to swap movies. That possible?" Cicero asked as he unraveled a pair of balled-up papers. The ticketmaster raised an eyebrow as he read the printed title.

"Yes sir. That will be sixty cents," the ticketmaster mentioned as he held his hand out for payment.

"Excuse me? Sixty cents to swap a movie? Do you have a senior citizen's discount?" Cicero attempted to negotiate. Rose could only look in embarrassment as she started to fiddle around in her purse.

"Don't you dare take out a single penny," Cicero ordered Rose as she rifled around her bag.

"Do you have anything to verify your age, sir?" the usher mentioned as he started to chew a piece of gum. His obnoxious chewing and disinterested disposition only made Cicero more annoyed.

"W-What? Are you blind boy? I got gray in my beard, and it hurts to piss in the middle of the night. What do you think? This is a movie theater, not the post office," Cicero retorted. Cicero grumbled as he placed two quarters and a dime into the man's hands to cover the new tickets.

Rose and Cicero walked over with Florence to find Niccolo attempting to open a wrapper of saltwater taffy. A few other movie patrons were sitting at a communal discussion table close by to the group as they talked about the last film they watched. A Hansel and Gretel retelling, the audience anticipated more of a divergence from traditional story beats but gave it a middling rating due to the use of orchestra music for pivotal scenes. As the movie experience was considered higher art by several people in the city, there were a number of chairs and other furniture for anxious movie-goers to talk about what they saw. Niccolo gave them a silent nod of acknowledgment, he hadn't planned on running into the pair, but their presence was appreciated.

"I take it you found us because we wanted to sit together for the same cinema. Well, welcome Rose. Cowboy," Niccolo said. He bit the wrapper and finally opened it, much to his relief. Niccolo ripped a piece of taffy and chewed on it for a while as they looked towards the room.

The theater was larger than either Rose or Cicero anticipated, the two saw a screen occupy the front of the room. There was also a stage present that had musicians dressed in suits who accompanied an assortment of instruments. Rose was confused at the endeavor, but Florence explained everything to her. As movies lacked sound, musicians were hired out to the theater to deliver exposition material for important scenes and in some cases, practical effects, to really sell what was displayed in the film. Rose looked up and saw a speaker, one where the narrator would comment on events during intermissions. Cicero looked at his pocket watch in disbelief as he heard from Niccolo that the movie would be two and a half hours in length. The last time Cicero entered a movie theater was almost twenty years ago, and it was only about ten minutes worth of animation.

Another usher went by and received mixed reactions from the other theater viewers. The ushers were quick to harass young couples that started to get handsy as indecency was bad for the brand. Niccolo sat next to Florence at the end and gathered all the tickets together to show they sat in a row. Rose looked slightly nervous as she noticed the clientele of the theater. Rose had seen no signs barring minorities from entering, but she noticed the usher's delay as he looked at her much longer than the others. Accompanying grimaces from both Cicero and Niccolo dissuaded the stalwart employee to go elsewhere as they already had their tickets validated at the entrance. Not wanting to cause any further issues, the usher left, and the show began. As the movie started, the four settled into their positions and silently passed snacks to one another. Niccolo pointed at the logo of one of the companies that sponsored the film which had a roaring lion. He marveled at how lifelike the imagery was.

"Do you think the lion is fake, or did they train it to sit there?" Niccolo asked aloud as Rose shrugged her shoulders in response. Rose focused on the changing scenery as the title cards started to play over the screen. She raised an eyebrow as she saw the title card was for a reshowing of a previous film.

"This doesn't look our movie, did we get the wrong one?" Rose asked Cicero in a low whisper. Rose's inexperience with the movie concept was something Cicero found very amusing and enjoyed it highly.

"No—These are advertisements you watch before the film starts. You know how it is, companies have to sell you the latest snake oil. Well I ain't buying. Anyway, get comfortable." Cicero took a scoop of popcorn.

The movie was an engaging endeavor. The promise on the posters said that the film would be the blockbuster of the year, a new category as movies finally breached past the niche category. *Go Forth and Prosper* was a best-selling book, just three years ago, and Rose could recall every line of the characters. Marketed as a romantic comedy, it featured a highly love-addicted young man who balanced several romantic prospects in the city of Chicago after doing a tour of duty in The Great War. The mystery was finding who would be the definitive choice. Under her breath, Rose whispered the dialogue of the protagonists as they appeared on screen with an accompanying title card, only to be surprised by a role that only had one line in the source material. Rose recognized a woman on screen. She wore an elegant sundress in the middle of the day that was reflected with a flash of intense light from a nearby camera to fill in the scene. The music around Rose played at a large volume as an array of trumpets accompanied a young man who went to buy flowers. Rose couldn't believe what she witnessed.

It's her! She actually did it. She made it into a film, and she has multiple lines. Rose thought as she covered her mouth in shock. The woman depicted as the gardener was her sister that had finally gotten her chance on the silver screen. She recalled her conversation with her parents, and had she felt so inclined to speak to them, it would be an interesting conversation.

Florence was enthralled with everything around her. Aside from the movie, the movement of the musicians, the position of the seats and the angles used to capture the motion for the endeavor all received high marks. The man had gotten into a suspenseful fight with a ruffian and the dodges from the character were well choreographed. She found herself practically bobbing and weaving in unison with the actor. She tapped her fingers on her handrest with the sound of the instruments and kept her humming low as she didn't want to disturb others. Behind her, another group was starting to discuss their theories regarding what would happen next. On the left side of this group were a few teenage boys who had their fun flicking peanuts at the focused moviegoers. Florence was surprised that children could afford to pay for the tickets to get in but also reasoned that many just snuck in.

"My bet is he's going for the baker's daughter. No-What are you talking about? She's easily the best choice. Brunettes do it best. Just watch," a woman mentioned. She seemed to be in an argument with her companions.

"Excuse me... Could you please keep your discussions a little lower. We're trying to watch," Rose whispered. Rose's gentle suggestion was ignored by the rowdier group that was sat behind them. Rose bit her tongue in annoyance but felt a bit of solidarity come from Niccolo, who slowly turned around and stared at the group. His frustration was more apparent as his face was clearly reddened in anger. Rose felt some sympathy, English wasn't Niccolo's first language, so she felt that he'd have a harder time regardless.

"Shut up! Quit your talking, I am trying to figure out what is happening, and I cannot do that with your yammering! If you want to talk, go outside! Bah, Americans!" Niccolo yelled as he got the entire attention of the room. Niccolo felt a bit of rage surge through him as other patrons of the movie stared at their row while the musicians did their best to ignore the scene.

"What the hell do you want? They were rude and I am right," Niccolo commented while Rose and Florence sank further into their seats. Cicero gave a muted chuckle as his eyes remained focused on the film.

The last remaining hour of the film flew by at an incredibly fast pace with the audience pinned to their seats hoping for more. Rose and the others stood up from their seats and clapped twice, once for the movie itself, and the live orchestra that helped the works come to life. It received a standing ovation as was customary for any finished film, but this gesture was also a topic of hot debate. In an age where cameras became more affordable, people could afford to be especially critical of the films their money helps produce.

The four felt some collective satisfaction as they talked among themselves outside the venue. Cicero stayed quiet while he listened to Rose talk about her experience with the theater. She was glad to have such a unique experience that she hoped to repeat soon. Rose was eager to schedule the next movie as she wanted something to really tear apart like the movie critics she saw outside. Cicero was a professional instigator when the time came, and he felt like having some friendly debate. He eyed the three of his companions and spoke freely.

"Alright, I'm gonna say it and get this started while we look for somewhere to eat. I didn't like the movie," Cicero mentioned as he lit a cigarette.

Cicero leaned back on the wall and chewed his tongue with a sly grin. Cicero prepared his noteworthy defense as he received the ire of Rose, Florence, and Niccolo. *Go Forth and Prosper* was a well acclaimed hit, in both movie and book form, and it only irked them further that Cicero wanted to immediately lambast it without time to stew. Niccolo decided to take on Cicero's provocation with full force.

"Of course, cowboy, always the contrarian! Please tell us your gripes. I would love to know the culture you Americans missed out on in cinema," Niccolo teased. He placed his hand on Cicero's shoulder. He twitched his nose slightly as Cicero blew some of the excess smoke in jest.

"It's supposed to be a romantic comedy, but I wasn't laughing other than how sad the main lead was. Now to sum it all up. He goes for the established saleswoman, has her own textile store. Responsible choice, but I have some doubts if the partnership will truly last. She rejected his advances, and he just says, sure I'll go the parlor and lift some weights? That's your plan? This is supposed to be a romance! Where's the flowers? The candlelight dinners? This gives men the wrong message. You can't expect to do the bare minimum and come out on top," Cicero explained while Rose and Florence shot a glance at one another. Rose gave an interested shrug at Cicero's words. Niccolo waved his hand to get his point across.

"I disagree. It is romantic Cicero; he sees that his current life is not enough, and he is working to bring discipline into it, so that he can be the one she deserves. The first thing starts with health in the body and good things will follow. He did this for himself and got her affection in the process," Niccolo debated.

You'd think they suggested the movie given how passionate they are about it. It's sweet. Rose thought.

"Don't get me started on the expressions. So fake and overplayed. They want big bucks for acting like they're in a funhouse mirror? Pshaw!" Cicero commented. Florence's face reddened as she was offended by Cicero's statements. She had a soft spot for thespians, actors, and the arts in general that contrasted with Cicero's crass opinion.

"Acting's a hard job, Cicero! They do all their own stunts, like trapeze artists at the circus. You know how hard it was to do that scene where they boxed on top of a moving train?" Florence cut in sharply.

"They're called carnivals and those are art. This is just a lack of noise, the narrative just falls apart by the second act and you just want it to end already. You know what—Rose, what did you think?" Cicero mentioned.

"Personally, I liked the music. I didn't realize that they played a live accompanying piece with it. It's a concert and a film all in one! I think the book was better, but they can only do so much. It's a cliffhanger ending so he can make a sequel," Rose remarked happily. She attempted to hold in a laugh as Cicero started to pantomime one of the characters from the film. He stumbled around as if he was a drunk who knew no better.

"If I could get a word in, I liked the use of color in the film! Such a great feat to accomplish with the screen," Florence remarked. She raised an eyebrow as Rose, Cicero, and Niccolo started to laugh at her.

"Bless your heart Florence, the movie was in black and white! We all saw it right?" Rose remarked as she wiped a tear from her eye. Niccolo rubbed his stomach and gave a nod.

"Actually, most set directors will make a tailored room in specific colors that is designed to reflect light off surfaces. The chosen hues all help contribute to mood lightin' and more to set the scene. I'm a photographer after all!" Florence said with a rosy grin that stifled the other's mocking.

"Point taken," Rose and Cicero admitted.

"Now of course, there's one more matter we need to discuss since we're all here. The Gala that The Baron and Baroness are hosting. It's in a few days. This is everything we've been working towards," Rose mentioned.

The four stood in silence as they realized the scale of the endeavor. Cicero's hands were pale as he squeezed the life out of them. He felt an embroiled rage. Niccolo rubbed his hands together in support. He was well aware of the opportunity that struck him. The Baron, out of the picture, would be an absolute uproar of loyalties in the criminal underground. Niccolo needed to act and provide the cushion for the downfall, and he hoped that with The Baron's defeat, he could show that Cirano was not untouchable. It was far more convenient for the man to be in fear if possible. Florence knew that the biggest shakers in town would be present, The Baron and Baroness knew just about everyone, and the thoughts of revenge were just as palpable. She didn't only want to punish those that ruined her life, her green eyes filled with a sense of justice that roared for the truth. All those with guilty hands would face the power of the press with camera in hand.

Rose held more muted thoughts. The Baron was an acceptable loss, he was responsible for horrid sins, and yet she couldn't bring herself fully into the fold. She above all else knew that The Baron was immortal. She wondered if this distraction would be enough to dislodge him for a time. As she learned more about her abilities, she found that with the inevitability of the rebirth, it became a futile endeavor to truly kill The Baron. Rose could only hope that she could retain the nerve to strike somehow, but how could it be done? It seemed like an illogical plan, but Rose felt she couldn't voice this properly to the others without coming off as a traitor.

The Gala

Rose honored the mandatory invitation to the event hosted by The Baron and Baroness. The event was supposed to honor their anniversary, and Rose was encouraged to bring all her friends. The Baron's words hung over her as she felt powerless and went through the motions. Not one to let an opportunity go to waste, Rose contacted Florence and Niccolo to remind them prior to the event to get prepared. Rose was bound by obligation; The Baron and Baroness had truly primed her as their successor to carry on their work.

Rose found the event to be interesting, a celebration of love that was still something kept secret between them. The Baron had mentioned public appearances meant they would be celebrating twenty years in matrimony as opposed to the cryptic thought of two centuries. Rose found it hard to fathom the truth about her mentors, that they were truly immortals who had seen the rise and fall of many. Yet they remained sane enough to enjoy milestones such as marriage. Rose thought about her conversation with Venus and wondered if she could make things work with Malcolm to be married that long.

Cicero's home was the meeting place for the group as they all held a mutual interest in arriving there. Rose adjusted her signature orange dress in the mirror while Florence gave her sign of approval. Rose looked behind her to see the rest of the team finishing up their tasks to prepare. Niccolo and Cicero debated length of ties and other meaningless gestures that older men debated to fill up the space.

"This is a load of horseshit, you know that?" Cicero complained as he squeezed into a suit that Niccolo loaned him. Claudia laughed as she watched the group contend with their own battles in stuffy clothing. It was rare that such events graced their lives and they needed to be ready for it.

"What's our plan of attack?" Florence asked as she caked on an extra layer of lipstick.

"Rose is the guest of honor. She's going to go up there and be the point of attention. I plan on putting two in The Baron the second I get close enough to find him. If I have enough bullets left, I'm taking out his wife too. It's all connected. Either help me or don't, just stay out the way," Cicero commented. Rose gulped at Cicero's words as her eyes met the carpet below her feet.

"Listen cowboy, I understand revenge is important. We need to coordinate. I help you, you help me. All I need is the bounty, so, you can get the satisfaction of the kill, but I need to place my mark as well. Understand? I planned on disguising myself as a server. I can get close enough to identify the target," Niccolo mentioned.

"They'll have security, Cicero. Lots of em, if they're anything like that mayor we saw some time ago. It'd be best if you worked with Nicki to take them out instead of fighting with each other. I don't know how you're going to get a gun in there. Rose has her... portal things, but those are a little obvious," Florence warned.

"The Owl—Cirano, might also be in attendance. I don't know if he will be, but if he is, that makes our job easier. I know it interests us all if he's taken care of," Rose mentioned, her low voice gathered the three's attention.

Rose stood next to the house and smoked a cigarette while her nervous shakes started to subside. She'd never attended an event of this scale and was practically terrified. A Shadow Bouncer was nothing compared to the sea of hungry sharks waiting for her in the country club. Rose did some earlier reconnaissance of the location; it was an extensive property built on the outskirts of Phoenix for the most ostentatious parties. Florence clapped as Cicero finally exited the home with his pressed suit and took a slow walk to the others. Rose sighed as she could clearly tell Cicero came prepared with an iron strapped to his groin. It wasn't his usual revolver, but something far more covert. She assumed it was going to be a joke, but Cicero meant every word regarding his efforts.

The drive over to the country club was silent, everyone knew their places. Rose only spoke on occasion to offer a quicker route for Niccolo to drive by. He ignored any traffic signs at Cicero's insistence for wanting to go as fast as he could. Roughly one hour on the road later, Niccolo identified what looked like a long stream of cars that started to pool in. The currently arriving cars were pointed in the correct direction by valet. The gala appeared to be even larger than they anticipated. Not only was the venue itself filled with people, but there were also structures located on the outside for the event. In an entourage of almost five hundred people, it was going to be a logistical nightmare for the group to communicate. Niccolo parked the car some distance from the others, in anticipation of a quick getaway, and to find their vehicle when all was said and done.

The four exited the car and stepped forward, giving one last look before slowly making their way to the crowd. Cicero recognized a few local celebrities from the newspaper that were in attendance. He hardly had any heroes at his age, but he was disappointed to see those that were supposedly for the working man betray their morals. Cicero's eyes peered through the blob of gray and black suits among them to search for either Cirano or The Baron. He and Niccolo both looked for armed security. Niccolo carried a tiny, silenced pistol in the back of his trunk and wrapped it up tightly in a handkerchief. He anticipated getting patted down and stuffed it in the interior of his suit jacket to hopefully skate by.

The country club was three stories tall and built with a modern design that echoed the Art Deco aesthetic of New York City. An elaborate mixture of black and gold emitted light that advertised its placement. The immaculate pruned landscape filled with grass was a testament to man's arrogance as it was a mountain to keep fed. Two giant fountains that spat out water at timed intervals were joined by commissioned statues of a couple in matrimony. Rose looked into the stone eyes of the model that represented The Baron. She hardly felt a difference between that and the living man. The pink sky that came from a setting sun was a bright bastion of light that illuminated the dresses of the women in attendance. All around them, the clamor for The Baron and Baroness grew restless. The pair were the hosts, and it was considered fashionable in high society to arrive late. Rose was unsure of where she needed to go, but it would be separate from the others.

Rose looked at Florence, who seemed frozen with the amount of stuff going around her. She quickly snapped her fingers to grab Florence's attention. Florence bit one of her fingernails as she noticed the crowd hadn't been let inside yet. She grabbed Rose's arm and held it tightly as she didn't want them to get separated just yet. Rose stood on her toes to get a quick glance above the crowd and saw that the enforcers for the event were finally getting things organized. There was a mountain of free wine and liquors being passed around to keep the guests happy as they stepped forward. Men were given a quick pat down and told to disarm at the gate while women passed by without issue. Rose laughed, if she had any room in her dress, she could easily bring her gun without a care in the world. Cicero and Niccolo walked ahead of Florence and Rose as they needed to be patted down longer.

Rose was stunned by the immaculate beauty of the establishment as security let her and Florence inside. The Baron had arranged for the country club to be modeled after The Garden of Eden; real fruit-bearing trees were planted for the venue. There were elaborate paintings on loan from various museum collections and music that reverberated through a series of phonographs. Nothing short of a hedonistic Roman spectacle, Rose could already see drugs pooling in from the women that hid bits and pieces in their dresses. The men entered shortly after them, reuniting with their groups. Rose waited by the entrance for Cicero and Niccolo who shared the look of awe. Regardless of their affiliation, they remained impressed, it was an elaborate structure and almost a labyrinth in its scope. The largest center room was a general eating area that was filled with the most elaborate dishes. Rose saw a flurry of seafood that remained ever fresh, despite being miles away from any water. Those that wished to eat were encouraged to sit down by security and were informed that The Baron and Baroness would arrive in due time.

It was Atlantic City, localized entirely within in a building, there were an assortment of distractions that Florence already looked at. She saw a photo booth, painting stations, conversation areas, various performances such as knife-throwing, amenities including pool halls, a reflecting pool, and an interior terrarium. The country club also featured a library, a perfect place for Rose to hide out her time until the big event. Cicero raised an eyebrow as he saw some of the men clamoring to rush towards the card tables. Niccolo complained as he knew he'd have no chance at trying to find his target in such a congested space. From the top of the establishment, the highest ranked aristocrats of the third floor could look down on the others. Cicero looked up at the glass panes. These areas were already populated with early guests that had a direct relationship to The Baron and Baroness.

"They're arriving late, eh? You go up there and squeeze as much info as you can. You're the guest of honor after all. I'll hustle here and win us some money at the card tables. The party ends when I get bored," Cicero voiced to Rose. He let her go with a wave while he lit a cigarette and made his way to the gambling table.

While Rose was aware of the plan and helped orchestrate it for Cicero to have his just revenge, she felt a strange feeling come over her. She was humbled by the sheer effort of The Baron and Baroness for her to be included and a centerpiece of it all. Rose knew they wanted her to feel at ease and comforted, all the while, more under the surface brewed. Rose denied it to herself, but she craved to fill the void of attention. She would do anything to get the approval that her parents lacked to give her, and an opportunity to have her own agency. Rose looked to find Florence and saw that she made her way to the opposing hallway.

Florence walked past Rose and gave an affectionate tap on the shoulder before continuing. She saw an elaborate ballroom where there was an assortment of dancers that were in sync to classical music. Attendees were arranged in a circle and clapped happily to such a display. She quietly hummed to the music as she overheard the conversation of others talking about things that gave little interest to her. Her eyes perked up slightly as she recognized Niccolo among the guests who was caught up in conversation with another man. She could tell from his body language he was looking for any excuse to leave as he was given a barrage of questions. Florence chuckled as she watched Niccolo further embarrass himself before deciding to come to his rescue. She tapped his shoulder and Niccolo turned around to an immediate sigh of relief as he distanced himself from the other man. Niccolo had his ear to the ground regarding the location of The Baron, who apparently had yet to arrive. The man was an art appraiser and attempted to ask Niccolo's opinion of the paintings, a subject he found completely boring. Niccolo looked for a way to occupy his time as he leaned against a wall.

"Wait. Before you set off again," Florence commented. Niccolo raised an eyebrow, he was more than happy to not engage and keep his eyes on a swivel.

"We should dance. I want to appreciate the music here before you and Cicero blow it all up," Florence mentioned as she held her hand out to Niccolo. She had a large grin as she watched Niccolo's eyes meet hers to the hand below. Florence yanked him forward and waited for an energetic jig to come across.

Left on her own now, Rose decided that her talents would be best used in following Cicero's instructions. Rose's directive was to make her way to The Baron and Baroness as quickly as possible. She was, after all, their guest and she needed to keep up appearances. Rose stood out among the many arrivals at the party. Rose noticed that even the help for the affair wasn't black, they were mostly Mexican. Rose heard bits and pieces of conversation from wannabe senators and other politicians, hoping to lick the boots of their rich benefactors for more money. At the base of the stairs, an armed guard stood by and looked over Rose. He was a tall mobster with an assortment of scratches on his face that contrasted from the carefully arranged appearances of people she encountered that were caked in makeup.

"Go on through. You're expected," the man said with a mischievous grin that unnerved Rose as she walked past him.

The second floor of the country club was just as rowdy as the first, but there seemed to be more organization in the chaos. Rose was met with a surrounding haze of cigar smoke that permeated the area and came to her dress. Rose noticed that The Baron and his esteemed guests were sitting on various couches aligned with silk cushions. The drunken yells of the lower floor were more inviting compared to those that remained here. Rose felt as if she was an invader in such a space. While the rest of The Baron's surrounding entourage were filled with drink, The Baron remained cold and unmoving. His charisma operated at the turn of a switch, he had no real use for these people other than meaningless social proof. It was evident to Rose that The Baron grew utterly bored with the conversation at hand. As a drunken man slapped the side of the couch and spilled a tinge of absinthe on the floor, The Baron saw Rose standing quietly out of the corner of his vision. His mood brightened immediately as he stood up and walked over to her. He looked into her eyes.

"Ah, Rose. I was expecting you'd make your way here at some point. Enthrall an old man, would you? Play me in pool in the next room," The Baron ordered as Rose complied.

"Is there something not to your liking? My wife even made sure to get the soda you liked," The Baron asked her. Rose was taken aback by such a personal gesture, but it was just one additional step the two took into knowing everything there was to know about her.

"I'm just being gracious to my host," Rose said, which prompted a simple nod from The Baron.

"I apologize for not seeking you out on your arrival. I like to have a moment to myself before we announce our presence to the rest of the social ladder and as you can see, I was occupied. Consider this the pre-party to the true festivities. It is only 6 PM after all," The Baron mentioned. The Baron glanced to one of the security to bar off the current hall for their game. Nobody else would be allowed to enter.

The pool hall was quiet as two tables with associated equipment were present. The noise of the outside filtered in, just barely for Rose to keep her sanity past the empty space. The Baron gestured to Rose to pick a stick tailored to her height. Rose heard a nearby radio start to play some low-tuned jazz that came as a relief to her while she had something to bring her mind towards. The Baron's words brought her focus back to the task at hand.

"You have my attention, as you are my guest. Are you aware of the rules? Speak," The Baron said as he stretched his arms out. He lit a cigar and puffed it to the side while he rubbed his chin in thought.

"I am. I'll take stripes, you can take solids," Rose mentioned while The Baron gave a proud grin.

The Baron appreciated pool to a great degree and Rose having her own preference meant there would be at least some skill to be had. He would give his all. Rose thought for a moment about how to establish rapport with The Baron, particularly so that she could leave as soon as possible.

Judging from what she knew, The Baron needed to feel he was in control of the conversation for now, and then she would pry in further. She remembered to look for things of pride when talking to the rich and successful, this is how she navigated her housekeeping job and could run the clock until it was time to leave. Rose racked the balls together for The Baron to break. He was a renowned expert, as his positioning alone demonstrated the amount of thought placed into his skill of the game.

"How did you get your start in business here? I know you have many contacts, but everyone starts somewhere," Rose asked, the tone of her voice came with a sense of genuine curiosity.

"Well Rose, you know the truth regarding my wife and me. I've been here for quite some time. But—I started out originally as a courier, bringing letters for people with egos far larger than my own. It was a wistful affair, headed through territory with hostile natives and mountain men that wore beaver skins on the frontier. After I learned the art from the Salem Witches, I visited other realms, saw what the other versions of myself were doing, and did it better after I killed them." The Baron explained. To him, it was a victimless crime to accumulate his wealth. He paused to take another huff of his cigar and exhaled.

"By the time The American Revolution started, I had people delivering things for me, and eventually, the railway company was born. If I recall, you were a housekeeper before our arrangement. Were you good at this occupation?" The Baron asked as he opened for Rose to hit her end. He watched with interest as Rose was able to land two balls in separate pockets.

"Good is a loaded statement. I did what was asked of me and retained enough dignity doing it. That's all I can ask for at my age. I want to become a teacher; I want to teach science," Rose said as she studied The Baron's reaction. For someone as well traveled as he, he understood the need of educators, but in the case before him, there was something that needed to be said.

"It is low-born work, but all work must have pride in it, otherwise it mustn't be done at all. They say those who can't do, teach. I associate myself with doers, and this is why we have conversation Rose. Consider your aspirations and why you are here with us, and not down there. You have potential. My wife sees it as much as I do," The Baron encouraged. He matched Rose's gambit with the ball, having enough skill to push her ball out the way, and corner himself up for a free point.

"Our goals may not align directly, but our interest in the multiverse requires many hands to understand. I'm not an agent of the State. I hardly follow such a concept, but there is something out there that requires our inquiry," The Baron continued as Rose nodded in agreement. The Baron placed his hand on Rose's shoulder and tilted his hat but let Rose continue as he knew she was ready to reply once more.

"Well, I'm not sure if I believe that. You say you don't believe in states, but you seem to have a vested interest in government. I recall reading you had some words regarding Blackstone Shaw. The Klan man. That's how I see him," Rose commented.

"Blackstone? Ah. Yes, I had him killed ages ago. He was a—union—man that was going to bust my entire operation if his bill got passed. Reform is popular, but cash is still king. Without it, my railway would never have reached completion. My guard dog took care of it and left his body parts through the post to other candidates as a warning. Though, I do miss the dirty work on occasion. To tell you the truth Rose, I consider it freeing to not have such cloak and dagger around you. I respect you, which is why I speak so candidly about what I do," The Baron admitted.

Rose felt a freeze come up her spine as she imagined the brutality behind Cirano and his men breaking into people's homes that opposed The Baron's will. Though Blackstone was not going to be missed, that sort of power was immensely dangerous. Rose felt that The Baron was unaware she knew of his connection to Cirano, an advantage she wanted to keep secret until the time was right. Rose thought about all she'd seen so far in her adventures. The scariest things she encountered were the monsters that masqueraded as human.

"What is your purpose in slaying the monster that be? You risk your life and limb for paltry rewards, ill treatment, and more. Is it a calling? A rush for danger?" The Baron asked, his tone as genuine as possible.

"I do it because it's the right thing to do. It's what I know God would want from me. He gave me the freedom to choose and so this is what I did. To be able to have my own destiny and save others, this is a selfless gift," Rose commented.

The Baron and Rose remained silent as they continued their game. Rose looked for inspiration around the room but could feel the walls closing in on her as time itself stood still in the room. She calculated her decisions carefully as she stuck her tongue out and attempted to match the angles. Rose had a goal in mind regarding her conversation with The Baron. She wondered if in this space, she could finally be bold and get the answer she wanted. She believed Cicero's story to the fullest and saw The Baron's death as necessary, but she wanted accountability as well.

I want to hear him say what he did to Cicero and his town, explicitly. He's willing to admit everything heinous and such, but I wonder what remains hidden. He can't deal with failure. That's his flaw. Rose thought.

"Thank you... Though, I thought about what you told me, there's something missing from your story here. What about the copper mine? This isn't the first time you've been in Arizona. There's a small town where many worked for you. A lot of people died. I understand nothing can be done about the plenty you've put to the gun, but this is my world as much as yours," Rose asked, which prompted The Baron to give a raised eyebrow. He narrowed his eyes at her question. It was clear one of The Baron's failed enterprises remained a heavy chip on his shoulder.

The Baron remained in concentration but recalled the incident with such clarity. He invested too heavily into the lackluster endeavors of the mine and took his statements seriously. The utmost perfectionist, The

Baron micromanaged every business venture with a supreme scope. He could not dodge the memories of stacked spreadsheets marked red with ill accounting for expenses. It didn't matter that The Baron had an untold amount of personal wealth, he thrived off his reputation as a competent industrialist. Every mistake The Baron made piled on him. His fingers grasped the pool stick with resentment as he saw the faces of the starving and tired miners that begged for their paltry sums. His own attempts to save the floundering business delegitimized his social standing, and that was one thing he could not fix with money. The Baron's memory of the cave-in was a capitulation to fate itself. The Baron was a slave to his pride, and those he viewed as expendable suffered for it.

"No such thing. I need to get prepared for the toast, so take as long as you like here. This was a close game, but I remain the victor. It would be good to remember that," The Baron stated. Although his tone remained the same, his expression left a piercing glare at their exchange as he walked off, leaving Rose to stand alone.

The Gala: II

Rose took The Baron's change of heart as a pure admission of guilt. Rose felt invigorated by Cicero's charge for revenge, even though she knew it would be fruitless. Before she could let the old cowboy end the show, she needed to make her appearance known to The Baroness. Her approach took her to the next set of stairs. She moved past a few drunken attendees kissing in the stairwell with a tinge of disgust. Much like the previous floor, there was an air of superiority that flew around her. A bombardment of expensive perfume irritated Rose's sinuses as she let out a large sneeze.

As Rose continued to meander through the foyer, The Baroness held out her hand for a glass of red wine and it was filled to the brim. She drank quietly as her eyes observed Rose like a hawk through the crowd. The Baroness screened out her admirers' voices.

I've been neglecting my job as a mentor; she needs to learn seasonal colors as well. The Baroness thought in slight jest of Rose's orange and yellow dress.

She clinked for another filled glass from a nearby servant and closed her eyes as the satisfying pour came to a stop. She closed her hand into a fist for the servant to stop pouring as she rose to address her guest above all else. Rose could hardly stand such attention to herself but gave a muted grin. Rose stood in the company of various politicians' wives, athletes, and celebrities with aims of their own, not yet evident to her. Few seemed to have the business acumen of The Baroness, with her jewel empire known by all. Rose hadn't realized it, but she in fact owned such a bracelet manufactured by her line and no doubt shipped by The Baron's company to her home once upon a time.

The Baroness broke her conversation to include Rose in the circle of women smoking and throwing dice at subsequent tables. There was a small pool of money that set the gamble, but it was merely just a transfer of wealth between each participant. In a way, it reminded Rose of time with her co-workers, but far less enjoyable with people she didn't know. Rose looked to see The Baroness in all her beauty, wearing a golden dress and pink carnation in her hair. Her hands were covered with sleek gloves that dared to not touch anything else.

"Oh! You actually came! Don't be shy, grab some champagne. I must show you my vast art collection, these I've done myself for the venue. Greatness is hardly recognized, but surely you knew that already," The Baroness stated as she extended a hand full of various jewels on her fingers. She gave Rose a tight hug that unnerved her severely. Rose felt a tinge of worry come down her spine. She recognized the amethyst around The Baroness' neck, her conduit for traveling between dimensions at will. Rose wondered if The Baroness had plans to use such a device today, or if it was mere oversight. The Baroness broke away from Rose for a moment as she extended her hand out to introduce Rose.

"These are some members of the Daughters of The Revolution. Their efforts have been quite good for us recently on the political front," The Baroness explained. She raised an eyebrow at Rose's reaction to the other women, who offered little to say.

"Uh huh. For you maybe, but not for me..." Rose stated with some resentment in her voice. Rose let out a small cough as she opted to take some champagne as recommended. She remembered Cicero's instructions and prompted the conversation to something more applicable.

"Politics aren't something I really consider party talk, how about your gem line? I saw there was an ad in the newspaper for a model girl," Rose said, seeing that some interest was generated in discussion.

Rose's statement was a lie as she was voracious in her studies of all sorts of things, but she wanted to get comfortable with The Baroness in this setting before asking more probing questions. The Baroness leered at Rose briefly but was marginally impressed at her ability to work a crowd and change discussion. She followed suit, prompting all to lean in closer to her words, as she workshopped a design in her head.

"Yes, I was looking to do a winter theme this year. Though we live in the Southwest, Old Man Winter is likely to be impressed. I want to make something beautiful, an immaculate sky-blue dress with silver inlay and a necklace with a gem so cold it makes your blood freeze. I pray such a stone exists for my collection," The Baroness mentioned as she gave Rose a targeted look. She naturally referenced the terms of their contract where Rose would assist her efforts in finding The Frost Gem.

"You know Rose, I had a business trip in New York that was very enlightening. Your friend Venus would make quite the model. We spoke, she's a fan," The Baroness stated with her hand on her shoulder. Rose felt slightly sick at the prospect; something felt off as she heard those words come from her.

Rose let loose a disarming smile at The Baroness' words to ease her concerns. It took little time for The Baron to arrive as he broke off their conversation. Rose's sweat started to betray her calm as she felt especially nervous. Rose met the eyes of The Baron; it was as if their earlier conversation completely vanished. He approached with a warm extended hand out to Rose. The Baroness already gripped her right with a tight grip.

"It appears we're all present. Wonderful. I suppose it's time we officially start the event." The Baroness signaled a nearby servant.

The clink of glasses amplified in its scope as more people followed this gesture. The sound cut through the minutia of people that were talking with one another, as each of their heads slowly looked up. A mass of people started to converge at the main center. Rose investigated the crowd to find a sign of anyone that she knew. Her eyes defaulted first to Florence's red hair; it stood out far more than she expected. Rose found Cicero instead, he was placed dead center in the crowd. Rose wondered if this placement was on purpose, the guards flanked every section of the outside. If he was going to pull off what he intended, he would need ample time.

"Dear attendants. Today marks the twentieth year of my betrothal to my beloved Archibald Conway. I-Maria Conway have seen the city grow to be incredible and a mighty display of ingenuity. As a working woman, I traveled the world, but none other than Archibald was able to get me to stop and appreciate the smallest things in life. With love, I ask you all to hear his piece," The Baroness opened.

"Thank you, my beloved Maria. It feels as if I've known you far longer than this. In truth, I can say it's been lifetimes. The flower to my spring rain. They say that marriage is about looking in the same direction to life as partners and I'd like to say we made that decision for quite some time," The Baron stated. He showed a sinister smile as he saw the crowd in awe at such a declaration of love.

This is all a lie, every bit on both. They told me they tried killing each other when they first met. Enemies to lovers, what an odd pair. Rose remained quiet as she thought about the story given to the public. Their love was genuine, as they sacrificed all to achieve their destiny, but the people here did not deserve the truth.

"With flowers, comes seeds. Our family today has been just Maria and I, but we have added a Rose to the garden. Her promise, her intelligence, all of it has come to pass as an extension of ourselves. Isn't that right?" The Baron mentioned with a strong pat on Rose's back as she nodded.

The people in the crowd let out a triumphant cheer to the happy couple above them as they grew rowdy in anticipation. Rose looked behind her and saw a camera set up to take a magnificently placed photo of the venue.

Rose wasn't camera-shy, but she found herself slightly nervous. Her gaze went back to Cicero, this time who held his pistol in the palm of his hands. Rose could see that Cicero was ready to strike, but she couldn't guess when. The Baron and Baroness flanked Rose on both sides and enjoyed the ovation they gathered for even just the simplest words.

As Cicero aimed his gun, the shot of the camera and the bullet from it shot off at the same time. A quick blinding flash filled the room as The Baron was shot straight in the head. The blood that came from the impact splattered onto Rose and the floor. Rose could see the impact of the bullet hitting The Baron as he had a look of surprise before his eyes glazed over. The muzzle flash and the camera reflected off the various mirrors. The sound ripped through the ambient music that accompanied their surroundings. The crowd cried in agony as they wanted to separate themselves from the madman that managed to bring a gun into the venue. All the decorum was abandoned as the rich stepped over each other to protect their jewels and other adornments. Cicero gave a loud cackle that exposed himself as if nothing else mattered.

With The Baron's face shot clean, his lifeless body tumbled from the opening of the third floor down to the first. It landed with a resounding thud on a nearby table. The carnage was apparent as security quickly withdrew their brass knuckles and beat those that were in their path to reach Cicero. Cicero accepted his fate as he knew there was no particular way for him to get out. He gave a wink to Rose, who still watched from the balcony. Rose watched as Cicero attempted to load his gun but was tackled by security as they beat him.

Rose quickly went for the stairs and attempted to reach the first floor to do anything. Her way was blocked as people started to swarm up the stairs in an attempt to escape the ensuing violence and possibly jump out a window. Rose felt incredibly claustrophobic as she couldn't breathe. She felt crushed by those around her; all she could see was an endless wall of black suits and multicolored dresses that she tripped over. Her hand reached out for The Baroness, but she did not come to her aid. The Baroness had other plans. She slowly retreated from Rose as she needed to communicate her next moves with the temporary death of her husband. She moved with a calmness that unnerved those that observed her, a move some considered heartless in the heat of chaos, but Rose knew differently. Rose's fingers dangled slightly until she felt a strange feeling come over her.

In the distance, the end of the third floor started to distort with a purple light. The opening was vast and Rose looked behind her with shock in her eyes. Rose subconsciously generated a portal with a torrential pour of water that quickly flooded the floor and started to fill the entire venue. The pressure from the gushing water burst open windows that propelled people out further as they were ejected from the area. Rose shook in a panic as the water grew even larger than she anticipated. She covered her eyes in fear of her power and hoped that injuries were minimal. At the opposite end of the floor, The Baroness stood with makeup running down her face but continued to observe without issue. Before The Baroness made her escape, she saw that Rose had made this portal appear and left with satisfaction on her face. The Baroness now knew that Rose would soon be ready to help her. Rose needed a way to think of an escape, and it was made. Slowly but surely, The Baroness knew victory would be at hand.

Cops and Robbers

With the downfall from the gala, much changed for Rose and friends. Out of the wreckage of the evening, the rising desert sun quickly evaporated the water left behind as people rose in utter confusion hours later of what occurred. Rose and Florence managed to rescue Cicero from among the unconscious attendants, but he needed some time to rest and recover from his injuries. Rose and Florence were together while they were on the outskirts of town, just moments away from Cicero's cabin. Niccolo was missing, Florence informed Rose that he was arrested on account of being recognized by some off-duty police that were present at the venue.

Just seconds from the safety of their home, Rose saw that Claudia was out on the porch with a shotgun. Claudia placed the firearm down. She sighted the pair and ran to Rose and Florence, who were straining to carry Cicero over. Claudia rushed over and practically carried him on her own with a strength that surprised them both. The elderly woman's frame was deceptive to the pair as she clutched Cicero with a vice.

"Give me my husband! What—What the hell happened?" Claudia asked in confusion as Rose and Florence started to explain the situation. Claudia let out an exasperated sigh at the affair.

"I knew this was a bad idea, I can't believe I egged this horseshit along," Claudia mentioned as she spat on the ground.

Claudia carried Cicero through the door to make an immediate rush to their bedroom. She'd done this plenty of times before, where she turned their sleeping arrangement into something akin to a field hospital. She had bucket loads of ether and other materials that were used to alleviate pain and bandages. For Claudia, having to clean up the mess that was left behind from the pursuit of The Baron was something she'd done for decades. Her breaking point was near.

"Claudia, I have something I need to tell you." Rose commented as she watched the unconscious Cicero slowly be undressed by Claudia. Cicero's breathing was stifled. Rose looked uncomfortable as she could see a few tears come down Claudia's face, but her expression remained unchanged.

"About The Baron... he's not dead. The Baron is immortal. He can't die at all. Or rather he can for a time, but he keeps on coming back. I don't know exactly how it works. Cicero needs to know what happened. I wanted to tell him, but I feared he wouldn't believe me, and it appears I was right," Rose mentioned. Rose felt a hard grip on her shoulder as the old woman's hand landed with a kind but firm thump.

"Don't. I know you want to, and I admire that, but let him rest," Claudia ordered.

"But—" Rose mentioned as she was stopped by Claudia's glare.

"Rose. He's spent more than half his life hunting this man down. Revenge is a tiring business and all I see when he comes home is being hurt. It was fine when he was twenty, and it was fine twenty years ago, but we're old now. I'm fifty-nine years old and I just want peace in this life. I'm not keen on being a widow," Claudia mentioned.

"I'm not saying stop hunting your monsters, those are saving lives and protecting folks that need it. But this revenge scheme, this long, convoluted plan? It's over for both of you. I would never forgive myself if you were hurt on account of Cicero's desire for revenge," Claudia commented.

Rose wasn't sure how to feel about this situation. She felt that Cicero needed to know the truth, but Claudia was his wife, and she did not want to overstep any boundaries. Rose knew she was in no immediate danger with The Baron as she remained useful for them. Rose nodded to Claudia and allowed her some privacy as she prepared to step out and let them rest. Florence overheard the conversation between Rose and Claudia in the other room as she sat at their kitchen table. She felt it was woefully unfair for Cicero to be left in the dark. She held her tongue but was going to make it clear to Rose that she had a choice to make.

Florence joined Rose outside for a smoke as she stared at the endless desert that was behind the home. There was nothing but miles of land and cacti that accompanied them. Rose chewed her tongue in thought while she met Florence's glance. She leaned against the back of the house and diverted her gaze to the crackling paint of the upper wall and roof. One of many chores that needed to be done around the house was to bring some extra life to the dying paint.

"Rose. I heard what you and she talked about. It's not right. There are people that are hurt because of that foul man, and he'll keep doing it unless we stop him!" Florence commented.

"I know. Claudia is his wife though; she knows him better than anyone else. I can't come disrespectful, they gave me a home to rest in," Rose replied, her voice clearly exhausted from earlier events.

"And as for Nicki, I need to get him out, but I don't know how. I don't think he's going to make bail for what's been happening and—" Florence mentioned as Rose held up her hand.

"I got an idea, but I'm gonna need time. Let me take a nap first. He's a hitman, he'll be fine for a few hours in the slammer." Rose mentioned with a sly grin.

As Rose took a nap and Florence bid her time, crime took no pause. The streets of Phoenix required a stronger hand than the thin-skinned locals, and this was the job of a young man with a determined vision. He had slicked back hair that was as black as his heart and walked with purpose. He saw them all as numbers on an ever-growing list of suspects. The man was an agent of the Bureau of Investigation called on to solve the murder of The Baron and disappearance of The Baroness.[1] To avoid suspicion, he was dressed in civilian clothing as an undercover agent. His iconic badge was hidden away in a pocket. He'd already had a hand in investigating petty crimes in the area on his own accord, as he was dissatisfied with the weak morals of the local police force. The BOI building was located in the heart of the city and first had its roots in Phoenix, starting in 1919. Years of corruption from political matters that interfered with the federal government's income was the target, but the outright disappearance of both The Baron and Baroness was likely to cause a financial collapse, if not properly addressed.

The man had a knack for conflict. He felt as if the world went beneath his heel as he was given unlimited federal power at the hand of his land. He walked forward down the street and made no eye to the locals. The sidewalk was his to own. His destination was a recent development finished by a contractor of The Baron, as he assumed that corporate climbing was the result of the murder. The Baron had many powerful enemies, but none that were as bold to make a direct approach on the man himself. The Baron's defense was ironclad when it came to corporate entities, if someone had access to him, it was by design. The man looked around with suspicion as he noticed a number of workmen that were on lunch break. As they were too low in status to orchestrate such a hit, he moved on. He scoped out every aspect of the property and took mental notes for a crew to gather evidence later. He minded the materials, the lay of the land, and other minute details that any lesser man would have ignored.

The man saw another well-dressed individual flanked by a taller man with a suit on heading in his direction. The three men slowly met at the intersection of the street with an alley that was near a residential neighborhood. The agent brushed paths with Cirano, who walked with a cigar

---

1. The name was changed to the Federal Bureau of Investigation (FBI) in 1935.

in his mouth. Cirano was accompanied by a newer contracting partner that would oversee the work laid out by The Baron as he recovered from his injuries. The two men shouldered one another without greeting and walked a few extra steps before stopping. The tension was high among them. Two immovable forces now insulted the other and there was no sign of a move for an apology. Cirano knew his status well, but the other man remained untested. There were plenty of those who knew exactly who he was, but there was also a prime ignorance that came from youth. Cirano assumed this was the latter. He was willing to walk away but felt a provocation come from the agent.

"Watch where you're walking next time, citizen," the man commented. His temper got the better of him as he turned around to see Cirano unmoved and instead laugh at such an endeavor. Cirano's associate looked away as he already knew his superior's approach to disrespect.

"Ease up, you some kind of Private Dick?" Cirano replied as he got a chuckle from his associate. Cirano enjoyed a good laugh from his subordinates when he made the effort at a good comeback. Brown-nosing wasn't popular among the mob, so it took good practice to find what stuck.

"You think this is funny? I'm on an important manner and gutter trash like you—You need to learn respect." The man said as he gritted his teeth. Cirano thought this was too easy as the man wore his insecurities all over him.

"Listen clown shoes, I go where I please. Now, I'm on my way. I can tell you've got some friends, and I don't need the heat on my case, so here. Take a pair of Cs from my wallet and fuck off," Cirano gestured as he withdrew two hundred dollars. Both of the other men were surprised at the amount of money.

"You lowdown urchin. I now have reason to believe you may be responsible for Conway's demise. Bribing an officer is a crime, you know! I've got eyes and ears all around. We know what you're doing, and a bribe won't fix this," the man said as he walked forward and poked Cirano in the suit.

"What's that? Conway's dead? Really?" Cirano said with a tease in his voice.

"You're a slimy little bastard aren't ya. I see you got no handcuffs, so, you looking to scrap this out? You've got some real stones trying to snoop around here. Sometimes I let people go because I like the chase, but I can't let an insult go unnoticed," Cirano's voice changed as he stepped closer to the agent. He blew on him and watched as the man closed his eye in response.

The agent took on Cirano's challenge with a demented smile as he was going to bag another bad guy to his roster. The two men were comparable in height and the agent himself enjoyed a good bout of boxing to relieve stress. He was used to using his position to bully white collar workers into admitting all sorts of crimes that would never have seen the light of day otherwise, but his approach with someone like Cirano was less than ideal. Cirano craved chaos and enjoyed it a great deal. The two made their way to the alleyway while the other man watched as a lookout.

While the man fully intended to fight Cirano out with his fists, his opponent had other ideas. Cirano made a stance where he was prepared to take a few jabs at the man and walk away, but his mind changed. Cirano goaded his opponent forward with a few faux jabs. Before he could react, Cirano brought out his gun and instantly shot him in the head. Cirano remained unmoved as the momentum from the shot propelled his target just a bit forward.

"You'd think a guy like that would have been heeled. What a rube. Go call the boss and tell him we have someone snooping around. He's particular about what we do with our bodies. Honestly we should just chuck him in the dumpster, but it's not my call," Cirano shrugged.

Sometime later, The Baron awoke in his home, perfectly accounted for as he once again walked among the living. He was truly unkillable and gave a low laugh to himself as he realized his ruse was finally complete. The Baron had called a hit out on himself that screwed Niccolo and his employer as he was also the primary distributor of the money. The Baron could not persuade people within the government to wipe his existence, so for a time, he arranged to use the Mafia to fake his death to lull his competitors into a false state of security while he laid low to plan further ventures. The dead paid no taxes and he would pose as his twin brother, once revived, to inherit the fortune. As The Baron willed this non-existent twin brother in all his current documentation, it would be an easy transition. All he needed to do was swap suits for a while. The Baroness had taken out a life insurance policy on The Baron a few years prior to their return. She planned on funneling the life insurance earned on himself to a Swiss bank and place the saved money back into well-earning stocks. This was a tested strategy for The Baron as he'd done this once in the mid-1700s, and again about fifty years earlier somewhere else in the world.

"Noted industrialist, Archibald Conway, murdered in anniversary special. Twin brother expected to inherit fortune. Thousands expected to mourn. What a ridiculous alias, I need something better," The Baron mentioned as he read the paper.

"Only thousands? I figured by now the Conway alias would have millions!" The Baroness' shouted from the other end of the hall. She walked closer to her husband. The Baroness hadn't gotten an ounce of sleep as she was busy dissuading visitors from attempting to give their best wishes to the supposed grieving widow.

"You've come back, and you seem younger than ever," The Baroness teased as she placed a kiss on his cheek.

Past the tender moment shared by the two in their mansion, the ring of a phone sounded. The Baroness wondered who would call their residence at this time, only a few people knew their direct line. Rose would always arrive in person as instructed, so they were aware it wasn't her. The Baroness looked at her partner before giving a nod of understanding. The Baron approached with a stern grab of the line as he wondered who would be able to interrupt his routine. Cirano's subordinate first answered the phone, but The Baron gave no response. He could hear a bit of rattling as the hands were exchanged.

"I need you to come down, got a rat snoopin' around, but I took care of it. You need to come by the new development as soon as you can. Shouldn't take you too long, just hop through your hole and get to me," Cirano mentioned as he coiled his finger around the line.

"I'll be on my way," The Baron commented. He slammed the phone down and left without further delay.

The Baron arrived from a nearby portal obscured behind a building as he neared the section of the development that Cirano alluded to. He hadn't bothered to consider the fact that Cirano casually admitted he knew his secret, it was secondary to the problem at hand. The Baron had only been confirmed dead for about twelve hours but there were already people snooping in on his territory. News traveled much faster than he anticipated, people were vultures and were quick to make plans that now seemed possible without The Baron's influence. The Baron quickly walked to Cirano as he was expecting important news regarding his adversaries.

"Did you examine the body? Allow me," The Baron mentioned. Cirano attempted to peek, but The Baron slapped his hand away as he wore gloves that kept his fingerprints from detection.

"Cirano. What can you tell me about this spy? Was he corporate? Did he belong to any other families in the area? I can compensate and let this fall to the wayside as a happy accident," The Baron proposed as he looked to Cirano for additional information. Cirano leaned against the wall and shook his head.

"He called himself an officer, but he didn't look any different. No badge or nothing on him. Why are you so keen on the details? We kill cops all the time," Cirano assessed. The Baron frowned at his words. The Baron's ability to be careful is what kept him alive for centuries, but he didn't expect such a pig-headed person such as Cirano to understand that. The Baron fiddled around the man's pockets and emptied his wallet for any sort of identification. He looked over a series of identifying documents that he sifted through and also noticed a badge that completely contradicted with Cirano's report.

"Agent Wilson," The Baron mumbled to himself repeatedly. Cirano looked over at The Baron. He saw the calm and collected nature of his superior melt away from such overwhelming anger. The Baron got up from the corpse with his face nearly red from rage. The Baron manipulated the badge in Cirano's face as he waved it around to prove his point.

"Get that shit out of my face, I can see it without you waving it around like some loon. What's the problem?" Cirano commented as he stepped back slightly from The Baron. The Baron rarely cracked as he always held control but all around he felt the walls starting to close. He feared that his direct administration regarding the railway may have been too much exposure of his position. He was just a few weeks out from laying out the last bits of rail to complete the job.

"Clearly, you are unable to see the gravity of your mistake, you incompetent ass! You troglodyte afterbirth! Time and time again, you have failed to think before acting and look at what you've done. I have doused too many fires because of your shortsightedness. War is coming to the streets and now—Do you realize how much shit we're in? You killed a federal agent! This is casus belli for them to seize my properties and nationalize them! This... does not bode well. We shall regroup a little bit later. I-I always have a plan," The Baron said as he started to hyperventilate.

The Baron had reason to worry when it came to the federal government. He lacked the resources to effectively fight off such a determined force. He hadn't paid taxes in years, and recycling through multiple aliases was clear identity fraud. In years past, his dance of deception was easier to perform, but people were more connected than ever. The Baron could simply escape internment or any other earthly punishment with his power, but he truly feared the loss and seizure of all his assets. To start anew and be poor once more was a fate worse than death itself.

Cirano hadn't realized the gravity of the situation, but as far as he was concerned, he was fine seeing The Baron in a panic. The Baron had painted himself as an untouchable force, but it was clear he had limits. Cirano admired his work ethic to a point, but he found the man to be a sniveling elitist that rubbed him the wrong way. He was a self-made man, and this was viewed as just deserved. Cirano had been busy with the growing gang war, but Rose was the last key of the puzzle. If The Baron was distracted trying to get the wrath of the federal government off his trail, it gave Cirano a clear opening to strike against his adversaries and force her into the fold one way or another.

Dino Danger

After a two-week recovery, Cicero was ready to get back on the trail. Rose had gone and done a few low-level bounties of her own to keep herself sharp. She felt a tinge of guilt, having decided to ultimately side with Claudia and hide the state of The Baron's true existence from Cicero. Rose and Cicero were used to the routine of having to deal with their monster of the week, but a new bounty that appeared on their list stumped them. Rose looked at the bounty board in the ever-familiar kitchen with a confused expression as she noted the contents of the report that Cicero had circled. She saw an assortment of photographs and citations that were linked to scientific journals. She didn't take Cicero to be much of a scholar, despite being an avid reader.

"This isn't our usual task, but we have an actual bounty. It's strange. We need to get a bustle of eggs from somebody that stole them from a local museum. A scientist that went rogue apparently. These dinosaur eggs that are fossils or something like that; the geniuses over the phone stressed that these were in good condition. So, we get the bad guy and retrieve the goods," Cicero explained to Rose.

"Do we know where he is? What do we do with him?" Rose questioned.

"Well that's up to us really. I'm hoping he doesn't cause trouble because then I'll just put him down. I'm not exactly marshal-friendly, but if he's worth something we can get the bounty and get a stiff drink back at our usual bar. All they want is the cargo. I've got the address and a map printed out. It's about an hour and a half out south of here."

"Not a problem. I'll just go around back and set us close by." Rose waved her hand playfully. A small inkling of blue emitted through her fingertips. Rose's skill seemed to increase exponentially as she grew more comfortable with her power.

"I know you can use your portals, but I think we'll need to take the horses to transfer our man and the cargo in one piece. Besides, I know that stuff makes you nauseous after a while. You don't need to impress me, Rose," Cicero said with a fatherly tone.

Rose and Cicero made their way to the barn with a tried-and-true approach of heading along with Mary and George. The horses yearned for the long stretches of land once more as their magnificent manes repelled the mountains of dust that followed the pair. The long road ahead was bumpy, and the pace was steady, as if the horses already knew the way. Rose had an amusing trick to show Cicero as the old cowboy decided to rear up George for a race.

"Hey Cicero, watch this," Rose called as she rubbed Mary's neck. While Cicero told Rose to relax with her portal making for the time being, she couldn't help but feel energized further.

As Mary went to a dash, Rose quickly generated a portal right in front of her and one behind her to make a perpetual loop where the horse's speed gradually accelerated. Cicero watched dumbfounded as he slowly saw Rose increase in speed. Rose was a sponge of information and had already started to apply tricks taught with her training by The Baroness. In a showcase of skill, she let out a devious laugh that impressed Cicero. Rose could feel the impact of her movement as the horse started to gain speed.

"As-you-can-see! I am moving faster each time I go through, the momentum of it all will push me and Mary faster until, we jet off as quick as we can!" Rose mentioned as she closed both portals and Mary was propelled forward with Rose on top for about thirty seconds of increased speed before leveling out with Cicero again.

"Wow, just like an old picture show! Where the horse skips around and all that," Cicero mentioned.

The pair continued their ride until Cicero stopped their advance with a whistle that stopped both Mary and George as soon as they heard it. Rose turned her head to see Cicero pointing in the direction of a few derelict buildings that were their target area. He unfolded the map and wiped his eyes from the ensuing dust that came from a nearby gust. He sniffed the air and ran his finger through the directions.

"The place is abandoned now but seems to be some sort of old hotel. It's probably where people used to stay before The Autumn Gates and the light rail got built. There's a gas station right behind us that's just as old. The Baron just sucked up any enterprise left, huh," Cicero commented to Rose.

Rose took in the sights and she was hardly impressed. The nearby gas station held no longer relevant prices for gas and had a few rusted older Model Ts in the distance. They were scrapped for parts and only mere skeletons remained of what used to be a suitable vehicle. What a waste. She wondered why this place was seen as irrelevant for travel. Its location would have been a port in the storm, but what took her breath away was what remained.

Past the sparse growth of cacti that surrounded the pair, what remained of the former hotel stood as a relic to roads less traveled. What remained of the melted asphalt now just revealed pockets of dirt and sand that cut through on the path towards it. Its brick and wooden veneer slowly receded under an oppressive sun that only continued to wear away at the paint. It once held a turquoise color and took the eye of all the prospectors and more that came by, looking for a reprieve on the road. The name in signage of its former glory was lost to history. It was named "The Pacifica" due to its sea-blue color of the interior walls. The Pacifica was accompanied by two other centers, a small-time casino for gambling purposes and a nearby general store. They were built during the Reconstruction era in the

1870s and was considered modern of the time with a blend of Americana and Spanish pueblo. Once the money ran dry, it became a hub for illegal activity as loose drug paraphernalia and cracked bottles were spread across the ground. One could move only a few feet and run into a needle.

Rose and Cicero looked at one another as the reality was juxtaposed with the information given to him. Cicero noticed on a second glance that some of the alcohol bottles still had a fresh smell that emitted from them. He felt that they weren't alone, and somehow, this place ended up being a hub of activity once more. Cicero could smell a scheme from a mile away.

"Uh, Rose. You should grab your gun if you don't have it already. I thought we'd be alone, but I think we might run into something." Cicero said with a bit of worry in his voice.

As the pair got closer, Rose realized that she could see movement in the distance. She crouched and advised Cicero to do the same as she gestured for his binoculars from his satchel. Rose adjusted her gaze to accommodate her glasses and nearly gasped in surprise. Rose realized that they weren't alone at all. The man they were looking for was guarded by mobsters. She recognized the guns they were carrying, a few had pistols as a sidearm, but the most dangerous ones were all paired with submachine guns. Rose was unable to find the vehicle's location and assumed it was parked in the back of the building. These had to be Cirano's men with how much money the guns were worth, but she was confused on what value this place would have to him. Strategically speaking, this made little sense for him to reinforce an area like this one, but she realized that the remoteness of an operation like this was the biggest strength. Nobody of any good moral character would want to be associated with a drug den like this one, even if just for reputation alone. She was convinced there had to be a distillery or something else of equal value that was being guarded here.

"Gangsters, at least three on the outside. No idea how many are inside. Ain't risking making a portal inside only to end up cheese, but I think I can get us closer," Rose mentioned to Cicero, who nodded in agreement.

"Well, if our man's in there, and we're out here. This is a real bind. What do you think we do? We can't just mosey on in there without a plan."

"We can try to sneak in. Knock them out somehow, and then—" Rose commented as Cicero cut her off.

"I'll give it a try. Just have to say, this'll be the first time you've ever directly come up against a human opponent, as far as I'm aware. If you find yourself in a firefight, end it quickly. Don't let them plead for your forgiveness, it's a ploy. These scumbags only care about themselves, you hear me?" Cicero answered as he got up to follow Rose.

Rose and Cicero took a lengthy approach in finding what path would be ideal to near the hotel without being spotted. As the pair stayed low, Cicero used his binoculars to keep track on them. It was obvious the mobsters weren't prepared for anyone to come around in the middle of nowhere. Their faces looked bored as Cicero watched one man dump a mag into the sand to amuse himself. Cicero nodded as he was more than happy to watch them waste away their tactical advantage.

"Rose, when we get close, I'll take out the two men and you go for the last guy. If he sees you, shoot. I don't care how loud it is, we'll figure it out. You get one chance with a gun like that one or you'll be dead on the spot. You'll want to use your pistol to hit em right in the noggin. I know you the body well, so hit that spot." Cicero gestured towards his Bowie knife on ha nd.

Rose and Cicero arrived in the vicinity of the hotel's entrance, or what would have been left of it. A small fence was hastily constructed to keep out vagrants from occupying the property, but it was easy to move through. Rose briefly froze in place as she slowly inched over. Cicero was far more experienced in this endeavor as he slowly unveiled his knife. Rose watched as he moved over and kept his silence. Cicero bagged the first man with his left hand covering the man's mouth, and the right hand with a direct stab to the throat accompanying it. The fluidity of the movement was enough to only have the sound of the man's gun drop out of his lifeless hands.

Cicero immediately grabbed the submachine gun and positioned himself against the wall of the house.

Rose quickly followed Cicero's lead as she took out her pistol. The mobster she needed to grab was urinating at the side of the house. While he was busy, Rose felt a shake in her hands as she held her breath. Rose's strength was less than Cicero's, but she held finesse as she used the blunt end of her weapon right where she was told to do so. The man stumbled over and spun around, only for him to be silenced by the rise of Rose's hand. Rose was startled by the sudden blast of gunfire that came from the other side of her. It was hardly anything like she'd heard before. She immediately covered her ears from the loud crack of the submachine gun as she feared for the worst. Rose couldn't help but call out for Cicero to make sure he was alright.

"Rose, I'm fine! These guns have one hell of a wallop. I might prefer my revolver still, but this is useful. Come on, let's clear this house. They definitely heard us if they didn't already," Cicero joked as Rose came towards him. Rose recoiled slightly as she noted the destructive power of such a weapon up close. The man's arm barely hung on the hinge as she looked at the bullet wounds.

"Yeah, someone doesn't like us! Rose, get into cover. I'm gonna use what's left of this and we'll breach," Cicero mentioned. Cicero heard the sound of a few bullets whizz by the entrance of the hotel as the men made some returning fire from the entrance. Cicero felt some of these were crack shots, they had to have had army training or something to supplement their marginally better aim. The men at the front were just a tease for the dangers that truly were within. If Cicero weren't concerned about the integrity of the bounty, he would have used dynamite to clear a path with little resistance afterwards. Cicero waited for the hail of bullets to stop as he fired blindly with the submachine gun to root out the others.

"Shit, there's a jam!" One of the mobsters complained in a panic.

Rose found it juvenile to broadcast their inability to fire the gun and wondered if it was a trap, but Cicero took prime opportunity to return the favor. Rose went right behind him and fired an additional shot from her pistol that caused the gangsters to disperse through the rest of the building. Rose could tell by where they were running, they were looking for spare ammo after expending the amount they could carry. The chase would be on their part now.

The interior of the hotel was already a wreck, but it was riddled with bullets from the sheer inaccuracy of their weapons. Rose witnessed a sinking leviathan of decay with molded carpet, long-empty boarded rooms, and Victorian-era dressing. The walls were peeled over with grime on every corner. Rose and Cicero opted to split up to find their target, keeping in mind the danger that came with the other men inside. Rose made an estimate from the number of men firing, there were about four remaining aside from the exterior that were neutralized. An even split between her and Cicero as they looked for their target. Cicero took the left, while Rose took the right.

Cicero barreled through the left corridor as with the quick draw of his revolver, he was able to nail one of the returning mobsters in the stomach. He kicked the man with his boot and laid a second shot into his head. Cicero winced slightly at the sound as it reverberated through the walls. Cicero felt a ring in his ears as he instinctively turned around to see a fully automatic rifle aimed straight for him. Cicero resisted the gut urge to try to resist, he recognized that thing could shred him to pieces. He knew that something was up though, as the other man immediately didn't start shooting.

"Consider him dead weight. Stay right where you are grandpa. I know who you are, you're going for ransom and making me a real rich man. You and that museum prick," one of the men said as he held Cicero up. Cicero felt the cold steel barrel pressed against his back as he was slowly led to a nearby room. He dropped his weapon and held his hands up. Cicero could only hope that Rose was able to figure out what happened as he found a way to escape. Cicero was pushed to the ground by the same man. One man holding a shotgun was on guard duty for the prisoner, but the man with the rifle decided to switch with him.

"Tom's looking for the other one, some woman—No, not one that got away. The one that came with him. I'll switch off, you take care of it," the man mentioned as he pointed to Cicero.

Rose remembered her experience with The Shadow Bouncer and quickly headed up the stairs. Given what she estimated, she would need to deal with two men, each with guns bigger than her own. She needed to think about this carefully. As she slowed her run to catch her breath, Rose barely registered the pump of a shotgun nearby. It was a common belief that a shotgun from stories or the movies was something used to blast at close range, but Rose knew she could be hurt easily at practically any distance. She was utterly terrified at being at the business end of one of these.

She took no chances as she hid behind a wall that led to a nearby set of rooms. The numbers at the top that labeled the room number remained etched in brass. Rose knew better than to pick the nearest one, she picked one in the middle. Rose noticed that the doors were locked, but that wouldn't be an issue for her. She found that aside from a regular lock, there was an effort to put wooden planks beside the doors, as if to keep someone inside. Rose cast a portal that allowed her to jump to the next room in search of the fossils.

Rose's panicked expression remained as her heart pumped once more with adrenaline surging through her. She quickly closed it behind her to briefly obscure her location as she hid from the two mobsters pursuing her, each on separate floors. Rose realized that as she entered the room to recover, she found that she was in the presence of another person. Rose was speechless. The wooden floorboards of the room and wilted wallpaper gave way to a lone figure sat in the center of the room. The window was boarded up with iron bars and planks to block out any light. The bed sheets were tattered and the structure itself nearly collapsed on the floor. She slowly found her way to find a woman with wide brown eyes tied with rope on her hands and feet. Her mouth was gagged.

Rose quickly went to the woman's aid and removed the restrictions on her mouth. Rose stared into the woman's eyes but saw little was there. The empty husks that remained slowly drifted upwards in silence. The weight of the woman's emotions stood on her. Rose had rarely seen such a look of despair, but with everything she witnessed, the world continued to oblige her. It wasn't hard to imagine as she kept seeing more and more start to make sense. Rose felt a sudden twinge of disgust as it wasn't just a drug den, Cirano's outfit was on the take for human trafficking. As her vision adjusted, she noticed the signs with rusted handcuffs and dried blood that littered the floor in scattered patches. Rose knew there had to be others in this place that suffered such a fate. The women there were victims of a greater and insidious war waging between the criminal factions of Arizona, and this was the price to fund it.

In her haste to find something to help the captive, Rose revealed a piece of paper stuffed into a nearby desk drawer. It was a copied carbon paper ledger with the price of women, their approximate age, and other details. Some were already sold to the highest bidder and never seen again. These were incriminating documents with not only signatures addressed in Cirano's handwriting, but the implicit agreement of high-profile executives and more that were responsible for placing these women into sexual slavery. Coerced at the heart of a gun, these mobsters would snatch migrant women along the border and use this location as a holding facility until the delivery and payment was secured. Rose realized this was the case as white women being stolen would have more ground for the police to respond. Rose surged with rage, as she immediately imagined herself in such a position.

What did they do to you? Rose thought in utter disbelief at the woman's treatment.

"I'll be back to help you. You and everyone else," Rose said. She summoned another portal to return to the hallway.

The footsteps of the mobster with the shotgun grew louder as he descended from the top staircase to match Rose's level. Rose panicked as she remembered brief flashes of the gangster that once pursued her in the forest before The Baroness saved her. He also had a shotgun that he used with fury, but now Rose could fight back. Rose positioned herself where she could see the man turn to fire, while she used a nearby reflection from a photograph frame to assist her behind cover. Rose was hardly as accurate as Cicero when it came to blind fire, but she landed a few solid hits that caused the opposing gangster down the corridor to hide behind a wall. She took the opportunity to reload as she only had one left in the chamber.

The man with the shotgun shot a blast that slammed Rose's eardrums and shattered the portrait with the spread of the shot, but the damage was done. The man was too weak now to properly shoulder his shotgun as it fell to the floor. Her eyes saw a trail of blood that was evident from shooting her enemy in the stomach and intestines. He hadn't gotten far as he could hear the clog sounds of Rose's shoes approaching. The man desperately attempted to withdraw a revolver and aim it at her. Rose kicked the shotgun out of the man's reach. Although he was fading fast, it was a ploy to get Rose in close enough for a clean shot. Rose watched as the man could barely lift up his own arm, the pain was immense.

Nah. You're going out like a man. Rose thought. With zero hesitation, Rose lifted her gun and ended the gangster's life with a headshot. Any revelations Rose had left about taking the life of a human being were no more. Her gut wrenched as she imagined the horrid pain the bound woman must have suffered at these gangsters. Rose felt nothing but empathy, as she would be the mechanism of revenge against these horrid rapists. She decided to harness her portal ability to look for the next pursuer.

It took little effort for Rose to detach herself from the situation at large, she remembered how every one of her hunts was supposed to help people.

Her mind raced about what would happen if Cirano won the gang war and took over the entirety of Phoenix and eventually the rest of the state. It was her imperative to make sure Niccolo had all the resources he needed to put things on the straight and narrow. It was immature for Rose to think she could get rid of everything wrong in the city, but she could do what she could. Florence reassured Rose that in the rift of what would remain in the power vacuum, there would be significant changes taking foot. Rose couldn't believe all of it, but she had nowhere else to turn.

Rose attempted to triangulate the location of the other man. She heard footsteps above her and gave a mischievous grin as she came up with a solution to her problem. Rose wondered if there was a basement to this place, not that it mattered. She paced her movement to match that of the mobster and used one portal beneath his feet to sink him through the third floor, and one at the bottom to go to the first floor. In a panic, the man fell through the blue void that Rose conjured and hit the ground hard. The impact was enough for him to break his arm as he landed on it wrong. A pile of dust accumulated through the hole as Rose sneezed. She used the opening of the hole as well, to place a shot along the man's back and would let him bleed out. She closed the two portals that she opened and did it quickly. Rose felt a bout of nausea as she coughed, but shook her head to refocus. Too many portals at one time without food would drain her energy, it was something that she remembered The Baron warning her about.

She then searched for Cicero and noticed the man holding the rifle. It was serious business, and she needed a plan. Rose took the staircase and made her way to the left corridor where Cicero once arrived. Rose knew she had a single shot to make this work. Her plan was to knock on the door to get the man's attention, and then use a portal to go through the wall and behind the man with her gun to shoot him.

Rose took a small prayer in a leap of faith to do this. She practiced the scenario in her mind for just a second before operating on pure instinct.

On the inside of the room, Cicero raised an eyebrow as he saw the man go to open the door. Cicero felt a sudden sinking feeling as he looked behind him in shock to see Rose's face emerge from the blue vortex. In a gracious move, Rose's brown arm extended back and let a shot fire from her pistol. She took two hits with the trigger as the first shot missed, but the second pierced the man's neck. The mobster fell to the floor as Cicero got up to make sure the job was done. Cicero recovered his revolver and quickly returned his focus to the captured disgraced paleontologist.

"Hell of a fine job, forget what I said earlier. Those holes you make are a blessing," Cicero mentioned as his gaze turned over to his internment companion. In his haste, he'd forgotten to address the man who Rose handled. Rose removed the man's gag and wondered why Cicero wasn't given such treatment. As the man spoke though, Rose already debated putting it back on.

"Now, let me explain. Our procedure is to make replica eggs for new exhibits from ostrich eggs or out of clay. In a stupor, I was going to pawn the collection for drugs, I'm a cocaine addict you see—" The man rattled off much to the annoyed sigh of both Rose and Cicero. Rose scratched her head at what value the museum had towards this person. He seemed to have a screw loose in his head as far as she was concerned.

"At least he's honest. Where are the eggs?" Cicero asked.

"I don't have them. I've been here at least a day, but before you two came along, they were here with me. They could be anywhere by now, but I do remember some going to the local farmer's market. The ruffians you killed, horrid gangsters thought they could turn a quick buck. Those specimens weren't just, no-no. They were the real thing. Color me surprised. A species I've never seen before in any scientific writing. If I still had my academy membership, this would be big news!" The scientist said.

Rose and Cicero exchanged a worried look at one another as they weren't sure what to expect. Dinosaurs were animals like any other, but if Rose's information was remotely accurate, they were going to be in for a difficult time regardless. Finding small animals was arduous, but tracking an unknown species was an endeavor that would be challenging. Their behavior would be variable at best, and even juveniles of a species could be an issue. Cicero also feared that if there were really live specimens and the portal remained open, the protective parent would be close behind.

The pair soon vacated with their target as the scientist wrapped himself around Cicero's waist. The grizzled cowboy complained in annoyance. As Rose and Cicero prepared to deal with what came next, Rose later explained to Cicero what she witnessed with the bound woman. Cicero stayed silent as he heard Rose's description and nodded. He knew this reality all too well. He understood the gravity of the situation and vowed to place an anonymous tip for the authorities once they got back to the main city. The pair could only hope they weren't too late.

Dino Danger: II

Two citrus farmers on the other side of town successfully haggled for the bounty of eggs and hoped to start a breeding farm. Ostrich breeding was popular among the upper crust in Arizona, the meat was highly prized, and the ostriches were fun for children to gawk at for a price. While the farmers recognized they had something else, it would still be worth raising the meal for meat. A few of the brood were placed inside a heated cage and given the same treatment as any other livestock. As the men were ready to embark on a new opportunity, however, a problem emerged. A few of the young soon hatched and immediately called out for their parent but received no answer. The presence of a purple portal manifested some distance from the farm.

What soon followed were two footsteps from a mighty creature of another world that saw the strange opening. It abandoned its sleeping area, a lush forest that was filled with other creatures much like it. From a dimension where dinosaurs were never extinct, this creature embarked through as a pioneer of a long-forgotten dynasty of animals. The dinosaur was a species known as *M. macrothorax,* one unknown by the paleontologists of the day. It was a brooding thirty-feet long megaraptorid that hungered for food and to protect its children. On its body were a layer of feathers to keep warm during the cold snaps. It was a gray and black animal with brown eyes that reflected the sunlight. With a name meaning the "Deep-Chested Shadow of Death", the Maip had massive claws in the shape of meat hooks that could rip flesh with ease. The animals' legs were tree trunks that were filled with vigor, each step had bulging muscles that left a definitive print in the dirt beneath it. The animal's tail moved from side to side as it supported sharp turns for the hunt. The creature emerged from the portal as it picked up the scent of the young.

The Maip was a creature of immense speed as it ran forward in dominance of an environment never seen before. The creature sniffed out the location of its young and headed straight for the farm. It let out a hellish cry that emitted a low whooping call. To the untrained ear, it appeared to sound like a demented bird. One of the farmers present on the outside was busy tending to the citrus fields as the mother ran at breakneck speed for its size. The farmer let out a scream in panic as he hadn't expected such a sight. He lacked a gun and could only hide as his defense. The unfamiliar beast was a fright that caused a clench in his heart.

Clouds of dust rose behind it in increased volume. The animal led a faux charge, as it tested its target to see how it would react. It ran forward and stopped just a few feet away from the man. The creature's head bobbed in a sporadic movement as it attempted to track the farmer's next actions. The scared farmer threw a rock at the animal and caused it to enrage as it ran forward. The Maip moved its head low and bit the man. The vice-grip jaw of its mouth eclipsed that of a crocodile as it refused to let go. The man was unable to let out a scream for help as he already fainted from blood loss and died nearly instantaneously. It gripped the man with its arms and ripped him in half with its jaws as viscera littered the field. The creature's mouth was reddened by the blood and a few droplets descended down its jaw to the ground below. Collapsed orange plants fell beneath its wake as it sniffed again.

The scent ran cold as the mother looked to find the next potential location for the eggs. The Maip received two conflicting trails, one from the currently hatched individuals and the remaining brood left. The mother made a tactical decision and decided to patrol for the eggs, there were more at risk. The dinosaur reared up with its hind legs and made a boastful display as its arms flailed alongside. The hunt was on as the creature made its way, using one of the city's skyscrapers as a landmark to approach. From its point of view, it resembled an immense tree from home.

Cirano and his men patrolled the city streets as they were fresh from an assault on a stretch of enemy territory. Cirano had since neglected his duties for The Baron as he yearned to stretch his legs and get into the fray. Cirano resented his role as an administrator and saw himself mostly as a glorified middleman for The Baron and Baroness. Peace was incredibly boring and not profitable in the ways he imagined, despite a historic buyout. For Cirano, it wasn't just about the money, he yearned the power and the fear that came from the mention of his name. Cirano recalled an earlier conversation he had with The Baron. He was fired recently from his position which made him a free agent once again. Cirano knew he couldn't return to working for the family he once did back in Chicago, for a new opportunity was present. Cirano enjoyed making a mockery of ransacking a property, now abandoned by The Baron.

Cirano Conners. My house is under investigation, and I need to secure my assets. Consider yourself fired. Do not contact me or my wife again, or you will be treated as an enemy. The Baron's voice projected through Cirano's thoughts.

"He fired me. Me! Yeah well, I've got all his shit still. Good luck with that," Cirano huffed as he exhaled some cigar smoke. Cirano felt his shoulder tapped by one of his goons and turned around to address the concern.

"Boss, ain't that your car in the parking lot getting flipped over?!" a mobster asked as he called for Cirano's attention. Cirano practically coughed on his smoke at the sight. He wasn't sure what to react to first, the dinosaur present in town, or that the car needed another payment before getting destroyed.

The Maip's appearance into town immediately caused a panic among the civilians that were present. The dinosaur's rage caused it to flip over nearby cars in the frantic search for its young. There was a mass exodus as people trampled over one another in an attempt to disperse from the beast. By now, the denizens of Phoenix were used to the paranormal occurrences that came by their town, but each time, it still incited massive panic for a number of reasons. Cirano watched as worried citizens didn't bother to go to the police station. They were surely unequipped for the job but were already mobilized as support for a house fire. Politicians had run on the promise to contain these threats but failed to deliver in just about every aspect. It was beyond their understanding and was currently only stemmed through attempted efforts to beat back whatever was found in the absence of Rose and Cicero, who could only do so much.

"Someone call Animal Control! What-What the hell is that thing?" a woman shouted as she pointed to the Maip. Cirano heard the woman's concerns and witnessed the beast for himself.

Cirano and a few of his men were unnerved at the sight of the beast and opted to also escape, but there was a problem. The Maip already set its sight on the fleeing people, in hopes that it could find a stronger traction to the scent. The beast ran in their direction and there was limited time. Carnage was already widespread as it ran into the middle of the street and roared at ongoing traffic. The present cars were frightened at the sight and attempted to reverse, causing mass accidents. The bravest souls of the bunch that were present attempted to try to scare off the dinosaur with any methods they could, but none were effective.

"Boys, we've got guns for a reason. Let's send that thing back to Hell!" Cirano declared as he attempted to load his submachine gun. A few of Cirano's men headed out to take the offensive. He watched as their aim wavered with the growing hulk of the dinosaur get ever closer.

A few pistol shots rang off with two making their mark on the dinosaur. The bullets were ill-effective as there was a small amount of blood that leaked from its skin, but it wasn't enough to last. The animal was irritated as it took on the provocation by Cirano and his men. The dinosaur understood that the weapons held by Cirano, and the others were the source of the pain and rushed directly at their location. The Maip lunged towards one of Cirano's men and immediately pinned him to the floor. His suit was riddled with blood as the creature let out another roar. Its leg claws pierced the man's chest, and the sound of ripped flesh were audible to the group of men. The man's body leaked blood like a burst balloon of flesh. One threw up from the devastation around him. Cirano himself was buffeted by the tail as he fell backwards and nearly shot himself with his finger still on the trigger. The sound of the gun firing off gave a loud ringing to his ears. The surrounding street was devastated as a pile-up of bodies started to grow under the chaos.

With the ongoing conflict heading towards a loss, Cirano recovered himself and ran with a few of his men into cover as they reloaded their guns and fired off bursts. The keen creature saw the flashing lights and attempted to shield itself by laying low towards the ground. The dinosaur let out a pained scream as the heavier caliber bullets started to damage it. The creature cried in agony as it mustered up the energy for another burst of speed. This rush was far too mighty for the group to contend with, and Cirano and the others abandoned the mission. The dinosaur would have to be properly handled by someone else, the risk was too great to let another person die by the beast. Cirano tripped one of his own men as a sacrifice for the dinosaur that was accepted happily. He looked behind him to watch as one of his associates was dragged by the leg by the bleeding dinosaur and his skin was flayed on the pavement from friction burn.

The ensuing carnage lasted for another two hours as the dinosaur gradually lost stamina and the search for its young slowed down. The police, originally arriving with only a net, realized the danger and dispatched snipers from the rooftops to put down the beast once and for all. With no knowledge on what to do, it was treated as a rogue bear or a wolf that escaped the zoo. A crack from the roof pierced the brain of the creature, but behind it lay a pile of upended cars, broken glass, and a trail of bodies. The clean up would take days and the trauma would take weeks to recover from. The animal's corpse baked in the sun like any other day. People were gathered around to give their inaccurate testimony to the authorities on what they knew of the beast.

Rose and Cicero eventually arrived in town to find that amid the chaos, the threat had already been stopped. The corpse of the mother Maip was riddled with bullets, but left a wanton path of destruction. Rose scratched her head as she wondered what finally caused such a terrifying foe to fall. Some mysteries remained unsolved, as the remaining egg bounty was never found, and the mysterious dinosaur young were left to fend for themselves out in the desert. Cicero assumed that without the parental guidance, nature would sort itself out and the animals would return to the dustbin of history.

"Well. I guess we lost our bounty on that one..." Cicero commented in irritation as he kicked a soda bottle away from him.

Now that Cirano was able to recover from the day's events, he thought of how to solidify his claim in a post-Baron landscape of the criminal underground. The first move that Cirano decided to do with his consolidated power was bring an all-out assault on the small town he bullied earlier. No longer needing to provide a cut for The Baron's projects, Cirano sought to cement the town's remote location as a repository for storing alcohol and other illicit goods. Cirano was aware of the town's reputation, but he banked on them wanting to enjoy their golden years as geriatrics hardly sacrificed comfort for the next generation.

The Lone Ranger

Cicero knew he had to honor his promise to help defend the town he cherished growing up in. The memories came flooding back as he saw these new age mobsters as nothing more than pitiful bandits that once ransacked their community in the olden days. Cicero defied his wife's wishes and rode off without delay. The atmosphere in the town was airtight as all feared Cirano's arrival. Much like a medieval warlord, he would send collectors that brandished their weapons to collect an unofficial tax of anything they deemed valuable. He didn't use the tried method of "protection money", it was extortion at its base form.

Cirano knew these people lived at the fringes of town and due to their criminal histories, many were not keen on getting local law involved, which made a perfect bed of activity for him to collect what little money they had left. The younger people that lived in the town were powerless to stop the threat, they simply wanted to enjoy the time spent with their loved ones in the community. Cicero shared this town with nameless legends who crossed paths with folks such as the legendary Bass Reeves and Jesse James and lived to tell the tale. Cicero's squad that wanted to bring a polite and armed response numbered around fifteen gunners in all.

"This is going to be a bloodbath..." Cicero said to himself as he eyed positions for the group to dig in for defense. Two men, a few years Cicero's senior, were armed with hunting rifles positioned at the roof of Mavis' bar and eyed the entrances. A few other outlaws were busy equipping the horses with everything they needed. Cicero had gotten word that Cirano's rampage was heading towards them like a developing tornado.

Of all places, Cicero's hometown was ultimately inconsequential with Cirano's new consolidated control of criminal enterprise and the pause of the railway, but it was about proving a point. One bold soul rebelled against the cause and threw a glass bottle at the back of a mobster's head for squeezing them dry. That mobster was fine, but the boy was met with a hail of bullets and given a closed casket for the parts they could find. The buried corpse in a shallow grave, treated by Claudia, was the last straw at the town's insistence on agreeing to such a takeover. The ongoing dispute reached Cirano, and he decided to send half his forces to the town to teach a lesson. This was one week ago and now the time was nigh.

Cirano's message was clear. He wasn't going to take any perceived disrespect. His men declared it a wash as just one person was the cause of all this, but he knew better. Cirano knew that if one person, a child no less, compared to them could pose resistance, the rest of the town would follow suit. Cirano had a tight grip on the city, and in the wake of The Baron's disappearance from public life, felt much more secure in forging the alliances he needed. The message was keeping them in line and to reinforce that there was no hope for their cause. Cirano had the police bought, but the task he needed them for was more complex. He ordered them to investigate an ongoing trail further out. By the end of this venture, he hoped to have Rose in his grasp and be taken prisoner at his warehouse for the final piece of the plan. He was going to force her to create a new universe where he could settle into his new position unchallenged.

Cicero let out a whistle that resonated through the town. There was no exact timing that Cirano and his forces were expected to come, but today was going to be the day. Cicero looked at the spots that his fellow outlaws were entrenched in, this was the most excitement many had in years. Two unlikely allies approached Cicero with the tip of their hat. Cicero nearly gasped at the sight, two of his old gang members that lived to old age were ready to fight. Their roots in the town were long gone save for the occasional drift of news that came by. Cicero was moved by such a notion and hoped their fight wouldn't be in vain. He saw an older black gentleman with a curled mustache and a big brimmed hat. He was accompanied by a pale Irishman with a bandolier and slick white hair. The first of the two men were armed with a bolt action rifle and a pistol, while his associate had a semi-automatic shotgun. They were prepared to go down swinging and wore their Sunday best for the occasion.

"Jedidah?! The hell you doing here? You brought Mick with you too?" Cicero asked in shock.

"Of course. We protect our own. I was running some rum with Mick down in New Mexico when we heard about your problem via telegram. Dropped everything and headed here, I'm sixty-six, but I can still sight an iron with ease. Hope we're not too late," Jedidah mentioned as his comrade agreed.

Cicero's reunion was cut short as his old ears picked up the sound of whirring engines that came by. Cicero quickly went to his hiding place and advised his old gangmates to do the same. A group of cars parked some distance from the town. One by one, a group of mobsters exited their respective vehicles as they were ready to strike. Fifty men in all were more than enough to take over an entire section of the city, let alone this town. The lead of the pack wore a tan suit that differed from the usual group. A subordinate of Cirano, he was the one that was going to get his hands dirty. The lead man scanned the town for anything out of the ordinary; it was always a quiet place that usually offered no trouble. The smell of resistance wasn't something he expected but Cirano wanted a clean and thorough job. He decided to bait the group into offering themselves up, but Cicero accounted for this. Cicero had tactically hidden those who were willing to fight in sections throughout the town, while those who were attempting to hide, watched through their blinds.

"We're going to give this one more shot. We want a value of two thousand dollars placed in the center of town! What do you say to that?" the man yelled. There was a moment of silence and then a crack shot rang from above. The sniper posted at the roof of the bar fired directly through the man's throat and he bled out on the spot.

One of the men on the rooftop shouted a rebellious yell against the mobsters. The men dispersed and started to fire wildly into the air as shrapnel ripped through the shoddy wooden defenses and sheet metal made as makeshift barricades. The violence was on an impressive scale as the sound was deafening up close. The loud charge of horses past the town's center square was heard as the outlaws on top of them took pot-shots at the mobsters that sequestered behind their car. Those that were too slow were gunned down, their heads popped like balloons of blood as their aim was unrelenting. The fast fire rate of their submachine gun counterattack, however, was more than enough to tear through the bond of rider and horse as blood spilled on the streets. The horses fell forward and the men that rode them were torn to pieces in a hail of gunfire. The mobsters split into two main groups, the first that held the attention of the active combatants, including Cicero and his gang members. The second group was more insidious; they started to shoot up people's homes and the resulting damage led to bloodshed as people attempted to hide from the destruction. Miles away, the sound of gunfire ripped through the silent canyon and disrupted the long-held peace.

Cicero saw that blow to blow, his men were winning the longer ranged engagements as they were able to scope in on the target, but casualties were sustained. There was no comparison for dealing with the power of a submachine gun and with all of Cirano's men armed with them, it was only a matter of time before they were mercilessly gunned down. Cicero looked to see the expressions of his townspeople as they were firing back on the opposition. He could tell they were scared, but invigorated by the purpose of dying for something as important as the town they grew up in. Few were filled with regrets of their ill-gotten gains in the outlaw life, but each one loaded their weapons with the intention of preventing the scourge of organized crime from taking another. Cicero watched some townsfolk older than he was triumphantly run into the fray with nothing more than a double-barreled shotgun as they attempted to at least injure their targets. The ensuing carnage was disgusting to witness as their bodies flailed in the wind that ensued. Cicero looked to throw a stick of dynamite and attempted to blow up the car that seemed to take the bulk of their cover.

Cicero beckoned to Jedidah to come forward, but his friend was hesitant from the streaming trail of bullets. He gave a familiar nod as he understood Cicero needed a stick of dynamite. The old man ran as fast as he could and tossed the stick, just barely landing at Cicero's feet from the other side. Cicero used a lighter to burn the stick and let it loose. The stick of dynamite collided with a nearby crate and its explosive trajectory missed the mark as tons of wooden pieces were dispersed in the air. The car was given some slight damage, but the group was pinned down. Cicero, additionally, had no idea the other forces split off. Cicero heard the obnoxious sound of a car horn in the brief seconds of reloading, and he was confused at the source of the sound.

When all hope seemed to be lost, Niccolo's men arrived in an armored car. Niccolo emerged with himself, and six men dedicated to the cause. Bill sped into the square and ran over one of Cirano's goons, with a satisfying crunch as his head rolled over. Niccolo opened the door with gusto and appeared out of the right side with his Thompson. He fired wildly, providing essential suppressive fire with little fear of the opposition. The rest of his men piled out the back and the tide started to turn as they immediately dispelled frag grenades with much greater kick.

For Niccolo, the outcome was completely ideal. Cirano himself wasn't involved in the fighting, but he was able to bring the war to the town where he could use the extra resources, just long enough. Niccolo also realized that by helping Cicero, he could appear to be the hero and could use this connection to cement the town for his own needs. Cirano was a brute, but Niccolo could shelve over some goodwill with some more favorable terms for the town at large. As long as they paid their share, nobody would bother them again and they would be free to do what they pleased. Niccolo already had victory in his eyes as the rest of his organization wanted blood for Andrea's murder.

"Niccolo?! I thought you were doing time!" Cicero yelled over the ensuing gunfire. He loaded his revolver and fired twice, hitting a gangster in the knee and then in the forehead. He retracted his arm just in time to avoid retaliation.

"Rose broke me out of jail with one of her portals! I owe her a great deal! Now, I should get into cover!" Niccolo shouted as he ducked beneath the car. He dictated orders to Bill and Frank who ran to recover the wounded as quickly as they could.

Rose... Cicero thought. Cicero had wanted Rose to be as far away from the town as possible while this firefight was underway.

Cicero had his doubts regarding Niccolo's sincerity on wanting to help his town, but he didn't mind the extra firepower that was surely needed. The combined efforts of Cicero's leadership with Niccolo's foundation from his men were able to drive back what remained of the others. The few mobsters that slipped into the deeper depths of the town were met with armed townspeople who attempted to beat back the menace with anything they grab. A flurry of stone and liquor bottles littered the streets as the mob used broken brooms and mops as makeshift spears. Cicero and the rest of the men cleaned up the opposition and were able to finally rest as the vultures circled above in anticipation for a new meal.

"Thanks," Cicero mentioned with a heavy delay as he looked to Niccolo.

"Naturally cowboy, we will talk the terms of what happens later. There is one other order of business to discuss. Bill, tell him the news." Niccolo pushed Bill forward.

"Mr. Cicero, sir. What we just faced was only half of what Cirano has. He has a warehouse located on the outskirts of the eastern city. It operates as an auto repair shop by day. I-I think we should take you along and we get going. We're going to finish the job," Bill explained. Niccolo had a slightly shocked reaction as Bill described Cirano's outpost in greater detail than he initially reported. Niccolo hadn't gathered the specifics, particularly with it operating as an auto shop. He raised an eyebrow at this slight omission. With nothing left to say, Cicero promised to gear for war as he left the rest of the town to bring the fight to Cirano.

Ghost Hunters

Rose and Florence were on the case and eyed a decaying two-story home in the interior of a growing Phoenix suburb. Houses once built to last were the chopping block for cookie cutter development spearheaded by the sprawling housing market. This building was one of many that soon needed to face demolition. Although company towns were out of fashion in the open, The Baron and other industry tyrants in the region maintained a tight grip on industry. Clarkdale was a stark reminder to the working class that they could be bought out at any point and once again placed under the yoke of the industrial heel. Rose and Florence were disgusted by the politics of it all and the soulless atmosphere throughout the community. Compared to the rest of the area that seemed to be teeming with life, however, it stood out as a gaping eyesore. The lawn's attempt at grass was left with only a shriveled amount of long decayed weeds and dirt beneath their feet. The house's windows were boarded up with wooden planks.

The ambient sounds of the street all but vanished as Rose could only hear her breathing. The place was long abandoned by the original occupants, the uncomfortable Edwardian architecture contrasted from the bombastic flairs of Art Deco and Spanish revivalism on people's homes. Rose originally intended to do this hunt with Cicero, but with the chaos of the gang war reaching his hometown, his loyalty overtook his need for the bounty. Rose opted for Florence to be her backup, as despite some inexperience for the task, she was more than willing to follow her lead.

Florence came prepared with her own satchel of supplies as her car was parked out front of the residence. She had her nail baseball bat and a camera filled with film. Rose still worked on her documentation for The Baron and Baroness and opted to include photographs of the things she encountered if possible.

"Well, ain't you gonna open it?" Rose teased as she looked behind her.

Rose nodded her head for Florence to use her baseball bat as she knocked away pieces of the heavy wooden planks. Rose raised an eyebrow as she noticed Florence's arms bulge with each strike, she was stronger than anticipated. Florence used the head of the bat to carve a path for the two to enter. She leaned low as her hair was prone to catching on splinters of wood. The door practically left its hinges as she made a bit more room for Rose to follow.

As soon as Rose entered, she felt an immediate shiver. Despite the heat of the setting sun behind them, the air felt constricting and cold. Rose felt as if her lungs would freeze as she slowed her breathing for every second to count. Her eyes scanned the room and looked for anything out of the ordinary. She saw peeled wallpaper that long lost its luster as it curled up with marks of decay. She noticed burnt photographs and smashed picture frames on a nearby dresser. Rose noticed there was some looting present, people lifting what they could from the walls, as the faint outline of former paintings remained. There was a staircase on the left side of the room, and a locked trapdoor that led to a basement. Rose could tell by the size of the trapdoor it wasn't any mere storage room. Basements were uncommon in Arizona which prompted immediate suspicion from both women. It was a choice that was common for those working on making their own home stills for alcohol to obscure the smell.

"So, run this by me again. What exactly are we looking for here? Feels like we keep running into bootleggers around these parts. Makes sense, nobody would suspect a crime in this rinky dink," Florence said with an affirmative touch to Rose's shoulder. She had a warm grin that contrasted heavily from her nearby surroundings.

Florence was a master at compartmentalizing her true feelings from the surroundings around her. A task like this was a tall order by any margin, but she trusted Rose and wanted to return the favor for her efforts in finding more information for her own goals. Rose and Venus coordinated a good effort over the phone to find that Florence's criminal family violated the American Antiquities Act by bundling laundered money into the artifact trade in the museum industry, just one more piece of evidence to bring to light.

"Some little boy done hanged himself because of bullying in this house. It's empty, but Cicero said there's a ghost around here. That's what the client seems to think," Rose explained.

"Do you believe in ghosts? Truly?" Florence asked as she placed her stuff down on a nearby chair.

"Well, if God's real, then so is the Devil. I guess that means everything in between too. With that in mind, and all the things I've seen on the hunt with Cicero, how could you not?" Rose reasoned.

"Hey Florence. Thanks for coming with me by the way. I'm worried about Cicero. I could do this on my own, but—" Rose added as she was cut off by Florence.

"It's better we're over here getting this bounty closed out than the skirmish out in the sticks. You're a real go-getter Rose, but what use would we be?" Florence said in support.

Rose decided to set down her stuff, though she retained her pistol in its holster. She was unsure if it would be possible to even harm a ghost. She scratched her head and attempted to come up with some sort of greeting. Florence patiently sat on the chair and watched as she wondered what was next in the process.

"Hello little boy? My name is Rose. I'm a Monster Hunter and I take care of scary things, but I don't think you're scary. We can talk this out. We need you out of this house—" Rose said.

Florence turned her head as she heard a small rattling sound come by the kitchen ahead of them. While Rose was occupied, a knife propelled itself at breakneck speed in Rose's direction. Florence quickly left the chair and moved Rose just in time, the knife only taking a sliver of Rose's cheek with a stream of blood. The metal was still sharp after all this time. She imagined it'd been dulled. Florence quickly got a handkerchief from her bag and dabbed the small bit on Rose's face. Rose was less than amused at the ghost's insistence on being a problem.

Boy, I will get a switch on you in a heartbeat. Don't test me. Rose thought as she felt movement inside her satchel this time.

She looked down below and noticed that there was an unusual calling for her notebook. The book felt cold to the touch as well, and it felt heavier as there were more pages in it than before. Rose was out of her element when it came to particular supernatural matters, it was easier for her to just accept what she witnessed and give little thought afterwards. Rose looked at her notebook and while she coursed through her various sketches of the entities she encountered, she stopped, and gave a look of surprise as she saw writing on her notebook that wasn't her own.

"Turn the page," Rose read aloud for Florence. The text was written three times, one in manuscript and the other two in cursive.

"There are three things you must do, if you want me to do what you say. Play with me when the sun goes down. Tell me a secret. Take me home," Rose read as the text started to materialize on the page.

Florence looked out the window, there was still some time before night would emerge. She gave a yawn as her nightly habits of searching the newspapers for any new leads of the criminal underground caught up to her. She felt a heavy desire to nap but found that would be a poor choice given the recent phenomena that occurred. Florence idled her time by knitting something to keep her hands busy, while Rose looked over her notes without end. Before they knew it, the ghost boy was ready to play, just as he mentioned before. Rose limbered up with a few stretches as she minded the large amounts of dust in the home. Rose kept her notebook open for the boy's correspondence and the first of the letters started to reveal themselves. She watched as the ink bled to the paper.

Her gaze met the pages as they formulated each letter. The ink first started as black, but gradually reddened with a trail of ink splotches. The loops of the letters were immaculate and well-practiced, a hallmark of the time and training the boy first learned his penmanship. Each second, there was an illustrated thought that was brought to life. Much like her own writing, Rose saw associated images drawn with the text. Some were endearing, while the others were much more gruesome. She noticed depictions of herself and Florence in multiple drawings that accompanied grave injuries. She saw her own bones exposed and Florence without a head. Pools of blood settled under the drawings of the two women. It was clear to her that failure to properly follow the rules of engagement was going to lead to their demise.

"I have two games. One is more fun than the other. Do you want to play hopscotch? Jump for yes, clap for no," Rose read as she shot a look at Florence.

I really don't want to know what the other game is. Hopscotch, it is. Rose thought.

Rose urged Florence to jump with her on the count of three and they did so in unison. Rose gave a slightly worried look at the foundation of the house as the already creaky floorboards gave way under their weight. With the jump of confirmation, Rose and Florence were urged to take the staircase in anticipation of the game. The upstairs of the home was more furnished than the bottom as dust overtook the rest of the furniture. A shriveled newspaper from over twenty years ago remained etched on the surface of a nearby drawer. Rose gathered that the boy was an only child with the master bedroom on the other side. The child's game area was the hallway between the master bedroom and the child's old quarters. Rose looked around in confusion at how the game would begin, but she saw Florence hold a piece of chalk in her hand.

"Oh my, here I am at thirty-three years old doing this. I can do a little jig if I have to," Florence joked while Rose nodded in agreement with her statement.

Both women were curious about how the ghost was willing to play, but it seemed to pit Florence and Rose against each other. A rock that moved on its own started the game as Rose volunteered first. She put her left foot first and had to commit for the rest of the squares. Rose had to mind her pacing, there were no punishments for losing the game as she was aware, but it caused her to be nervous anyway. She retained a sense of dread in her as she chose her movements carefully and made it to the other side, minding the rules. She had to use the same foot on her return as well. Florence had a more gregarious presentation to her as she toed the line of the points, with her feet barely making in the square. Florence's return was not as graceful as Rose's was, an early childhood injury made it more difficult for Florence to maintain balance for that length of time. She fell and laughed it off. Rose felt unsure if both had to win the game, but despite her worries, the first demand by the ghost child started to evaporate with acceptable payment.

Rose was anxious about the second demand. A secret had to be something inherently vulnerable, and she often lacked the openness to bring these up. She intentionally kept much about her vague at best, with some anecdotes she provided as social cover for herself. Rose really only confided in Venus and Cicero to a lesser extent, and there was plenty that Rose hoped would never see the light of day.

"A secret. Well, this is embarrassing, the best ones are. Last week, I had a dream. I was a baby in a little bed, wrapped up tight in some sheets but something spooked me. I called for my mama, but it wasn't my mother who came in. It was The Baroness. She walked towards me and scooped me up. She put some tea into me, and I was a still baby. It was warm, I felt the warmth as her wrists supported my back. I felt safe. The lift of my tiny neck, I had to do that hold before. I... I shouldn't have these thoughts. My mother is here on Earth, she's alive and I know her, but all I see is a stranger," Rose rambled on as she constantly checked the notebook to see if that would suffice.

It's not often Rose says something that makes me really surprised! Not sure what I should say here, maybe I should just do my turn. Oh, but what would be good enough? Florence thought. Florence wasn't sure how to react to Rose's tale but rubbed the back of her neck in slight concern about the health of their relationship. Florence gathered the attention of the spirit as best as she could while Rose sat on the floor with folded legs.

"When I first tried to escape the hospital, I took a car. It was 1917 and the country just started off to war. There was a big party going on so nobody would notice. I bribed an orderly to let me use the bathroom on my own, and then I climbed out of a window. I took the car in the middle of the rain but ran into a deer-no-no Florence, it wasn't a deer. It was a sickly old man on the road. I was so desperate not to come back, I tried to hide the body. I got caught and I paid a real bad price for it," Florence said while Rose coughed at the admission in surprise.

"You know Rose and... Clarence. This is really freeing to me!" Florence added as she came across the name of the deceased boy in an old family album.

"I know it's not what you'd imagine, coming from someone like me. But—I told Nicki about what really happened at my stay in the hospital, and he was truly the first person to see me the whole of who I am, despite missing some... things. I think that we found each other at an odd time, and it works. I don't know what this all means just yet, but I'm not gonna knock on a good thing. I don't want a family or anything, the idea of woopie alone makes me gag, but I always had to pick up the pieces and be on my own. I don't have to worry about that. Trust, I have no illusions of the work that's done, I sought his kind out for revenge to root it out. Sometimes, Niccolo can be really stupid, but he's sweet. He's reliable and doesn't judge, even though I go into the breach, the trenches—Nicki always had my back. He didn't have to work with me, I'm a grown woman that's made her choices." Florence commented as she felt flustered over her words. Her blushing subsided as Rose placed a hand on her shoulder in sol idarity.

I didn't expect all of that, but it makes sense. I don't know how she can stay so positive all the time knowing that lies behind her. I can only think about how much guilt she probably has. Rose thought.

Once Rose and Florence finished the boys' tasks on the second floor, a rumbling sound throughout the house came all at once. Rose held on tightly to Florence in a hug as the rumbling soon stopped. This was accompanied with only the sound of a latch that unlocked. Rose remembered the next phase of the plan, which was to take the boy home. What did that mean exactly? He was a ghost.

Florence recognized this latch sound as the opening to the trapdoor that led to the basement. She recalled that this was originally locked, but it appeared Clarence had control of this portion of the house as well. Florence led first as she extended her hand out to Rose to grab. Rose gathered their things and she reflexively held out her pistol. As the pair descended the second floor, Rose noticed there were an unusual number of mirrors present on the walls. Once Rose or Florence walked past one, the glass exploded into small shards behind them. The women increased their speed as they shielded themselves from the debris. The basement once upon a time was a place that held company, it was furnished with a couch and carpet. Florence lifted the latch and the two entered the basement.

Rose could only hear her heartbeat as Florence silently held her hand against the wall. She froze, unable to go further. Rose understood this feeling well, but they needed to push through. Rose placed her hand on Florence's shoulder in confidence to lead them through. If Clarence wanted them dead, he would have done it by now. The low light of the basement contrasted with the already dim atmosphere of the rest of the home. At the end of the left corridor, a closed door accompanied the sound of a blowing wind. Rose stepped forward and approached the door with a big padlock on it.

"Stand back." Rose lifted her pistol to shoot the lock off. Her and Florence's ears rang as the lock fell to the ground.

Florence nodded to Rose and opened the door as they went inside. The tale given by Cicero was laid bare. The lone stool used for the deed was overturned some distance away and the clothesline was long since rusted. Rose couldn't fathom what would drive someone as young as this boy to kill themselves, or to even gather such knowledge. Not far from their position, a lone pile of bones and shredding clothing remained. Any smell of decay was long since gone. Rose gasped for air as she realized what had happened.

"They left the body?! They, they left the body. It's just bones! There's nothing but bones!" Rose screamed in horror. Florence looked for her camera. She needed to document the site to include in their report, regardless of how gruesome the scene was.

As Rose struggled to hide her tears, she noticed a spectral gray image start to permeate from the remains. The cold feeling remained as it grew larger before them. Rose felt as if she could see pale blue eyes slowly degrade in color until they were a resounding empty black. Florence was ignorant of this as she already placed her eye and focus on the scene with her camera. She racked a quick spool of film. While Rose anticipated a fight of some sort, she was surprised at the outcome. The shadowy image that started to appear vanished at the sight of the large, blinding ray that emitted from Florence's camera. Rose rubbed her eyes and saw they were once again alone. She touched her chin in thought.

"You caught his soul in this photo. We'll have to burn it later to set him free for good. We should get the bones out too," Rose recalled Cicero's instructions.

After an awkward silence between the pair, leaving to go home was the first thing on their minds. Rose hadn't imagined how traumatic that would be for her as a veteran and she thought of Florence who had to unearth such long forgotten memories. The duo made their way through the house and saw there was an unusual amount of activity on the outside. The police were gathered for some sort of investigation, but the root cause was unknown. Rose started to panic as she noticed the swarm of police getting closer. She noticed they had a stream of rifles and shotguns at the helm.

"Hands up! Right where I can see them, now! Drop your weapons," a police officer yelled as he pointed his revolver at Rose.

Florence protectively stood in front of Rose. She defiantly raised her neck at the crewmen who cared little for the display. It was for naught as the two women were subsequently handcuffed and placed under arrest in the back of the car. Rose was struck with a nightstick by one of the senior officers, while Florence could only look in anguish. Rose knew that it was possible to hatch an escape plan of with her portals, but she was powerless to take Florence with her. Rose looked outside the window and noticed that there was a mass exodus of police officers from this location. She was shocked as it seemed there was this many for just them. What did it all mean? Florence watched as they passed her car.

"What do you want for this to go away? Money? Something else? I know people that can help you or make your day terrible." Florence attempted to negotiate. She bit her tongue in annoyance as she figured most of the police here were spineless and could take a quick buck with ease. Now was the sole time she found police officers with something vaguely resembling integrity. The police officers driving the vehicle made zero attempts to speak with Florence. Rose kept her head down as she couldn't fight off bullets in her direction. Florence assessed that the route that they were taking was one off the beaten path, they'd already passed the junction for one police station. Florence was skeptical about what to make of this news.

"You're not taking us to the station boys, it's south," Florence protested as she tried to wrestle herself out of her confinement while Rose said nothing.

The two policemen exchanged a glance with one another as Rose and Florence slowly lost their resolve. Rose had her thoughts on what the politics regarding their capture entailed. As she drifted to sleep, she heard the driver finally answer Florence.

"We know."

The Owl: III

Cicero took a moment to catch his breath as he was taken aback by such a request. His blood was still pumping with adrenaline as he defended the town with his saving breath, but he felt that he needed more information and to get properly equipped. Cicero only had his regular revolver and lacked his shotgun and other weapons that were essential for heavy combat. Cicero pleaded with Niccolo for a chance to gather his supplies before embarking on the mission. Niccolo agreed to let Cicero get situated first before heading straight to the compound. Niccolo anticipated that he could use surprise to their advantage as it was likely Cirano expected the men to return home soon after their shootout. Niccolo's knowledge of Cirano's forces being split in half still gave him some worry, but given their victory, proper planning would win out. He mobilized the few men he could in order to perform a wide search of the city for Cirano's warehouse in an attempt to bring him out. He assumed his earlier gambles of getting Cirano to attack the town worked, although it was already Cirano's intentions to do so.

"Get in cowboy! What are you waiting for?" Niccolo chimed as he enthusiastically loaded a new magazine into his gun. Niccolo was overjoyed to see that he could prove to Cicero his word was worth his weight in actions as well. He already looked around to see the town starting to rebuild itself, and with the cemented defeat of Cirano, he could start raking in on the cash.

"Yeah. If you want to see Rose again, you should come with us," Bill commented.

As Bill and the other men drove to Cicero's estate, they shared a smoke outside the property while Cicero gathered himself. Bill wondered what his life would have been like if he picked a different path than working for both Niccolo and Cirano. He lacked a lot of core skills, but he showed up when it mattered, which made his presence valuable. His betrayal to Niccolo, he felt was worth the cost of what was attributed to him, but it wasn't something that was done passionately. Frank shared a laugh as he watched Cicero avoid the passion-filled slaps of Claudia through the window at such an idea of joining them on their mission. Their conversation was audible to a considerable degree as Niccolo pretended not to notice. Niccolo was sadly reminded of his own ex-wife and the debates they would have late into the night about things that no longer mattered. He chose to put his mind on other things as he heard the door of Cicero's home finally open. Cicero emerged a short time later with his weapons and a slightly embarrassed look on his face as he met the eyes of the others.

"What can I say? My wife loves me," Cicero commented.

The four men in the car remained quiet as Bill traced the route back to Cirano's warehouse. Bill knew the most efficient way to get there but attempted to take a few missed turns here and there to sell the facts regarding this information. Bill realized he made a grave mistake as he mentioned Rose's involvement in all this. Bill knew bits and pieces of Rose as he overheard Niccolo's conversations with Florence but knew little of her personally. Niccolo intended that his monster hunting business with Cicero stayed as separately as possible when it was required. As far as Niccolo knew, Rose was nowhere to be found. Cicero found Bill's earlier statement to be suspicious, as he knew Rose was going to hunt ghosts on her own as they agreed to earlier. Cicero couldn't shake the feeling that something was off, and he decided to forward the question to the rest of the car to see how they felt about the matter.

"Now hold on, something about this isn't right," Cicero questioned as Bill turned down the street. Cicero watched as Bill signaled the car to let a few pedestrians pass by while Niccolo checked his watch.

"You, big fella. Bill, was it? How the hell did you know Cirano was going to be here? We've been looking for Cirano for ages now. Hadn't had a lick of sense where he was, and you just found him. You also mentioned Rose earlier. What's that got to do with her? Should I be concerned?" Cicero commented. Bill kept his mouth quiet as Cicero's question hung over the rest of the men and Niccolo.

"Well Bill. Aren't you going to answer the cowboy? They are partners, so this information is important," Niccolo mentioned. Niccolo looked at the rearview mirror to see that Cicero was deep in thought.

Bill floored the car as he drove past a few other lanes to reach the outskirts of town. He was hoping to use the speed of the vehicle to change the subject as quickly as possible while beelining for the outpost. The car came to a sudden halt that nearly catapulted the men and their respective weapons around from the momentum of the stopped car. Niccolo was increasingly angry by Bill's behavior, and it showed in his irritated expression. The four men exited the car and slammed the doors, while Bill started to shake like a leaf in the wind. He could hardly meet Cicero's eyes, let alone that of his superior.

Bill completely boiled down as he realized he gave up the game with just a simple admission. He hadn't bothered to account for Cicero's sharp ears as he paid attention to every word. Bill started to sweat, and he rubbed his palms on his jeans. The group stood some distance away from the auto repair shop that lacked any sentries or anything on the outside. A first guess would have been that Cicero and company blew them apart back at the town, but Cicero wondered if they were actually stepping into a trap. Cicero eyed the structure and noticed the reinforced entrance that would require more than just slick hands to open.

"Uh..." Bill mentioned with a stammer. Bill could feel his chest clench from the pressure on him. His breathing slowed as he stared down Cicero, Niccolo, and Frank. Frank met Bill's eyes, but he could offer no sympathy for the man before him. In the private conversations between goons, a man's business was his own, but he was right next to the boss and knew where his pay was coming from.

"Niccolo, I'm sorry. It wasn't supposed to be this way. That wasn't the deal," Bill muttered as Niccolo started to vibrate with rage. Bill could hardly lie his way out of such a direct question, and he crumbled as Cicero remained unmoved by such a display.

"I-I had some trouble. I... I've been working for Cirano. Not in any way that impeded the business, he'd ask me questions, and I'd give him information. He gave me the money I needed to deal with my debt to the Irish and to take care of my ma. It was innocent enough. He told me that he was going to plan something with Rose, and I didn't care, but then he mentioned Florence as well. I'm sweet on her and I don't want her to get hurt," Bill mentioned with confidence. Bill knew there was no way out from admitting this and he tried to keep himself together. Bill was keenly aware of what Niccolo was capable of from his leadership style and that of Cirano's.

"Bill. This is a lot of information. I need to know something. This was a burning question in my mind. How long was this? I remember the bank job that we did not going as well as I planned, was this your doing?" Niccolo asked as Cicero watched quietly. Niccolo withdrew his pistol and aimed it at Bill.

"It's been a while, sir. He knew about the bank job. The safe is what was cleaned out, but I never told him about the trucks. The truck is what we grabbed, and we got a lot of money, you know that. I chose us. I needed to give something so that he knew I could be trusted, but I never exposed us," Bill pleaded.

"We got some of the money, but not all of it. Our organization needs this money, every last bit, you were told this the day you joined our family. This is so much more than simply making quota. We are fighting the fascists back in Italy to take control of Venice once again. Mussolini has total control over it, these knuckle-dragging fascists, the ones that are probably raping my wife and child as we have this conversation. All this, for gambling debt? You could have declared bankruptcy! You weak, spineless, fool!" Niccolo mentioned as his voice raised to a harsh scream. He gritted his teeth in anger as Bill could only hang his head in shame.

"Look at me," Niccolo ordered as Bill slowly raised his head to look at Niccolo. Niccolo paused as he took a deep breath and fired his gun. Bill hit the pavement with a bit of blood that leaked from the bullet wound and the back of his head. Niccolo was angered at such a betrayal as he had high hopes for Bill. Niccolo pinned the gun next on Frank who was quick to disavow any involvement he had with Bill, much to Niccolo's satisfaction.

"Do you have a problem?" Niccolo asked as he noticed Cicero watching the entire time.

"Not one bit. I was in a gang once, silence is golden. Not only did that oaf put Rose in danger, but it's also likely there's a trap waiting for us inside. That low down coward can take a dirt nap with the rest of the trash," Cicero bluntly stated.

"Frank. Hang back and cover the exits. Cicero and I will go in and deal with the rest. If there are really fifty men, so be it. They will die by my hand," Niccolo stated with disgust as he kicked away Bill's corpse.

As Niccolo and Cicero made their peace before attempting to enter the facility, Rose and Florence were upheld by the gangsters that remained as Cirano's personal guard. Cirano was routinely paranoid and had applied some last-minute defenses to his main warehouse. Between deserters after the dinosaur attack and the shootout in town, Cirano hadn't had the time to replenish his numbers and was running low on bodies to throw at his problems. Cirano was busy with Rose while Florence remained under watch by his remaining guard. Rose looked at Cirano as he stepped forward. She could smell the alcohol on his breath with disgust.

"I know who you are. You're The Baroness' little project. I was hoping we could get acquainted under better terms, but I'm in a rush right now. The chips are low on the table for me. Funny, how things work out that way," Cirano stated as he adjusted the collar of his suit. He held out his nickel-plated pistol directly at Rose as she kept her arms up and back against the warehouse walls.

"Where's Florence!? You captured us both, why is she away from here?" Rose asked as she waited for her answer. Cirano scoffed at the mention of her.

"Suppose it doesn't matter now. She's got no tactical use to me, but we'll see if anyone's sweet on her to come by. I know nobody's looking for you. Now to the task at hand. I read the notes in your file they kept on you. You can make portals that can go anywhere." Cirano answered, his voice echoing slightly in the room. Rose kept her silence as she saw the man's wild nature take over. Rose hid her confusion regarding Cirano's statement of a file but knew that arguing was not the way out for now. She gave a subtle nod agreeing with his words.

"Good. I was right then. Make me a portal, a purple one. Not the blues. I know the difference." Cirano said as he inched closer to Rose. He toyed with the gun as he moved it around and watched Rose's eyes fixed on the weapon.

"The Baron and Baroness fuck over everybody, but I'm not some fink. I am gonna come out on top. You can make purple portals under duress. Well, I'm gonna give you a stressful situation." Cirano grabbed Rose by the neck and aimed the pistol towards her temple.

"It's not that simple." Rose said as her body tensed up with the cold metal on her forehead.

"Make me a goddamn portal, or I'll blast your brains all over this fucking wall! That's as simple as it gets!" Cirano yelled.

Rose closed her eyes and focused hard as she pieced together an amorphous blob. Cirano gave no estimation of what he wanted, so Rose was left to imagine what would fill the canvas. Cirano noticed the visual space around the potential portal warped, his eyes trained on the location. At once, a purple vortex was conjured as a light appeared through nothingness. Rose remembered a world of giant mushrooms she'd seen before and prompted this as her destination. The portal's image materialized like a well-crafted portrait as pieces of it took form. A pleasant smell leaked from the opening that resembled a fresh pine tree. Cirano himself couldn't believe that such a sight was real and that his vision would soon be realized. Unlimited riches and power were in his grasp. Now that Rose was a proven asset with her abilities, the possibilities were endless. Rose still felt the cold steel pressed against her and wondered if she could come up with a plan.

In the midst of the warehouse, Cirano's remaining men, a force of eight, made a stalwart defense against the combined might of Cicero and Niccolo. Armed with shotguns and pistols, they lay down lead at the sight of a small mouse. They were on edge and had every right to be. Niccolo heeded Cicero's observation and also noticed the vault-like entrance of the warehouse, packed with reinforced steel. Niccolo came prepared with his signature submachine gun, a few grenades strapped to his suit and a pistol taken from the back of his car.

"Let's do this and go home. Claudia's got chili brewing, I just know it," Cicero stated.

Cicero gestured to Niccolo, who removed the pin from a grenade and hauled it at the door. The explosion was more than enough to dislodge the lock placed on it, and the men inside began to worry. They hadn't expected this much firepower to be brought out. The two men walked inside and held their guns out first, signaling their entry to the passersby. Cirano's men were aware of the growing tenacity regarding Niccolo and the dedication to his order. The silent but effective cowboy also remained a matter of concern. Cirano's men were smart and were loyal to the money rather than the man. An attempt was considered among the survivors that they could use some form of reason to get out of this alive. In a last-ditch effort to save their hides, one of the men walked out with Florence. While she was aware of the severity of the situation, her upbeat attitude gave a snarky delivery.

"Oh, is it my time to shine!? How wonderful—" Florence said before getting elbowed in the face by her captor. She frowned but couldn't do much else at gunpoint. Her face brightened as she heard the explosion and out came the unexpected Cicero and Niccolo standing at the far end of the repair shop.

Florence looked above as the overall ambient light darkened. The high sun soon vanished behind a wall of clouds that blocked nearby rays. It was monsoon season, and the torrential rains became a backdrop to the sounds outside. The dark clouds obscured the men who stood on awnings in grey and had their guns trained on the pair. Stacks of boxes and other assorted goods were piled high throughout with both in the middle. Florence was pushed further out first, with her captor right behind her. Florence attempted to squirm while Cicero nodded his head to dissuade her from adjusting position. He had his eyes focused on the kill while Niccolo attempted to make conversation as he planned.

"There are supposed to be two of them. Where is the other?" Niccolo asked as his eyes searched the room. One of Cirano's henchmen from above replied to him.

"The black is with Cirano, his mind is cooked sunnyside up. Boss flew the coop about destiny and fate. We're here to get paid, make us an offer and we can all leave," the man commented as he gave a grimace to Niccolo.

"You're surrounded anyway, I suggest you drop your gun and forget about this," the man holding Florence said. Cicero and Niccolo's attention turned to him as the two brought out their pistols. Cicero guided Niccolo with his eyes to focus on the above targets, while Cicero had his sights on the matter at hand.

"You think this is some picture show? You can't expect to take all of us out," one man scoffed at the two from the awning.

"And there's Billy The Kid with that gaudy hat! Ride off into the sunset, cowboy," another voice called out as he teased Cicero. His yellow and gray stained teeth were visible from the darkness.

"I take it you surrender then. Look boys, we got places to be. Go ahead and drop your gun and I'll cop a feel before I let her loose," the man said as he blatantly groped Florence. He took the two's silence as a means of surrender.

While Niccolo switched his firing mode to auto, Cicero was just a smidge faster on the trigger. Cicero fanned his revolver without a second thought, two bullets were all he needed. One to disarm the man as the gun fell to the floor, and another to go through his skull. Cicero wasted little time as he focused on recovering Florence from the grubby hands of the mafiosos. Bits of his brain and blood leaked onto Florence as she stepped away. The man fell to the floor with a hard thud as his body took the shock. The man was dead before smoke left the gun. In the chaos that followed, the men opened fire while Cicero and Niccolo scattered to find cover. Florence crawled on the ground towards the pistol before getting away. Bits and pieces of shrapnel reflected throughout the vicinity as gunfire was exchanged. Two for two, Cicero much preferred fighting against monsters than human opponents, but he still was able to deliver.

Among the commotion, Florence yelled out that she was going to try to grab Rose while she could. Her voice was barely audible over the gunfire, so she hoped for the best. Niccolo opened fire on the awning, concentrating a burst on the men at the top, while Cicero loaded his revolver behind a box. Bits of shrapnel reflected from the awning as glass from the windows broke and spilled out to the floor below. As the awning was rusted, it took little time for the piece to collapse, leaving some of the men to hang on for dear life. The target of Niccolo's rage fell to the ground as their lifeless bodies reached the floor and landed on boxes or the ground. Cicero switched to his shotgun and pumped a gangster in the stomach while he keeled over with a pulled grenade. Niccolo noticed this and reflexively grabbed Cicero by the shoulder, distancing himself just enough to avoid the shrapnel.

"Agh, my ears!" Cicero complained as the explosion rang through the closed space.

Niccolo continued to fire down range, suppressing the remaining gangsters in hiding while Cicero took crack shots with his revolver. On the opposing side, one of the gangsters slinked out in an attempt to intercept Florence. Florence heard the man's footsteps and held out the gun, quickly shooting it and nailing him on the foot. She hadn't anticipated such recoil from the pistol, but it landed its mark. Florence made her way to the door where she saw Rose get dragged and shot the lock off.

As Cirano was enamored by the vision of the portal, he hadn't realized that Florence now made her way inside. Rose's eyes lit up in excitement as she saw that Florence managed to get herself out somehow. Florence held the gun with both hands as she yelled to grab the pair's attention.

"L-Let her go! Or I'll shoot you dead," Florence threatened as Cirano offered a laugh. He felt he was in control of the situation despite Florence being freed. It mattered little to Cirano what happened next as his vision was achieved.

"You and that little peashooter?" Cirano mentioned as he took his pistol off Rose to aim at Florence. Cirano shot the gun but was off by just a hair as Rose took advantage of the gap. It was only for a few seconds that Cirano decided to threaten Florence, but Rose grabbed his arm and used enough force to alter his aim.

Cirano countered Rose's attempt at bravery with a punch in the face. Rose felt her head spring back as she took the hit. Rose's mouth was bloody as she spit out some after biting down on her tongue. She let out a harsh cough and attempted to defend herself as well as she could, but the strength difference was mighty. Cirano grabbed Rose and forced her to the floor with a throw. Rose felt her bones creak as she attempted to get herself up.

Florence ran to Cirano and jumped on top of him and started to hit him over the head with the pistol.

Out of the corner of her eye, Rose could see that the other gangsters were occupied as she recognized the sound of Cicero's revolver. She felt invigorated by the fact that Cicero was risking his life to save her, not that she had any doubts to begin with. Rose knew she had to act quickly and think of a way to save herself and Florence. Florence was thrown off Cirano as he backed her into a wall and she felt her back crack. Cirano got up quickly and curled his hand into a fist as he was aiming to strike Rose once more. The purple portal remained open as he walked past its hue. Rose snapped her fingers and summoned a blue portal beneath Cirano's feet, and one at the top. Rose placed Cirano into a freefall that continued as he attempted to move out, but was trapped under his own momentum.

Rose waited for Florence to pick herself up as she looked to Rose for what to do next. Once Rose thought Cirano had enough, she removed the bottom portal and watched as Cirano hit the floor with a loud thud. There was enough force from his movement that Cirano's head hit the cold floor and blood seeped from his forehead. He was still very much alive but put into a daze. Rose decided to give Cirano exactly what he wanted and looked towards the portal. As Cirano attempted to get himself up, Rose gave a mighty heave and pushed Cirano with all her strength through the purple portal. Cirano had gotten what he wanted, but was so filled with fury, he attempted to run back and claw at Rose. Rose closed the portal and watched in silence as the last thing she saw was Cirano shouting curses at her. He would now have to contend with his new reality and whatever else came with it.

Rose and Florence looked at one another and hugged tightly as they waited for the rest of the violence around them to calm down. Roughly twenty minutes later, Cicero and Niccolo emerged victorious as Rose heard their banter over the matter. Cicero rushed through the door and had his gun trained, ready to put Cirano down. Niccolo immediately checked on Florence but also looked over Rose to see if there was anything else that needed to be taken care of.

"It's alright. It's over," Rose explained what happened. Cicero had a worried expression and gave Rose a tight hug. It was unexpected as he was hardly the emotional type, but it was appreciated by both parties.

"Your first kidnapping and you got yourself out of it, what luck! Not many can say the same," Niccolo commented as he put his hands on Rose's shoulders.

Cicero and Niccolo recommended they make a quick exit from the repair shop before the authorities came and gathered the evidence of what happened. With the town finally saved, Rose could rest easy as there was at least some closure for Cicero. Cirano was removed from the playing field and Niccolo was able to make the necessary moves to start incorporating his territories. At the end of the fighting, there was a still calm among the four of them. Niccolo was satisfied with his outcome, though he was not given blood for Andrea's death, the power vacuum was more than enough to make up for the loss. Florence remained unsatisfied; she hadn't been able to completely resolve her goal but was happy to have helped take on such an endeavor. For Rose and Cicero, however, The Baron's presence still loomed over them both. Cicero lived in ignorance at the true outcome of The Baron's death while Rose shouldered the secret.

The Frost Gem

Now free of her obligations with Cicero for the time being, Rose had one last task to do. Rose arrived in her mentor's favored dimension at the behest of The Baron's letter with a strange list of supplies she needed to gather. Rose reviewed the list as she was to bring a shovel, a coat with finger-tight gloves, and her weapon. She was proud of her current progress under The Baron and Baroness' guidance; blue portals were trivial for Rose as she had plenty of practice after her escapades with Venus. She could even indulge herself to show up at home and grab an ice cream cone from her favorite vendor and be back before anyone's notice.

She used her powers without much question put behind them. There were far worse people out there who could have gotten this gift. While she enjoyed the wide berth of her abilities, the purple vortexes were ground that Rose still needed experience with. Not only would Rose have to contend with contorting the bends of this reality, but she would need to control the other to travel through. She recalled her embarrassment as she flooded The Baron and Baroness' anniversary party with a resounding pool of water that she generated in a panic. The Baroness saw this and rather than be cross with her, she could hardly suppress her joy at such a revelation. Rose was aware that The Baroness expected a lot from her and today was no different. Her eyes met The Baroness present with her supplies as well, various cold weather implements. The Baroness prompted Rose to dress the part and studied her patiently as Rose looked forward.

"Do you remember what you were supposed to do?" The Baroness asked as she folded her arms. Rose held her hands to her side. She took a deep breath from her nose and exhaled as she held her hands out in a tight grip and started to strain. Rose's vision grew less and less as she clenched her entire body in concentration. As she attempted to focus, the space that was in front of her slowly contorted as she was creating another vortex within this dimension. Blades of grass that were at the bottom of the space bent in unnatural ways. The Baroness walked over and gently placed herself onto Rose in a guiding motion. Rose could feel the touch of her bosom on her as The Baroness whispered into her ear.

"You're trying to force it, let it be natural. Remember the poem. Did you memorize it?" The Baroness asked. Rose gave another nod to confirm her statement.

Whose woods these are I think I know.

His house is in the village though;

He will not see me stopping here

To watch his woods fill up with snow. Rose thought. She allowed her body to grow cold. It was first her fingers and toes, but she felt a gradual cooling across her entire body. It took all her willpower to keep her teeth from chattering as she cycled through the visions in her mind. The Baroness had a peculiar request as there were several worlds filled with snow, but there was an exact one she searched for. It was the same one every time, and previously she failed to do so. Rose decided to briefly break her concentration as she had a burning question.

"Why do you always ask for a world filled with snow? I've gone through at least ten and each one of these isn't the right one. Are you sure this exists?" Rose asked with some skepticism in her voice.

"Yes, it exists. This is why I am testing your abilities. I know that you have the strength to do what must be done, but do you believe in yourself? It seems unlikely," The Baroness retorted as Rose bit her tongue. A ripe challenge was one she was always willing to take on, much to The Baroness' satisfaction. She knew she had to be careful when addressing Rose as she didn't want to upset her. She chose to defuse any doubts with a string of humor.

"Besides, I am from Mexico, you know what humidity does to my hair?" The Baroness responded with a stifled chuckle that put Rose at ease.

Between the woods and frozen lake

The darkest evening of the year...

The only other sound's the sweep

Of easy wind and downy flake.

The woods are lovely, dark and deep. Rose thought as she at long last brought the vision given in the poem.

Now that Rose had gathered what she wanted, she opened her fingers and gradually provided a large enough space for a clear reflection from their current abode to the next. A rush of cold wind shot through the vortex and gradually cooled the space around the two. The Baroness was warm in her coat as Rose did the same. The Baroness remained in awe at such a display from Rose. The Baroness could do this from mind alone, as this was where the power was truly stored, but the hand motions helped with visualizing the target. Rose looked at the vortex's opening and saw a snowy woodland in perpetual winter. The Baroness knew this world better than no other, where the eye of her affection, The Frost Gem remained just shortly out of reach. Now that Rose could conjure this from will, with the right primers, The Baroness felt as if she could continue her plan with a much more powerful asset for her.

"I've searched for years... Rose. This is it. This is where I found it all those years ago. It's been... at least two centuries now. Now, I can understand everything," The Baroness said, her words oozing with joy.

Rose gave no response, other than a muted smile at The Baroness' words. She massaged her temple and shook her head. The after effect of the purple vortex felt as her entire body gained a sudden shift in weight. Rose took a second to grab her bearings and saw the hand of The Baroness, open and inviting. The two emerged through the portal as one. Rose chose to leave it remaining open for their backtracking.

The woods were filled with massive evergreen trees that seemed unending around them. The women stood on top of the snow as it dispersed their imprint. Rose felt an unusual presence and imagined that the gem knew of their desire to plunder it. Was this some sort of sentient thing that the pair was engaging with? The movement of the tree's branches met a sudden gust of wind. Rose shivered with every bit of cold beyond her as she tried to figure out where to chart the course. She'd hardly had any experience with the cold, her native Southern roots and then the warmer Arizona sun made her ill prepared for such temperatures.

"I can only take us so far... I wanted to come closer to it, I can see it, the gem in my mind, but I can't get us directly there. We'll have to hike the rest," Rose said in confusion.

"This is... natural. For some reason, the gem has a neutralizing effect on our power. This happened to my husband and I on our first venture. I had only gotten here by accident and finding it with intention has been bothersome, but thanks to you, much more can be accomplished. I wish to remove this factor from the equation and stabilize it for our goals," The Baroness commented as she pulled the hood over her coat closer to her.

A silence that accompanied the gusts of wind came between Rose and The Baroness, but as Rose pressed forward, she turned around to hear the woman's voice. Through the glisten of the iced over landscape, The Baroness' call resounded further than expected.

"Rose, I figured we could chat on the way. I owe you a conversation after all that happened. I shouldn't have left you with no contact, not without telling you that The Baron also shares my power. After he was shot, I was distraught slightly, I knew he would be fine, but I needed to be sure. It's been a while since we had violence so close to us..." The Baroness mentioned. Rose was aware of The Baron's immortality; she heard it from the man himself after all. Rose decided to keep some of her knowledge to herself.

"Speaking of violence, this begs the question, have you taken a life yet in your travels... with intention?" The Baroness added as she watched her breath materialize in the air.

Rose took her time to think of her answer sufficiently. As the pair traveled further through the woodland, a large obelisk far in the distance was visible where the treeline vanished. The gust of wind that moved snow around as a smokescreen settled and the ruins of a greater civilization were revealed. Giant black and gray pyramids jutted out from the abyss present before them. The Baroness gave the foreign objects a look of familiarity and recalled their presence. She pressed forward as she examined her pistol that had leather wrapping at the bottom to keep the gun safe from frost. There wasn't a sign of life anywhere aside from the pair of them, and a small rabbit that was barely visible amid the snow. The rabbit's singular red eye shone with the reflection of the ground. Now that she felt calm, Rose replied in earnest.

"Yes. For some reason, the place I was supposed to clean out some time ago had gangsters swarming the place. They wanted us gone, so we shot first... It's just, I didn't recognize this crew. They were different. Very well trained," Rose responded. Rose obscured her true feelings regarding her rampage. She wanted to be sure The Baroness viewed her as someone not willing to fall subject to their emotions, much like how The Baron feared.

"Tell me about it, the kill, what did you feel?" The Baroness asked.

Why is she asking me all this? Rose thought.

"You once told me that these things required tough choices to make. I've made them," Rose said with asserted confidence.

"Word is the big players that be established a truce. Perhaps one to last or something more sinister. Say Rose, if you were the voice amid all that male bravado, how would you handle an enemy that came at your footsteps? What would you do? Take as long as you like. As you can see, our way is apparent. Let us continue north to the obelisk, I feel that I can now translate the text that will most likely be on it." The Baroness explained as she felt a burst of speed to outpace Rose ever so slightly.

"Well, that depends. I've seen what's been written in the papers, and I don't like it very much. Back before my daddy drank himself stupid, we had a garden with all sorts of vegetables. One problem though, is we always had weeds. No matter what we did, ladybugs, pesticides, we always had 'em. So I got a knife and I started cutting all the weeds myself, straight from the root. Took a while, but the vegetables were safe. So I'd do that. If you leave one weed out, the rest will follow, so you need to be quick with it."

"I am intrigued. So, why all the "weeds" then? Wouldn't just one change be better than any other?" The Baroness asked as she adopted Rose's code. She wiped away snow that cooled her face while she kept her attention on Rose.

"Every weed wants to be the big weed. Plants are hungry beings and squabble for water with their roots that get everywhere. Innocent people trip over those roots and can hurt themselves. Better to snip the garden and salt the soil." Rose said coldly.

"My... my... Well, if I ever need gardening, I can trust you know your way around a shovel."

"I think I see something..." Rose said, where the sound carried her quiet voice.

Rose's eyes followed a looming shadow that grew larger in volume as bits of light illuminated the expanse to them. Rose waved to get her attention, but she saw that The Baroness received this as an invitation rather than a warning. The curious rabbit that followed them hid in the snow and remained still as a looming specter came over the twilight. It was a Frost Vampire that was more animal than human as it glided towards a source of fresh nutrients. The Frost Vampire was a hulking creature akin to nightmares of primordial minds that feared the dark. It held piercing yellow eyes, a set of four protruding horns, interlocking jaws with jagged teeth and wings from the back. The pattern of flight was unusual to Rose as its wings were too small to support its body; it used its mind to float through the air as it remained bipedal and headed closer. Rose wasn't willing to test if this entity had any sort of intelligence, as her priority was staying alive.

Rose had little experience with shooting flying targets, but the creature's center of mass was large. She felt the encroaching feeling of frostbite slowly creeping in on her gloves. She knew she had to land a shot quickly. Rose looked behind her and instinctively ducked as she saw the raised hand of The Baroness with her pistol. The distinct crackle of her Borchardt C93 resounded throughout the landscape. She didn't intend to hit the target, but to instead distract the Frost Vampire for Rose to get an opening. Rose held out one hand and zeroed in on the target. She noticed that as the Frost Vampire opened its mouth, a resounding sapphire light came from it. A closer look from Rose revealed the presence of large icicles slowly forming. The icicles were launched by the Frost Vampire into the snow and made a low cracking sound that hurt both women's ears as it reached in volume. Rose's first shot missed entirely, and she found it more difficult to see with the growing wind. She needed to find a way to get closer to the target. Rose ran ahead and quickly conjured a blue portal, much to The Baroness' surprise, with the opening timed on top to where the creature charged another volley of ice missiles. Rose grasped her knife and ran through the portal. She was about ten feet in the air to meet the floating creature and grasped on its back. Rose had zero hesitation as she embedded the knife into the creature's neck and blood started to spill.

The Frost Vampire flailed around to deter Rose off its back. Her grip was ironclad as she anticipated taking the beast down with her as a cushion for the landing. The only thing that broke her concentration was the voice of The Baroness down below as she heard it over the creature's low growl.

"Rose! Jump now, I've made a place for you to go!" The Baroness called out as Rose saw the growing vortex for her to jump through. The Baroness was keenly aware of Rose's resolute trust in her as she didn't need to check on her.

Rose let go as she was ordered and fell back first as she neared towards the ground. As she looked above to see the sky growing before her, she saw the familiar blue light of the portal surrounding her as she gently rolled out to the snow below. It was instantaneous as she got herself up without issue and wiped off the snow. Rose closed her fist and the portal she summoned soon vanished with it. The Baroness offered her hand to pick up Rose as the hunt remained afoot.

She closed her portal from so far away. Interesting. And-that move to appear above the creature? I'm rarely impressed like this. My teachings have carried on well. The Baroness thought.

The pair pressed on for another half hour in the snow until the ground became much harder. In the distance, a lone building that stood above the ruins of a frozen civilization was a fortress of solid ice. A low hum filled the pair's eardrums like static from the radio as the vibrant gem of yore became aware of outsiders somewhere in the vicinity. Rose inhaled deeply and felt her chest cave in agony. The Baroness marched forward, crawling along the snowy ground as she felt the heavy weight of the gem's raw power now grounding them as they got ever closer. She knew that once the threshold of the gem's ability was breached; it was only a matter of time until it could be grasped.

Rose raised her hand in vain to try to summon another portal to get them inside, but she felt a block on her abilities. The ice fortress was strangely inviting with a door left ajar. Left with no other options, the pair walked inside as the snow gave way to paved frozen brick. It was an effort for the pair to enter, but compared to the harsh conditions of the outside, it was a bastion of beauty that reverberated harmonic music throughout. Rose could see her reflection on the walls as she felt a slight sliding motion as she moved forward. Rose looked to The Baroness for input on their situation and noticed her dissatisfied expression.

"All of this... was not here before. I remember just a simple pedestal where the gem remained," The Baroness recalled to Rose.

"It looks like someone's lived here. You said it was what-two hundred years or so since you first went here?" Rose asked.

"It was one of the first places I went with my husband after we agreed to travel together with our abilities. The ruins were present but all this is new. We are not welcome in this land, be prepared for the worst," The Baroness replied.

Is this denizen a follower of Ithedra? I recognize these engravings from the notes we took twenty-five years ago from the fortune teller's temple. Like that woman. This gives me more questions than answers. The Baroness thought and recoiled as she noticed a series of familiar glyphs inscribed in the ice. Rose offered no reaction as she was content with navigating the long corridors that led to nothing but empty rooms.

Rose noticed there was one room that stood out from all the others at the end of the icy corridor, one that remained occupied. The inhabitant was an ice wizard belonging to this civilization. His eyes were removed, gouged out by his own fingers, but he could see with a new form of vision. His feet didn't touch the ground as he floated like that of the Frost Vampires. Rose wondered if their creation had similar origins. His chest was caved open as well, with the replacement of his heart being the Frost Gem that they searched for. His attempts at words were completely incomprehensible to Rose as she called for The Baroness' attention. The Baroness came quickly, her desire for the gem trumped above all else as she pushed Rose out of the way.

"Give us the gem. You don't know how to handle its power. I've studied it from a distance for years," The Baroness explained to the ice mage.

The ice mage's head turned to the pair at her words, where his mouth opened but nothing else was given. The Baroness had no patience as she withdrew her pistol to threaten the man before her. Rose started to have some doubts on the gem's importance, given the conditions the person involved had with it. She noticed an assortment of now frozen solid books, also written in an incomprehensible language. She remembered seeing the runes spawned from the mummy having a similar form. She wondered if Venus had any sort of archival information at the museum to start doing translation work on such a task. The Baroness' provocation caused the ice mage to make an unusual moaning sound as two sentient blocks of ice started to take form. As they did so, the gem's glow intensified.

Rose saw no other choice but than to defend herself. She gathered quickly the gem was the source of their adversaries, so rather than go for the blocks of ice, she decided to make her target on the ice mage's flesh. The man's hands were nubs that were replaced with icicles that replaced his fingers, lethal and yet remained with the same dexterity. His face was half frozen and served as a rudimentary form of body armor. Rose couldn't imagine the agony it took on to have such a form and saw killing the man as a mercy more than anything else. Rose loaded her pistol with silver bullets and hoped that her weapon hadn't frozen in that time. She moved The Baroness aside and dumped her magazine while The Baroness sought to dispatch the ice blocks. Each bullet made its mark, with a crackle of ice accompanying it. Rendered insane, the man was hardly a conscious threat, and Rose knew this. After some time, Rose took a deep breath, and it was over. The man fell to the ground with an assured thump and the gem was dislodged from his cavity. Unlike the gem she'd seen before, Rose saw this was still filled with energy. On a closer look, Rose understood why it was such a sought-after item. She noticed that it held a glistening core and had ice coils that surrounded the item like a cage. It seemed almost alive.

Without further delay, The Baroness was practically shaking from the pressure as she went forward for it. The Baroness hastily grabbed the gem and felt the cool touch of it that glistened. It was a more powerful high than opium as the surge and rush came through her. Rose looked in shock as she saw the opposing woman's eyes change from a dark brown to a glistening sapphire. The gem's ethereal light glistened further. The Baroness felt a torrent of knowledge flow within her, incantations written by the ancients now made sense. For just a moment, she was able to understand the symbols that were inscribed on the floor and in the pillars, she noticed in previous travels. All these marks of Ithedra, but there was more to it than that. She recognized the name of a being not yet known to her. This was a being known as Khelkid, the rest of the text considered illegible. This knowledge was coupled with darkness, a creeping malevolence that ripped at the edges of her sanity. Her hands started to emit light blue and she started to twitch uncontrollably.

The Baroness assumed that after centuries of traveling the World Between Worlds, she would be able to handle The Frost Gem without complications, but work still needed to be done. It was a hasty move. Rose approached the twitching woman and pushed her to the ground. The gem rolled on the floor and The Baroness quickly reverted to herself. The Baroness wiped the drool off her face as she quickly realized she'd foamed at the mouth from such a raw insertion of power. Her senses returned to her as she met Rose, who looked at her with pursed lips. While Rose met the first gem in her travels with curiosity, she looked at this with scorn. Rose felt an unusual presence that was associated with this object and slowly retreated from The Baroness. She wondered if it was all worth it.

"Oh... I see. In my haste, I touched the gem with my hands instead of putting it in its proper container, and it became an ever-increasing bit of madness. Thank you, Rose. I would have taken the place of that... wizard, had you not helped me," The Baroness said. She gently scooped the gem into a leather bag with a thick glove.

"Is this thing really going to save the world? It seems to have ruined this one," Rose asked with disbelief in her voice.

"Of course, it was only the man behind it and his madness. This can be controlled and will rid of us the evils that plague our society. I will unlock its secrets; it gave me a message. You and I, have a new world to build," The Baroness mentioned as she gently guided Rose to the entrance of the fortress. It was her prerogative to keep Rose on side, but from her perspective, Rose's task was complete. The rest was extra. The culmination of centuries of planning had finally made its way to her and she basked in the glow of its hue.

Rose and The Baroness didn't look back as the pair left to see that the last sign of life was extinguished. Rose had done her duty and knew she was going to be compensated heavily for her efforts, but she wondered if she did the right thing. These gems were an unusually powerful entity that brought someone as powerful as her mentor to their knees. She hoped that this anomaly could be contained and no longer cause suffering to those it beholds once it was properly understood. Like all things, Rose decided to let the consequences come when they did.

Epilogue: Florence

Florence was asleep in her hotel room as she heard a loud and rough crash near her window. She darted up in a daze, startled by the sound. A small rock thrown against the window made its mark again. She fumbled around in the dark and looked to turn on a single light. The dim glow revealed an outline of her room as her vision slowly adjusted. Florence looked out the window to see the source of the sound, and it was Niccolo who was parked out front.

She recognized the shape of the car and was intrigued by the purpose of this visit. It was about a month since their last time together from the fighting with Cirano and the other factions. Florence thought it would be best to pack her bags and go to greener pastures, but she couldn't find herself leaving until she got what she came here for. Cirano was no longer important, but bigger crime still remained in the power vacuum that followed with both The Baron and Cirano gone. Florence was incredibly confused, Niccolo never visited the hotel directly, nor did he ever come at night. She quickly got dressed and made her way down. She turned as she heard Niccolo's voice call out to her.

"Your discretion is appreciated," Niccolo mentioned. Florence remained confused at Niccolo's cryptic wording.

The two met each other's gaze as Niccolo gestured towards the trunk of his car and opened it. Florence was taken aback by the cargo. Inside the trunk was a man wrapped up in rope and gagged with multiple layers of felt. Florence shivered; she hadn't realized the reality had set in. Niccolo managed to somehow find her uncle ultimately responsible for years of misery put on her. He was aged considerably; Florence knew the man lacked any sort of guilt regarding his actions.

"It took a lot of favors, but I arranged a false meeting for his business to look at opening office here. A friend of mine forged some documents and I made sure they came to the right place," Niccolo explained.

"It's really him. Uncle Kay..." Florence whispered. Florence hadn't imagined a situation where she'd be able to finally see some sort of retribution. The memories of her late twenties were filled with horror of the endless sea of white and people that drifted in and out of reality. Florence's indomitable will kept her alive through forced sterilization, sensory deprivation, and a bout of whooping cough. All of it was pinned down to one man and the fact he sold his soul to keep his standard of living regardless of who suffered.

"You helped me, and now I am helping you. This is what we agreed to do. So, what do you want done with him?" Niccolo asked. Niccolo had an assortment of tools kept by from the mine that could easily turn from crushing rocks to crushing skulls with some ingenuity. He raised an eyebrow as Florence closed the trunk and got in the car's passenger side.

"Let's take a drive," Florence commented while Niccolo said nothing more.

Niccolo stopped the car some distance from town as Florence tapped his shoulder to do so. The pair spent a half hour on the road and Florence pointed to veer off the path. Florence remained quiet as she heard the sound of a curious coyote approach the moving vehicle as it came to a close. She made a low whistle that caused the animal to retreat slightly before its attention went elsewhere.

"I can't begin to think of a fate worse than what I was put through, but I know jail is somewhere even the rich still hold power." Florence rubbed the dirt beneath her shoes. Niccolo raised an eyebrow at her statement but saw her eyes go towards the shovel. Niccolo went by and attempted to grab it, but Florence took the initiative.

She started to dig a medium-sized hole. She strained as she did so, but her anger was a prime motivator. Her muscles bulged as she labored through the moonlight while Niccolo smoked a cigarette. He withdrew his pistol and handed it to Florence as he expected her to enact justice with a shot to the head.

"I don't need that awful thing. Put that away," Florence mentioned. Niccolo paused as he realized what she intended to do. Niccolo approached the trunk and carried the squirming man. Niccolo's fingers were wet as the man urinated himself as he met Florence's face. The fear was palpable as the man saw not only the consequences of his mistake take physical form once more, but how the young woman he betrayed, now embraced a much darker side.

"Nicki, could you be a dear and throw him in? My arms are tired," Florence requested.

Niccolo complied with Florence's request as he hauled the man aside into the pit. Florence recovered her strength and with each heave, started to smile more. Her green eyes reflected the moonlight as she gave no triumphant speech or words of intimidation. Florence approached this as if she was simply taking out the trash. The heaviest load of dirt was the first, but she took her time as she could see her uncle reflecting. His panicked motions were for naught as he attempted to roll out, only to be betrayed by the lack of his strength and fall back in the dirt. As the man soon accepted his fate, the fact he heard nothing from Florence unnerved him and wondered if she any humanity left. He never imagined that someone would have gone after him and he feared that there would be others to suffer the same fate.

The last piece of dirt on the top was more than enough as there was nothing left but a large mound out in the middle of the desert. The pair appreciated their isolation from it all. Florence anticipated it'd take a century to find him once the dirt settled and the scavengers did the rest. Florence was appreciative of her craft and sat on top of the mound. Each step was taken with extra emphasis as she drove home the fact she couldn't be walked over any longer. She looked outwards to the landscape and thought she could feel an ambient shaking in a feeble last effort of a dying man below. She imagined the suffocation, the uncomforting weight, and the horrid feeling of loneliness.

"How did it feel? The justice. All of it. There's no going back now. He was very powerful, but you knew that going in," Niccolo asked.

"You know, I almost forgot his name already." Florence patted the soil beneath her.

Epilogue: Rose

R ose was packing her bags with clothing and other necessary supplies as Venus looked over her shoulder in slight jealousy. The pair were sitting in Venus' apartment as Venus quickly examined Rose's now larger wardrobe. She had an immediate judgmental look at Rose's outfits, and chucked the ones she thought were gaudy, and gave a nod of approval on the best pieces. After everything that happened, Rose gave her a concise synopsis of her quest. Venus could hardly remove her jaw from the floor as Rose casually mentioned her friendship with The Baroness and how this was the culmination of all that occurred. To Rose, it seemed nearly unimpressive as she tackled such a wide variety of situations, but it remained an epic story.

"I can't believe it. You not only got to meet her, but she's your teacher? Lord above, I need an autograph! A photograph, anything!" Venus stated as she clapped in happiness. Venus remained enamored with The Baroness, but Rose felt it was for vastly different reasons than her own. Rose laughed. It was fair, she was an incredibly successful and attractive woman. It shocked her that she didn't beat off a wave of suitors even with The Baron at her side.

Rose gave an embarrassed nod as she hadn't realized that Venus knew far more about her fashion work than she did. Venus rattled off an assortment of photo shoots and celebrity collaborations that The Baroness signed on for her company. Rose knew The Baroness for her other attributes but obscured the truth about her exact origins to Venus. She didn't want to complicate matters more regarding how this connection was built and wanted to keep her safe. Rose was already aware that The Baroness had visited Venus and did not want her involved in this business.

"Of course cuz, I got you. Though, I'm learnin' a whole bunch of other stuff too. Say, uh—How are you and your lady friend doing?" Rose replied as she attempted to make small talk. Rose was hoping to get a diversion, so she didn't need to talk more about her ongoing plans. Despite her ease with The Baroness, she felt nervous about the inability to perform.

"Oh, things are... pleasant. Not with Tasha anymore, I needed to go tend a new pasture. Let me tell you 'bout Junebug. From Harlem, she works at a record store as one of the clerks. So friendly, beautiful dark skin like the Queen of Sheba and a smile that hits harder than Jack Dempsey. Yeah, she talks a lot. I like to listen, so not too bad." Venus leaned against the back wall of her apartment. Rose shot Venus a glance before continuing to organize her suitcases.

"Wonderful. So, what did y'all get up to?" Rose mentioned while Venus passed her a few folding hangers for clothes. Rose struggled to keep her bags together as she was a chronic over packer and fit the inflated articles of clothing she brought. After owning so little for such a long time, she and Venus went on a shopping spree and Rose had little experience with such excess.

"We had supper a few times, the way Yankees like to eat it," Venus mentioned with a tinge of disgust. Venus brushed her hair and looked at a handheld mirror as she did so.

"Oh..." Rose said with a disappointed tone of voice. Rose lamented the idea of eating in the city, as for all its grandeur, not a single person knew how to apply spices correctly and there was a woeful lack of butter. If your chest didn't clench after you ate it, there was no point in the endeavor.

"So, I take it you're seeing her again?" Rose asked as Venus burst into laughter at her question. She dropped her brush and met Rose's face as she adjusted her glasses. Rose shook her head in slight judgement at Venus' decisions but couldn't throw stones at a glass house.

Rose was preparing for a year long work study with The Baroness to harness her abilities. She found there was more at stake with Rose remaining essential for her plans regarding The Frost Gem. Rose still required a heavy deal of training to master travel between universes, as with the chaos of everything happening, her haphazard teaching sessions were not adequate for The Baroness' demands. The Baroness sought to keep Rose as long as possible and visited her parents' home to explain the details. She disguised her venture as a mentorship program for young women and Rose was plucked from one of many. This was true, Rose was in competition with herself and the other copies that were unable to use her abilities. Rose recalled the conversation as unpleasant to witness, but necessary for her growth.

Rose also thought about her first mentor. Cicero was able to hang up his hat for the time being as with the public death of The Baron and Baroness' disappearance, the otherworldly portals diminished significantly in scope. Cicero felt he could finally take some much needed rest with Claudia as The Baron was dead and gone. For when the call came, he had backup in the form of Niccolo or Florence as trainees that could contend with the powers that be. Cicero knew Rose deserved a vacation and assumed that she would return home. He'd try to send a letter or two when he could.

"Well Rose, looks like we're all packed here. I'd see you off at the train station, but you know. You can do your thing," Venus said as she gave Rose a tight hug and an affectionate peck on the cheek. Rose returned the greeting in kind as she took a deep breath and started to concentrate.

Rose stepped outside to spare Venus the trouble of cleaning up afterwards once the portal was created. Rose recalled her mentor's location by humming a song that reminded her of the birds that inhabited the trees. She used her hands to practically rip open a tear as the portal she summoned was smaller than anticipated, an irregularity compared to her blues. Rose emerged right where she wanted to be, a solid log cabin that was sequestered in the middle of the woods. She stepped in and looked behind the portal to see one last wave of Venus before it closed. Rose was now alone as she saw a woman in the distance wearing an unusual outfit. Rose recognized The Baroness and waved.

"Pardon the dress, it is not how I usually am shown to you. I felt homesick, this is what women wore in my village when I was young. The festivals come and go, but I am the only one who remembers," The Baroness mentioned. She wore a white skirt accompanied with cloth that surrounded her hips. It appeared to be stitched together rather than machined by a sewing machine or store-bought. Her ears were exposed underneath her hair and were pierced with small pearls. She wore no shirt either, something that gave Rose slight embarrassment given the nature of their connection. She'd seen Venus naked more times than she could count, and it hardly elicited a reaction.

Rose was vaguely aware of The Baroness' Maya heritage, it was something not often discussed between the two, but she assumed she would learn much more. Rose hadn't thought about her family's past much aside from what she already knew. It was depressing and she'd rather think about the future. Once Rose recovered her nerves, she addressed The Baroness with an important question. This was also a question that she thought of herself, but never bothered to search because she feared what would happen if she did on her own.

"Where's The Baron? I figured after everything happened with the gala and all, he'd want to talk things out. All I got was a letter from him to meet you here," Rose asked.

"He's away helping me with something. For now, it will just be us in these woods. You and I will connect with nature and this will help you. The cabin is more rustic than what you are used to, but your needs will be met," The Baroness mentioned. Rose wondered what esoteric things The Baron could be up to as he was now divorced from his tenure in Phoenix.

A man with that much determination and will was not one to go quietly. It mattered little though as Rose knew she had much to learn from her mentor.

"Do you trust me?" The Baroness asked.

To a point. "Yes... I do," Rose replied with a smile, her defensive thoughts taking over.

As she extended her hand out to Rose, The Baroness let out a warm smile as Rose accepted the invitation, just as she did once before in the opulence of the mansion. Rose's subconscious was in constant struggle when it came to recognizing the faults of The Baroness, she'd experienced such a failing at the search for the Frost Gem, but Rose's doubts were ultimately clouded by her sheer admiration of the woman. The door closed behind them and Rose's training had just begun.

Also by Xavier McClean

The Jih's Journey Series:
Jih's Journey
The Khelkid Series:
Khelkid
Khelkid: Second Earth
The NEVADA Series:
NEVADA